Pandemonium

Pandemonium

Encroaching Shadows

MOIRA BARRIE

ARCHWAY
PUBLISHING

This is a work of fiction. All of the characters, names, incidents, organizations, and dialogue in this novel are either the products of the author's imagination or are used fictitiously.

Archway Publishing books may be ordered through booksellers or by contacting:

Archway Publishing
1663 Liberty Drive
Bloomington, IN 47403
www.archwaypublishing.com
844-669-3957

ISBN: 978-1-6657-2512-5 (sc)
ISBN: 978-1-6657-2511-8 (hc)
ISBN: 978-1-6657-2513-2 (e)

Library of Congress Control Number: 2022910901

Print information available on the last page.

Archway Publishing rev. date: 07/05/2022

The fear of death follows from the fear of life.
A man who lives fully is prepared to die at any time.
—Mark Twain

Chapter 1

The heavy wooden door creaks open, bringing some much-needed light into this desolate area. As much as I enjoy seeing the light, there are two reasons it would be shed here. I've only been here one day, so it is not time for me to come out and pretend all this torture never happened. Am I strong enough to deal with this again? Curling into a ball on the cold, damp floor of the cellar is the only way to protect myself without letting her see me cry. Weakness is not an option. *Pull yourself together.*

Her shadow appears before me, giving away the object she is holding, but my hazel eyes won't leave the view of the harsh floor. My skin welts from the concrete constantly rubbing me. The few memories I have left are my only salvation, but her evil voice interrupts my thoughts and trails through my mind. She is pacing around me, circling the object on my bare back. One blow and then another, each time more painful than the last, all at her discretion.

"Why are you doing this to me?" My voice quakes in fear as I use all my strength to lift my head to meet those cold, dark eyes. There are no lights in this darkness. My eyes have become accustomed to the dark—so much so that when she sheds light in here, my eyes burn, surely another one of her tactics. I haven't eaten in days, and I'm sure if there were flies in here, they would be attracted to me.

Her voice is raspy. It reveals the pleasure she feels from my pain. Her teeth barely show as she grins at me. "Because I can. Because you are a dirty little bitch like your mother. Because if you tell anyone, I will kill you." She spoke with a promise—a promise I know will come true one day, just not today. "Now tell me where your mother is—"

"No!" My terror is reflected in the scream I can barely let out. I can only imagine what she would do to my mother. *Wait, my mother.* This must be a dream or a memory. Someone is calling my name, but no one would find me down here, locked up and caged. She takes a needle out of her jacket pocket and stabs me violently in the arm. My young, fragile body takes in the bright-green serum that cools me from head to toe.

The woman says I won't remember what happened, but she was wrong. I can still feel the lingering pain and my body convulsing with each blow to my back. I can hear the whip cracking.

It is her. The imposter. The mother I thought was mine but wasn't. I must kill her.

I slowly wake and see a dark-haired, dark-eyed man standing by the foot of the bed. I pretend to sleep on. This large bed is soft and comforting, and yet the feel of the concrete floor is still fresh in my mind and senses. With one eye barely open, I can see him rubbing his hand through the salt-and-pepper scruff on his perfectly sculpted face. He is looking at me inquisitively, like he has many questions to ask but cannot find the words to do so. Having a stranger just watching me is creepy, but we are at a standoff right now. He won't speak, and I won't wake from my fake sleep. We both know it to be true.

I stretch cautiously, moving my leg in search of Laila, but there is no feel of her. Normally, as soon as I make any movement, she is by my side. The panic starts to run through me, and the electricity is boiling, making the huge canopy and the covers on the bed shake. I can hear the crackling of a fireplace in the room, slowly burning. The embers burn out before they touch the cathedral ceiling. I can sense everything in the room without even opening my eyes. I can almost visualize the paintings on the walls; they are a nice contrast to the otherwise dark interior.

Doors fly open and slam against the wall behind them. It takes every ounce of my control to not jolt out of this bed. A fury storms in, and the footsteps behind it are loud and intense. A familiar voice speaks. "Is she still asleep?" The Irish voice puts me at comfort a bit, and all the electricity in me stops building.

"Yes, son. She is."

Oh my, he has the same sweet accent as Aidan. I slowly start to open my eyes to see that he and Aidan bare a strong resemblance. Clearly these men do not age, as the man at the foot of my bed looks way too young to have fathered Aidan. Marcus had once mentioned that Aidan is the strongest of his kind. Does that mean his father is also a werewolf?

I keep flashing back to the night at my house. My mother—well, not my mother, some imposter—and the burning flames. I move to touch my arm, surprised it is not broken from the heavy beam that fell on me, and both men turn immediately at my sudden shuffle. There are two sets of eyes locked on me, one dark and the other Aidan's intense blue.

I need to say something to break the silence, as I can feel my eyes getting bigger with each passing second. One thing comes to mind. "Where is Laila?" My voice is small, almost unheard. I cast all potential rudeness aside and raise my voice. "Where is Laila?"

Aidan turns his eyes away from me, something he never does when he is speaking to me. In fact, he always insists on eye contact. Why isn't he answering me? I shoot my eyes to his father, hoping they hold the answer I am looking for.

"Ava, I would love to catch up with you. It has been centuries, after all. Right now you need to have a discussion with my son, which I do not care to be a part of. When you two have finished, please come downstairs and have some breakfast." His voice is kind—a genuine spirit I can tell.

"I cannot wait to speak with you. I have many questions." I fold the blankets down and hop out of the tall bed and onto the dark wooden floor. I am in the same dress I was wearing at the charity event. I roll my eyes at my state and slide over to give Aidan's father a hug before he departs the room.

"You will never change, Ava." He smiles and returns the hug as though he hasn't received one in many years. He hugs me close, stroking the back of my head, and it reminds me of a father's hug to a daughter. Warm. Sincere. Filled with love. He holds me at arm's length. "I am glad to see you are in one piece and not badly injured." My eyes shoot to Aidan over his shoulder, and he releases me, knowing full well I need to have a serious conversation with his son. Why is Aidan always the one who can give me the answers I seek?

I hear the door close, and the footsteps are removed from earshot. "Well ..." He knows exactly what I am referring to. "There were faint barking sounds when the log fell on me, so I know she followed me in the house ..." Every sentence is a runoff, just waiting for him to complete it.

"Ava ... I am so sorry."

Tears swell in my eyes as he moves closer to me. My mind is imagining the worst. He needs to get it out. I put my hand out to his chest to stop him from coming closer.

He lets out a gasp and speaks with his head down. "The house was on fire, and she ran in behind you." He raises his eyes to meet mine, and my hand slowly drops from his chest. "By the time I got upstairs, she was by your side, barking, trying to wake you up. Her bark led me right to you. I saw the joist lying on top of you, moved it, and picked you up into my arms. I kept calling her to follow me, but she wouldn't. I had to get you out of there. I have this ..." He trails off and moves away from me to walk to the other side of the room. He opens a door that leads to a large walk-in closet.

I move my head to see him, but I've lost sight of him. When he reappears, he is holding the box.

It's the box I ran into the house to get. The box that made me lose her.

He moves closer to me, but I am rendered speechless. I cannot hold it, but he keeps gesturing for me to take it. Sadness and tears overcome me, and I sob. "What happened to her?"

He shakes his head in response, and I ask the same question again, each time my voice projects louder.

This is the worst thing I could have possibly imagined. She means so much to me. This cannot be true. I need to know it isn't true. I sit on the floor and wipe away my ears with the end of my dress, and he takes a deep breath.

He kneels down to meet my tear-filled gaze. "I tried to go back in to find her once you were safe. I couldn't locate her. I came back outside just when the right side of the house started to crumble down, and that's when I decided to leave. I needed to keep you safe." He reaches his hands to my face to try and console me, but it doesn't work.

"You should have saved her, not me." I know that is a ridiculous statement in his eyes, considering most people would save their loved ones before their pets. Laila is more than a pet to me. She is my family.

I know he won't regret his decision, and I can't expect him to. But he feels badly. I can see it in his eyes. He pulls me onto his lap and lets me cry softly into his chest, rubbing my face into his shirt. I breathe in his smell and an hour passes in a minute. Finally, I compose myself.

"We should go downstairs." He wipes the tears that are streaming down my face, and I scoot off him.

We stand and I maneuver to leave the room, but he grabs me and holds my face in his hands. With intense eye contact, I look into those deep blue eyes. "Ava, I am sorry. I couldn't lose you again. I love you."

Despite the gut-wrenching feeling in my body from losing Laila and knowing how he feels about me and how I feel about him, I can't say it back. Not right now. My mouth won't open to let me voice those words. I force a half-assed grin, and he reciprocates, sad eyed that I couldn't say the words back. I'm going to use this moment and spew a bunch of questions in hopes for some answers. "How did no one find me before? Vernon knew who I was. So did Shane. I don't understand. The way everyone made it seem was that I was being hunted. How did Kieran and I make it through the portal together? I know Marcus told you. Please give me more answers." At this point, it isn't even begging. It's a calm demand.

And he opens up. "I do not wish to talk about Kieran right now, another day. No one came for you because no one believed it to be you. There have been many people who have been tortured to find your whereabouts. And without any powers showing on your end until recently, the Grimmers and Militia had no reason to believe the theories. Plus, I would travel to different places, and they would assume I was visiting you. It was all a ruse."

With a disgustful knock on the door, he is gone and out of sight.

Aidan and his father are speaking outside of the room as I am changing into something that is not a long evening dress. At this point, literally anything else will do. I rummage through his elaborate closet, looking for something of his to put on. Fancy clothes, fancy clothes, come on anything but fancy clothes. Gotcha! His sweatpants slide right up and are much too long for my legs and not as loose on the waist as I would hope. I scoff at my own body issues, even at a time like this. But thankfully, the drawstring band makes me feel a little better, and his T-shirt looks more like a dress on me than anything else, even on my curvy body. Sometimes I wish I were conventionally skinny; body dysmorphia can be real. If I were just donning the T-shirt, I'm sure Aidan would think I looked sexy. But considering I'm in an unknown house, with god only knows how many people, I can't even think of having mad-at-him sex right now. Imagine that being our first time. No thank you. Plus, for everyone else's sake I should keep pants on, I'll just roll the pajama bottoms up at the waist a few times and good to go!

Exiting the closet, I realize I haven't had a chance to snoop yet. Now, I'd like to say I am one of those girls who doesn't snoop. But I should be honest with myself. Isn't it suspicious that he miraculously comes into my life? I want to find out more about him.

This isn't what I expected his room to look like, but on the other hand, I didn't think I'd ever be in his room, especially after his disappearing acts. There is no television, no bookcases, and the room itself is very dark, minus the crackling fireplace. He has very eclectic taste, and I'm guessing this old-worldly room matches the rest of the house, a modernized gothic. The floor-to-ceiling doors opens to the bathroom, closet, and hallway. That's probably where Aidan is waiting for me. I make my way to the door but start to walk slower when I hear him conversing with his father and a few other voices. Of course, I do not recognize any of them; it's not like there has been time for proper introduction.

I can be as confident as can be out at the bar and talking to random strangers. I could pretty much make friends with anyone, from the old lady who likes to play bingo to a group of college guys or even a toddler. But then again, the toddler and I will probably be on the same wavelength, done with life and ready for a nap. Still as open and as friendly as I can be, on the other hand, I am selectively social, and him just dishing information on me out to people feels incredibly violating and personal. As I press my ear softly to the door, I can't help but wonder why Aidan is even talking to strangers about me.

"Well, if it is as you say it to be, he must be her Shaddower. I have never heard of a Shaddower living for centuries. But given the situation and how powerful Ava has grown to be, it is quite possible he was reborn—just as Victor was. We should seek out a Pureck for more answers." Aidan's father is speaking of my Shaddower?

"It makes sense. That is why she would not believe Dillion was Grimmer. Dillion is smarter than he appears to be and a threat. He knew as long as Dino was near her, she couldn't read him, even when she touched him ..." Aidan's voice drifts off in contempt.

"Dino must be very powerful then. Ava's powers could be suppressed by him to the point of potential destruction. Does she realize how powerful she is and how much stronger she can get in just a short time?" A female voice speaks up. She sounds bitchy, but what do I know? Maybe she's the sweetest person on the planet. Never judge a book by its cover—or the sound of its voice?

"She has no idea how powerful she is." Aidan's words are short and clipped. I can tell he is beginning to grow uncomfortable of this conversation. Maybe I shouldn't doubt him so much. Maybe there is something to this that will come back to me in pieces.

I pull open the door as an older man is speaking to Aidan's father. "Elijah, she must remain here." He is shocked with dismay across his face when he turns to see me looking directly into his light brown eyes.

Elijah, that is Aidan's fathers name; it has quite the ring to it. It sounds as wise and strong as he appears to be. I can feel my lip curl into a half smile. Before I can even render what his face looks like or what he is wearing, the old man scurries off like a rat.

Then boom, back to reality, "Why must I remain here? I

don't know any of you. No disrespect meant, but why would I stay here?" I lock eyes with Aidan, just waiting for him to answer.

Another smooth accent answers instead. Elijah smiles at me. "Come, we will speak of it later." He extends his hand out to mine and then places my hand on his arm.

He is leading me down a tall wooden staircase in the center of the room. Even his manners alone have a calming effect. This place is truly beautiful, its old-world style making it seem almost like a castle nestled away—somewhere? Wherever I am. In its vastness, it holds many exquisite paintings on the walls and a lavish fireplace with old, elegant dim light fixtures and decor.

My mouth drops open in awe at the centuries of history that cover the walls and shine throughout, and I cannot help but question the comforting feeling. "Have I been here before?" My body seems to relax on its own, without any help from me talking to myself with reassurance.

"Yes, Ava. I wish you could remember."

I turn to look over my shoulder and lose all sense of self. Wait—that's not my sense of self but more like my footing. As I begin to fall, I can see Aidan's sad face. But luckily Elijah still has hold of my hand. He grasps firmer, pulling me back onto the stair before Aidan can even blink an eye.

As odd as it may be to some, I feel comforted knowing a part of me still exists; a part of me is me. Hey, it might be the clumsy part, but at least it is something. The illusion of self is shattered with growls and drool and ferocious words as we approach the main living room.

My hearing fixes on a beastly conversation—nope not conversation; it just turned into an all-out fight. The closer we get, the clearer it becomes. Can't I just have one normal day? You know, slippers, hot chocolate, a fire, and a movie? Where are those days? I sigh in disbelief. At some point, I'll have to accept my new path. The cherry on top is the argument is about me. How sweet. I can hear the sarcasm in my own thoughts. I'm not surprised as the words become clearer; some people find me to be a burden, others say a risk, and a few say my presence here is key and that I could be of great use to them. Not like what I want matters in the slightest. There is some common sense in me right now stopping me from touching each and every one of them to see their true intentions.

The voices become quieter. If they could sense us coming why wait so long to pipe it down? The second my feet touch the elegant old-school rug—which belongs in the queen's castle and cascades, perfectly molding to the staircase that leads to the dead center of the room below—some start to change into their werewolf forms, further proving they do not trust me. It is amazing how quickly they change, clothes ripping to shreds and lying on the ground as they do, with all their hair stood up on end. Only a few remain human. I need to make a mental note to thank them later. The looks from those in werewolf form could kill, like I'm sure they would, so my appearance here would come to a close—or a death, whichever.

I have entered the lion's den or, more literally, a wolf den. I squeeze Elijah's hand and, in the same second, feel the stairs creaking behind me before a huge gust of wind blows over my head, nearly knocking me over. Aidan appears in front of me as a werewolf. As he glances back over his shoulder, his eye beam with intensity toward me. He snarls and focuses his attention on the brute who was scowling at me. He cleared a twenty-foot staircase with no issues. He circles the other wolf, growling and showing his teeth. I'm only used to Laila protecting me. This is something entirely different; the sheer size of them would frighten anyone.

The other wolves have moved away and backed against the walls. I've watched the Discovery Channel enough to know this is a showdown of dominance. It doesn't take much but one growl and eye contact on his part to have the other wolf submitting to the ground within seconds. Normally when I watch these showdowns on the television, there is a fight and someone walks away with a tail between his legs. But here you can tell there is still respect; just people are unhappy and don't know how to convey it any other way. Change can be terrifying. And let's be honest, I'm not sure everyone even understands what's going on. How can they when I can barely? He turns to look at me with those piercing blue eyes and turns back into the handsome sweet Aidan I met in Mexico.

I stare at him awkwardly, not realizing he is completely shirtless, and I don't mean to, but I can feel my mouth gape open. How is it possible he is wearing no shirt but has pants on? I'm just confused.

Before the words can come out of my mouth, Elijah answers my puzzled look. "Thankfully, we do have a witch in favor." That's all he says as he points to a bracelet on his wrist, once again leaving me with more questions than answers.

If this man doesn't put a shirt on, I don't know how I will ever be able to concentrate. *Please put a shirt on. Please put a shirt on.* I've completely forgotten my mouth is still wide open. How embarrassing. There is definitely a primal pull between me and Aidan. Elijah and I remain the last on the stairs until Aidan is directly in front of us and offers his hand to me. Resisting the urge to just ogle him up and down is increasingly difficult. Something in my gut is sinking, and I look back at Elijah, in my own way questioning if it is safe. He nods approvingly. He knows his son would do anything to protect me, even fight his own family. Still, I can't help but question, Why all of this for me? I am surely not the girl he spoke of before. No one is the same. I am not who he remembers me to be.

"Do not mind those in wolf form. For some, it is easier than appearing human, and this is a safe home for the pack." He pulls me off the stairs and into his arms, my toes not reaching the ground. I instinctively nestle into his skin. He breathes in my hair, which brings me back to my senses, as it must smell like ass after being through a fire and not showering.

As I breathe him in, I have lost concentration again. "Can you put a shirt on please?" I blush and speak quietly enough so no one else hears me.

He pulls me back and puts me on the ground, but not without smirking and winking first.

As he leads me through a long corridor, he swipes his bracelet in a way I can't completely see, and he has a shirt on. Maybe that's what Elijah was talking about. But it still doesn't give me any answers—like who is the witch? Can't there be an owner's manual for all of this stuff. The hallway echoes, and I know Elijah is trailing behind us, having brief conversations with randoms about, what else, me of course.

One even makes a rude statement, purposely being louder than necessary. "She is not one of us. She should not be here."

As we enter the brightest room in the house I have seen so far, I sigh in disbelief. "Not to be ignorant, I am appreciative of your help, but what am I doing here? Really? Clearly your pack doesn't want me here." I don't even know if I wanted that to be a question but more of a statement. I shouldn't be here. I shouldn't make the rest of his pack, or family, whatever they are, on edge. I imagine this is a whole different level of exposure for them, and I can't help but feeling guilty. There is also a slight worry someone might eat me. But what can I do about it now? I am here. "Will someone try to attack me?"

"Not with me here." He turns his neck harshly and stretches it in anger and lets out a low growl, sounding every bit werewolf in his human form—leaving me absolutely speechless.

So, he can still growl like an animal without being one? Hopefully, soon I will get some answers. In the meantime, I will just enjoy this little bit of normalcy in the kitchen. The kitchen is absolutely beautiful and doesn't make me feel like I'm in another world. It is modern in comparison to the rest of the house, almost as though it doesn't belong, just like me. There are skylights and huge windows to bring in all the natural light throughout the kitchen.

"Take a seat." He points to the gray and white marble countertop off to the side of the kitchen. I take a seat on the bar stool, watch, and think. How was I ever happy with someone so controlling in a past life? Yes, he's sweet and kind, but even having me sit down was a demand not a question.

It is time for me to get out of my own head for five minutes and just enjoy the show. It's obvious he can cook, much to my surprise, just by the way he moves around the kitchen with ease; he's in his element. He slides orange juice down the counter to me, and I catch it right before it falls off the edge and send him a playful smile and giggle. "You know, I've never had a man cook for me before."

He is cracking eggs with one hand. In my book, that's a professional move. So I clap, but the golfers clap—got to throw some sarcasm in there somehow.

He laughs but soon again becomes serious. "I have cooked for you many times. I wish you could remember. Surely there is something we can do to make you remember."

At first, I thought he meant something sexual, but with the way he is shaking his head, I can tell it's more serious. Aidan dawns a Martha Stuart-like cooking apron, something only Madea would wear, and it brings us back to a lighter mood.

"It is good seeing you two like this again. Unfortunately, there's nothing we can do for her memory right now. It will have to come back to her on her own."

I almost fall out of my chair. How long was Elijah standing in the kitchen doorway? I know just from the look on Aidan's face that his father's words rest deeply in his soul and sadden his heart. He looks like a child who has lost his puppy—just how I feel right now. If it weren't for all of this craziness, I'd be laid up in bed for weeks crying about Laila. This is a helpful distraction, but it doesn't help my heart.

"How long will it take? Can't we talk to Isolde?" He is looking to his father for answers, which he doesn't have.

Elijah simply replies, "I will reach out to her, but please do not get your hopes up, son."

Despite once again not knowing who or what they are talking about, I try to lighten the mood. "Mr. Cross, please sit." I stand and pull out the chair next to me and sit back down. "I was just about to watch a brilliant show called *Aidan Is Trying to Cook: Will It Kill Me or Be Delicious?*" I make sure to use my best Alex Trebek voice.

Elijah lets out a laugh. Clearly, I was the one to keep Aidan lighthearted in the past. He walks over to take his seat, in the same effortless, casual, but every bit powerful saunter. "Again, please just call me Elijah. You once knew me as father-in-law. You and Aidan were only days away from marriage, before, well …" He trails off and stops himself before any happiness evaporates in the room. "Never mind." He coughs, "My son is actually a very good cook. What are you making?"

"So." The so lingers too long in the air before I belt out. "Can I ask you two some questions?"

Aidan shoots me the of course you can look, confused as to why I would even bother asking. Elijah returns my question with a polite smile and a hand gesture that says, by all means.

"OK, so where do I begin? You said I have known you both for centuries, so you never die?" And the thought never occurred to me to ask, But I can? How is any of this supposed to make sense.

Elijah shakes his head. "Werewolves can die. Some have longer life spans than others. But the average life range is around two hundred years." He pauses for a moment and takes a deep breath. "But we are different."

Before I can even ask a question, Aidan picks up where he left off. "Ava, there's no way around it but to just say it. My family was cursed, long before I even walked this earth. It's a curse that lives in the bloodline of men in our family, now only remaining in my father and me." He puts a plate in front of his dad and continues. "My great-great-grandfather, well, to put it as simple as possible, he pissed off a Pureck by breaking her heart. She let out the small amount of evil her body harnessed in that instant and used it to curse the men in his bloodline to live a lonely existence with heartbreak. The only power she didn't foresee coming was that of soul mates. Soul mates aren't found for everyone; this is a yin and yang of the universe. My mother was taken from my father by her curse. After giving birth to me, she left him to raise me and …" He pauses, not wanting to finish the story. He gets choked up but puts his hand to his mouth to cough it away. "She left him to raise me on his own. Seeing her eyes in my face is his constant reminder of the curse upon us. The curse has caused us heartbreak when we are the most in love and available for ultimate vulnerability. Only when we have suffered enough heartache can we be killed, when our hearts are ripped from our chests."

I hop off the stool and start walking over to Aidan. As I walk past Elijah, I stroke my hand over his shoulder. "I am so sorry, Elijah."

He brings his hand to mine and gives it an easy pat and tries to fake a smile. Just the instant touch, and I am able to feel his heartbreak, he has been vulnerable all of these years since then. My powers are getting stronger, and I am able to see the moment his wife was taken from him. Elijah's left arm wrapped around his wife as she lay in the bed, fading from life as she held her son.

I finish making my way around the countertop with ease. It must be the power; the vision did not stop me from moving. It is as though I am walking back in time through a memory to my future without hesitation. I am cognizant of where I am heading.

Aidan opens his arms to me, and I shuffle into them, escaping the memory of the past and the pain that went with it. I lean up to give him a heartfelt, soft, quick kiss on the lips, one my body wishes would last longer. But I pull myself away. "I am so sorry, Aidan."

"It's OK, my love. It's not your fault." He brings my hand to his lips and places a chaste tender kiss on my palm.

A thought hits me, a question I'm not sure I want the answer to. But all I have been doing is complaining in my mind about not knowing anything, so now is the time to ask. "Do I keep dying because I am your supposed soul mate?"

His reaction when I said the word *supposed* was not so thrilled; in fact, I will go with angry, so much so his father speaks for a question directed to Aidan. "You live again though the Pureck's soul who enchanted you." Elijah speaks to me as though I am his daughter, soft and sweet. "I am not certain of your enchantment, Ava. Each time, it seems to be different, and I'm positive the only one who knows the true extent of it is the Pureck. I know you keep coming back until your responsibility here is finished—until you've made the impact the universe has set out for you to make."

Twiddling the ring on my index finger, without even remembering it was there, relaxes me. She gave it to me, that imposter. Twiddling it round and round. What do I do with it? It holds all these memories—yes bad ones but some good too. Should I just get rid of it? Without speaking to anyone, I make a hasty decision to take it off, saunter over to the bin, and throw it away. Before I even get the chance to sit back down, Aidan and his father both blur over to the bin and try to scoop it out of my hand, but I don't let them.

"What?" I turn around, somewhat angry that they have tried to snatch it when I am just trying to throw those memories away.

Aidan keeps trying to grab it from my grasp. I eventually give in.

"I'll get it off myself, I don't understand what the big deal is."

I swat away his frantic hands and gently ease off the ring and place it in the center of his hand.

Instantly, the ring burns the palm of his hand, leaving a perfect circle as it drops to the floor. The three of us stand uncomfortably quiet, staring at this literally small but giant problem I sense we are about to face.

"Ava, has your mother—I mean fake mother—given you many trinkets over the years?" Elijah is speaking to me but looking directly at Aidan, concerned.

"Dad," he mumbles with worry.

"Perhaps you are right. It is time for me to reach out to Isolde." Without even acknowledging me, he looks at Aidan with concern and doesn't break his eye contact with his son as he speaks to me, "Where did you get that ring? The way it hits the sunlight looks almost magical."

"So, what does this mean? Can someone explain it to me?" Clearly, I have no idea what is going on, and I know it's not good. At some point, someone is going to have to break the silence and explain to me what is going on here, so chop-chop. Gosh, I want to yell at the top of my lungs and make someone talk to me. My frustration is boiling, and with that, so is the force in my body. I unintentionally let out a small pulse that manages to get their attention and break some of the dishes along with it.

They are utterly unphased by what happened—no shock at the broken glass scattered across the floor. Elijah takes a deep breath as he musters the strength to speak. "Ava, for how long have you been wearing this ring?"

"I don't know—on and off since I was sixteen. It was a birthday present from the possessive fake mother of mine." My eyebrow raises to him in curiosity. Just once I would like to not have to probe for information, for it to be given willingly.

"That just goes to show how powerful you are getting—if you are somewhat able to resist the power of that ring. I'm sure she used it for many things. But ultimately, it was to suppress your powers and your thoughts. Rings like this are only effective when worn. But when you wear it, your thoughts are swayed in the direction of whoever cast the spell on the ring. She could also use it to track you."

Fear strikes my face, but he is quick to reassure me. "It won't work in here. We are protected by magic well beyond the power she possesses. It would take a lot more than her to break through these walls. This ring could be used for many things. Now, we have to figure out exactly what charms she cast on it. I will have to consult some old friends to see how we can reveal this magic."

He doesn't say another word just bends down to wrap the ring in a towel, places it in his pocket, and leaves—leaving me with so many unanswered questions. What sway did this ring have over me? What actions had I taken that weren't really my own?

"Look Ava, there should be no stress about this—"

"*Are you serious? No stress?*" I cut him off midsentence. "How can you possibly say that? I've been wearing that thing for years. I can't even remember what actions were not my own"

He places a chaste kiss on my lips to shut me up. And boy does it work. I'm just stunned he would actually do that mid rant. I glare my eyes at him intensely, nudging him on to finish what he started.

"We have so much going on in your life right now. Yes, this is horrible. But in the big scheme of things, it could be worse. At least we realized what this is, so we can investigate it. And maybe it will potentially benefit us somehow. Let my dad do what he does. He will get some information from someone, believe me. As far as what you are probably thinking, you might have done things under her persuasion and not known about it. But you cannot change it now. So let's just try to not be angry and enjoy what limited time we have before shit inevitably hits the fan, please."

He is almost begging me, so what else can I do other than nod in agreement. But I will not let this go. I need more answers, and he knows it.

"Come sit down and finish your breakfast. I will fill you in on my thoughts."

I do not move from my spot, and he is forced to pick me up and sit me back down on the stool.

"My father will be back soon, and you can ask him some questions. But for now, eat." He gracefully places an egg, bacon, and cheese omelet in front of me and then starts slicing melons with ease. If that would have been me, my finger would be lost already. "There are certain types of trinkets witches use."

Wow, he's diving right in. I wasn't expecting this. FINALLY.

"These trinkets have all different powers. Yours looked like a blood trinket, which, when you go back hundreds of years, was used for tracking."

"So, wait. Stop. My blood was in there? Wouldn't I have remembered someone taking my blood?" I already regret the question before it's asked. I'm not trying to hurt him anymore than the fact I can't remember our previous lives together.

He skips by the memory part of the question and continues on. "The blood trinket requires blood of both involved—in this case, your fake mother and you. Then you would have to wear it in order for her to track you. The point now is, with this, maybe we can have a witch extract the blood and use it to locate her with a new spell. The old magic is barely undetectable, and we wouldn't have even seen the ring if you hadn't taken it off your finger. Her magic hid the ring as long as you were wearing it. It was undetectable to anyone other than you two."

"Thank you for sharing what else you think is going on. But right now, my brain is just on processing overload, and I need to take a minute to digest this all." I start to quietly eat my food and just process everything I'd heard.

Who knows how much time has passed at this point, but

Elijah is sitting back down next to me. I must have just zoned out. Emotions are swimming through my veins, and I am drowning in them.

I'm mulling over what Elijah and Aidan have said. I have an impact on this world, but how I do that is beyond me. With each moment that passes, the powers within me grow and captivate my whole body. With every step I take, I can feel more of the ground beneath me. The Pureck's powers of nature surely rubbed off on me.

Aidan reaches out to take my hand, pulling me away from my own thoughts. "Come with me. I have something to show you." Once again, it's not a question but a statement.

But without hesitation, I take his hand as he leads me away from the table and, hopefully, away from this nightmare for a minute or two.

Chapter 2

Follow him I do—right into another argument; it echoes down the corridor as soon as we leave the kitchen. Only one topic is on their mind—me. Do I belong in this house? What danger could be brought them by me being here? Even with the place well protected and enchantments hiding it, they could become sitting ducks. A few argue that my presence here is key and that I could be of great use to them. The repetition of that conversation is getting old quickly.

I'm not surprised no one has made a move on me considering I have their alpha by my side. Marcus was right. It is clear Aidan is the pack leader. And with that authority and dominance comes respect, whether they like me or not. And as I am learning, that applies not just to his pack, as he's the alpha among them all.

There are now no words spoken, just fierce looks. Without releasing my hand, Aidan doesn't speak either. He just lets out a low roar, and those in form slowly back away into the corners and, once again, submit. Once they're in their place, he leads me back up the elegant stairs and into his bedroom, a place I'm suddenly wishing I never left this morning.

"Ava, I am so sorry. For everything."

I look up deep into those eyes, and I know there is nothing but sincerity.

We both sit down on the edge of his bed and look into each other's eyes. And even in a house of wolves who probably want me dead, he makes me feel oddly safe. I lay back, staring up at the ceiling and pondering the thoughts over and over in my mind, trying to resist the urge to sleep just from pure exhaustion.

The only way to not sleep is to ask questions. "I do not understand why your kind does not like me." That's putting it lightly. No one wants me here besides him. But he shouldn't just pull rank on this if no one else wants me here. I'm not even sure I want to be here. But what else can I do? The thought of being attacked by more than one werewolf is less than comforting. If Efron were here, he could impart some wisdom and tell me what they were thinking. Efron, Kai, Kieran—oh Kieran, I hope he's OK and keeping everyone together. At least them being together makes me smile, and I'm sure Aidan notices.

He didn't speak when he noticed my mind going down a rabbit hole. Now, my attention is back, and I forcefully nod to him to move along.

"What were you thinking?"

I don't answer because I don't want him to be uncomfortable. So I just shrug it off, and he takes the hint. "It is not every one of my kind who dislike you, Ava. Those you saw fighting were the younger, less knowledgeable among us. They don't have as much wolf time under their belts. They are the ones in werewolf form, because they felt scared and threatened. They do not understand your power as their parents did."

He continues on, but I agree, I don't even know my own power. How can I expect anyone else to? My thoughts drift me off again, but I hear Aidan's voice bringing me back.

"Their parents followed the cause. Some who are here you have actually met before. Some of us here know what peace looked like; some of us here no nothing but war. We have many generations under this roof now, and with that comes a difference in cause. They have grown up with tales of your powers, not being able to see it for themselves. They just want to remain alive. They are fighting an ongoing battle internally, which I help them to mold and understand. This isn't an easy time to be a beast. Some Elders here and my father really try to provide shelter and guidance."

I shake my head, just wishing I could remember something from my former life; anything to hold onto that would help me understand.

"Aidan, give me your hands." I sit up suddenly, startling him a bit. He is perplexed at the change of topic but gives me his hands anyway. If I can focus enough, I can explain. "I have been working a lot with my natural gift, searching for the good in people. It has developed the more I focus and actually lets me search memories sometimes. Earlier this morning when we were talking around the kitchen table, I was able to see into your father's past when his hand grazed mine. I could see the very moment he lost your mother. Maybe if you think about a. moment we shared before, I could see it."

He nods in agreement, just as skeptical as me as to whether this will even work.

I close my eyes, trying harder, searching his soul for a visual—but nothing. I open my eyes to see his lingering back at me, hopeful, until I shake my head and slowly release his hands from mine.

"You can see the good in people and have even been able to see into the pasts of others, but not me—when I have so many memories of you. I just don't understand." His voice is sour, wishing I could just remember.

"Aidan, do you remember the first night we danced in Mexico?"

His lips turn up into a smirk, eyes fond with memory. "How could a man forget, Ava?"

He kills me. Just the way he speaks lures me in every time, as though it was the first time. "I embarrassed myself by telling you I had dreamt of you before. Now I want to tell you what the dream was about."

His eyes widen with longing, trying to catch a glimpse into the part of me he has never seen before. This man knows me so well and for centuries. But can I be the same as I was then? He is always eager for me from me eager for me to remember, eager for me to come back and be me, eager for me to be the Ava he knows. Ye, he is so reluctant sometimes to give me more answers.

"I couldn't believe you had walked into my life that night, because I had been dreaming of you for years, almost for as long as I can remember. I didn't know your name, just that, night after night, you appeared to me. Sometimes, I would just dream of your eyes and sometimes of your face. Other nights, I would have terrifying dreams of bombs going off, but you were always there. You would show up and place your hands on my waist, and I would feel safe. I felt as though I had known your touch for so long and that your gaze was so familiar to me. I just didn't know how. None of it made sense because it felt so real. A part of you has always been with me. Now we are here like this. I can see that it pains you that I do not remember. Can't you see that, even though I don't remember, you have always been lingering in my mind, you have always been with me? I don't take the word lightly, and I know you loved me in the past, and I loved you then too. But those feelings feel embedded in me. I love you, and I cannot express how or why because it doesn't make sense to love someone so soon. But I do. I feel like I get to fall in love with you all over again."

"Ava, I—" Aidan is at a loss for words. He grabs my hips and pulls me closer to him as he pushes my hair away from my face, leaving his hand behind my neck. He inches his face closer to mine, and I close my eyes, feeling the connection between us. It's there, centuries worth of memories I don't remember, but his touch is so familiar. His lips touch mine in a kiss that is filled with years of love and passion that is hard to control.

Yet somehow, I manage. I slowly pull away, and he leans his forehead down to rest on mine, not moving his hands away from my face. I keep my eyes closed and just inhale, breathing him in. I cannot let this intensity between us go too far. That's the other aching feeling I have; no matter how badly my body wants to, I keep pulling away.

When I open my eyes again, a different man greets me entirely, but still Aidan. His long hair is exchanged for shorter hair in a slicked down style paired with a neatly trimmed beard. Very Cillian Murphy in Peaky Blinders, and I'm loving it. Still very much dapper, he is down on one knee in light colored pants, shirt, and vest. His pocket watch jiggles as he reaches into his vest pocket to pull out a ring. The background is a blur, but the ring is crystal clear. It is a beautiful ring with a huge sapphire surrounded by diamonds on a thin white-gold band.

"Ava ..." His voice trails as he kisses me again, bringing me back to real time but with a concerned look on his face.

"Aidan." I can barely keep the tears from welling in my eyes. "I just saw you"—hesitation rolls out of my mouth; how am I to know if any of this is real?—"with me. You were down on one knee and holding a sapphire with diamonds ring." Could I really have caught a glimpse into the past? He looked so happy and in love, or was this a memory of him with someone else?

He shakes his head in disbelief. "Ava, that was when I asked you to be my wife. I was just thinking of that moment."

"I wasn't sure if it was a memory of us or of you with someone else. It's hard for me to decipher these moments when they happen."

"There has never been anyone else, Ava."

I quickly speak to keep his mind off of what hurt I just caused him. "Perhaps I can see the moments when a person is truly vulnerable, not expecting me to go into their memories. You looked unbelievably happy. I want to see you that happy in this lifetime, not the past." The memory I now possess is cause for celebration on so many levels. This truly shows me how he feels, and at the same time, I am gaining more control over my powers, whatever they may be. I bite my lip and close my eyes just to replay this memory over and over again. No scenery to be found, just a happy Aidan; I like it that way.

"The happiest day of my life—you agreed to be my wife." He manages to make everything look elegant as he smiles and moves off the bed. Looking over his shoulder, he checks on me as he saunters across the room. He grabs a box covered in flowers off the dresser and walks back in my direction. The antique is not something I could see Aidan buying; it is very girlie and not masculine in the slightest. He sits back down and places the box on my lap. I carefully run my fingers over every nook and cranny and over the smooth top. It feels so familiar. I look at him with cautious eyes; he yearns for me to open the box and nods his head approvingly, and I reach for the latch and key.

I place my fingers on the key in the front and gently turn the fragile, old bronze key latch. "This box was … I mean is yours." He corrects himself and shrugs apologetically.

It plays a soft tune, a melody I remember my mother humming to me as a child, but I do not know the words. I start to hum the tune. I don't know how long I was humming for, but I catch a glimpse of Aidan reminiscing. He is happy, happier than I have ever seen him before, granted we do not have that much time under our belts in this life. The beautiful engagement ring is the main focus of the contents of the box. It is on a stunning white gold chain now. I take the ring off the chain and slip it onto my finger, just out of curiosity and, with no surprise, find it is a perfect fit. My hand almost reaches itself out as far as possible on its own without control, like all the newly engaged couples I see on the internet. I stare at the magnificent ring. It is so simple and elegant. No doubt my old self has the same taste as my new self. Enough of living in fantasy land or the past. I have to take this thing off.

"Please don't." He stops me from taking it off. "Leave it on, please." Now he is the one begging me.

Even though this is the happiest I have seen him, I cannot help but shake my head.

"Let me explain."

He takes the ring off my finger and puts it back into the box.

But I don't stop talking. "Aidan, I can't. I accepted this ring before with a promise that went along with it. If I were to wear this ring now, I would expect the same promise to be upheld and the same question to be asked of me. I mean, we aren't even officially boyfriend-girlfriend yet, and you disappear all the time." I look down at the ring he has placed back into the box and take note of the picture of Aidan and I surrounding the bottom of the box. We truly look happy and from a different century. I cannot help but let out a groan, "I cannot believe you let me wear that hideous dress and, god, that ugly hat! At least you look handsome. I look like I am in a burlap sack!" I scoff. Seriously, that picture needs to be hidden from the world, but I suppose it has been.

Thankfully, he is ignoring my ring and girlfriend rant. "You always look radiant Ava, and a lot less skin was shown back then, which I am grateful for. I had a hard enough time in Mexico with other men seeing you in your bathing suit. One day soon, I will be able to call you my wife again." A mystery lies in his eyes; he's working something over in his mind, and I know he will not tell me.

Yet, I cannot help but giggle at the smirk on his face right now. I would do anything to make this man happy, but even if he asked me to be his wife now, how could I say yes? I don't even know who

I am anymore. I'm trying to be who I was destined to be without losing sight of myself in the process.

He reaches into his pocket to pull out a tiny envelope and drops the contents into my hand. I'm not even asking where this came from. He beasted out not long ago and had magical pants put on, so at this point, how can I even be surprised?

"I can finally give you your birthday gift." A megawatt smile beams across his face and makes my heart skip a beat.

I place a sweet, innocent kiss on his cheek before I even open it, which has him smirking even more. He needs to know it's the thought that counts above all else, no matter what is in my hands.

"Aidan, where did you find this? How did you know what it looked like?"

There in my hands lies the necklace my mother gave me, the one that was ripped off of me that horrible night in Boston's back alley.

"It's a replica."

That's a fact, down to every detail, even the cross with the roses wrapped around it in the front.

"I knew the necklace you spoke of. I have seen you wear it. Actually, you never took it off. The original had an enchantment so only you could open it. I do not have the ability to do that, so I went with the modern technology and enabled a fingerprint scan." Shrugging it off, he seems nervous.

But I cannot believe what I am holding in my hand. It must be a trinket from my previous life if I had it now. Or what's the story behind the necklace now? I place my index finger on the back of the locket, and it pops open, showing a picture of my real mother and me. My judgment isn't clouded anymore. I know it is her. My finger runs over the photo, and I sob into my hands. My memory has been tampered with, and I wish I could remember more of my real mother.

He pulls me onto his lap and consoles me. "The picture you

had before was just of your mother, but I figured you would want one of the both of you. I have had this picture for centuries; I've been waiting to give it to you."

So many emotions are running through my body; all I can do is lunge at Aidan more. Thankfully, he holds me close as we fall onto his soft duvet. Tears still stream down my face as I place kisses all over him, while repeating thank you through sob-filled words.

With an ounce of his strength, we are both upright. "Let me put it on you."

I swivel around on the bed, and he clasps the necklace on and notices something I almost forgot about. "What is this?" He picks up the key necklace and turns it around.

"Honestly, I'm not sure. My father gave it to me in the box and wrote that I will know what to do with it when the time is right. Beats me."

Aidan turns the necklace back around, and both of them fall down my neck, past my collarbone and right beneath my breasts, safely hidden under my clothes and fitting perfectly together as though they are one necklace.

"Since we are sharing now, perhaps I can enlighten you on a question you asked me in Mexico."

The openness has me clapping like a toddler or a sea lion. I cannot believe he is opening up. I sit in silence and wait.

"This scar." He points to his head. I remember, but what is going on? "You gave it to me."

"What? I hurt you? Why?" Well, that puts an end to our happy-sad conversation.

"Stop it. Don't make that face. Let me explain. It was a week before you agreed to marry me." He stops the conversation to smile at the thought, but I smack his leg, insisting he go on with the story, "So, even though you hated me at the time, you loved me enough to agree to be my wife."

I let out a huge laugh. Something about it just resonates with me, even now.

"Anyway, you had acquired the power of telekinesis somehow. But it was linked with your emotions, so when you got mad, everything in our house moved. You unintentionally sent the whole kitchen in my direction. I was able to doge most of it, except this knife." He opens the box back up and points to a knife that is cracked down the center.

I touch the knife, and the whole memory comes back to me. But in this moment, I am choosing to keep it a secret. I don't know why, but my gut tells me to. "I'm so sorry. I didn't mean to." They're the only words I can come up with. Should I even apologize for something a previous me did in a past life?

"I know, but hey, I survived, didn't I? Mostly because I couldn't die, but still I survived. Here I am, still in love with you after you tried to kill me." That boyish grin is going from ear to ear.

"Is that a hint of sarcasm I'm hearing in your voice. And all this time, I thought I was the funny one." I poke him in the side to get him riled up for the fun of it, before I nudge him for more information. "So anything else you want to share while you're in the moment?"

"Well, there is one more thing." Sweet words practically echo out of his mouth, and he plants a tender kiss on my forehead.

"Oh, goody! Hit me with it." Giggling is something I have missed doing, but I love how open he is being with me. Hopefully, this lasts longer than just for today.

"You are always commenting on how my eyes change color."

I purse my lips out and nod while closing one eye—my, that's so true face.

"Well, my love, you are the reason my eyes change color."

Ignoring the sweet "my love part", I get brazen. "What exactly do you mean?" Now is a horrible time to point out that

Kieran has seen my eyes change. I thought it was Aidan who made them change until Kieran told me he had seen it. I wonder how he is doing. I can't help but have this feeling he needs me right now or that he is helping me with something, like I can feel him in my heart searching for me.

"For a werewolf to have changing eyes is very rare—in fact, nearly unheard of anymore. Only one special being can have a strong enough effect on a werewolf to make them have physical changes, and that person is a soul mate.

"So, I am your soul mate?" This is something he has said before. But until I saw the memory of him proposing to me, it was all just words.

"Yes!" He pulls me down on the bed, and I rest my head on his chest as he holds me close. "You can control the beast in me. You can change me to human if you need to. My eyes are blue with passion for you. I am at your mercy, Ava Buchanan."

Chapter 3

I am enjoying the wordless silence as I take in the feeling of the water washing down over me. It is refreshing, considering I haven't experienced any silence since Mexico. My wandering mind takes me on a journey to those beautiful eyes. I have him. This remarkable man is mine. Once, he was just a figment of my imagination. And now, he is here. Why must my mind drift from happiness to sadness? Laila. Any moment I have that isn't filled with talking leads me to heartache. It feels like a bulldozer ran through my heart. I am brought back to the flash of fire as the heavy beam falls down on me. I fall to the ground in the shower; there is barking trying to save me. My baby. My life in flames consumes me as the darkness encroaches and removes all shadows from my sight.

The water cannot mask my tears. While my body runs warm, my tears are cold to the touch. What is the point of me wiping away my tears when they blend in with the water hitting my face. For someone who doesn't cry, I feel like I have done it a lot today—or at least I've tried to hold it back. But no more. I will sit here and sob, remembering her. Looking at the clock Aidan has set up on his bathroom wall, I see that over an hour has gone by. It doesn't seem like enough time to mourn Laila, but I really need to figure some things out and have more questions to ask. I am making it a point not to cry any further, even though all the pain remains, and part of my heart is missing.

I decide it is best to turn the shower off and go on the hunt for Aidan. I'm new to this world, but part of me wants to go hunt down my fake mother and speak to her, maybe convince her I am still lacking my memories. She might lead to where I need to be—you know, to sort out my destiny and all. Or am I being foolish? I just don't know what the right thing to do is right now. Hopefully, a sign will come out of nowhere.

I wrap myself in a towel and walk out of the lavish en suite bathroom to the over-the-top closet. I have never seen a man with this many clothes in my whole life. How does he even live this double life? I'm exhausted, and he has been doing this for much longer than I have. How does he even have the time to go to work and meetings? As I approach the bed, I notice multiple bags from many different stores, including Neiman Marcus, Nike, and Bloomingdales. I take the contents of all the bags and throw them on the bed to see what all is here, and not one inch of bedspread is showing. I'm guessing Aidan thinks I might be staying a while if he went out and purchased this many clothes for me. All of this is too much for me, and he spent way too much money on this. A pair of jeans or leggings would have been fine, but I need to remember to thank him for the gesture anyway, instead of saying it is too much.

Thankfully, there are some comfy clothing options. So, I opt for yoga pants and a tight zip-up Nike sweater, looking like I'm going for a run fresh out of the shower. I brush my teeth and quickly brush my hair and throw it into a high ponytail, almost too high, like a '90's ponytail high. But who cares? The main advantage of me running hot now is I don't ever have to worry about dying off. I am dry within seconds. I'm ready and on the loose to start the Aidan manhunt in this mansion.

They must have been collecting art for centuries. Not one

hallway is left bare and without some form of talent. Walking through this maze of galleries us like strolling through a museum. I wish I had the time to stop and stare at every single piece; each hall is dedicated to a time frame or artist. IT seems like there is a theme to everything. I didn't even have time to notice earlier that, when you come down the stairs, there are a few sculptures around. I walk through the kitchen once more, on the opposite end of the last time I was here, but at least now I know my general location in this palace. As I exit the kitchen, I can hear Aidan and his father speaking. The conversation appears to be coming from the study on the left. The door is barely cracked, letting a small amount of light into the hallway.

"She needs to be here. She can protect us. I know you want to protect her, but we cannot ignore the obvious." Elijah's tone is much more serious than I have ever heard it before.

"I am not sure that is best for her. Everyone will know she is with me. I just want her safe, at least while she is figuring all of her powers out. Perhaps I should call Marcus."

I feel like shouting at him, but I want to hear what they have to say without me being present. Maybe this will be more honest. I don't have anywhere to go. Walking closer, I am sure to be careful of my footsteps to not disturb the conversation; after all I'm sure they have supersonic hearing or something. I know absolutely nothing. No worse feeling.

"You want to leave her, too? Just like her father did. How do you think that will make her feel? Do what is right for your pack." I can tell Elijah is trying to get a rise out of Aidan, but I am not sure why. Is he purposely trying to hurt his son?

"She is everything to me; you know that. I will keep her safe at all costs. She is not meant to be a pawn for you or anyone else to play with. You cannot sacrifice her for your own benefit. I will not allow it. Would you sacrifice Mum if she were here?" I can feel the disgust coming from Aidan from outside of the room. Now is my time to walk in.

"For fuck's sake, think about someone other than—" interrupting their entire conversation only seems logical to me at this point.

Or perhaps this wasn't the best time. "Hi," I mumble as I crack open the door.

Elijah looks shocked at my appearance here. Or perhaps it's the fact he couldn't sense me coming. Either way, I should have knocked or announced my arrival or something. I need to think a little more sometimes before I just act. Aidan swiftly moves over and embraces me in a tight hug; his speed and hug have me winded. Elijah is up and at his liquor cart pouring himself a glass before our hug is even over. He is pouring himself a glass of Macallan circa 1939—crazy that stuff is still around in here. I can smell the dried furies and earthy peak smoke and sweet toffee flavors from here.

"I've just come to let you know I am going for a run to clear my mind." For whatever reason, I feel the need to whisper. The air in the room has grown cold and filled with tension. I had no plans of going for a run, but I feel this is my best exit strategy.

"Shoes would be helpful. Let me get dressed and I will run with you." I look down at my feet and smirk that he is right. I have forgotten my shoes. But in fairness, I really wasn't planning on it in the first place.

"I know you are trying to keep me safe, but I will be fine. I can tell I have interrupted something and want to let you guys get back to it. I didn't mean to intrude. Plus, you are forgetting I can run faster than you now." I smirk and let out a giggle, mostly to make it seem as though I didn't hear anything before. I playfully shove him. This charade wasn't just for Aidan, but for Elijah as well.

He leans down and places a tender kiss on my forehead. "That was not a question. I will be upstairs in twenty minutes. Wait for me there."

I roll my eyes at him, knowing full well he doesn't like it.

"Here, add this to your collection." He takes a key off his chain and hands it to me.

Is it a key to his room? Or house? I'm not sure. Does this mean I can come and go as I please? I mouth a sweet thank you, stand on my tiptoes, and place a sincere kiss on his lips. Who knows when I will be able to taste that kiss again? My mind is made up. I need answers, and I am not going to come between Aidan and his father. He pulls back and studies my face. He knows that the moment we just shared meant more, but he doesn't know what.

I exit the study, and immediately Elijah and Aidan continue the conversation when they believe I am out of earshot. I make it to the top of the lavish staircase and get hit with the sense I am not alone.

"So, you're the one who makes his eyes change? The stories are true? You do exist." A flawless auburn-haired woman is circling me. I wish her voice matched her looks, but it doesn't, filled with spite and anger.

"My name is Ava, and you are?" I use my most professional customer service voice just to be an asshole.

"I know who you are, but you really don't know who I am? Has he told you nothing? And look what I have found." She flashes me the ring my fake mother gave me, in some bag, but way more durable than a Ziplock. I guess it will keep the ring from burning her. How she got it away from Elijah beat me. I know she is referring to Aidan. These are the times I hate that I love his mysterious ways. I shrug my shoulder, giving her the nope, as strong as possible. Her blue eyes are intent on me as we now stand about five inches away from one another. I raise my eyebrows egging her on to speak more, preparing a snatch-and-go plan. "All of those years he was pining away for you. I expected you to be …"

She takes a long pause as she scans my body with her eyes and circles her fingers. I could have predicted what she was about to say. "Well, more."

Woman just beating on other women, because I don't look like a Victoria's Secret model like her, how original. What are we, twelve?

She is really starting to piss me off. I have no time for this pointless conversation. So I retort, "Well, aren't you classless. If you are just going to keep judging me, we have nothing to talk about." I walk past her and toward Aidan's room.

"I am Aidan's girlfriend." Well, that was enough to stop me in my tracks. I'm glad it did, as I almost let my anger blind me to forget about the ring. An unknowing sense of possession has grown stronger in my body, causing that electricity to emerge. I don't know how to control this.

I need to control this. "Please choose your next words wisely. But if you wish to continue this conversation with me, you will have to walk and talk." I turn on my heel, pleased I didn't fall. And the beautiful, for all intents and purposes, model walks besides me, imparting some information.

"You are feisty. I didn't see that coming. My name is Isabel. I am with Aidan." At least her voice isn't cold anymore. Maybe I can get her to give me the ring instead of this turning into a brawl.

"You've made that abundantly clear." Why is the hallway back to Aidan's room so long? For how long will we have to banter back and forth? Granted it's been less than five minutes, but still.

"I don't think you understand." She stops me by grabbing my arm, and she is hurt. I can feel her heartbreak when she touches me. "He left me for Mexico. For you." The pain in her heart is still fresh; it's so new.

"I am so sorry." It's true. I am. I didn't intend to disrupt anyone's lives. ut I don't know what else to say to her. I feel for her pain, but at the same time, I cannot give her any closure.

"I live here in this sanctuary. I was in that room"—she points to Aidan's door—"until he returned from Mexico and told me you were alive. You took him from me."

Here we go. This is what I was expecting—the blowout, meant to be directed at Aidan. But it's my lucky day, I guess. I pick up the pace and keep walking to the room. She is trailing off behind me spewing out word vomit. She is so caught up in her own world right now she barely even stops talking enough to notice me running back and grabbing the ring from her pocket without her even feeling it.

And as I am standing face-to-face with her, I truly apologize at her stunned faced. "Look, my intention wasn't to mess up anyone's life. I wish you the best."

Her rage really should be pointed at Aidan. She can be mad at me all she wants, but I didn't know she existed. And that isn't my fault; it's his.

I guess something about that set her off. Maybe it was my words or the fact I caught her off guard, and she doesn't seem the type that happens to often. "He and his father only want you here to protect us. They will give you up to the highest bidder if they have the chance to."

And just like that, her words strike a fear inside me and just make my decision easier. But with how loud she was, there is no way Aidan and Elijah didn't hear it.

I open the door and have every intention of flashing her a rude look before I slam the door. But honestly, she deserves my sympathy, not rudeness, despite how she is. But she turns herself into a werewolf and is barreling towards me. Maybe she just doesn't like me, or she's realized I stole the ring from her. She changed without making a sound, so now is not the time for a dramatic departure. With a deep breath and a what the fuck mumbled under my breathe, I quickly move in and lock the door behind me. I'm betting on the fact this door will be able to hold her for a little bit, considering Aidan likes things protected.

Within a matter of second, I find a backpack and a piece of paper. I throw some clothes in there, but her pounding on the door distracts me and prevents me from grabbing anything that could be of use to me. She is pounding on the door louder and louder. The claws start scratching, like nails on a chalkboard, desperate to get in and get to me. The door starts to rip in one spot, wood puncturing through to my side. I place the box Aidan and I looked at earlier on the bed, so when she gets, in it won't be destroyed in the wreckage.

I scribble a note as fast as I can in chicken scratch, hoping he can read it, as my time here comes to a close:

> Aidan,
> I heard you and your father talking.
> I'm doing this so you don't have to make the decision.
> You have my heart.
> Also, talk to Isabel. She needs closure.
> Always,
> Your Love

My note doesn't convey everything I want to say, but it says enough. I place my last words on top of the box as the door breaks open. But in a blink of an eye, my aura pushes me, and I am already climbing out of the window. Her eyes lock on me as she growls, and drool comes out of the side of her mouth. With a sorry glance in her direction, I hop onto the drain next to the building and I'm sliding down the drainpipe adjacent to the window.

Aidan's voice starts echoing outside. He must have grabbed Isabel. The last thing I heard was a wolflike cry and Aidan's stern words. "What have you done with her, Isabel?"

I want so badly to console him, but that's not what's best for him right now. Letting go of the drainpipe, there is a free feeling that reels inside of me, and I bounce on the top of a fruit stand. The wind blows through my ponytail, releasing my hair in the same fashion it always does, not comforting me this time, it can't overpower my anxiety, even though it tries again. On the second bounce, I break through the tarp but land perfectly on my feet without knocking anything over.

In a matter of seconds, I am gone, lost in a group of tourists, hoping a pack of werewolves doesn't follow me as I turn the corner and then another corner and straight and another turn. I am lost. Lost in the city.

"Ava! I was just coming to see you!" It's a familiar voice. I couldn't be any happier. He does not blend in well at all. He stands in all black among the lively tourists, with heavy-duty combat boots and a hat. His salt-and-pepper scruff is tamed and sculpted perfectly against his jawline, stopping at his neck. He looks fierce and ready for a fight that could come at any moment.

"Marcus!" I am overjoyed and begin running to him through the crowd of people but end up at Aidan's front porch somehow.

Damn. Where is the shining light when I need it? Could my sense of direction be any worse. I had to have been walking and running for at least twenty minutes and end up not where I want to be. We have to get moving. I grab his arm and zip him a few blocks away as fast as possible without risking exposure.

His feet dig into the ground, stopping me from pulling him any further, and he holds me at arm's length before giving me a big hug. He is starting to become suspicious as to why I moved our location. He starts inquiring, "Aidan told me about the fire. Are you OK? What are you wearing?" The last bit of his sentence was a slip. I can just tell by the tone of his voice he didn't mean to say it as he sneered at my homeless look.

"I'm fine, Marcus. How is Kieran?"

His eyebrows raise with displeasure.

And I am reminded of time and the fact I am still too close for comfort to Aidan and Isabel's home. "I have to go." I'm so sorry to cut off Marcus when I want to spend time with him more than anything and he could actually help me. But I have this ring, and even though I know I can trust Marcus, Isabel is still in Aidan's, and she wants to rip my head off, not to mention I know where Marcus is going, and that would defeat the purpose of keeping him safe. I need to stay clear of everyone, until I can get some headspace and figure this out or come up with a plan; I just need something without everyone breathing down my throat about who I should be or what I should do.

"Where are you going?" He looks concerned, and I probably look frantic. But for obvious reasons, all of this is out of character for me. He knows there must be something going on. He has to; he knows me better than that.

"I don't know. Look, Marcus, I am running out of time. What aren't you telling me?" There is an encroaching presence getting closer, every hair on my arm is standing up on end alerting me, like a lighthouse sending a signal to me. On top of that, Marcus is holding something back. Maybe it's the fact Elijah wants to use me.

"I don't approve and didn't want to tell you, but he insisted it was important …"

I shoot him the I-don't-have-time-for-this look.

With a sigh, he finally starts getting the words out. "Kieran has been trying to contact you."

Dense footsteps are getting closer, and my feet take off, not knowing who it is and not caring to know, someone from Aidan's pack. I leave Marcus with no words. His last look seemed he was ashamed to tell me that Kieran is looking for me, like he has somehow betrayed Aidan.

Trying to camouflage into the crowd, I find a comfort and funny side to it knowing at least I am better at this than Marcus tends to be, and he's the one who lectured me on it time and time again. There is nowhere for me to go. What do I do? All my belongings burned in the fire, along with any potential clues she might have left behind that could have been used to trace the fake mother. Once again, I'm lost in the city and lost in my mind. At least I have this little thing. I roll the ring around in my fingers, and it is now giving off some serious *Lord of the Rings* vibes, like it's calling me to put it back on; that must be part of the charms she put on it. Fucking creepy.

I have no cell phone and just the mere contents of this pack to hold me over. I have no money and no food. So, things are really looking up for me. The heavens begin to open all at once, pouring down on New York City. Across the street stands an old alcove for the fighting couple that needs to reconcile their differences, a convenience for me to push them out of it now at this very moment, a good old-fashioned red phone booth.

Do I feel bad for kicking the couple out? Yes! But with this new shelter, I am able to rummage through the backpack and manage to find some spare change at the bottom. The coins roll around in my hand as I zip up the pack. I feel sensory overload, with the necklaces dangling between my breasts, a reminder of Aidan, and the ring trying to lure me in. But it's also a sign I probably shouldn't be calling the only number I know by heart. Hopefully, he picks up the other end. After all we have been through, I still feel as though he'd do anything for me, despite everyone telling me otherwise.

This could be poor judgment on my part or the judgment of a hopeful heart.

Chapter 4

This suite is absolutely amazing, all 720 square feet of it. The swanky decor of the W Hotel in downtown New York City is something like the rich and famous would enjoy. It's certainly not a place I could normally afford to pay for—unless I was splitting it with someone. The modern elegance is beautiful. I flop down the circular bed and try to enjoy the chic oasis, but enjoyment is something I feel guilty for even thinking about. I need to track down my mother. I just need to stay here long enough to figure out a game plan or find a witch. But where do I get one of those? A serious con to being new to this world is I don't have the connections. As I bend my head back to sigh in disbelief over the situation, the amazing floor-to-ceiling windows have me wonder. Maybe in this huge city someone could help me, but it is also Aidan's stomping grounds. He's a city boy, and I'm more of a country girl. What future could we possibly comingle? Why am I even thinking about this? Why am I having such doubt? I wish I could keep my mind on track for at least a minute.

The staff left a quite lengthy brochure, chocolates, and champagne on the bedside table. I skim the packet; it really doesn't lie. I read to myself in my head in the most uppity customer service voice I can, making exaggerated body movements, so posh, darling. *Lounge in the tranquil sitting room creatively designed with backlit acrylic panels … an organic silk and wool animal print rug … soothing earth tones … Stay connected and inspired in the stylish multilevel work area.*

Work! Shit! I still can't believe I left Harrison high and dry. Surely no one would be tracking my work phone anyway, knowing I'm on the run, because what kind of person would have the world chasing her and still feel bad about work? Oh, that's right, me! I pick up the hotel phone and quickly dial my work office number. I know they are closed right now, so I hit his extension and leave another brief message, as I always do! I apologize over and over again on the phone, beg him to understand, and give as much vague detail as possible. What are the chances, when my life returns back to normal, I will get my job back? Slim to nonexistent. But I feel better, as if I'm holding onto my humanity letting him know none of this was his fault. None if it is anyone's fault.

Room service should be here any minute, but my mind still wanders. I wish Marcus would have answered my previous question. If I love someone, but they do not love me back, could they kill me? Or does the feeling have to be mutual? Based on what Elijah said, he isn't even certain. How do I get the answers I seek? Maybe I need to find a connection to the Pureck somehow.

Did I make the right decision? There would no doubt come a time in my life when I would have to be selfless with a passionate love, but was it today? Hopefully, Aidan understands my reasoning, although I doubt it. He has such a lack of trust in me for some reason. Could it be because I don't have my memories? Making him choose between his pack, his father, and me isn't right. No matter what he chose to do, he would get backlash from his sanctuary, and that's just not right. Surprisingly, talking to myself has calmed my nerves. Afterall, he has a family, and I don't. Knowing what that feels like, I could never do that to him.

Someone is knocking stridently at the door. The knock grows

louder and louder, not something I would expect from room service at a proper establishment like this. I rapidly open the door, "I didn't think you'd be here so fast!"

Dino's arm wrap around me, comforting me. How I miss his arms.

"I was close to the area when you called. Luckily for you!" He shoots me a playful wink, and it is like we are back in Mexico in our own time. I fiddle with the ring in my jacket pocket, debating whether to tell him. But I hold back. My gut is telling me not to; now is not the time.

His boyish smile beams. How could that ever be fake?

"Thank you for this, Dino." I wave my arm around the room. "What would I do without you?" That is the question, isn't it?

"You will never have to find out."

Aidan and his father seem to think Dino is my Shaddower and that he is the one who can mask my powers, make me not see the good or bad in people if he is nearby. I dare not ask him. Even if that is so, we still have a bond of friendship that cannot be faked. He has always been my person. As Meredith Grey would say, he would do anything for me, and I for him. Plus, he could be my unintentional Shaddower. What if he doesn't even know about this world and then I bring him into it? Maybe he didn't choose this life or even have any knowledge of it. Shaddowers are born that way, just as I was. Everyone has a choice how they life their lives; maybe he lives it by the saying ignorance is bliss.

Walking around the room, I give Dino the brief rundown of what happened. Of course, I'm sure to leave out all the werewolves bits and what I have been up to in my free time recently. Basically, all he needs to know is that Aidan's "family" didn't want me there. Dino has always been my sympathetic ear, and normally he won't pry into situations. He is trying to now, though. But I won't fold.

We are finally situated and eating the room service food. He has extended the room here until Tuesday to give me some extra time, although I'm not sure why. Maybe just out of kindness, as I currently don't have a home. The fire? I haven't even told him about the fire. I don't even think I need four days to figure out my next move. The less time spent here the better. I'm like a sitting duck in this place. I know Kieran and Marcus are both close by. If I can catch one of them alone, I can seek some guidance. I ramble on and decide to fill him in about the fire too, but it seems like he already knows. He isn't reacting the way I would expect him to if this was fresh news.

"I told you, Ava, he is a jackass." Dino's cold words distract my train of thought, or perhaps he was just trying to break the unusual silence that never happens between us.

"He isn't. He is just trying to protect me in his own morbid way. I would never make him choose between his family and me. That is just not who I am; you know me. That's why I left, but I left everything behind when I did. So, I appreciate you being here for me," I say, thinking a sweet word will lead him away from any Aidan talk. But it isn't working. The truth still stings more than I expected it to. Do I accept a life without this soul mate? What do I even feel right now besides confusion?

"He's an overbearing son of a bitch. He left your dog in a burning building. He's definitely buff enough to carry you both."

I want to vomit with the way Dino is phrasing things today. He is constantly trying to make Aidan out to be the bad guy. Is that my best friend talking or my Shaddower?

I always find myself defending Aidan to everyone. "Dino, he didn't intentionally kill my dog. He tried to save her, but he said I was more important." The loss of Laila is so fresh in my mind, and the last thing I want right now is to be reminded of that pain. It will push me over the edge. He places his hand on the top of the table, and I oblige his silent question by placing my hand in his.

"We could rule the world, you know? If you decided to be with me, we could have it all. Anything your heart desires." There is an evil promise hidden beneath those words. He is my Shaddower, and he knows it. I have no doubt in this very moment. But for all he knows, I have no clue of this world yet. I should play this out to see what kind of information I can get. He probably knows more than I do. The low rumble in his voice tells me he knows who I am.

Keeping up with the lie, I close my eyes for a second as though I am pondering what he said. When I open them, I smile an innocent smile, a shy one, that I am hoping will lead him to say more. This is the first time I have seen what Aidan sees in Dino—the lies, deceit, and the manipulation all come forth within seconds.

"Dino, you know I love you," I make sure to squeeze his hand tightly. "My heart is broken right now, and I don't want you to think you are a rebound. You deserve better than that. You deserve me at my best." I'm hoping he plays right into my hands.

He walks with that walk around the table to get on his knees in front of me while I still remain sitting on the chair. He places his hands on my thighs and looks deep into my soul. "Ava, if you want this, if you want me, I will help mend your broken heart. We can do anything together. Please see that." He is trying to hide the evil in his voice, and I know what is coming next. I close my eyes as he slowly stands up and leans in to kiss me. A chaste foreign kiss on my lips. It doesn't feel right; I am using his emotions toward me, fake or not, to get information.

I slowly pull away, "Dino ..."

"I know. I know. It was too soon for the kiss, but I know you want this, Ava, and I won't leave your side until you feel safe." Evil still lurks beneath his thick lashes.

Oh, that's just peachy. Now I will have someone else up my ass, until I figure out how to get answers and get away, again.

"Tonight, let's go dancing! I'll call Sofia since she's in town. That's bound to lift your spirits. Plus, what do you love more than dancing?"

I find it suspicious that everyone is in this town right now.

Could Sofia have a part to play in this too? No one has mentioned her to me though, so she might be safe. And this all could be a coincidence. I nod a slow yes to his proposal.

Dino and I haven't spoken since dinner, and there could be worse things in life, like everything else that is going on. He has disappeared off the face of the Earth and simply and shortly said he would pick me up fifteen minutes before we are supposed to meet Sofia. Life without a phone, especially in this case, has been more difficult than ever. I could even tell in a text message if Sofia was up to something; she is such an easy read. There's a sinking feeling in my stomach that tonight isn't a good, good night, cue The Black Eyed Peas. Hopefully, at first glance of Sofia, I will be able to tell if something is going on. I am going to have to rely on my instincts, even if they haven't been the best when my Shaddower is around.

Staring at myself in the mirror, I am almost unrecognizable to myself. What happened to the normal girl who just wanted to travel and work and live a normal life? For all intents and purposes, I was happy. I just want to be wrapped up in a blanket by a fire, drinking a beer with my pup by my feet. I still look the same, but I don't feel the same, and it shows. My natural waves fall down past my shoulder, and the minimal look is taken to an extreme.

Dino left a dress and mascara on the bed for me, but I don't trust wearing anything he has placed out for me. I grab an outfit from my backpack and don it, making sure to put my previously worn outfit back into the bag. Sneakers are the go for me tonight, and I know I'll be incredibly underdressed compared to who all I am going out with, but I'll just say tonight is for comfortability and not to find a man. There has to be a way for me to get away tonight. It has to happen.

Before Dino gets back, I make a beeline to the kitchen to place whatever knives are in the kitchen in the pack. Of course, I feel bad for stealing. But maybe I'll send them back in the mail when I am done with them, along with an apology note. I need to make everything seem as normal as possible tonight before I find my escape. My conscious will have to live with it for now. This will have to do, considering the rest of the room is entirely child proof.

Dino arrives quiet as a church mouse and startles me. "Ava, are you ready to go?"

I walk into the living room with the backpack slung over my shoulder, and Dino looks me up and down. "You seriously cannot bring that. Let's buy you a small purse or something, or I'll stick whatever you need in my pockets. You shouldn't have much."

He's right. I don't even have an ID. He keeps arching his brow looking at my outfit. I know this is, by no means, the going out norm. His hands are placed tightly in his dress pants, dapper as ever.

Now is the time to play my card. I reach my hands out to him and pull him in close to me, "Who am I going out to impress anyway? I thought we decided earlier we would give this a try …" My words trail off, and he smirks at me but not before placing a too long kiss on my lips; but I lean into it.

"Aidan, who?" He laughs and pulls me into a deeper kiss.

My body can't give my lack of comfortability away now. *Pull it together, Ava.* And I do just that.

We meet on middle ground, even though this shouldn't be a discussion. I change my shoes and place my sneakers into the backpack and sneak the ring into my pocket without him knowing. I wear over-the-knee, black high-heeled boots with my jeans, a white tank, and a leather jacket, kind of looking every bit badass.

But I shoot him a friendly reminder. "Dino, you need to stop caring what people think."

And just like that, we are out the door hand in hand as he escorts me to the elevator. With just the slightest touch, I am able to read his mind, and I am not sure why. I am getting bits and pieces that I know I shouldn't be able to access. The elevator ride down as our hands are entangled his facade is fading away. He is surrounded by the same darkness I saw in Victor's eyes on the tarmac at the airport. Is that how Victor found me? I try to search his soul for answers, but there isn't enough time. Whose side is Dino on?

My best bet is to sneak away and find Kieran. I can trust him; my heart knows it. Marcus would be ideal. But his allegiance lies with Aidan, always has and always will.

Chapter 5

"Sofia! You look radiant as ever!" I smile from the inside out, definitely keeping up with appearances. But should I even be surprised at this point she doesn't reciprocate with the same actions? Like come on, at least pretend to be best friends with me. Now what? How is she involved. I swear I should move out to the mountains, leave everything, and pretend none of this ever happened. The world would survive without me, right?

She looks flawless as usual, but her face is filled with uncertainty, almost as though she doesn't want to see me at all. I'm on the fence as to how she could possibly be involved. I've been around her loads of times without Dino present, and never once has she been anything but true to me and our friendship. *Sofia, I am sorry if somehow, I got you mixed up in all of this without you even knowing. This isn't fair.* I pull her into an embrace, even though it is unwanted on her end, but I am seeing a vision of her and David fighting—fighting about me. He is throwing things at her and yelling in a venomous tone as she falls to the floor covering her face. I try to search her mind for more, but Dino joins us, creating a group hug, and I am not strong enough to see past it.

My instincts are kicking in as I pry. "Where is David?"

We all pull away from the hug at the same time.

"Last time I saw you two, you were inseparable. Is everything OK?"

Quick to change the subject, she fakes a smile. "He'll meet us out later. Come. Let's go dancing." She just kicked into an Oscar-winning actress with that performance, but I know better. She grabs me by the hand, and it is hard controlling the electricity that is boiling inside of me.

Dino follows closely behind us into the club.

Sadly, I didn't get carded, but I am still part relived given the fact I don't even have an ID on me. Ah, the sweet sting of a double edged sword. I knew this day would come, but not yet! Come on! With everything going on, we could still pretend I'm young enough to get carded. The Mean Fiddler is quite the unique place; and honestly, if this were my normal life, it's a place I'd probably get tanked at from having too many shots of Jameson. The Irish pub, in every sense, reminds me of Aidan, especially how it seems the only Irish people in New York have migrated to this bar tonight. Upstairs is a bugger bar with a large dance floor and plenty of room for socialization; downstairs, there is a smaller bar, but the room is equipped with karaoke. For the win! At least one perk of the night, even if I don't get to participate. What am I even doing out anyway? Aidan will find me. I hate having to pretend and keep up with a ruse, but I need information.

Even in a happy-go-lucky place like this, the atmosphere between Sofia and me is almost unbearable. She doesn't even want to speak to me, at all. The mingling between us is so fake she moves across the room. Our normal, happy-to-see-each other relationship is not here. It has disappeared into the past. I just want one normal thing back into my life, and I was hoping Sofia would be it. Clearly not. Is the argument between her and David the root cause? Is she that much in love with him that she would give up her friendship with me? There must be more to the story. I want the music to take over me and distract me—to take me back to Mexico, a simpler time.

As I push my way through the crowd, a stranger grazes my side. Without even realizing it, I must have given him a shock. He is lying on the ground in pain, not certain what part of his body to hold. I cannot be here. I panic, and the flight-o- fight instinct is leading me to flight. I want to stay and help, but I am losing myself with every second that passes. There is too much going on, too much inside me that I am unable to control. The passersby are not sure what has happened. They are looking around the room for answers, until the bouncer comes over and explains it as a drunken mess.

Somehow, I have managed to find Sofia, and we are standing inches apart. She is glaring at me in awe. She must know. Somehow, she knows who I am and what I am capable of. But that was just a small fraction compared to what I can do. Fear is written across her face, and she is pointing to the man the bouncers are carrying out, screaming in pain. I shove her hand down, not wanting to attract any attention; grab her arm; and try to remain as calm as possible while pulling her away. "Come with me. We need to talk." I can sense her body remaining still. "*Now,*" I harshly mumble under my breath, and she complies.

I never imagined having to be this kind of person with my best friend. Her eyes are frozen over, and she is just rolling through the motions, unsure of what to do. I don't blame her quite frankly, but after all of these years, I would have expected more from her. We are walking past the downstairs bar, but people are heading in the opposite direction, no doubt to hear the screaming man. The dark hallway makes it hard for me to read the signs, but the chatter of the women that fill the ladies bathroom, gossiping about hoping they find their dream man this night and wondering if their makeup is still on point, leads me. It would be too much of a hassle to make them all leave the bathroom, not to mention suspicious. I don't care how many movies I've seen where they kick people out of the bathroom; that just doesn't happen in real life. Sofia looks surprised as I continue walking past the ladies room to a janitorial closet—small, good lighting, and convenient. I lock the door behind us.

"Tell me what you know. Tell me why you and David were fighting about me."

The fact that I've never been this blunt with her before has her shook, but I need answers, and I need them now. She keeps shaking her head, telling me she doesn't know anything. Her eyes. She is hiding something. Aidan said Dillion was a Grimmer. Perhaps he is the one who has spoken to Sofia. I reach out to touch Sofia's hand but give her a little shock accidentally. Thankfully, it was just friction, the remanent of what I had used on the stranger.

"Ava, not here." She looks around the tiny room we are squeezed in.

Despite the fact that I am standing on a bucket, not caring that my boots are ruined, I give her the come-on look. She keeps shaking her head no. So for her, my friend, I nod in compliance. This has just reassured me she knows something. As soon as I unlock the door, she shuffles past me, happy to be free of the space and me. She takes me by the hand and leads me through the crowd of people. We must be getting somewhere if she feels comfortable enough for this right now.

Someone has called an ambulance. I'm sure the scanners will report the man said he has been shocked, which means I need to leave. Like ten minutes ago. I am trying to walk past him without making eye contact but fail miserably. I am hoping he can see in my eyes how sorry I am. He holds my glance for what seems like an eternity as he is placed onto the stretcher. Our eyes lose contact as he closes his eyes, sending chills throughout my body and bringing wind into this saddened street. The gust has everyone surprised, making Sofia look back at me over her shoulder. I suspect she thinks this is also my doing. As I exhale, frost covers the air in front of me. I know she saw that much. The wind continues to flow between him and me, and I know he is going to be OK. The screams have stopped, and his heart is beating. I can focus enough to hear it.

Dino is missing in action, which is suspicious enough—probably out conjuring up some darkness or whatever it is that he does. I still can't help but search around for him in my peripheral vision, but the most suspicious of all is how calm and collected Sofia is all of a sudden. As if to answer my unspoken question, her voice is filled with angst, "We are going to my hotel. There we can talk, and you can explain all of this to me." She seems determined, and she hails a cab down within a split second. If there is one person on the planet who will listen to me, no matter the absurdities spewed, I always thought it would be Sofia, but now I'm thinking the only person is Kieran.

We ride in stillness as the cab driver takes us to the location. I'm not surprised that we pull up to the Waldorf Astoria and the bellboy greets Sofia by name. She still has that way with people; good to know some things haven't changed. I just can't help but keep wishing her warm, friendly demeanor were directed to me, instead of the cold, distant, determined Sofia I have never experienced before.

Part of me wishes this were all just some dream I could wake up from and go back to my normal life. The other part of me knows deep down, everything happens for a reason. I have some greater purposes; I can feel it now, even if I can't comprehend the reasoning at the moment. One day, this will all be over, and I will return to New York City and experience it like I should have—with a walk through Bryant Park and to see the Christmas tree light up, shining miles long, all while being cheesy and holding the hand of the one who loves me and sharing a kiss as the night fades away. One day. Just not even close to today.

Even under these odd circumstances, I still want to take in the beauty and elegance of the architecture of this hotel. But Sofia is pulling me through the main doors and into the lobby with great haste. The marble floors are making Sofia slip around, and I smile on the inside; if only I could share some of my newly acquired grace with her, I would, even now. The lift doors open, and she hits the button, all while maintaining a serious posture and without speaking to me even for a second. She snarls at the few people who join us in the elevator right before the doors close. They continue on with their casual chitchat, and I am so envious. Normal. That's all I want.

"We are staying in the Towers Penthouse Suite." She smiles wickedly once the last person leaves the elevator.

"Good to know." I roll my eyes at the Sofia I didn't know as unintentional sarcasm rolls off my tongue. I've pissed her off even more, but what else am I supposed to say? Her eyes are piercing with greed as she speaks with a sense of entitlement I find revolting, and I have to let her know. "What is going on with you? You aren't being yourself. What do you know?" The elevator door chimes as the big doors tuck behind the walls, and we exit in unison.

"Let's just get to the room. I can make some tea and we can talk—about everything." Jeez, tea has me having flashbacks to my mother. "I know what you are hiding. Why didn't you tell me?" It seems as though she is pleading with me, but now I just don't trust her.

I think honesty is the best policy here. "Because I wanted to protect you. Hell, Sofia, I didn't even know what was happening to me. How could I explain it to someone else?"

She keeps looking at me with regret as she slides the card into the door and the low ding releases the locks. I am about to turn away, to go anywhere but here—the fright on her face is scaring me. The double doors fly open without her touch, and I am pulled into the room before I can even get my senses together. I keep my eyes locked on Sofia, and she mumbles sorry, and the doors slam closed in her face; the last thing I notice is tears flowing down her cheeks.

My feet are dragging across the floor, until I start to kick and scream for my life. The arm around my throat gets tighter and tighter. Before I can build up the energy to send a pulse across the room I think, *This could be my chance for answers.*

Whoever they are who have hold of me, place me in a low sitting chair and have my arms and wrists bound to the chair. As if the rope burn on my arms isn't enough, they start binding me down with zip ties, even on each one of my fingers. They are being very thorough, and I have the feeling I should be more scared than I am, but my need for answers presses on. One thing they did right was tying me tightly enough for not one muscle of my upper body to be able to even move a centimeter. Out of nowhere, one of the guys slings my backpack across the room. That came from the other hotel. They must have broken in. Or Dino gave it to them. They must be looking for something, and I know it's not the ring; no one knows about it because no one could see it. I sigh in relief. They aren't going to find anything in that backpack, not even a cell phone. I have nothing. I smirk, thinking about their wasted time.

The body moves around to the front of me. "No, David!"

Sofia's lover is the one who has kidnapped me, not Dillion. He bends down in an attempt to tie my leg to the chair. But before he can even make the move, I swiftly and with as much power as I possess, kick him in the nose. He is knocked back on the glass table and doesn't even scream or seem phased in the slightest. His blood covers the white couch behind him. I can only imagine what the Waldorf will charge for that. Why can't my mind focus? Come on, Ava! I manage to stand awkwardly with the chair attached to my arms. If only I had Aidan's strength at this moment. Then I'd have no issue unbinding. Pulsing out will only send me flying.

Where is the other guy? I know two pulled me in, but where is he? I listen for footsteps, ready for a fight. They come closer and closer to the room.

Dillion! Now this is more up to snuff with what I thought was going to happen. But he catches a glimpse of David sorting himself out and raises a brow at me. He's impressed and smug about it. He is quick, almost as fast as Aidan. He is running over to me, and within half a second, he is here, looking down on me. He grabs my face and brings me in closer to him. He can feel my struggle as I am trying to get away from his strong grasp.

He leans down and places a violent kiss on my lips and bites me hard on the side of my mouth. "Oh, how I wanted to taste you, Ava."

I could throw up. First Dino and now this? Do men think the key to ruling the world is me? Forcing my hand isn't the way to gain my affections. What the hell is going on here? He pushes me back to look at all of me from head to toe, and I spit in his face. It's the only thing I can muster the ability to do right now.

"Now, that isn't playing nice."

I'll show him nice. I'll shock him to nothing if I can get my hands on him. I need information. I have to stay levelheaded and get my shit together. He shoves me on the chest, knocking me down onto the chair, and I let out a squeal of pain; part of the wood from the chair has broken during the fall and pierced me in the side. While I am down, David comes over and binds my legs to the chair tightly, using everything he has within arm's reach, and then he sits the chair back up, and I plop forward, groaning at the wood that is stuck in my side.

"If you would have accepted me, this would have never happened." Dillion's words are poison to my ears.

David steps to the side, and Dillion leans down, resting his hands on the arms of the chair. The weight of him makes the wood inch further into my body. I try not to give any signs of pain away, but I know it's written across my face. He leans down lower in front of me, so our eyes are at the same level, moving his arms from the chair to my legs. My body chills under his touch and he runs his fingers over my body.

"Let's just ask her the questions and get out of here." David's voice is quaky; he is definitely not the one in control here.

Dillion is running the show and, apparently, on his own good time. He completely dismisses David, not even a head shake or acknowledgement of any sort; he just points for David to fetch my backpack. David walks over and drops the contents of my bag on the floor and rummages through what little it holds.

"I see you must have been preparing for something. We followed you to your hotel room. You have knives. We were hoping for more. Toss me one of those." Dillion stands and starts to circle me, until he is behind me with one hand on my neck. David throws the knife to him, not without skimming my hair. I watch as a few strands of my hair float to the ground. The knife was just inches from my face, as though it was done intentionally with that perfect placement. I am in a different world now, and this confirms it. Dillion traces the knife over the front of my shoulders and across my neck. I hold my breath, in hopes he doesn't nick the skin before he gets the answers he's looking for. He grazes the knife again over my shoulders, deep, drawing blood.

"Brave Ava, trying not to show pain. You forget. I know all about you. I know you can feel pain," he keeps whispering him my ear.

I hesitate but make eye contact with David, who look scared to death, maybe of his friend or what he knows is about to happen—torture to get answers I don't even have.

I can't keep quiet any longer as Dillion starts to shift in front of me, moving like the snake he is, "This doesn't make sense.

Aidan said you were a Grimmer, but I saw good in you, Dillion, in Mexico. I saw it. How could you even claim to want me, and this is what you do?" I was searching for anything in his face, something. I shake my head, surprised he has now placed the knife on the floor. He is now full frontal, and I try to keep the vomit down in my mouth, as David just lingers in the background. He was definitely someone's loyal Saint Bernard every step of his life, I can tell, unfortunate he doesn't want to be loyal to the right kind of person.

"I suppose I could explain a few things to you, naive girl."

Great. Now he is going to talk. All those episodes of *Criminal Minds* I have watched have finally paid off. Keep him talking. Buy enough time for me to take in the scene and plan my escape. He and David both look normal, dressed in attire that shows they are ready to go out. How can they be a part of this world? How am I a part of this world? Appearances really don't matter.

Dillion grabs my face, stopping my wandering eyes. "You will make eye contact when I speak to you. After all, I am doing this as a courtesy to you."

"I'm sorry. You're right. Can I ask you a"—I mumble under my breath to play the part—"question."

"Yes." He pulls the chair I am sitting on over right in front of the bloody white couch, and he takes a seat, making sure we are inches apart. I am really tired of people invading my personal space.

"David, where does he fit into all of this? I know you are a Grimmer, but I know nothing of him."

David squirms at the question, making it clear he had no intention to play the game Dillion does. He shakes his head toward Dillion as he leans against a wall, silently pleading for him to not entertain me.

"Please, I am lost in all of this. I don't even know what is happening to me. I need answers. And if you had treated me differently, maybe we would be in a different situation."

"Since David is reluctant to answer, I shall oblige. You see, Ava, you didn't figure out David because he wouldn't touch you. He was a bit superstitious of you, but I knew your powers hadn't fully developed. Plus, with your Shaddower around, you couldn't see anything but good in me. Where is your Shaddower anyway?" Just pure putrid. Everything he says.

"Clearly not here." Man do I need to learn to use sarcasm at the right times, instead of all the time. Now isn't the time for snarky remarks. I hope a shard of glass has pinched him in the ass. "Why me? Honestly, what's all the fuss about?"

He isn't playing the game anymore. "Dino left you. Sofia left you here for her love of David. Poor thing didn't stand a chance. Insecure girl. Aidan is nowhere in sight. Why not just join me?" He stands, putting his hands in his pockets, and jumps over me and what is left of the table—all just to stride back around toward me. Is he showing off now? What was the point of that?

"I would rather die than kill innocent people."

"In time, my dear, all in good time." He places another kiss on my lips, and I turn to the side. But there is no avoiding him. In that instant, I notice a large window; perhaps I can use that as my escape. No other options in sight; obviously, I can't just take the elevator down.

"I still don't understand. What do you want from me? What do you have to gain from this? From me?" I know there is good in him somewhere, even if it is just a little bit.

"Oh, Ava, you are the perfect tool. If only you would embrace it. My story is almost as sad as yours—except the ones I love didn't betray me; they were taken from me. The Militia killed my family when I was a child, leaving me alone and helpless. I never forgot; any memory wipes they tried to use didn't work on my blood. A pack leader took me and explained to me the world we lived in, and from that moment on, I followed him, until he passed away. Now I am the leader, and it is time for me to avenge my family and all others the Militia has done wrong. I will kill them all and anyone who stands in my way. They will feel the pain I felt as a child."

So, he wants a bloodbath. "Revenge shouldn't motivate you, I know they were taken from you. And like you said I know the pain, but this—"

"*Enough of this*!" David cuts me off, knowing I would get more out of Dillion. I keep turning to look at him mesmerized by the lightning he is rotating around his palm. "Let's get her back to base now."

"Who the hell is that?" Dillion asks David about the knocking on the door.

David walks over and peers through the hole and opens the door. "It's Sofia."

Her love for him is real, I can see it in her face. As he bends over to give her a kiss, he extinguishes the lightning in his palms.

"Might I have a word with Ava please? You two can sit in the other room. I just … if this is the last time, I am going to see her …" Her voice trails off, and she is afraid to make eye contact with me. "I have something I need to say." She starts to cry, either at the state I am in or what she has done to me. Or maybe it's something else. Whatever the case, the waterworks won't stop, and it even makes David uncomfortable.

David tries to protest her request. But Dillion lets it slide. I truly might have been getting somewhere with him. I don't understand why we all can't work on stopping the Militia together. Dillion brings David into the other room.

There are so many things I want to say to her, but she needs to speak first. She sits down in front of me and places her head on my knees, "Ava, I am so sorry."

I try to shuffle her off of me, but it is no use. I still can't budge.

"I was, well, I am, so in love with David that I am blind. I should have known. Then he began to talk about who you really are, and I didn't believe him. Not until tonight at the club." She lifts her head and tries to search my eyes for answers. I know. It's what I do to everyone else.

"I'm not the bad guy here, Sofia. How could you do this to me? Betray me this way? I wish there were words for how I feel."

"I see that now. They said they wouldn't hurt you, but I just had to come back and see for myself." Her voice is so small I can barely hear her.

"Well, they lied. Surprise, surprise." *Honestly, Sofia, and they say I'm naive.*

"If we could get these binds off, do you think you could escape? You can't make it through the hotel without them catching you."

I quickly glance around the room. It's fortunate she has had a change of heart, but they have taken my knives, so even they didn't trust her.

"It will have to look like there was a struggle, so you don't get in trouble. I will headbutt you, but don't make a sound. Then I think if I start running down near that door"—I shift my head to show her—"I'll have enough momentum to break through the window and hope for the best."

"You could really do that?" Her eyes flash to the window in disbelief.

"If you're willing to help me, that's my best shot, And best case, I land on the roof across the way."

She pulls out a knife from the side of her dress and starts to cut away my bindings. I silently stand and shake off the remains. I give her an apologetic nod as I headbutt her in the face and run to the back door without seeing how she is doing. I catch a glimpse of her bleeding on the floor and the door from the other room beginning to open. I press off the wall with every fiber and power I have within me and run.

The door fully opens, and Dillion is transforming into a hairy beast as David is shooting lightning bolts my way. But my body absorbs them and uses them as more force as I break through the window. I can feel the glass shards digging into the side of my face that is exposed. Glass digs deeper into the side of my face as the inertia pulls me forward. I consciously don't look down, keeping my head forward on the target and just praying I make it. The wind picks up, helping me push forward to my destination. The wind presses against my back the whole way and I feel like I am flying in the sky. My adrenaline pumps as my fingertips latch onto the brick building with my legs dangling. Innocents below look up to me and marvel at what they have just seen. In the time it takes them to pull their phones out, I am already concealed on the top of the roof, no longer in danger of falling to an uncertain death.

David and Dillion stand in the window of the Waldorf Astoria knowing better than to attempt this jump, especially Dillion in human form. They can't beast across or send lightning bolts shooting across the sky without causing terror in the humans down below. All I can hope for at this point is that Sofia will not be harmed and that she changes the direction of her life.

Chapter 6

The wood piercing my side hurts more the more I try to take it out. But with one swift motion, I grit through the pain and pull it out and toss it to the ground. I don't even have time to think about where to find bandages. Making my way out of here is my only thought, considering Dillion and David must not be far behind. But I can't run too fast, or they can probably see my aura. Talk about a double-edged sword.

Jumping from building to building, I realize my depth perception is off, making my knees buckle. Something is happening to my body, but can I move through this at the same time I am running for my life. Every fiber of my being is trying to shut down the premonition before it happens. I need to not think and jump; the only thing I need to be concentrating on right now is making an escape and getting far enough away to gather my thought, but the premotion is too strong. I'm halfway to the next rooftop when I cannot stop controlling it anymore and the vision takes over me. But this is real time, not a premonition; it's a live feed right now.

Aidan is fighting Dillion in the hotel room of the Waldorf. David and Sofia are crouched in the corner of the room. David is trying to hide Sofia, but surely Aidan must know she is an innocent in all of this. I have never seen him attack this way. I keep trying to shake my head loose of this feed, but my body cannot stop. I can't even see in front of me. The live feed is real, and I'm there in my mind. Aidan bites Dillion, and they both slowly start changing back into their human forms.

Aidan turns his glare to David and Sofia. Within that split second, Dillion runs out of the room holding his neck, trying to stop the bleeding. But Aidan doesn't go after him. He just lets out a deep growl and focuses his eyes directly on David. "You." The desperation and anger in his voice make for a tone I have never heard in him before; he is a different person.

"I'm just a pawn in all of this. Please don't hurt her." At least David redeems himself trying to save Sofia, and he isn't using his powers, almost as though he is silently pleading with Aidan. He doesn't want this fight. And then he asks, "How did you even find us?"

His final question, without question, causes Aidan to rethink his position. I can see it in his eyes. He is furious—if you are that innocent, why care how you were found? "Her." Aidan points to Sofia, but it's almost as though he can sense me watching in. He shoots a glance around the room, letting me know he isn't going to harm her. But then his eyes change, and darkness takes over. He is grabbing David by the neck and, even in human form, has managed to lift him a clear foot off the ground. In an instant, David is lying on the floor lifeless. Aidan has snapped his neck. Sofia's cries echo though my mind as I slam down onto the next rooftop.

I must have been out for a couple of minutes. I'm coming back to consciousness, and I see six people, all surrounding me in a circle. Well, isn't this just great? My bearings are off, but there are four men and two women, all sporting the same intense face and uniforms, not trying to hide themselves under masks. The glow of the illuminating streetlights makes their silver uniforms easier to see at night. They look like some cult, for sure here to capture me as well, because why wouldn't I be hunted down by more than one person in one night, especially after the scene that was just caused? Not a huge fan of my new standard nights to be honest, I go without it.

One man separates himself and starts slowing walking towards me. Clearly, he is powerless, as he reaches behind his back and pulls out a sword. His blond hair is nearly as long as mine, and his brown eyes are glazed over as though he has no soul to speak of. Maybe he's under a spell; at this point, nothing would surprise me.

"Riley, attack, now! Hurry, before she's up!" Some young, white-haired, dark-skinned, gray-eyed woman points her wand, and he is off in my direction. She is dressed differently than the others, relatively normal looking. I knew it had to have been a spell.

Before I can even think of what to do, it's like all the instincts in my body take over, and someone else is operating it entirely.

I run toward him. As soon as I get close enough, I drop to the ground, ignoring the burning on my knees as I slide right between his legs. I am up and standing before he even gets the chance to turn around, and in one motion, I roundhouse kick him and knock him unconscious. Riley tumbles to the ground, and I look for an exit. But there is none, and I am significantly outnumbered.

Some other goon picks up Riley's sword and is put under a spell. The sword must be the key here somehow. I must make a mental note not to touch it. The man takes heavy strides toward me, the sword firmly in his right hand. The rooftop shakes with his every step. With each step he takes, my breathing becomes steadier. Now is my chance; he is close enough. Using every instinct in my body and all the training I've received, I swing my leg around. In one movement, I kick the sword from his hand, and it flies into the air and off the rooftop. I land steadily on the ground and send a pulse to my attacker. It must have had an effect with the spell. The pulse doesn't just knock him out; it makes him explode.

Blood splatters across the faces of the four remaining attackers. This man is now just chunks of human flesh that will be left to rot on a New York City rooftop.

Before the last remaining four have a chance to attack, the witch stops them with a raise of her hand, while muttering some mumbo jumbo in a language I don't understand but sounds a lot like some of the things my imposter mother would say. She flicks her hand in my direction, and with that comes bursts of light. The light is trying to immobilize me, but just as my body did on the battlefield, it soaks the light within itself. The witch turns her head to the side, confused as to why I have not fallen but, rather, appear stronger. I remember Marcus saying this was new and that I had never been able to do this before. Why is it some things hurt me and, at times like this, my body soaks up a would-be attack? I don't understand.

With a flick of her wrist, the four remaining aggressors attack in unison. As they jump on me, I continue to shock each one, building up that electricity higher and higher within my body until it stops. Pain radiates from my side where the wood was stuck before, throwing off my concentration. One of them has managed to find my weak spot, hitting it over and over again. In just the second it takes me to recover, there is a bag over my head, and I'm held captive to the blackness. Why can't I shock them like I shocked Cornelia, without a touch? I try and try, but my body just won't comply.

"What do we do with Oshea? We cannot leave him!" Guessing from the tone in her voice she and Oshea were more than just friends, and she doesn't want to leave him here on the roof.

"We leave him. Now," the witch announces for all to hear.

"Regina, he isn't dead yet. He's still breathing. We take him with us."

Just based on the whispers, the woman denouncing the queen bee's rules is in for a world of hurt.

A loud gunshot goes off, and then the roof vibrates with the sound of a body hitting the ground. She killed him. Shivers run up my spin. She killed the woman just to make a point. Even without my sight, I know what is going on. She killed her for wanting to save someone she cared about.

"Anyone else want to save Oshea?"

There was no response.

"I didn't think so." The witch begins to hum an innocent song, and her footsteps travel in the distance, leaving the bodies of Oshea and his lover. Her cheerful song leads the way.

A deeper voice speaks up. "I'm glad we followed the Grimmers. They lead us right to her."

So, they are not Grimmers; they must be Militia then. Or perhaps someone just hoping to sell me off to the highest bidder. A terrible force strikes the top of my head, and I doze off into my contemplations, barely cognizant and not sure if I am sleeping or awake. Thoughts of Aidan's face captivate my mind, drifting, drifting, drifting into another vision.

He is talking to a group of men. "The meeting must be pushed back." His voice is very CEO and insistent, and he paces back and forth in front of the men.

"We will not push the meeting back. However, another will be held tomorrow evening. You must be in attendance. It is nonnegotiable with your status here. How will that make us look if you are not in attendance?" An older man speaks to Aidan with a cautious voice as the other men who surround him nod in agreement.

Then they disappear in a flash before my eyes can scour the crowd for faces. Aidan is left standing in a room by himself. He is searching for something, traveling a distance.

A harsh light temporarily blinds me, and I am shaken back into my reality. My legs are shaking as I rock back and forth. I look around trying to restore my sight. Stop it. My worst nightmare. As if the shit isn't piled high enough. I am on a boat. Vomit starts to creep up my throat, but I swallow it back down and make myself gag. Wind gushes across my face, easing my seasickness and mind and bringing with it the smell of fresh water. The sun is rising to the east, and this helps me get a grasp on time; it must be around six thirty in the morning. This is my nightmare, to be surrounded by water on what appears to be a small yacht. Still, for the size of the boat, the little motion is driving my stomach wild.

The motor turns off, and I quickly navigate my vision to focus on the driver, who isn't that far away from me—until my hearing points me in another direction. The radar keeps beeping. There has to be a map on this boat! I search the captain's quarters and try to focus the best I can to look at the map; according to the coordinates, I am currently floating in the middle of Lake Champlain.

A short, fragile-looking old man whacks me upside the head. "Eyes forward, or else I will cut them out."

Well, isn't he the pleasant one? I was going to say things could always be worse, but having my eyes cut out would be less than ideal. Plus I'm already pretty messed up. I do as he says. Now that I have a location, there must be an escape off this boat.

There are five people within my immediate vicinity;, there could be more. Definitely, the witch is below deck; no way she would leave.

"Lex, where do you want these?" a young, child-sized ship hand asks the older fragile man as he holds up cinder blocks with ease. His power must be that of strength. He looks too meek to be able to lift giant cinder blocks otherwise, and this isn't the sort of life where you have time to go to the gym three hours a day to get a good pump in. If they aren't Grimmers or Militia but have powers, what side are they on?

"Right in front of our guest," Lex, still standing behind me, says happily.

My hands are tied in bindings in front of me but with duct tape this time. The young boy walks over and drops the cinder blocks in front of my feet, leaving me with sympathetic eyes. Lex shoos him away, and the boy returns with substantial chain. He wraps the chains around my legs, which are already duct taped together, and attaches them to the cinder blocks.

"There, that should hold." He looks up and gives Lex the nod of approval and is gone from my sight.

This boat is too clean to be used for kidnappings, it's definitely more for entertaining, and part of me thinks this kid has no idea what he has gotten himself into, not that it matters what I think at this moment.

Lex moves to face me, blocking my vision from everything but him. He is old, very old, and appears to be withering away. His dark eyes once held love, but now show he is heartless after a loss. Why is he fighting? I need to hone my powers more to not rely on physical touch.

"This is how it's going to work. I know your fear of drowning."

As surprised as I am that he knows that fun fact about me, I cannot acknowledge it. My face shows no hint of anything at all.

His eerie voice continues. "Don't try to be strong. We all know it to be true." He runs his hands through his long gray hair and stops to play with his beard, matching in length. "I am going to drop you down and give you time to think about our questions. And when you arise, I expect answers."

"Sir, shouldn't we wait for Regina?" The young deck hands voice shakes as he looks at Lex.

"She will have her turn. Don't you worry, boy. Get the creatures ready."

This geriatric is not messing about. He wants answers and wants them fast. A thousands thoughts are running through my mind, but number one is wishing I could hold my breath longer. Hopefully my connection to nature helps me though this, or else I'm toast. I will die of drowning before he even gets the chance to question me.

He attaches a chain around my waist that is held together by an industrial carabiner. "When you look to be struggling and fearful of drowning, the struggle will be shown by the amount of tugging you do. Trust me. I've done this a lot." A smirk crosses his eyes. He loves this. "Young Jack here will pull you up." He points to the small boy with red hair walking away. He can't be more than thirteen. "And you will give me my answers or continue to live your nightmare until you do."

There's no doubt struggling will make this situation worse. This would be a great time for every instinct in my body to kick in, or whatever other powers people claim to tell me I have; anything would be great. Jack is back at my side and has lifted the cinder blocks, me, and the chain in his arms. He recklessly moves to the edge of the boat, holding me above the water.

"Where is your base?"

Lex becomes enraged when I do not answer, like I'd cave that easily, even if I knew what he was talking about. Marcus said we all have a placeholder inside of us that points in the direction of the safe zone, like it's a calling, but that we learned how to use it at a young age. I still haven't figured that part out yet.

Jack dumps me over the side of the boat, and the weight of the blocks drags me down into the dark water. Plummeting farther down into the depths of the lake, I panic when I gather the strength to open my eyes and pull on the chains, but there is no movement going up. With each foot I drop down deeper into the water, my struggle is harder; I try to rip the chains loose. This situation is not ideal. I'm sure all my open wounds are getting infected, and with a lapse of judgment, I suck water into my lungs.

My prayers have been answered. It is like the water is a part of me. Could I be dreaming? I take bigger and bigger gulps of the fresh water, and I can breathe it all in. Gills painfully open on the side of my neck. They must only appear when I am immersed in water. The bass swim near me, making eye contact as though they are trying to tell me something. The ruse must continue. I must fake a struggle, so Lex doesn't suspect I have died.

The good news is, with how far down they've let me go, there is no way anyone can see me in the murky waters. The chain tightens harshly on my waist as I am being pulled up to the surface. As soon as the air hits my face, I gag water out of my mouth. Time for the show.

Jack pulls me on the chain with ease as he is removing me from the water. But my body keeps hitting the side of the boat. At this point, I might have gone overboard on the gagging water bit, but I need to sell it. I lift my shoulder to my neck and feel reassured when the gills are gone; it's my secret. The redhead drags me violently from the side of the boat onto the floor, and I try to curl into a ball, but his foot on the cinder blocks won't let me.

Lex walks over to my injured side and kicks me sadistically over and over again. "Answer my question. Where is your base?" Another blow, this time directly in my stomach, causes me to vomit.

"Take her clothes off."

Two of his flunkies surround me with knives, stripping me of all the clothing I have on. The ring. I cannot let them take the ring. I'm lying here in just a bra and underwear, and they have me vulnerable;--it's a perfect time for me to make my move. I make a quick move and snatch the ring from my pants pocket without them catching on to it. Somehow even with my hands tied, I was able to get the ring into my bra without them noticing.

"I see you are hurt." Lex circles back around to me, kneeling callously next to me, and someone passes him salt—just like they were able to read his mind and anticipate his next brutal request. He pours a mound of salt onto his hand and then into my open wound, enjoying every second of pain he causes me.

I kick and scream as the burning hits my core. *Come on, Ava.*

Get over this pain and zap the man. But that would ruin my escape plan.

"Now, where is your base?!" He smirks at me, thinking I am going to cave. His disposition gives him away, he thinks he is victorious.

"Screw you, asshole." These are words that otherwise would never have been spoken from my mouth, but I want him to toss me back in.

"Make her heavier. She will sink faster." He kicks me in the side once again and walks away. Members of the crew tie clothing around my waist and neck. I guess that's all they had left at their disposal. Jack picks me up and slings me over the side of the boat, launching me at least twenty feet away from it.

"What the hell is going on out here? Duct tape her mouth next time and send her in." The witch's voice fades as I fall deeper into the water.

With my newly acquired skill, I get straight to work bringing my duct taped hands to my mouth. Pulling and gnawing the best I can, I at last bite away the restraints. My skin rips loose on the tape, but that's the least of my worries. Time is my worry. It seems that all the fish in the lake are swimming closer to me and bringing with them a denser covering fog. They are here to help me. "Thanks, guys," I mumble to them under the water. I still haven't gotten the hang of this yet. Plus, breathing under water and talking to animals are two totally different things, right? I'm not Cinderella—far from it. Perhaps this has something to do with my connection to the Pureck, something I do not understand but have been grateful for constantly.

With my hands free, I am able to come up with a game plan. With my main fright becoming void, I undo the duct tape from my feet and bring my knees to my chest, trying to muster the strength to move the cinder blocks. But I don't have the capability. I grab the carabiner that is attached to my waist and pull it down to my feet. I fasten it to the chains tied to my feet with the cinderblocks attached and use it as leverage to release the chains around my feet.

There is no doubt at this point they are close to bringing me back up. I release a few air bubbles and lightly tug on the chain to simulate a struggle. I swim off with the clothes still attached to my waist and neck. I plunge deep down to the very bottom of the lake, and not only can I breathe underwater, but my swimming skills are intense. I made it to the bottom of the lake within seconds. This is an empowering feeling, with the fish by my side pretending to be my protectors, I swim low and far. I look back to see the cinder blocks slowly being lifted from just within my line of vision.

I search for the shoreline, knowing Lex and the witch are about to witness the truth. I dart out of the water, pull one of the sweatshirts tied to my back over my head, slip it on, and run into the wood. My internal warmth has the clothes dried within seconds, and I cop a feel of myself to make sure the ring is secure; it is.

A loud banging stops me in my tracks, so I turn to see a black, bright green cloud swirling above the lake. The witch has found out of my deceit, and she is not going to be pleased about this one. The cloud begins to disperse in all directions, and the engine on the boat starts. Perhaps she can track me through the cloud; sorcery and its abilities have no limits. With every fiber of my being, I concentrate and prepare to run as fast as I can without pushing my aura to show.

Chapter 7

With my hands on my knees, this is the first time I have felt winded from running. But no one is meant to run as long as I just have. It's midmorning and a sigh of relief barely exits my lungs as I have managed to evade the witch all night. But out of the corner of my eye, I see there are small creatures barreling toward me. I do a 360 rotation, and they are coming at me from all directions. I've only read of these creatures in books. While they are slow and seem relatively unskilled, they are large in numbers, and I have no choice but to muster my strength to begin running again.

With around forty goblins running toward me, coming from all directions, in the split second I stop running to access the situation, I have put myself into a worse one. The goblins are covered in mud but sport heavy mallets and bright yellow fangs. I press forward, kicking many of the less than two-foot tall creatures to the side. I throw and kick as many of them into one another as I can, but the exertion is getting to me after not having a second to truly breathe.

The goblins stop from progressing any closer to me, and I know the terrified looks they're wearing are because of me. They could take me now if they wanted—if they just kept pushing.

Whatever has stopped them gives me a second to actually look at these creatures. With the mud sweating off of them, they vary in color, from light skinned to dark skinned to dark green, all with the same bright yellow eyes and fangs. They take shelter beneath the trees and hide from the daylight as growling comes from deep in the woods. Huffnalgers emerge on the edge of the woods releasing high-pitched growls.

As though in answer to my unspoken prayer, knives are being flung in their direction. By whom, I don't know. But they've stopped changing in my direction, only stopping momentarily to snarl at the one wielding the knives and figure out where he is coming from.

I've managed to grab some of the knives that were overshot and landed within my reach. With knives in each hand, I cautiously begin my approach of the dark wooded area my foe remains perched in, temporarily distracted. Navigating my way, I hide behind trees. A few goblins come out and attack my feet. With new energy rising within me, I don't even need to kick them. My body gives off a natural shock when they grab me, sending them skyrocketing. The little creatures only stand a chance in high volumes and working together. I'm the crocodile Dundee of goblins with my new energy burst. I can't help but wonder if they are the witch's doing. Or are they just defending their hidden home?

One blue-nailed huffnalger jumps out of the woods and is running toward me. With ease and concentration, my body kicks into gear, and a knife glides out of my hands, zipping toward the beast. The knife hits it right between the eyes, but one knife isn't enough to stop this large creature. So, I release the other one. But before the knife reaches it, it falls to the ground and lets out a squeal, like an injured fox sound. Hearing it almost breaks my heart hearing, even though it was going to kill me.

A man covered in black from head to toe jumps down from

high in the trees and lands gracefully on his feet within inches of the injured creature. He walks over to the beast and pulls the arrow out of its side and slides it back into his quiver. With a series of acrobatics, he is in front of me with a bow drawn to my face. "Next time, aim for the heart, not the head."

Even gulping down whatever saliva I have in my mouth is hard right now, so I nod, and he lowers his weapon but does not remove his mask.

"No!" I shout as he moves back to the animals with his sword drawn. "Don't kill it."

He doesn't even flinch at my words, and with one swift swoop, he beheads the animal in front of my eyes. As the beast falls silent in death, low growls come from the woods, angered at the loss of their own. I start bracing myself for the next one to jump out of the woods, but it isn't just one; five Huffnalgers creep in our direction.

It's been more than known to me throughout my training that it's nearly impossible to kill, outrun, or survive these creatures. They are able to strategically deduce situations; maybe surprise is a huge factor to play. Clearly, these intelligent beasts hadn't seen a masked man come to save me come into the picture.

"Meet me ten miles due east if we get separated. There is an abandoned gas station. Neither wild Huffnalgers nor ones who have tamed by a master will show up there without a master. It is too far out of their comfort zone." His smooth voice is smaller than what I thought it would be, and all I can see are his dark brown eyes; they are almost black. He knows the terms of those creatures, but I have no reason to trust him, and I also have no reason not to trust him. I smile in agreement, and his arrows and knives attack.

The masked man keeps tossing me knives between his shots, and we are working as a team. We lead the Huffnalgers to the goblins, using the trees as cover. We hop on the top of the goblins to make our way up into the trees and jump from treetop to treetop, using this angle to find the perfect shots. The knives stop coming. He is out; we are out.

"Go!" the dark-eyed man yells to me.

I cannot leave him here alone.

But he insists. *"Go!"* he yells, his order demanding than the last time.

I jump down and out of the tree and run, dodging the slow-moving goblins and leaving my aura chasing behind me, hoping no one can see it hidden under the shield of the trees.

I come to a sojourn on the boarder of Vermont and New York, knowing this a could very well be a trap. But with how my days have been going, what's one more risk? My only option is to take risks. Wandering aimlessly around this place, it's hard not to notice the lack of things—no children, no cars, no people. There's just a run-down, desolate, and useless gas station through the thick of the tall grass. An old, tarnished sign barely hangs from the cracked roof, and it's blowing in the wind. The wind is such a comfort to me; it clears my lungs and my mind. Obviously, I have no idea when this thing was built, but they probably don't tear it down for historical reasons.

As I move closer, I pick up the pace. I leap off the ground with my momentum and land on the creaky roof above the gas pumps, searching the roof for the best place to sit. I pick the most stable spot with a support beam directly underneath, and from here, there is a better view into the distance. From here, I'll keep a lookout, waiting for the masked man's arrival.

The wind blows through my hair and against my face, luring me in, making me listen to its calm voice surrounding me. The unspoken bond with the wind is telling me he is here. I open my eyes to see the tall grass beginning to sperate in a path. The man in all black stops at the edge of the grass, not taking a step onto the pavement, skeptical I am here. His eyes land on me sat on the roof, and I do not move, don't even lift a hand to wave in the air. I hold my position.

He runs and pushes his weight off the hood of an old junker car, and he is out of my sight. There is fumbling beneath me, and I know it's him, although I am unsure what he's doing. His hands creep up the side of the roof, and the masked man is pulling himself up. His unique set of movements, like those he used in the woods, have brought him up to the rooftop where I sit. The closer he gets, the more I notice his black outfit is covered in soot and blood. Maybe he didn't want me to see what was going to happen after my reaction to him killing the huffnalger. He starts to peel back his mask as he gestures his intention to sit down next to me. I nod in agreement.

He turns and faces the other direction as he crosses his legs and sits down. His mask falls to the rooftop, and his thick, pitch-black hair shines in the sunlight. His dark slanted gaze is set on me. Even with no expectations, he isn't what I thought he'd be. His porcelain fair skin, without a wrinkle, would be radiant if it were not for a thick scar that protrudes down the left side of his face. It looks like a number three has been drawn on him in a scar, starting from the center of his forehead down his chin. His hand reached out for the intended handshake, and I indulge him. Even with his black gloves still on, I can see evil lurks behind his soul, waiting to be released. But he has good intentions now and doesn't want to harm me. Shadowy darkness is waiting to overtake all that he sees in his mind, like a thick cloud; something could set him off.

I smile and stand, making sure to be courteous. "Thank you for helping me back there. I appreciate it." Short, sweet, and to the point.

The second his hand is released from mine, I jump off the roof and begin to walk off. At this point, my bearings need to kick in.

I am not even sure where everyone is—if Kieran is still in the city or Marcus.

"Don't I at least get your name?" His words whisper against my ear, and I feel the ground move beneath me as he lands off the roof.

The dark soul in him places a hand on my shoulder, and I quickly pivot in his direction. My long hair whips across his face, accidentally, but he remains still. We are at equal eye level, and my defense shock is boiling within me.

"You already know my name. However, I do not know yours." I could see he knew me and that he doesn't want to hurt me. But still that darkness lies; it's terrifying. I shouldn't even be entertaining this conversation. I quickly turn on my heel and start the getaway process all over again. But his closeness follows me; his nearly silent footsteps shift the ground beneath me. Thank the Pureck for that, Ava.

"My name is Ray Smith. I am an undercover agent for the Resistance in the Militia. Come with me. I promise no harm will be done to you. How else would I know you were being tortured on a Militia vessel?" Ray has perfected his words, but I can see through them. Even with his mouth gushing sincerity, there is something that cannot be trusted; it makes my skin crawl.

"I really do appreciate what you did. I am grateful for that. But with so many people after me … I just … I don't trust you." I do not want to give him any hint of what powers I may or may not have. My upper chest starts to cool, while the rest of my body is overheating. My organs, my soul, everything is trying to get my attention. Visualizing the cool spot, I see it is a small circle. This is it, the beacon. When I focus, I can see the coordinates—coordinates found within me that are not directed back to New York City. I stretch my neck and think about the distance I need to go.

"Don't." Ray speaks up. "I know the location of the meeting.

Both you and I need to be in attendance." He is exasperated with me.

My conflicting soul search has me confused what to do with him at this moment. "Where is the location?" I'm testing him since the location is no longer in the city.

"They changed locations. It is no longer in the city because it's not safe. There were attacks, lots of them. It has been moved to Adirondack Park in New York, about thirteen miles away from the main trail. The entrance is located next to the stream."

Well, he has me beat. He rattled off the exact coordinates that were in my mind, but also in greater detail. "Fine, let's go." I'm not pleased. But at this rate, he knows the location. So, either he's really telling the truth, or I'll need to defeat him somehow if we get there and he's an intruder.

I get into a running position, but his baffled look stops me in my tracks. "We need to walk or hitch a ride. I cannot run like you can."

This is great. Now it will take us at least three hours to get there by car, if not more. At least we have daylight on our side this time and not the creatures of the night.

I need to remind myself of who I am, the human side of me. "Sorry. I forgot not everyone can. Let's try and hitch a ride. We won't make it in time if we walk." If only Aidan could see me now; he would have plenty of things to say about my reckless behavior and trying to hitch a ride from strangers.

The long walk to the main road is quiet, and without any belongings, we look every bit homeless and lost. Who would stop to pick us up anyway? Honestly, there is a man dressed in all black, carrying knives on his back and a girl who looks like she's been tossed off a train and rolled around in the dirt, not to mention no shoes or socks. It's a surprise I'm even able to walk at this point with how raw my feet are. No one in his or her right mind would stop and pick us up.

"You have to ditch the knives and swords. We need to look the part if we want someone to pick us up." We stop about five hundred yards short of the main road, still enclosed by the sound of birds singing and corn row after corn row. "You can't look like an assassin." I roll my eyes at his look that conveys he's unwilling to let go of his toys. "Honestly, boys and their toys." I giggle, and he lets out a little laugh too, as cheesy of a joke as it is. This feels nice, a hint of laughter after this madness.

"Fine." Displeased and reluctant, he strips himself of the swords from his back and his knives stashed all over. He tosses them into the cornfields. He still isn't giving off the best vibe but loads better than before.

"Stand still."

He looks both uncomfortable and inquisitive as I move closer to him. I remove his gloves and throw away his mask that he's gripping for dear life. He squirms under my touch as I mess with his hair and try to make him somewhat welcoming. "One more thing. Smile, please, or fake laugh—something other than the Joker serious face."

His pale cheeks turn flush for less than a second. Fed up with my demands, he still manages a smile, but he looks like a serial killer. He has all of his teeth showing and mouth wider than I thought it could stretch; his eyes looked crazed, as if he's never smiled a day in his life.

"Come on, man. What gives? Relax. You look like the crazed lollipop guy from *Chitty Chitty Bang Bang*."

He shakes his head at me, attempting to maintain the silence we started earlier, despite my persistent jokes he clearly doesn't find funny. This is going to be one long road trip, I realize as we begin in utter silence down the main road.

Mile after mile, we walk. Today would be the day there are no cars traveling in the direction we need to go. Hope is starting to evade me, until a loud, old, single-cab yellow Ford 150 pulls over on the side of the road, cutting us off midwalk.

As we apprehensively approach the truck, the driver manually crank lowers the passenger side window down and yells to us, "Stop right there!" He is an older man, at least older than his truck. "Do you kids need a ride? Where are you heading?" From the tone in his voice and the way he speaks, he reminds me of a grandfather. If I were to have one, I would think that's what he would sound like, an old war veteran with a raspy voice.

"Yes, sir. We are trying to get as close to Adirondack Park as possible." My voice is sweet and innocent and his eyes begin to light up, like I remind him of someone he has known. I have created a whole sweet backstory for this man in my mind already without even speaking much to him.

"Young lady, you can ride in the cab with me. This gentleman will have to sit in the bed of the truck. I can take you about ten miles outside the park."

"Thank you so much, sir." I wave and send my megawatt smile in his direction and hit Ray on his shoulder in excitement, a bit harder than I should have as he shoots me a dirty look. Honestly, what's up his craw? At least now we don't have to walk. I skip over to the truck, and Ray slowly saunters behind as I open the passenger door and slide in.

"Well, isn't he expeditious," the old man with kind wrinkled eyes notes as the truck moves when Ray uses one arm to hold onto the truck and jump into the bed with one swift movement.

Truth be told, I am not sure how to respond to his observation. "He is really big into working out and showing off." I do not even give him time to interject before I change the subject hastily. "Thank you again, sir. I truly appreciate it." Now Ray just needs to have some manners and thank the man as well.

"Anything to help those in need." He puts his truck into drive, and we slowly pull away from the shoulder and moved onward to our destination.

I am admiring the trees surrounding the road on both sides; we're no longer in cornfield city. Before long, I've spaced out completely, admiring how they sway.

"So everyone has a story. What's yours?"

I know he's probing asking how I ended up on the side of the street, but I decide to just stick with the bigger picture. "Funny you ask. I have asked myself that same question for a long time." I turn my body from the window in his direction and see Ray's back against the glass, arms crossed in front of his body.

"And what conclusion have you come to?"

I like this old man. Even without much speaking, I know he is intelligent with life experience. He has crazy, long light eyebrows that curl up to the middle of his forehead, and his mustache accentuates his inquisitive smile, even when he speaks.

"Well, sir, to be honest with you, I am still writing my story. So far, it's about love and loss and overcoming obstacles that came into my life without me even knowing how. So, thank you for helping me over this hurdle. By the way, my name is Ava."

"Pleasure to meet you, Ava. I am Louis." He casually extends one hand over to me, while keeping the other firmly on the wheel.

I shake it with a smile and can see the loss of his wife and daughter. He in fact did serve in the Korean War, all of which brought him years of devastation. He took his pain and turned it into something good and lived life how his wife would want him to. I remind him of his daughter because we have the same eyes and blond hair.

Our hands separate, but I can still feel everything he went through. "My apologies, that is, for Ray. He's not much of a talker."

I tap on the glass and Ray turns around with a forced smile—still looking every bit serial killer. No wonder Louis sat him in the bed of the truck even though we all could have squeezed up here.

"Perhaps not someone you would normally associate yourself with?" He questions me about Ray, but his tone is warning me. Perhaps that's just his instinct from all the years of being in the army.

I shoot him a look that hopefully answers his question and shake my head. "I really like this truck."

The schoolboy in him lights up like the Fourth of July. "I bought her new in 1973. I just don't have the heart to get rid of her. She holds so many memories." He taps the dash of his truck and rubs it in a sentimental way. It reminds him of everything he has lost but cannot part with. Without me having to read into his mind or heart, he tells me everything about his life-- from childhood to war to marriage to fatherhood and the loss of it all.

Chapter 8

"Now, if you walk straight for about six miles, you'll reach the edge of the park. From there, you're on your own. I wish you the best of luck, Ava." He embraces me for a long hug that makes me wince. I still haven't managed to take care of any of my open wounds.

"Thanks again and thank you for your service to this country." I smile at him, hoping he knows how thankful I truly am.

"You take care of her." He directs a firm voice to Ray.

Ray waves this off and smiles but mutters under his breath that I can take care of myself and some other jibber jabber I can't really hear. I'm too busy watching Louis get back into his car and making sure no one is following him as he pulls down the desolate road. It's rare you meet strangers anymore who are willing to help you, not to mention drive you hours in their car.

"You could have been nicer to him since he helped us out. After all, you are really the one who needed the ride." Sure, Ray has helped me. But could he have been anymore rude and snotty to the person who helped us, and mostly for his benefit?

"He is just a passerby in my life. He means nothing to me, not someone worth my attention."

Wow. I just keep disliking Ray more and more. "You're a

jackass." Shaking my head at him, I walk off the beaten path, through the muck and to the treeline of the park.

It looks like a forest from this distance, beyond the thick padding of the trees nothing is visible. There is nothing about Ray I trust at this point, even if he did come to my aid. I keep my detachment from him very serious. There surely has to be a reason behind him helping me. I wonder if he is who he claims to be. But at this point it would be strange if I grabbed his arm to search deeper into his mind; he would have his defenses up.

While I start to pick up the pace, he trails behind me. I run to the trees. I miss the feeling of the wind flying through my hair and the good chill it sends up my spine. Ray, crap. I turn to look for him. He's about two miles behind me. I sit on the ground and run my fingers through the dirt. Walking through the trails barefoot is going to tear my feet up, but at the same time, I'm excited for that connection. I stretch out my legs and wiggle my toes into the dirt. My toes play in the dirt, but the dirt doesn't stick; it runs over the top of my feet and then to the bottom, like it's magnets running over my body, trying to massage my feet. I place my hands on the ground next to my feet, and it is strange to see the dirt graze across the surface of my hands and feet, moving in its own pattern, exfoliating my skin and healing the wounds on my hands and feet.

I lay back and enjoy as the dirt begins to wash over my exposed arms and legs. First, the wind spoke to me and then the fish; now the ground is exposing itself to me. When I focus, I can hear the creeks within the park babble, the birds chirping, the frogs hopping around, and the few people who walk the trails. I know their exact locations. The dirt quickly shift off of my arms and legs before consuming my whole body and collapsing into my hands. I sit up, not shocked to find Ray's footsteps getting closer to me; nature doesn't trust him either.

My body feels weaker than normal. Or perhaps all the adrenaline is finally wearing off and I'm starting to feel the side effects.

I place my head in my hands and take nice slow breaths but I'm interrupted by Ray's hand touching my shoulder and reaching out to help me up. The tree roots are moving beneath me, and as I stand, the wind blows through. My hair lifts the leaves off the ground, and they surround me. They're circling me, creating a barrier between me and Ray; the wind has created a cone of silence, whispering to me I cannot trust him, another alarm to keep me on edge. I close my eyes and shake my head in acknowledgement, and all at once, the leaves stop and fall to the ground around me.

"What the hell was that?" Ray yells as he approaches me.

"Come on. Let's go while we still have daylight on our side." Completely ignoring his question. I begin to trample off into the woods, and he follows me.

"I do not trust these woods. They move on their own." The assassin, for all intents and purposes, is scared of Mother Nature. How funny. I do not acknowledge his statement but, rather, just press forward through the wild lands into the raw, uninhibited elements of nature. Maybe we will find an actual walking trail.

After miles of walking, we are getting close. I can sense it in my body. I keep my head down and push my way through the trees and bushes, not minding them swinging back and cutting me in the face. I keep moving, until I come to an edge of water and stand on the only rock on this side of the creek. The sounds are absolutely enchanting as the water flows slower with each passing second. There is a stillness here that cannot be duplicated. There's but an incredibly beautiful and wild creek surrounded by pure green, even in this brisk weather. Ray's shoes give him away; the swooshing sound echoes through the otherwise peaceful woods. This is definitely off the beaten hiking trails in this woods.

"Who thought this area would be so marshy? Let's find the entrance so I can dry off."

Just his voice gets on my last nerve, but still, I remain calm, like dealing with customers at work I cannot stand. "You said you knew where it was, so lead on." I open my arms wide to encompass all the spaces that are before me and do a little spin.

"They change the portal location constantly. We are looking for an 'S' within a circle, and that will lead us in."

Great, how descriptive, and surely easy to find in the vast woods. There is a lot of land to cover.

Trying to take deep breaths and gain my composure and focus helps me concentrate. And there before me is the answer. I see the starry, bright, illuminated sign, just as it was for the last portal during the training battle. It points in a direct line to one of the smaller trees. I want to follow the brightness, but should I with Ray here? Something inside is drawing me to it—to walk a line like I'm on a tightrope, not one toe out of line. It's like I have no control over my body. My feet sink into the creek water, not obstructing anything; no ripples were made. I just follow my body's desired course.

Once I am out of the water, I instinctively tiptoe closer to the weakened, fragile tree. I place one of the branches in my hand, trying to feel its life, and in that moment, the last leaf falls slowly to the ground. Looking down, I find I am standing on a pattern, with the leaves in a distinct color piles. The green leaves have formed a circle and the red leaves form the letter "S" within them. Ray was right.

So subtle and unsought—how anyone else could find this exact spot is beyond me. It would take hours if not days of searching without the beacon inside of you. But I guess that is the point of all of this. Cautiously, I turn to find Ray, but he is already walking in my direction. Before he gets close enough to me, I take a step back unintentionally, and I am being sucked into the portal.

The suction of this portal is different, like there is no space to even breathe, and there's a scan going across my whole body that stops on my face. The portal whips me in all different directions, until I am upside down with my hair dangling above an unknown, colorful abyss. It is a laser, and it scans my face another three times before it violently turns me right side up and drops me. My ankle moves in a direction it's not meant to move as I slam down onto the ground, and I hear it crack. Like what the actual fuck? Can any more shit be piled on top of how my day is going? How my life is going?

"Ava! Are you OK? Don't block the portal. Someone could land on you!" Kieran's sweet voice and hopeful eyes are barreling toward me.

Before I can even stand, he is grabbing me by the waist and helping to lift me up. It seems like he is always helping me, and I am always groaning in some form of pain, especially now as I try to put weight on my ankle. And perhaps it's from the stress, but my side is seeping blood again.

"What the hell happened to you?

I miss his concern because, for some reason, it comforts me.

He picks me up and cradles me in his arms as though I am a child. "I am going to get you to a room and take care of you."

I breathe him in as I let my head linger on his covered chest and enjoy the feeling of cotton against my bruised face.

Out of the corner of my eye, I am trying to gain focus on where we are; it looks like an underground military bunker, with surprisingly bright lights. There are many long, blank corridor walls and metal doors that lead to separate rooms. The floor looks like it is Rhinolined in shining silver. Surprisingly, the space looks big without any windows in sight. We do not pass one soul; there is nothing but silence and the sound of Kieran's fast beating heart. He kicks in one of the heavy metal doors with his foot, and it swings open. The room is larger than what I thought they would look like. It's probably forty feet by twenty feet with a queen-size bed against one wall, a bathroom off to the side, and a small kitchen running flush against the left wall. The same panel lighting from the hallway runs throughout the room. He places me down on the bed and shakes his head.

"Where are your shoes? What happened to you? I've been calling …" His voice trails off as he stops pacing in front of me to make eye contact. "I was worried about you."

He shuffles his hands through his hair, looks me over from top to bottom, and bends down on his knees in front of me. He takes my ankle in hands and examines it and then pulls the side of my shirt covered in blood. I don't even bat a lash as he lifts my shirt. His face looks displeased as he places my shirt back down and brings his hands to my face. His eyes carefully examine me. I do not speak, just watch him move as he goes into a cabinet and comes back with clothes. I feel bad. This man was worried about me and I had no way to get in contact with him, no way to get in contact with anyone.

"You need to shower, and then we will take care of your wounds." He stands over me, in black and green camouflage pants tucked into black boots, with a green cotton shirt tucked into the pants.

"I'm sorry." I barely mumble my words looking into those intense green eyes.

"You have nothing to be sorry for, Ava. I do want to know what happened. Stop apologizing!" I can't tell whether or not he's mad at me by the tone in his voice.

He bends down and picks me up and I place my arms around his neck. Our eyes lock to each other's, and he pulls away as he begins to walk.

He walks me into the bathroom and places me down on the large countertop that holds double sinks. I try to swing my legs, but he stops me. Kieran is watching me as his hand is behind the blue shower curtain; the knob squeaks as he tries to adjust the temperature. Everything in this room is white, minus the shower curtain. Even the bedspread is white. It looks so sanitary.

The sound of the water bouncing off the shower floor is relaxing, and I close my eyes, not remembering the last time I slept. But the urge to want to fill Kieran in is keeping me awake. I let the steam of the shower run under my nose, and I breathe it in and Kieran. When I open my eyes, he is close to me again, as close as possible, leaning both his arms on the countertop. He stares into my soul with such concern.

"Ava, please don't be mad at me. I am sorry I raised my voice. I was just worried about you. There is so much we need to talk about, but first …" He brushes my hair behind my left ear with his finger, and I lean into his touch. It feels so nice to be comforted and not worried about what attack will happen next.

Before he can finish his sentence, I am overwhelmed to ask, "I bumped into Ray Smith. Do you know him? He said he is one of us. He came here with me." I was hoping his answer would prove my thoughts correct about him.

"He has been with the Resistance for about three years. He was doing some undercover Militia work from what I heard—before the ring got busted, and he had to flee. Where is he now? He will be OK."

My eyes lower to the ground and my intertwined fingers. "I'm not worried if he will be OK. Kieran, I don't trust him at all. His thoughts are frightening." I shake my head, but he grabs me and places a tender kiss on my forehead to stop me from rambling.

"We will talk about everything, I promise. But for now, you need to get in the shower." He lifts me off the counter and goes to leave the room.

But I grab him by the arm and stop him. He looks at me with surprise, unsure of what I'm going to ask. Truth be told, I'm unsure why I grabbed him in the first place. I'm unsure of myself right now. I look down at the floor and up to his eyes and then back down to the floor. Words want to come out of my mouth, but they won't budge.

"Kieran …" What do I say? How do I say it? I cannot ask this of him. I shake my thoughts away and let go of his arm. "Never mind."

He looks disappointed as he turns to leave the room. With his back to me, he speaks. "I've put clothes on the edge of the counter. Come out whenever you're ready. Yell for me if you need anything." And he leaves, leaving the door cracked behind him.

I take off the nasty clothes that have gone through hell and back and toss them to the side, along with my bra and panties, being sure to secure the ring and my necklaces. I hobble into the shower, disgusted with the thought that I was about to ask Kieran to shower with me. For the life of me, I still don't understand how I can be uncontrollably drawn to people like this. The only one who can give me full truth is Cassiopeia. How could I see Kieran and all thoughts of Aidan fade? Aidan—a man who is supposed to be my soul mate—hasn't even seen me naked. And here I am about to ask Kieran. I lie to myself, trying to convince myself I was only asking him in for support because I can't stand properly. I was craving intimacy. I went from having no prospect to this.

This feels like a weird love triangle that's more like the death of the Bermuda Triangle. I can't even find time to myself to just breathe.

I lean my weight against the shower wall and let the water flow over my body and all my open wounds. I pick up the soap and begin to wash myself, over and over. The feeling of clean is something I will never take for granted again. I am trying to wash away the day, month, and year—everything. It doesn't work. The memories remain. Shampoo is lathering in my hands, and I bring it to my nose. The lavender is enchanting. I rub it into my scalp and throughout the end of my hair. The bottom of the shower is filled with water mixed with blood, dirt, and other debris, slowly go down the drain. The lavender and aromas of the bathroom take the pain away, and my voice lets loose in song, trying to feel like my old self.

Singing made-up songs about the trials and tribulations of the past few days, trying to even jokingly throw a rap in there, is my release of the moments. Just as I am comfortable feeling clean and ready for the next thing life is going to throw my way, my footing changes accidentally to my bad ankle. The pain is not as intense now, but shocking since I didn't see it coming. When will I learn my lesson not to get carried away in my own slow jamz? The shower floor is soapy and unforgiving as I slip, grabbing the shower curtain to maintain my balance. But it is no use. What is it with me a causing scenes in bathrooms?

The thud of my fall sends reverberations off the walls in the bathroom, but I don't make a sound. Within a second, Kieran is in the bathroom in dismay at the state he finds me in. I cannot help but laugh. Could the past few days be any worse? I'm talking about hysterically laughing, out of control. Now here he is looking at me like a lost boy. Thankfully the curtain has somehow fallen right over my bikini area.

Kieran is not sure what to make of my crazy laughing, but he walks over closer to me. And instead of picking me up like I thought he would, he lays down next to me, placing his arm around my back with the other hand rearranging the shower curtain to cover all of my body. His modesty is making me glad I didn't ask him to shower with me earlier. What was I thinking? Stupid, stupid girlish fantasy.

"Thank you, again." I look at him and blink slowly as my giggles are coming to an end.

Now my abs hurt, or rather my nonexistent abs hurt. Just adding that to the list of pains. The shower water is running all over us, but neither of us moves. And I just lay everything on him. He doesn't break eye contact with me or even motion to turn off the water as my laughing stops and I tell him everything. Kieran's eyes are locked on mine and hanging off of each word about Aidan and his fiancée; about Dino; about me stealing the knives and the man at the Mean Fiddler; and about Sofia, David, and Dillion. I can feel a tear drift down my face as I continue on to tell him about how I am most afraid of losing myself. He wipes away my tears, which are mixed with the shower water, and lets me just talk. He doesn't say a word as I ramble on and on. I tell him about the boat and the ring, every injury I sustained, although he can visibly see all of them. I mean, every detail I can think of I spill—because I trust him, more than I trust anyone else.

He makes me breathe as he cups my face, and somehow, his touch brings wind into this nature-free room, and it stills my heart. Silently, I remind myself it's OK to be vulnerable with someone I trust, to let my guard down, and to not pretend to be strong and that everything is OK. My whole life has been a lie. As if I didn't have it hard enough in my fake life, now I find out even my real life is a pile of donkey doo.

I think he can tell I don't want to talk of it anymore, at least not right now—that I have gotten it all out there in the open. So, he tries to joke, "I should have just joined you in the shower. We could have prevented further turmoil. By the way, you have a beautiful voice." He shakes his head and laughs his statement off; if only he knew I was thinking of asking him.

He lifts me up. The feeling of his hands on my bare skin sends shivers down my spine, and the mood switches to confirm he feels it too. There is an electricity there, one so different from me and Aidan, it makes me cold, but in a good way. As I exhale, my breath is showing in front of me, and I am shocked by its appearance.

"That's odd. It's the same color as your aura." He looks just as confused as I am as we both reach out to touch my breath, which appears as colored vapor.

That is a first for me. He helps me up and wraps me in the

shower curtain. Before he allows me to move, he dries the floor and passes me the clothes that were laid out.

"I will be right out here while you change." And the kind gentleman leaves me to change in privacy, despite the feeling we are both pretending didn't just happen.

He lifts his shirt up. He's going to change into dry clothes, and right before the door begins to shut, I catch a glimpse of his stomach. The man works out—abs for days. But that's not all. He has tattoos that seem to tell a story on his body. Now I wish he was really in the shower with me so I could learn every inch of that body and what story those drawings and art on his body tell.

Chapter 9

My legs dangle over the edge of the bed, and I hum to myself while Kieran looks at my ankle. "You're lucky. Even though you feel pain, it seems you're already being to heal. So, I just wrapped your ankle. Just curious as to why it's healing faster. Now let me look at your side."

My ankle is perfectly wrapped. Sometimes, it's nice being taken care of. I feel like, for my whole life, I was always the one taking care of others. Now, that has seemed to change a bit.

I pull up the side of the shirt Kieran gave me, and he shakes his head. "We'll need to sanitize and stitch this, along with your head, to keep anything from getting in."

I chuckle. I'm no stranger to stitches. But since Mexico, I've been stitched up a decent amount. "Perfect." I playfully shake my head in his direction.

He turns to walk into the kitchen to rummage through cabinets. While he does, I pull the shirt off over my head. I managed to wash the bra with some soap in the sink. Although I would prefer this bra to be burned, I am not left with much of a choice. Plus, it is the safekeeping spot for my ring at the moment. I can't go walking around knocking people out with my boobs. They come around the corner before I do.

When he turns around to walk back to me, he hesitates, staring at me.

"Honestly, you would think you have never seen a woman before. I am not naked. I'm just trying to make your job easier." I giggle, and he visibly relaxes. I'm not trying to be judge, but he looks like the kind of man women throw themselves at on a constant basis. But I guess he is the gentleman kind.

He advises me to turn on my unwounded side, and I listen without hesitation and place my hand behind my head for support. I feel like I'm posing like Rose in *Titanic*. I look at him, and he is intensely focusing on preparing the needle and sanitizing it and my wound. I'm guessing this is like ranger scouts 101 to these kind of men, brought up in this world. He moves his hands slowly around the needle and places the needle in my skin. His hands maneuver the needle perfectly, so I do not feel a thing.

"I want to hurt whoever did this to you, Ava." His voice is cold, not like the welcoming Kieran I have come to know.

"Well, that's because of Dillion and David. They're Grimmers. The Militia is who tortured me on the boat. So, there's a long list, but they aren't worth your time. Karma will get them." Is it silly of me to still believe in karma?

He scoffs at my remarks, but I am just being honest with him. When he finishes both my side and my forehead, he puts antibacterial ointment around the stitches and wraps gauze around my whole waist. My forehead is left exposed.

"I look like a mummy," I joke.

"At least your sense of humor is still intact." He smiled, sat me, and sat up from the bed. "Give me five minutes. I will be right back."

"Where are you going?" My brow creases as I unintentionally frown.

"Don't worry. This will definitely cheer you up. Promise."

I shrug my shoulders as he runs like a flash out of the room, leaving the door open behind him. I lay back and let the softness of the pillows frame my face. And finally my body is 100 percent relaxed. Focusing on my body, as I have grown to enjoy doing, I'm thankful for my hearing heart and pumping lungs.

Kieran's voice is distant, but I can hear him. Sitting up so quickly I almost get light-headed, with my eyes scrunched closed and turn my head toward the door, I am listening. But the talking has stopped. I hear only the sound of feet coming in my direction. Perhaps in my lethargic state, my mind is playing tricks on me.

A sudden force pushes me down, and a wet tongue is running across my cheeks, making my eyes open with excitement.

"*Laila*!" I scream and wrap my arms around my beautiful blue-eyed pooch. Tears fill my eyes and stream down my cheeks. She will not stop licking my cheeks, and I do not mind one bit! To say I am overwhelmed with joy is an understatement.

The feelings rushing through my body are insane. "Kieran, how? Why? Just thank you!" I do not know what is possessing me. But overwhelming happiness and a mix of emotions fill me. I jump from the bed, ignoring my stitches, and run over to him and jump. He catches me, and I wrap my legs around him and give him the biggest hug I can possibly muster. He spins me around, and when I pull my head out from the corner of his neck, I look him in the eyes and place a kiss on his soft lips, and he kisses me back. Equally as passionate on both sides, we share a blissful moment for a picture-perfect first kiss. The soft kiss turns into more passion.

I am the first to pull away, but I search his face. He is taken aback by my actions almost as much as I am, but he cannot wipe the grin off his face. Perhaps it's the joy of having my dog back—that, somehow, he saved her. But in this moment, he is the person I trust more than anything—the only person who hasn't told me a half-truth to save my feelings and the one person who actually wants to get to know who I am not and isn't thinking I'm someone from the past.

He places me down on the ground, but not before sneaking in one more quick kiss, and a smile reaches my eyes. Laila, sat right between our feet now, is taking turns nudging my hand and his hand. Cloud nine is real, and I am the number one occupant at the moment. Moving backward until my butt hits the bed, my eye contact doesn't break his. Laila moves from his side and jumps on the bed next to me and spawls across my lap. I instinctively pet her behind the ears. I've never been at a loss of words so badly in my life—for the moment we just shared and much more.

Finally, with a shake of the head I speak. "How?" It's the broadest question I could have asked, but he knew what I mean. Tears are welling in my eyes again, and its official—this man has seen me cry more than anyone else on the planet.

"Poor thing hasn't slept since I found her." He sits beside me on the bed, and Laila scootches over so now she is laying across two laps, looking happy as ever and relaxed. Kieran once again wipes tears from my face and then begins to spoil Laila with even more affection. "I went to your house after the charity event to see how your night went. I knew you had a lot going on, and I selfishly wanted to convince you to come to New York City with me for the meeting." He shakes his head and takes a deep breath before continuing. "I was so worried about you. My stomach sank to the ground when I was about a mile from your house. I could see the fire, and my gut just knew it was your home."

He wraps his left arm around me and pulls me closer to him. "As I was pulling up, there was a truck pulling out. I thought for a moment he could have been the culprit, but I was more concerned with your well-being than stopping and interrogate the man. I stopped in front of your house, and it looked like it was going to collapse. Then I heard the barking coming from inside. I figured if Laila were in there, you had to be in there, too. So, I ran into the house and followed the barking. I had to force open the door to your room. But when I did, she jumped into my arms. There was a support beam that had fallen behind the door, and the windows were melted over with some sort of metal. It was like a spell was placed on your room, making it impossible for anyone to get out, but not in. I looked for you and couldn't find you, so I either thought someone took you for bad, or someone saved you and left her behind. I promised myself I would treat her like my own until you returned. I knew you were alive somewhere; I could feel that in my gut too. I just had to find you. And here you have fallen into my arms before I even had the chance to look, considering I exhausted the phone call method."

I gaze into his eyes, "You went into a burning building to save me. I just … I don't know how to thank you. You have taken such good care of her. This is why Marcus told me you were trying to get in touch. Things are making sense now." I look to Laila, and she does look so happy as she sleeps now with both of our hands rubbing her.

"What is it, Ava? You look hurt? Talk to me."

Hurt is an understatement. Since the moment I met Aidan, the passion has been intense, but he constantly hides information from me. "The man you saw driving away had me in the truck. And well, he lied to me. I hate that my face always gives me away." The truth is simple sometimes, but it doesn't stop the hurt.

"Who is he really to you?"

I contemplate how to answer.

But he is getting impatient. "Tell me, Ava!" Now Kieran is standing and pacing in front of me, trying to work through his own emotions. Seems like that's a common thread between the pair of us.

"Aidan. He told me he went back into the house and looked for Laila, but she was nowhere to be found." I stop myself and think to answer what he asked of me. "His name is Aidan Cross, the supposed soul mate of mine for centuries. I don't even know how to process that myself. In typical fashion I will say it's complicated, and unlike other girls, I really mean that." I can see pain across his face, but I continue on. "I don't want to feel sad, so I'm trying to focus on the fact you saved her, and she is here with me right now." I pat the empty space next to me and shoot him a bright smile to urge him to take his seat back.

"I don't want to upset you, Ava. We can talk about that later. Let's talk about something else. Where is your mother?" He moves to sit behind me, legs dangling at the side of mine, and I feel a brush running through my hair. I laid so much out in the shower I cannot believe I forgot to go into detail about my mother. I mean I talked about the ring but forgot her.

Well, here we go. "She is not my mother. Apparently, she's an imposter. I don't know. I have half a mind to go off and find her myself." The crazy part about all of this is she liked Kieran. She spent time with him and me after the battle. We'd spent nearly every free moment together after that night either training or just staying up all night talking. Why did she like him? Or was it just because he was not Aidan—who could expose her lie?

"What do you want to talk about? Ask me anything?" He's trying to calm my nerves, and I appreciate it. He speaks softly as he keeps brushing my hair, and honestly, this is probably the most intimate thing I have ever experienced. I have never had someone brush my hair; even my memories whether fake or real, don't show that level of concern. He's just brushing my hair, no need to read too much into this.

"Why did you hate me so much? Before the battle, you refused to even speak to me, even when I tried to talk to you."

The brush stops moving and Kieran shifts awkwardly on the bed. "Ava, I want to tell you, but I don't want you to hate me. I don't know if, at this point in our relationship, I can stand you being mad at me—when all I want to do is be close to you. It's your call." The unrestrained honesty from him is one of the reasons I enjoy his company. He's not afraid to be vulnerable around me. But during the battle we had to form a certain bond to survive. Or at least that's how it felt; it unwillingly pushed us together, much to Marcus's distain.

"I won't be mad at you. I just want to know. Things are different now. Always honest with each other."

The brush begins to move again. This is definitely the longest a brush has been run through my hair. But at this point, it's like a massage, and I'll take it.

"I don't want you to think less of me, but I need to explain everything so you'll understand where I'm coming from. I grew up resenting my mother because she left my father when I was a child. She constantly told him that, when the time came, he would make the wrong choice. So she had to leave him and take me with. Neither my father nor I understood what she was talking about. At that time, I was only eight years old. You sure you want to hear this?" He exhales deeply.

I turn my body and maneuver myself, so I'm facing him, looking him directly in the eyes, and my legs wrap around his lower back. He needs to know my sincerity. "Yes. I want to know everything about you. Please tell me."

He shifts me off of him and pulls away to speak and looks down at the bed. "One day, my mother told me I have the ability to turn to the other side—to go bad essentially. The only way to stop this was for me to accept the love of the one she had blessed. With those words, I left my mother alone, with the intention of proving her wrong—to prove that I could be a good man and that I am a good man, without accepting love from someone I didn't know. That my destiny was in my own hands. I hated you for so long, not even knowing who you were, Ava.

"My mother is Cassiopeia, the Pureck who granted you those powers. I hated you for what she has said, and I hated you for taking the powers that should have been given to me. I didn't realize they were instilled within you before I was even born and walking this planet. I was jealous of you and hated the idea of loving you. Yet here I am. Doing just that.

"I know we don't have centuries under our belt and have a lot to learn about each other, but I care about who you are now, not the person you were. I don't know what it is about you, Ava. But my mother was right. She said that, when I met you, it would all make sense, that it would be an overwhelming yet natural feeling for me once we got to know each other. That's why Kai and I joined Marcus's class, a class neither of us needed. It's no secret that he and your father were close, based on what my mother had told me. So I knew you'd end up there somehow. Kai is my ride or die, so he gladly came along to help prove her wrong. My mother warned me there would be another love in your life and that I would have to fight for you. But with each step I would become a stronger and better man for it. Now I understand it—what she was talking about and why she chose to give you those powers and not me. You heart is truly made of gold, and your born gift is truly something amazing to see. Don't you see? Even though you have a soul mate, we are connected. She made it so."

"Kieran." I pull his face up, and he finally breathes. Our eyes lock, and I am at a loss for words. I felt that connection with him too. I have so many questions running though my brain, and I'm not sure which to ask first or if I should just console him. "Help me to understand. How can you be destined to be with me when I am destined to be with Aidan? I thought soul mates were a rarity? Or does accepting my love mean an unconditional love? Can destinies intertwine?"

I don't ask this question to him but only to myself. Am I supposed to give up Aidan to stop Kieran from turning to the other side? He has done fine without me this whole time. Why now?

"Ava, how can you be sure he is your soul mate?"

It's a good question, which I don't have the answer to, other than that's what I've been told. Marcus has claimed it; Aidan has stated it himself; and even my father mentioned a soul mate in the letter, although not by his name.

"Another question." He's bound to be displeased by my misdirecting the topic. "How was I able to breathe underwater? I have a fear of drowning—have ever since I was a kid—so I avoid water at all costs. But I was able to swim with the fishes like I was one of them." Even saying it sounds ridiculous. He must know more about my relationship with Cassiopeia than anyone else; this is my guess as to why. My connection with nature is overwhelming and becoming stronger; perhaps it has to do with that, or at the least he could offer some insight.

He throws his head back in thought, grabs my legs, and pulls me in even closer, like I'm almost on top of him at this point. "You have no idea how powerful you are; it is frustrating honestly." He drops his head and places his hands on either one of my shoulders. "Did you kill someone?"

I guess I managed to leave a few things out of my shower rambles, probably because I was so emotional. "What kind of question is that?" I remove his hands from my shoulders and instantly become defensive. Without any intention, that electricity is building, and my energy must have woken Laila as she is up and sitting between us. Normally when I get like this, she's by my side, growling at the person who my energy is directed at. But not now; she looks sad at my defensiveness, and it brings me back to calm.

Moving as gracefully as I can, I shift off the bed and walk over to the kitchen to cool myself down, but I push myself up onto the countertop to sit and sigh as I reluctantly answer. I don't want him to judge me or think less of me. "Yes, but I had to. I had no choice." I lower my head and think about the dying body on the rooftop in New York City, thanks to the witch Regina.

Laila is first to jump off the bed. Running over to the counter, she places her paws on top while standing on her hind legs. Killing is not something I ever thought would be a part of my life, a part of who I am, but I was outnumbered. Vomit rises in my throat just thinking about it.

"Ava, I am so sorry you had to endure that alone. I can't imagine how that felt for you and how it still feels for you. This is another reason my mother chose you. You wouldn't kill unless you had to. The power, that power, could drive someone crazy with bloodlust." His voice grows closer and closer to me, but I still remain looking down, disappointed in myself but also understanding there was no other way.

His words softly graze my face as he leans down, whispering in my ear, "Ava, you have the ability to acquire the power of others."

Confused, I feel there's no other option but to question what he means. "Come again?" That came off more sarcastic than I intended it to.

"When you kill someone, you acquire their powers. This makes you very dangerous in the wrong hands. You could be the strongest killing machine. Think about all of this for a second. Think what others would do if they had that skill. If someone with a less than pure soul had the ability to take other powers? The Militia? The Grimmers? Does this all click now as to why they want you? I'm sure there are more reasons, but this is a huge factor. I mean think about it."

"Kieran, I just feel so vulnerable. All of this information—everyone seems to know more about me than I know about me. You're the only one who cares who I am in this life, not who I was in past lives or what I could be used for."

I look up to him, and our eyes lock as he places his hands on either side of me on the countertop. Je didn't tell me any of this to kiss me, but I can tell he wants to. My eyes close and wait, but a low, judgmental scowl makes my eyes open, and I shift off the countertop. I didn't even hear the door open back up as he storms into the room.

"What the hell are you two doing?" Marcus looks more displeased than I have ever seen him before, like he literally boil over. His aggression is catching me off guard, and I reach for Kieran's hand to protect him.

The sight of our hands intertwined stops Marcus in his tracks. "Ava, Aidan is here. You must go see him."

He is not my father. Why is he trying to boss me around all of a sudden?

"Why?" My tone is small and clipped. I meant to come off more assertive than that. As Marcus moves closer to us, Kieran postures himself in front of me.

"Why? Get your head out of the clouds, Ava. This isn't fun and games. You have responsibility. Go see him, now!"

I look at Kieran. His eyes are filled with anger toward Marcus. This couldn't be more awkward and uncomfortable. I stand, lifeless.

"This is ridiculous. I know you are trying to do what you believe is right. But I am hoping eventually my happiness and what is right can be one and the same. I am just going to go." It wasn't directed to anyone in particular, just a random statement as I hold my head high and make my way to the door.

"Ava, you have a big heart, and that is beautiful. Don't let anyone steal it from you. It is one of the things I love about you." Pardon me? He just said that with such certainty. "But you are the classic people pleaser. You need to learn to say no, or you will end up hurting yourself in the process of making others happy. What do you want?"

"To be happy." I barely get the words out as I am about to walk through the doorway.

But I am stopped by Aidan. He looks as though he has been digging through the trenches, covered in mud. His hair isn't perfectly placed like normal but, rather, a mess. I stand here, literally and figurately torn between which direction to go. He lied to me about Laila. Why? Aidan's eyes narrow to Kieran, his neck jerks to the side, and long black hairs start growing out. His shirt begins to stretch at the increasing size of his body. Before I can even witness the transition complete, Marcus runs over to me and drags me into the bathroom, Laila following closely behind us.

"They were never supposed to meet. That wasn't part of the plan." Aidan is talking to himself in frustration or to Marcus… I cannot tell. Is he talking about Kieran and me? Some other people? Marcus is trying to shut the door, but a force is pulling it off the hinges.

Aidan is a beast again and ripping the door off to throw it in Kieran's direction. He scowls at me with those penetrating blue eyes with such disgust. He should be disgusted in himself. If I am his soul mate,why won't he take the time to get to know me and who I am now?

Kieran locks eyes with me for a second as he raises his hand and stops the door from impaling him and uses his powers to send it violently against the wall, smashing it to pieces. Aidan's heavy footsteps leave dents in the floor as he walks toward Kieran, drooling and letting out deep fierce sounds from within him.

I cannot take it anymore. I start screaming for them to stop. But neither of them is listening to me. The room is being trashed. I would like to think Aidan wouldn't actually cause Kieran harm. But seeing him now, I know there's no question he will. Kieran confidently grabs knives from the kitchen and hones them as his weapon. This is the last thing I wanted.

Marcus tries to stop me, but I squirm out of his grasp and run into the room to get between the two men with my hands spread apart. Aidan is too large and doesn't see me, while Kieran is trying to fend off Laila as she pulls on his pants with her teeth. Aidan's sights are set on Kieran, and he doesn't even notice me. He has tunnel vision, even while I am trying to get his attention. He has tuned out all sounds and vision to anything other than his target. His large paw is raised in the air, and I don't have time to move before it strikes me down.

Comprehending what has happened is still leaving me in shock as I lay once more on a floor bleeding. For someone who can be so powerful, here I am, injured again. Aidan's eye switch to me, and fear comes across his face as he realizes it was me, not Kieran he struck down. Aidan begins to change form back to the handsome man I know, not this feral beast.

I bring myself to stand, posturing for all of them to leave me alone. "Please, stop this," I beg as I hold my arm that is bleeding profusely from the perfect claw marks that run horizontal from my arm and slightly onto my back.

Marcus runs out of the bathroom, and for the first time, I see his power. He uses a force field to keep everyone apart and away from me, granting my wish. And I make my departure from the room with Laila by my side, giving everyone time to cool off.

Chapter 10

I am meandering down the hallway as their voices begin to fade from my mind. With no destination in mind, I follow Laila. She has at least been here longer than me. We walk the hallway for over an hour without seeing one person, and out of nowhere, my body begins to convulse as I am fighting being taken to another place beyond my will. Another vision. But I lose once more. I must try to control it this time.

Victor is in an interrogation room, with all glass walls, and the floors are bright red to match the ceiling. The room isn't sterile looking. In fact, it looks like a place where decapitations are performed, as blood is splattered against the glass walls. He sits shirtless in a large metal chair, in the otherwise empty but grotesque room. A man dressed in all white comes storming in the room and starts yelling at him. I cannot see his face, just his blond hair and the back of his body. Some machine is altering his voice. Or maybe it's just my imagination. It's hard to make heads or tails; it's like I'm getting pieces of the picture and not the whole picture. The man whips him across the face and yells at him; it's unclear what he said.

"Where is she?" The man hits my brother again. Victor is resilient. The man walks over to the door and brings a large machine in. He quickly turns it on and holds the nozzle as high-powered water marks Victor's chest, knocking him over, leaving his chest red and raw.

"I wonder if she can see this. You have linked souls, correct? Ava, see us hurting your brother?" He looks to the sky, searching in what direction to yell for me. "Come save him!" He sprays him while he's down but, this time, on the side of the face, making it appear as though Victor has serious burns.

I have to help Victor.

He is my brother.

This is a new lifetime.

He cannot be hurt because of me.

Yes. Yes. *Yes.* I will help. I scream, but they cannot hear me. The man keeps torturing him.

The man takes a long serrated knife out of his side pocketknife holster and walks over to Victor. He picks up his weakened hand and cuts him in the center of his palm purposefully. With the blood seeping out, he takes the blood and writes a location on one of the bare walls.

Water splashes over my face and I am awake, lying on the floor of another room in the compound; the lights on the ceiling give it away. Once the water is cleared from my eyes, I can see her. She's beautiful with the most amazing aura; it glows multicolored around her. I don't even have a chance to speak before I am greeted with a smile and a helping hand up. "Sorry about that. It was the only way I could think to separate you from your vision." Before I even ask, she answers me. "I, like you, have been around for centuries, so I can tell when someone is having a vision or premonition, no matter how rare it might be. I am Kerri. The Healer."

I have heard a lot about Healers throughout my training. They are people who live century after century, like the Purecks. However, they only have one purpose, and that is to heal, without bias. They cater to all. Unlike people who train to heal others, like doctors, they are naturally gifted and can see within someone to sense the problem, and occasionally, healers can have other powers as well.

"Pleasure to meet you, Kerri! I am Ava." Gratefully I take her helping hand up and look around her room. It's definitely a Healer's room. It's not like any of the hallways or bedrooms I've seen. The walls are filled with trinkets. There are comfortable rugs places around the room. Even dream catchers hang from the ceiling. This room fits her personality from what I can tell. Her soft blueish-green eyes filled with wisdom light up the room, showing pride for everything she is surrounded by, and her shoulder-length dirty blond hair frames her face perfectly. It's so hard to even place age anymore in this new world I live in, but she looks to be around the age of Marcus. They must know each other.

We make our way to the comfortable, soft, plush blue couches in her room and take a seat. There is no awkward silence. I feel a huge sense of comfortability with her as I jump right in. "When I touched your hand, I could see you back in Salem at the witch trails. I know they believed you to be a witch because of your healing powers."

"Men with small minds will always be afraid of things they do not understand." Her voice is elegant and graceful as she speaks her truth.

"I can't imagine what it must have been like for you throughout the years, dealing with different hardships." It's my truth to her.

"You don't have your memories, do you? I can tell there's a block. Something's tying up your memories." She stares into my eyes inquisitively.

I proceed to tell her about the ring and my fake mother being a witch. I only give the important details I think she will need to know about my memories. No need to lay my whole life on this poor woman's plate. She probably already has enough going on, so short and sweet and to the point, nothing more.

"Something is holding your memories back—could be your fake mother, could be the amulet she uses to harness her spells. Either way, it seems there is only one common link to retrieve your memories back, and that is to confront your imposter mother. For she who did the spell can also undo it."

Wow, this information is great, and I am eating it up like an apple pie on Thanksgiving. She makes us tea, good tea, not that shit tea my mother was giving me and chat.

Being in her presence truly heals the soul and spirit. She talks about her history, and I listen. She can feel others pain through their bodies. That's how she's able to tell where the true issue lies. She can search each vein, each neuron, every cell to find the true place of injury. Sometimes she even has to suit up in gear a witch made for her to help protect her so the pain doesn't transfer to her body. She speaks of Native American burial grounds she likes to protect to keep dark spirits away, and in turn, they give her the gift of temporary foresight, so she saw me coming. They only show her the foresight they believe she needs to see. I've never met anyone more fascinating.

She pulls out tarot cards and wants to do a reading on me for fun and study my palms, and her brow furrows as she tells me the result. "The hermit card has come up. This is showing me that you are going through a time where you may be feeling a little lost or that the path is unclear. You might not be sure of what way to go, or you may be struggling with making a certain decision. You need to listen to your gut, as you are being guided in the right direction. I do see there is someone who is manipulating you for their benefit; it's almost like they are tricking you into doing things that benefit them and that they are not taking your views seriously.

"It is better to be alone than to be involved with or around someone who doesn't value you or treat you well. Or maybe this is a decision you need to face in the coming weeks. This card suggests that you choose the option that puts *you* first. Being the kind of person you are, though, you find it hard to put yourself first. This is also a time when you may be faced with some decisions, and some of those you might not find easy. But the answers you need will come to you in the coming days or weeks. With this, you will be able to move forward, letting go of someone who is not helping you. There may also be someone in your life right now who is slightly narcissistic; you will need to let go of this person eventually. You must surround yourself with people who make you feel good, people who encourage you, inspire and support you, but most of all respect you.

"It seems like someone needs to make an effort as well for things to change and improve. It can't all just be one-sided. Don't settle for second best in life just because you don't want to be alone."

Boy, this got intense really fast. She is holding onto my hands now, tighter and tighter. Her hands start to shake, and I look to her.

But her eyes are closed and then suddenly burst open and are bloodshot. "There is a gentleman spirit who is trying to communicate with you. He passed suddenly and has a very fatherly presence around you." In her shock, she lets go of my hands.

"Dad?!" I yell around the room and then quickly draw my attention back to Kerri to make sure she is all right.

She fans her hand at me, showing she is good, and I look around the room. Every chime, every dream catcher, anything with the ability to make noise or move is doing so. The sounds are beautiful and not hectic as the wind swirls around the room and back to her. Spirits are trying to talk to her.

She stands and moves with grace as the spirits push her toward the door. She stands by it for a moment as her long, colorful dress robe shifts in the wind before opening it. Her delicate hand pulls on the knob, letting in my patient pooch, who has been waiting there for who knows how long. She closes the door after Laila enters.

"Interesting," she mumbles to herself and brings herself to stand in front of me. "Here, allow me to heal you, please. Before you can say no, I insist."

She navigates me to what looks like a massage table, and I hop on and lie down. She starts working on me, laying all sorts of products all over my body. Some look like seaweed. There are oils. To be honest with myself, I can try to say I know all of these things, but I have no clue. I casually ask her if she knows anything about making something that could harness my ring so I don't have to worry about it tracking my location. She doesn't respond, just keeps working. All I know is all of these things together don't create the best smell, but I am not going to interrupt her work. She has one lone clock on the far wall; it is the only blank wall in her room, just white and the clock.

I must have dozed off at some point during her healing because hours have passed. I wake to find Kerri nowhere in sight, just a note laying on my stomach on a post-it:

> You will know where to go
> Let Laila lead the way

Cool. Interesting. How descript. There have been weirder things written and said to me recently, so this isn't anything to sweat over.

Laila leads me down a long hallway, not much different from the others, expect this time I see actual people crowding around one door. This is it—the meeting everyone has been talking about. You would think people are lined up to get into a concert. They seemed jazzed to be here; at least some people do. Others look like they're looking for solace. I try to peek my head around and see what is going on. I am not even able to get descriptions of people engrained into my mind before a handsomely dirty man is standing right in front of me.

"What do you want?" I can't help but be a bit snarky toward Aidan.

He was clearly expecting another reaction from me. "I know Marcus broke up the fight. It shouldn't have gotten that far."

Laila is at my side sensing my unease and skeptical to let him get close.

"Ava, Kieran is fine. I am fine. Marcus is fine. We are all good. I got out of control."

Yeah, you're telling me! Isn't that obvious? Laila is growling at Aidan, showing all of her teeth. I love this crazy pup.

"I thought you said I could make you human?" My eyebrows raise in his direction.

"You did. It could have been worse."

Worse than this? I look down at my arm that is freshly healing. I am a literal walking mess. But thanks to Kerri, it's not as bad as I could be.

"Ava, you ran off. You left that note." He tries to come closer, but my hand is raised to him in resistance.

"Aidan, you have a family. I couldn't make you choose. I'm not even your girlfriend, you were with Isabel. It wouldn't be fair." Even with all the hustle and bustle going around us he manages to make this conversation intimate.

"You are my family. When will you understand?" He looks down at me with those still blue eyes, and I know how much he cares for me. But I will not take his family away. Not to mention, can he really be my soul mate? I feel like the word has been used so much by others it is losing its meaning. He doesn't wait for my response. "Come, we have time before the meeting. Let's go somewhere to talk."

In an odd way, I owe him that much, I follow his lead with

Laila right next to my side, down one corridor to another and another, a never-ending maze. This walk is long, so I try to break the awkward silence. "Why are you all dirty? It's unlike you to have a hair out of place. You also … kind of smell." I try to clear my throat, but a laugh comes out instead; a hint of a smile touches his eyes, and the awkwardness evaporates.

"I was searching for you. You let your guard down, and I was able to see you, just like how I found you in Mexico. You were on a boat, tied up and in pain. I was able to track your vision and see you were on Lake Champlain. But when I arrived, there was no boat and no you. I didn't know what happened to you. Then I saw you smiling with an old man, and he said something about the Adirondacks, so I knew you were coming here."

There's no question that he is concerned for me and worries about me. We've established this. But would I be a fool to trust him? "I appreciate you coming to look for me." For whatever reason, I don't want to go into detail with him like I did with Kieran, even if the opportunity arose.

"I love you, Ava. I made a vow to keep you safe, and I intend on keeping it. No more running off."

"Do you love me? Or the person I was before? I don't have those memories. I am not the same person. Plus, you might not say that after the conversation I want to have with you later." Even my words sadden my soul.

"I won't lose you again. That is a promise." His eyes turn dark and dangerous. Boy, he means business. I know he lied to me, but how deep does the rabbit hole go? Could I forgive him?

We are here, the destination. He opens the door into a huge suite, at least four times the size of Kieran's room. It's not the classic sanitary military style I've been accustomed to seeing but elegant and modern. There is an all glass wall that looks out into the forest, not a soul in sight. Is there something like a wait list to get a room? Everyone seems to have one. Maybe I can ask Kerri.

I feel like she would help me without being judgmental about my lack of know-how.

I aimlessly wander around his living space, and he is tinkering around in his all tile and marble kitchen. The wall behind the bed is all brick and gives a nice contrast next to the glass wall. This is how the other half lives. I am, by no means, slumming it back home, and I am fortunate. But this is a different level of money. Or perhaps it's respect. I don't know. There is such a vast difference between how he is treated and how others are. One of my hands gently grazes the glass wall, and there is a ripple effect.

"This is my own portal out. Only I can exit and enter through this site. Here, drink this."

My hand reaches for the drink and I take a swig of the pale, cloudy, vile drink, sure to keep some distance between us. It's not fair to him, my confusion. "Yuck. What is that?"

"It will help the pain, even if you do have a scar, a constant reminder for me." Little does he know I have already been healed immensely more than I thought I could be.

"OK, so no one can see in, right? What about the randoms walking in the forest?" There is a little bit left in the vile he handed me, and I swig the remanent back.

"We are able to see out, but when anyone other than me is approaching, they will walk right over us. It's like any other portal, just specific to me." He moves from behind me and comes next to my side, looking at me quizzically. My body has taken in whatever he has given me; it's a familiar feeling, like it's alerting me somehow. It's like an animal is running rampant through my body, from my arms down my side and to my ankle. It is not painful, just invasive.

It has healed whatever was left over to heal from Kerri's healing. When the feeling stops, my body stops moving, and it is refreshed. It's like I have had a million Monster Energy drinks. It feels good to be able to stretch my whole body and not wince.

"It's a serum, one my mother had in her book of potions. I've been making it, and it does wonders. I am not happy about this." He growls at himself, gesturing toward my scar, letting the beast out through his teeth.

"Don't, please. You had tunnel vision. You didn't know it was me." Hopefully, consoling him will work. But maybe I should just rip the Band-Aid off at once and get it over with. "Why did you lie to me about Laila? Kieran said he heard her barking, and she was locked in the room. How could you leave her behind?" There is so much disgust rolling off my tongue.

"When will people stop trying to turn you against me? First Dino and now Kieran. Ava, I don't expect you to understand why I made the decision I made. You are an emotional being. I lied to you because I knew you would not understand." He moves away from me and sits on the red comforter that is placed without a wrinkle on his bed. He sinks his head into his hands. "I love you so much. I would do anything to keep you safe, which meant getting you out of there. The house was on fire, and there was no way to tell if the witch had used spells or not. Ava, the house could have blown up the second I got you out of the door. When I went in to get you, I begged the dog to follow me out, and she didn't." Laila is growling besides me, but he ignores her and continues on. "I know you love that dog, but I love you more. And I made the decision I thought was best. I do not expect you to understand. I should have gone back, and I didn't. To be honest, if I were placed in the same situation again, I would make the same choices—your safety above all else. Your love blinds me."

I couldn't make eye contact with him once while he was speaking. I just stared out the window, and now I turn to look at him. He has taken his head out of his hands, and a tear is rolling down his face—a sole tear. He isn't upset over the decisions he made; he is upset that I'm upset over his decisions. "No more lies. You need to be thankful she is alive, and nothing has happened to her."

"Ava, I want you to be happy. I want to be the reason you are happy."

Well, there it is. He wants to be my reason for happiness—while I just want to be happy with myself and then, hopefully, be with someone who amplifies that. My burst of energy is gone, and reality has set in once more. "I will happy when this war is over and I don't have to worry about facing death every day, even if it is inevitable."

He reaches for my hand, but my protective pooch won't allow it. Aidan moves his hand away. "I guess she will need to warm up to me."

Duh, you think. You did leave her in a burning house.

He shrugs, but his eyes show he likes a challenge. This isn't just a challenge. This is my life. "I am very protective of you. I do not like people getting in the way of my being with you. I can see Kieran wants to be involved in your life. But let's not beat this dead horse. I simply don't like him." He looks repulsed.

"For your information, you were right about Dino. As much as I hate to admit it. I know as my Shaddower I'm not supposed to sense things about him, but I can ..." I trail off, just so disappointed in my best friend. I mean I'm living life hoping so many people will change, and that's not a reality.

"Ava, that's not how all of this works. Dino could be good. He could be evil. That is his choice. The other thing that is sure is he was meant to balance out your birth powers. The only one who has all the answers is Cassiopeia. When did you see Dino?" His voice went from sweet and comforting to stern in an instant, and now he looks down at me in an overpowering position.

"When I left you, I called him for help. His was the only number I had memorized outside of work. I had nowhere else to go ..." Again, I trail off into silence. I don't need to defend my actions to him. I made the decision and cannot take it back now. Plus, if it weren't for that moment, I would still be thinking Dino was an angel sent down to save me.

"You didn't have to leave me." Oh, I can tell he wants to start an argument. Why not? Seems like all we do is argue, even if it's passive.

"Yes. I did! Your girlfriend was trying to eat me alive. You and your father were arguing over me. I was not going to be the reason for such havoc. To be quite frank"—I start to get snippier—"I don't want to hash this out right now." My arms are folded across my chest; he is not getting me to cave.

"Fine, let's go. The meeting starts in twenty minutes." Now he is trying to one up my level of coldness. Aren't we quite the temperamental, non-couple soul mates? Who knows what we even are? There's nothing I hate more. The passion and intensity can be so dysfunctional.

It's like he purposely wants to make the situation worse. Granted, I'm not helping. Something comes over me as he turns and grabs the doorknob, making his way to leave the room. I pull him toward me and force him to turn around. Before he gets the chance to analyze what's happening, I kiss him—hard, passionate, and with all of me. I wrap my arms around his neck, and he is fighting it at first, until he caves to me. He grabs my waist and takes control, picking me up and pushing me against the wall. We lock lips, yet our mouths search each other's.

I pull away breathless as he is shaking his head at me. "I cannot stay mad at you for long." A smile grazes his eyes, and I wish I felt the same.

There is nothing but regret. I've kissed two men today. What the actual fuck am I doing? Maybe I shouldn't be with either, like Kerri insinuated, take time for myself, even if the world around me is crazy.

"One day, I will call you Mrs. Cross," he promises, and my heart sinks.

Quickly, before he can say anything, out with something, anything. "I keep asking Marcus, and he avoids the question. So, I understand only someone with a linked soul can kill me. I need clarification. Does that mean any linked soul? Or does it have to be mutual? Just because I love someone, they can kill me? Or is it a connected love-linked soul? Does that make sense?"

He cocks his head to the side and slowly releases me to the ground. "Interesting question. Why do you ask?"

Do I need a reason? It is my life. He grazes his finger along my jawline waiting for my response. "Kieran"—just the sound of his name, and Aidan's eyes turn dark—"mentioned something, and I need to know."

"It is someone you link souls with, a two-way connection. That's why your brother was able to kill you before. You have linked souls with your family members, but that's obviously not by choice. When it comes to love and linked souls, there is a difference; the love has to be mutual. It has to be powerful enough that you share a soul with the other person and are willing for them to see into your deepest thoughts. For us, we are destined. But there are other kinds of love; if the soul is given, the options are endless." It seems as though he was reluctant to tell me; his voice was quiet as he was speaking to me.

He grabs me by the hand, and we exit the room, heading to my first ever meeting with the Elders.

Chapter 11

Kerri is sitting next to me to the left, and she taps my side, reminding me to stop twirling my hair around my finger. There is just such an eclectic range of people. And what is up with these uniforms? I thought the idea was to not draw attention to us, and walking around looking like a uniformed cult probably isn't helping. I'm not even sure what the main topic of discussion here is. There is supposed to be talks about the safe zone, but something uncomfortable is lingering in the air. Laila is beneath my feet, her ears up and on alert. The room is cold, too cold even to me; a few degrees lower and I would probably see a penguin walking around in here. No one else seems to be bothered by it. Maybe it's the status quo. I've tried to make casual conversation with a few randoms, but no one will speak directly to me, just over me or to the side; all gazes pass over my face—trying to hide the truth, knowing I can see it with a touch. I am beginning to feel I am only here due to mutual connections and not my ability to contribute. But what do I know? No one will speak to me after all.

Next to Kerri sits a man, practically withering away in his seat. Even so, his spirit is as bright as his orange eyes. His old leather coat almost matches his age I'm guessing; he wraps himself snugly in it as he is contemplating what to say to me. He talks to me but doesn't mind that Kerri is listening. "I hear you have the power to shock those who you feel uncomfortable with." His raspy voice reminds me of our drive here.

"Yes, it has developed to be more than that," I whisper back as to not disturb the crowded table. People are still piling into the large room.

He runs his hand along his long face; there's a long pause before he continues. "I would love to draw your blood for a sample and see what you are made of. Nonetheless, I bet if you focus hard enough, you could project that shock through your body, much more than a defense mechanism."

I'm not sure what to say back or whether to divulge his line of thinking at this point.

Kerri catches on and interjects. "There's a potential for all things to be limitless. We'd better pay attention," she states simply enough to break the chain of the conversation.

Aidan is sat to the right of me, holding my hand under the table and giving me a tight, reassuring squeeze every now and then. I keep trying to break free of his grasp. I need to be able to hold my own in some aspect, not just be here as Aidan's sidekick.

The elder sat next to him at the head of the table has dark skin but very light blue eyes, dreadlocks, and is donning a cloak similar to the one Higgins Crawlford wore during the training fight, except his sleeves are cuffed up under the elbow, with blue rims that match his eyes. He is solid, sitting tall with confidence, a point for all others to emulate and look up to, but he has worry lingering behind his eyes.

More and more people are filling into the vast, military-styled room that matches the rest of most of what I have seen. The table sits about thirty people, with standing room for others. Surprisingly, there is little chatter around the crowded room; everyone is just waiting. The silence is deafening. Ray walks into the room. Our eyes lock, and he tilts his head, a quick hello to me that just sends that electricity through my body; it is staring to boil, but somehow it is subdued.

"What is it?" Aidan's concerned voice is something I will never get sick of; it is genuine.

Looking back on all of it, I realize my fake mother never looked truly concerned. And if she did, now I know why. She always had herself and her intentions lying on the table, but I was blinded. I pick up my left hand and swirl the locket around in my hands, placing my finger on the back so it plops open, not forgetting the other key that dangles from my neck as well. My real mother—she is beautiful. He smiles down at me, looking at the locket he gave me.

Without interrupting the conversation I'm having with Aidan, Kerri slips me a black band with a small box in the center. Aidan is looking in the other direction, and I keep casually talking to him about how I don't trust Ray as I read the note Kerri put in the center of the box:

> Wear me around you ankle.
> Put the ring inside.
> No one can track it.

I mouth a sweet thank you to her, and she nods in acknowledgment, making sure to draw no attention. The man sitting next to Kerri must have overhead my rambling to Aidan about Ray. "I don't trust him either. By the way, my name is Judd."

Aidan chirps in. "Ava, you have no reason to lie to me. I believe you. He serves a purpose here, giving us information on the Militia. He is a rat." Aidan clarifies to Judd and me, but that just makes my opinion of him even stronger.

"How do we know he is not playing both sides? He helped me. For that, I am grateful. But still? What did you guys put him through to prove himself? Are we forgetting I can see into souls now? Dark shadows have eaten his whole soul." That's the best way to describe what I have seen inside of him. When my hand felt his touch, there was so much pain in his soul it blocked me from seeing further. Normally, there is hope lingering; but with him, nothing.

"We will talk about this, but not here, not now, Ava. These conversations are meant to be private." His stern face is back and on full force.

The way things are done here is totally different than how I would handle them normally. I'd just be out front and open. He can sense my disregard.

"Ava, this is something you used to have mastered. It will come again, time and place."

Ray finds his seat to the right of the head of the table on the other end. And these seats better not be arranged by importance, or we are in trouble. Could my powers be wrong? Certainly not. I try my best to respect Aidan and not search his thoughts. But maybe I should. Or would I rather be blind with trust? Two women share the head of the table on the other end. One has pale, perfect porcelain skin, just like Ray's. Her long, blond, curly hair is tied back in a braid that nearly reaches the ground, with tendrils lose all over, some falling in her face. Her brown eyes match her elegant dress, showing off her perfect posture. The cold must not affect her one bit as her brown dress is almost see-through.

The other woman is sour-faced, with large dark eyebrows that do not flatter her aging face at all. Her light brown hair is frizzy with chunky purple highlights. It is stuck all up on end; it looks like she has had her finger in a light socket for the past twenty years. Gathering from the wrinkles on her face, neck, and hands, she has had a long life. Perhaps sitting next to the non-aging beauty makes her appear older upon comparison.

Aidan is consumed in a conversation with Mr. Elder at the head of the table, so I turn to Kerri and Judd. "Who are those women?" I nod my head down the end of the table, which Ray must have noticed, because now he is giving me a death glare.

"They are actually sisters. You can't tell just by looking at them. And that boy staring at you is the blond's son." Judd speaks to me.

I stare at the women, trying to find the resemblance; and it's there, just not strong.

"Ferma is the dark haired woman, and she has the ability to change scenery, to place one reality upon another. You had an encounter with her son once," Kerri chimes in. Either she was there to witness the ogre-like man from the training war or word travels quickly.

"We both were there, watching from the boxes," Judd adds. These two must know each other, judging from how comfortable they are to converse with one another. "Ferma has perfected her skill. Many with that power have to stand still and focus to bring one reality upon another. But she can walk and talk, all while instilling a new reality upon us. With enough practice, the only one immune to her is you. A few here are cursed with immortality, and she is one of them, as is her sister, Freya."

Kerri picks up where he left off, quietly of course. "Freya is the older of the two sisters. Her husband died when the Militia killed him and left his body in flames in front of her house."

I try to turn to them to keep this conversation more private, but Aidan will not let go of my hand. He turns and shoots me a look that says, *no.* I sigh and try to shift as close to them as possible, with my arm awkwardly held behind me.

"Kerri, you are a healer. I thought you do not choose sides. Why were you at the battle? And how does an immortal birth a baby? I am just going off of movies here." As always, so many questions, so little time.

Judd gives Kerri's hand a reassuring squeeze, and she places her hand on top of his. "Judd and I have been friends for quite some time, so he knows all about this. Healers do not choose sides, or we are not supposed to. My duty is to heal, and I will do that. However, what the Militia and Grimmers have done, what they are trying to create, I cannot stand behind. There is a clear difference between right and wrong. I will heal those I encounter, so I trying to keep a distance as much as possible, as to not pick a side and let someone die. Freya had a soul mate. And when that happens to an immortal, they are able to conceive, even though he was not immortal himself. In fact, he was a blue-collar worker, who stole her heart; but it was written in the stars for thousands of years." Kerri begins to get reserved, as though she is disappointed in herself.

"Freya is special. Her mother was a Pureck who only possessed one power, and that was to read minds. When her mother passed, she gave Freya the ability to read minds. Now she has multiple powers, including moving objects with her mind. We respect the immortals. But they fear you, as you are the only one who can turn them mortal, so the story goes."

Judd is becoming apprehensive to share more, and Aidan is staring him down. My guess is Aidan knew all of this but, again, likes to keep things to himself—in his own odd way, to protect me.

"How many Purecks exist now?" It's an opened-ended question to either Kerri or Judd, and I'm hoping that Aidan's glare won't stop them from answering my last question.

Kerri chimes in, not fearful of Aidan, but Judd holds his finger up in protest, and she swats him away playfully. "As far as I'm aware, there are currently three walking this Earth. Cassiopeia is the strongest of them all and the one whose spirit is with you. Her life here will not be much longer as your path gains more purpose. The other two aren't as strong and remain in hiding. They will come to us in our time of need to help, but you won't notice. They will fly under the radar most certainly."

"Couldn't they just stop all of this? If the three of them united?"

Judd raises his brow to me, and a smile reaches his eyes as I literally scratch my head, confused. Looking around, I notice that the whole room is jammed full, leading out into the hallways, which are crowded as well.

"Brilliant, like you father. He asked the same question but soon realized it was not their purpose here in this life. The Purecks will not work together. Cassiopeia has picked a side, while the others have not. we hope they stick to their roots. But time can turn even the purest soul dark under the wrong circumstances. Everyone, I mean everyone, has an Achilles' heel. It's just about finding out what that is." He ignored Aidan's scolding look to answer, which I appreciate. But turning over my shoulder to see Aidan's face shows Judd is in the doghouse.

At least there is some comfort in knowing they haven't picked sides and would rather stay out of it. As wild as it seems, that is more ideal than them going to the opposition.

Hundreds of people have to be here or listening in. There isn't an open inch of room I can see. Kieran is standing on the side of the room across from me. I cautiously wave my left hand at him and then bring it to cover my face. How can he forgive me? He must have noticed me talking to Kerri and Judd. When I move my hand from my face, he is still looking at me and mouths, *It is OK.* I don't know if he forgives me, but at least that is a start. The relief is overcoming me as I sigh, all while not breaking eye contact with Kieran. Aidan must have noticed who I was looking at because he is picking our intertwined fingers up from under the table and slams them down on the table out in the open—all while looking at Kieran.

I try to squirm out of his grasp. Kieran notices and becomes uncomfortable with how uncomfortable I am. Aidan shoots me a glance, a mean one at that, as I fight to get my hand free. Aidan is doing this to make a statement and mark his territory, but I don't need to be involved in his egotistical pissing contest. Kieran makes a quick move to come this way through the crowded room, but Efron and Kai appear out of nowhere and grab him by either arm. Kai speaks into Kieran's ear, and he relaxes but still makes eye contact with me. I shrug my shoulder apologetically and scoot down in my chair.

All eyes are locked on Aidan and me, not just Kieran. All eyes. My face is flushing. How am I supposed to handle this situation? *Like, take a picture; it will last longer,* I say internally in my best stepbrothers' voice. And something makes me think Kieran knew what I was thinking, since I can see a smile crack on his otherwise displeasing face.

What the actual fuck? Aidan stands to speak. I didn't realize he was speaking here. I'm always one step behind. "Thank you all for coming. We have many important things to discuss. Please listen to Humphrey as he starts the meeting off. We will be open to all questions at the end." He addresses the whole room formally.

He must know so much more than what he has been telling me. And Humphrey? Not the name I would have picked for the dark skinned, light-eyed elder.

"I will spare everyone the pleasantries and get right into it. The war has been going on for centuries, even if some of you were too young to notice it. But now the Militia and Grimmers have both produced stronger numbers than we could imagine. They have been recruiting. Thanks to an informant, we know there are different levels of the Militia—the grunts, who don't know much about anything; midlevels, who follow blindly; and the hierarchy ends with a blank face leading them. Our informant"—I know he is talking about Ray; I shoot him a glance, and his lips curl up into an evil smile—"was in the trenches and worked his way up yet still never saw the face of the leader, just that of second in command. Both oppositions are looking to advance further."

Humphrey continues, "Thanks to our informant, we know the Militia will set out on their attack starting next week. They have not yet located our newest safe zone, so we will all hole up there and disperse forces accordingly. We are hoping that, on the Militia's hunt for us, they take a few Grimmers out in the meantime."

"What about the Grimmers? What is their plan?" one random voice quakes over all the silence.

He is not reprimanded, but Humphrey reminds him, "Hold all questions until the end. However, I will answer this one. Grimmers have only had one plan, and that is to expand themselves. They want to take over every person, every city, every country. They believe they are the superior beings and need to be treated as such and not live in hiding. We do not know much about where they stand with the Militia, but I wouldn't be surprised if they tried to use them to their advantage."

There was a great deal of chatter going on back and forth about what could be done to stop each one of the groups and what types of numbers and skill sets are need to do so. It becomes a very militarized conversation.

Freya stands, her elegant loose dress falling to the ground. "We know the Militia and Grimmers have the same mentality, and that is to stop anyone who gets in their way. Many years ago, they tried to rise up, but we had fate on our side, and they went back into hiding. What we request now is for a small number of men and women to come forward, who will help us locate their bases. We know the general vicinity in which they seem to have large numbers, but we need an entrance point for all locations. This might seem like a suicide mission to some, given the small forces, but it is essential to report this information back to us."

A hologram appears in spots throughout the room with one in the center of this table. The map shows the main Militia locations, one is near where the torturer wrote for me to go. Now I am certain this needs to be my mission, and I must hold back the location until I gather further information.

Aidan releases my hand as he stands and places his two hands firmly on the table. My fingers are getting all the feeling back. The blood circulates quickly. It's hard not to focus on this feeling, but his voice distracts me. "I know what we are asking is putting some in danger. We only require a few people to search and report back. We know their numbers are great. But we need to know what machinery they have on their side—rumors are circulating—especially the Militia. Grimmers we can handle as they come to us, as we have always done. The unknown is the most frightening aspect."

Humphrey chimes in, "Tomorrow, we will travel to the safe zone and speak to the recruits and others who are willing to volunteer. We will travel throughout the day and in small groups to make sure no attention is brought to our portal. There will be spies everywhere, hunting us and looking for our entrance. Make sure to be on guard always. When we get to the new safe zone, there will be thousands of us there to discuss further strategies when reports come back to us."

It is like they have rehearsed this exact conversation. As Aidan takes a seat, Freya goes into further detail, but I don't pay attention. Leaning over in Aidan's direction, I whisper into his ear, "I will go in search of the Militia base."

"No fucking way!" He is much louder than I expected him to be, and people turn to stare at him.

When he realizes the attention, he has brough upon himself he runs his hands through his hair and gestures to Freya to keep talking, with an apologetic wave that isn't raised off the table.

With all eyes back on Freya, he feels comfortable to speak again, more softly. "I just got you back. No way are you leaving."

"But I thought the whole point of me being here was to be put to use. Let me help. I am doing this." This time, I'm not asking for permission, but more or less just informing him.

"We will talk about this later." He scowls.

Based on this meeting, I know he is in charge of arranging the groups to leave, and there is no way he is putting me in a group. Freya said the maximum is five per group, with five groups going out to potential different locations. Those invited to this particular meeting were ones they could entrust with this task. So why even invite me? Why not kill two birds, unknowingly to them, with one stone? Save Victor and locate a Militia base? They are sending the groups out soon, it is hard to fully keep track of what is going on with Victor residing in my mind. They request the groups return within five days, by November 14, with whatever information they have.

"Now we are open to questions," Humphrey announces.

All are silent. Aidan isn't allowed to leave the meeting, so now would be the perfect time for me to cut out; even though there could be more information to gather, it is just not worth me being here.

I stand, shocking Aidan, who grabs my hand. But I let my fingers slide through his. I bend over and give him a kiss on the cheek. It makes him smile, and I know it was the only way I was getting out of this room. It was my reassurance to him that I was not leaving. The crowd parts like the Red Sea in my path. and I get to the heavy metal door and glance quickly over my shoulder. Aidan is watching my every move. As I push open the door, my peripheral vision shoots me to Kieran, making his way over to the door as well. I don't wait for him, so there is no scene caused. And I make my exit, but not before hearing a familiar, mad, female voice over the crowd, Isabel. "What of the girl? Will she—"

The door shuts, and I am almost wishing I stayed in the room, although the questions clearly wouldn't have been asked with me there. My very presence held people back from asking what was truly on their minds. This hallway is much brighter than the others, and I will never get used to the heavy walls and mazelike feel of the bunker.

I sigh to myself as I lean my head against the wall for a moment of peace, which is soon interrupted by another familiar voice.

"Ava, we have to talk." Marcus is standing behind me, not Kieran, much to my surprise.

I look down at Laila. She really want to go outside. I know Kieran took very good care of her, but a walk through the woods would be nice.

"Shoot, Marcus." We walk and talk through the hallway, mild pleasantries, until he gets to what he really wants to say to me.

"You cannot see Kieran."

Great, this again, as if my internal debating wasn't strong enough; now I need it from more people. Honestly, who has time for this? "Marcus, Kieran is a great guy. In fact, he's one of the only people who actually care about who I am not, not who I was. Why do you dislike him so much?" I stop dead in my tracks to look him in the eye. "You never had an issue with him before I came along, according to him."

"That's because I didn't know who he is. He is Cassiopeia's son." For once I can tell he is being extremely truthful with me, and it is making him uncomfortable.

"Yes, I know."

Marcus looks shocked. Is it a hidden fact that Kieran trusted me with?

"How do you know?" He doesn't skip a beat in questioning me.

"Honestly, Marcus, that is a silly question. He told me. We are open with each other. Why does all of this matter?" I figure I'll take advantage of his openness while it lasts.

"Did he speak to you of Aidan? What else was said?" He is really pushing here and getting closer and closer to me, causing discomfort, not because I don't trust Marcus, but because it is more pressure and more questions bringing the anxiety all the way from my toes to my chest and now my face is blushing. My heart starts beating a million miles a second.

I begin walking again and tell Marcus as much as I can, without breaking anyone's trust—which really doesn't leave me with much to say. "All he said about Aidan was he wasn't sure I was meant to be with him and that his mother was right about me. Very general statements."

"What does that mean?"

Marcus, stop with the inquisition. Just because my dad trusted you doesn't mean I will betray Kieran's trust. "I can't say anymore; it's not my place to tell." Simple as that.

Thankfully, Aidan's door is in my line of sight, and I'm hoping I can somehow get out through his portal.

"And what has Aidan told you of Kieran?" Marcus grabs me by the arm, softly, not in a harsh way. "Ava, this is serious. I am trying to help you, but I don't know how to help if you won't talk to me." He is frustrated and I am not sure why he is taking it out on me at this point.

"Aidan doesn't tell me anything. In fact, he hides stuff from me. All Aidan has said is he does not want me seeing Kieran. Why? What do you know?" It's time for me to turn the inquisition around on him.

"Just as you said before, it is not my place. I would have assumed he would have told you. It has to do with his curse, his family's curse."

"Marcus, can we catch up later? I'm sorry to brush you off right now. I'm just processing a lot and need some headspace to think away from everyone. Can I catch up with you later?" I don't wait for him to answer, and I make my way to the door, leaving Marcus behind.

He leaves me with a few parting words. "I know you will

love both of them, Ava, in different ways, but you should be with Aidan."

I turn to look at Marcus before I walk through the door, but he is gone. How does he know I will love both men? If it has something to do with Aidan's curse, Aidan should be the one to tell me.

Laila is in the door before me and picks up a piece of paper that was on the ground. I bend down and give her a scratch behind the ears. "What is it, girl? Want to go for a walk?" I take the paper and just like to always notice that my voice to her is so sweet, like a really good customer service voice.

The window is almost the twin of glass, but does not hold its weakness to shatter, but still perfectly shows nothing but darkness of night.. The time has once again escaped me, but the light green of the trees illuminates the forest slightly, leaving it with a breathtaking ambiance, something I have grown more and more fond of.

I open the note:

> 9:00 p.m.
> Meet me outside the portal, alone.
> Kieran
> P.S. Alone doesn't mean you can't bring Laila.

He definitely gets me. But why would he even think I would bring anyone else? Unless I bumped into Kai or Efron, it isn't like I have many friends here at all. I am a total outsider. I have about an hour until I need to leave, and I know the meeting will be hours longer, so I don't have to worry about Aidan showing up and ruining my plans. I saunter over to the kitchen, turn on the fire-burning stovetop, and light the note on fire. I hate feeling like I am deceiving Aidan; it is just this feeling that resides in my gut that I have no control over. But it hurts me to know it is the only way to keep him calm and from beasting out.

Perhaps Kieran knows more about Aidan's curse and would be willing to share with me. The paper burns and turns into ash, which I take and put in the sink and watch the water float all traces of it away.

Chapter 12

It was an absolute shit show trying to go through Aidan's portal; it bounced me back, causing me to look a little bit like Cousin Itt. Then trying the other portal in the main entrance of the building took me ages to figure out; apparently, you need to do a body scan for it to operate. After many trials and tribulations, I am outside but not after landing horribly on my ass when the portal shot me out of the other end. Sooner or later, I will get used to this.

I have about thirty minutes or so until Kieran shows up, and there's a desperate need for me to get back to my roots a little bit and remind myself of who I am. What better way to do that than put pen to paper.

"Where is my notepad?" Searching everywhere, I can't seem to locate it, so why not ask my super helpful, always intuitive pooch. Laila walks over to me, notebook in paw, or mouth rather, and she drops it by my feet. We search for the perfect writing spot and have found it, right near the heavily wooded area. So if someone else needs to enter or exit the portal, I am just out of viewpoint.

Sitting on a boulder, I slowly chant to myself in a new way that comes to me naturally, almost like the sound of wind chimes. And the earth gracefully moves beneath me. The leaves and dirt surround me on three sides, giving me privacy but not blocking my vision from the creek. The nature swirling around me feels natural and doesn't bother Laila at all, and I feel at ease—at ease enough to write:

> Dad,
> To be honest, I am not sure why I am writing you a letter, knowing full well you will never read it. As crazy as it sounds, I need to get a few things off my chest, and you're the one I feel wouldn't judge me or my decisions and would help provide me with some clarity. Maybe writing these things down will help me put things in perspective. Or who knows? Maybe there will even be a sign you're listening to me and can provide me with some guidance.
>
> I understand why you did what you did, why you left. You wanted to protect me and keep me safe. It was a selfless decision for you, and I can't imagine how hard that is on you. I love you for that. But at the same time, I am angry with myself for spending so much time thinking you abandoned me, when that wasn't the case at all. Every person I meet who knows you talks about how brilliant you were and how much I remind them of you. I understand why you left, but I just wish I could have known the person they speak so highly of.
>
> Now, Aidan says he wants to keep me safe, but he wants to shelter me from everything, even helping. I feel like I cannot be honest with him all the time and have to hide parts of myself.

I wish there could be some way you could be here with me to help clear things up. I have so many unanswered questions, things others won't answer for me. Aidan said he saw you. Did he mean in a vision? I have seen you in visions. Is it your spirit coming to leave us clues? Or are you alive walking this planet somewhere and projecting yourself here? What of my real mother? I have some memories of you from childhood but none of her. Who was the imposter pretending to be my mother? I need guidance with Victor also. I saw the evil in his eyes in Cancun. But he is being tortured. And I cannot leave him there if I can help, right?

People either look afraid of me or seem to not trust me. I don't know who I was before, and people are looking to me, but I cannot remember. Kieran trusts me, and sometimes I think Marcus and Aidan do, too. Some have no faith in me, and others, too much. I have an unbearable weight on my shoulders, but they are looking to the person I was before, and I am not sure I am that person now. I understand that I have to give everything to save innocent lives and help this war come to an end, which I have no problem with. But how can I do that if some people tiptoe around me or omit the truth? Aidan is so fearful of losing me again. Dad, I just don't know what to do. I feel like, no matter what decision I make, I will hurt someone. Sorry for rambling, but not sorry, considering it is really just me reading this and, well, Laila.

Marcus told me earlier today that he knows I will love both Kieran and Aidan but in different ways. What choice is he telling me I have to make? I do not have enough information. How can I be expected to choose, if, in fact, being with Kieran could save his life and keep him from turning dark? While at the same time, I am destined to be with Aidan. Then Aidan's curse—there is definitely a piece of the puzzle I am missing, and it has to do with his curse. This is a key part, but he leaves it out. Well, he leaves everything out if I am being honest.

On the bright side, I am getting a pretty fantastic grasp on my powers. I can morph just by thinking of what it is I want to be, almost down to a science. And I no longer need to close my eyes and concentrate. My closeness with nature is amazing. Even now the wind, leaves, and dirt surround me. It is beautiful.

My birth power seems to be causing me the most difficulty. And now I understand part of your letter more. There's no doubt I have always been able to see the good and evil in people. But I cannot constantly think I can change them and bring the good to the surface. I met a Grimmer named Dillion, and time and time again he has pulled one over on me. But I saw good in him. Or was that Dino blocking my vision? Perhaps some people cannot be saved? Perhaps the evil is too strong for that little bit of light to shine through? I hate believing that is the truth, but I am not sure what to think anymore.

I wish you were here.

I wish I could remember my real mother.

> I wish what my heart wants turns out to be the best thing for everyone.
>
> How do I get the answers I need? How do I find my old fake mother to get my memories back. I actually think I know what to do—that will be best for everyone.

A sad weeping dog on my lap has interrupted my writing, so I cuddle her of course. But the sound of approaching footsteps has me on edge.

Kieran appears through the swirling wind of leaves and dirt. "What are you writing?"

It's like nature just let him through. But I guess he can do that because of his mother. In his playful, boyish way, he jumps over a rock to sit next to me.

"I connect with nature too, maybe not on as large of a scale as you, but it helps me and heals me. Ava, nothing is silly. Out with it."

Why would I think he would just breeze past it?

He shoots me that boyish grin, knowing full well I will cave to those green eyes.

"I'm writing a letter to my dad. I know it silly because he is not here, but I was hoping he could help me figure some things out. Or at least writing to him would allow me some time for perspective." I shrug. What else can I say?

"Laila is crying."

We both pause to look at her. Kieran is confused as he sees her sprawled across my lap. He rubs her behind the ears, but nothing.

"She started crying right before you got here. This hasn't happened before with her. I'm worried. Speaking of crying, I normally don't ever cry. I mean, I can count on my hands how many times I've cried, and the vast majority is from when all of this started.

I am sorry I am such a mess." It really has me baffled and breaks my heart to see Laila cry real tears.

"You are a beautiful mess. She is probably just happy to see you and overwhelmed. She has gone through a lot in the past few days. And as much as all of this is a shock to you, imagine it must be a shocker to her as well. Or maybe she is sad you are confused. Dogs can sense that kind of stuff, you know? So, what are you trying to figure out?" His voice is so soothing to me, in the most comforting way.

"Maybe you can help me. At this point, you know me better than anyone, and we have spent more time together than I even have with Aidan. You mentioned your mother and her telling you someone else would be in my life. What do you know about his curse?"

"First things first. I'm glad we have developed this friendship and deep connection. But I'm still not 100 percent a believer of prophecies. I think everyone has a say in his or her own life. Was my mother right that I would develop feelings for you? Yeah." He shrugs it off. "I'm drawn to you, but I know you have a lot going on and a lot to figure out. So, just take me out of the equation for you. I will be here for you as a friend, but I am not going to pressure you to be with me because of some prophecy or not. If we find our paths to each other, great; that's what I want. But you have the world on your shoulders right now, and I know you feel like it's crashing down on you. You don't need pressure from me on top of that.

"As far as Aidan goes, I didn't even know he had a curse." He stops talking quickly as if he's just realizing he was rambling more than normal.

But I admired everything he said—he is thinking of me and not himself.

He looks confused, probably the curse thing just now sinking in. "Ava, I know it's a lot to take in. I meant everything I said. That kiss meant something to me, and I know it meant something to you too. I don't know what's going on with you and Aidan, and I don't think you even know yourself. I never wanted to be on his bad side, but I was before I even met him. He knows more than what he's telling you. That much is clear. The only way you'll be at peace is when you find all the answers you need."

"You're right. I don't know what is going on. He has loved me for centuries. I saw a vision into his past, one where I agreed to be his wife. I could see our love for one another." There should be a but at the end of my sentence; it won't come out.

"Ava, the past is the past. You can appreciate it, but you also have to move forward and decide what you want—not the old Ava, who you are now. This decision is yours alone. It's not about what anyone else wants. I will support your decision, but I will be here for you always. My heart will always be fighting for you." His words are always so powerful and honest.

My head instinctively lowers, thinking there is so much more to add to the letter to my dad, but later. I imagine my dad was here now; he'd be laughing at the mess I'm in.

Without moving my head, I say, "Kieran, I love how raw and honest you are with me."

His stare isn't breaking from my face. I can sense it. He's waiting for me to say more. But what can I say? At this point, my heart just aches thinking about breaking anyone's heart. I tuck my hair behind my ears and stand, only for the wind to breeze so quickly past me it all falls out of place.

"You sing beautifully."

Crap, how could I not realize I started singing when I stood up? It is my way to help my mind concentrate and process things. Why is it I can't control that around him? It's a habit I don't mind in the privacy of my own home. But not here—not in front of him or anyone.

"I have to go." Suddenly, all my body pressure rests on my

turned heel as I make my way to the portal, fully knowing he isn't going to stay put.

The wind pushes him toward me, not even giving me a second before his hands are on my waist standing in front of the portal. His hands move across my hip in one swift motion as he places himself in front of me. Just that touch so tender sends the wind flowing through my veins, and my heart pounds, as nature works in unison and literally pulls us closer together, causing us both surprise. With his free hand, he gently sweeps his fingers across my lips; my eyes close at his touch once more.

The wind pushes the leaves around us, and they graze my lips right before we are intertwined in the most passionate kiss I have ever experienced in my life. My hair is tousled in the wind; nature floats around us creating a cocoon, just me and him. Shivers cover my body, and I reach my arms to his face to pull him closer and feel he has them too. Water swirls outside of our cocoon, and as our lips separate, the cocoon bursts and water flows over us and back into the river—soaking me from head to toe.

We laugh in unison. Surely, we must look absurd. The midnight darkness of the forest is lit by the orange moonlight radiating purple and pink. A deep breath released from my body, I have no tension whatsoever, and as I open my eyes, there is pink in front of me—my aura, showing my emotion. How do I know all of this is real? That this isn't just an act? Not just Kieran, but Aidan, Marcus? Anyone to fulfill the destiny they want. Kieran is real. Or is this all his mother's doing?

He breaks the silence and rambling thoughts of my mind. "You will be happy to know Higgins is under review and is no longer receiving sensitive information. He is strictly on a need-to-know basis. That was the last thing they said in the meeting, before pulling him out in some magical restraint cuffs. If they prove their facts, he will be condemned to death for working with the Grimmers."

Death? Not the romantic close I was thinking I would have for sure. Laila is pacing in a happy way around us at the news. People who says dogs don't understand us are crazy; she knows.

"I thought we were the good guys. So, why death?"

"He knows too much, Ava. As much as I don't relish the idea of taking a life, I understand it would save thousands. If he gives out any information, people will be slaughtered; make no mistake of it. He could sell the information to the highest bidder. It's not like he's someone low on the totem pole. He's an elder who knows all of our locations."

The thought still makes me sick to my stomach, no matter how logical it is.

Pushing myself back quickly, my words barely come out, I am smiling ear to ear being suctioned into the portal. "Bye, Kieran."

Laila jumps into my arms, and we are gone. Nothing like a dramatic exit.

Chapter 13

Kerri managed to get me my own room. I'm not sure how she pulled that one off, but she did. And I am so grateful to have my own space for once. The room looks almost identical to Aidan's. It's crazy to think there are these monstrosities of a room in comparison to the others I have seen, even through open doors. These must be reserved for someone special—or someone who has money.

We bumped into Marcus on the way to my room, and he advised in a very serious voice that he would let Aidan know where I was staying. I hope now Marcus doesn't find issue with Kerri, since she was just helping a girl out. While settling me in, she did some of her voodoo to my mind; yet Kerri was unable to let the block down, but it did provide some clarity to confirm to me my suspicions that my fake mother's tea was, in fact, a memory blocker and also suppressed my powers. In the cellar dream I was having, it was her; she was torturing me the whole time. Her brew must have been strong for me to forget that interaction with her or forget it was her. It's still kind of crazy to me that she was watching over me and waiting for the right time to turn me over to whoever she was working for. All of the dots are starting to connect in my mind, and it is a maze to put all of these pieces together; there are so many moving parts.

I'm thankful Kerri has gone when a loud knock on the door rumbles my room, and without hesitation, he opens it before I can answer, "How was your walk?" His inquiring is almost as though he already knows the answer.

"I didn't do much walking to be honest." This bed is comfortable. My body is so tired I do not even move to greet him but let him come sit down next to me. He is not going to like where this conversation goes, but I at least have to be honest. It isn't like a normal dating scene; this is so serious, all the time.

"Well then, what, pray tell, did you do?" He turns his head to look at me as he gracefully sits down and starts running his fingers through his hair.

But my hand meets his to stop it midway. When all of this comes out, it isn't going to go down well, but how to say it? "I wrote a letter to my dad, which is stupid since he isn't here. But it helps." Why my words were so defensive for no reason is beyond me. That's not even the worst part. With Kieran, I can talk openly about Aidan and not feel bad about it. But the other way around, and a knife is jammed in my chest, making it hard for me to breathe.

"Ava, it is not stupid. If it makes you feel better, it's how you cope."

Why do I always expect him to be harsh? That wasn't harsh at all; it was actually sweet and endearing in a way, without any rage.

"Thank you." That's all I can muster for now.

But his inquisitive look is making me panic. It sucks when you want to move, but your legs are cemented into place by a dog.

"What else aren't you telling me?" He has an advantage. Having known me for so long, he can read me—not like I make it hard for people to read me. But even when I try to not give it away, he is on me like white on rice.

Here come my defenses again, making me almost hate who I am when I am with him. "I should ask you the same thing." That sounded bitchier than intended.

"What do you mean?" His sour face is now standing, looking down on me.

Might as well get all the arguments and confrontations done at once, one break instead of many over time. "Honestly, for such a smart man, how do you not get it? How do you think I will be OK being thrown into this mess and you not being honest or purposely withholding information from me? You are holding back about your curse. And I have a feeling it's a pivotal piece of information. Please." Hopefully, the pleading gets him to finally not omit the truth for once. I stand to look up to him face-to-face, so he can get how serious this is to me.

"How do you know I am holding something back?" He raises a brow at me and motions his hands closer to me like he wants some love, almost playful, to the point I struggle holding a smile back.

There's always an opportunity to joke something away, but not this. "I could say I have known you for centuries. So, give me some credit. But instead, I am going to nip this right now. Why are you being toxically invasive and trying to be playful to change the subject. I love it when you are playful- given how rarely that is the case- and you know it."

"All right, I have a proposal for you." His words leave a lump in my throat. "You tell me everything I want to know about your walk, no short answers. In return, I will enlighten you about my curse and why Kieran gets under my skin. Fair enough?" He raises a brow.

"Yes." It is fair. But it's odd that he doesn't want to know everything about the time I was missing and is focusing on my walk. Maybe he already knows about Kieran, although I don't know how, considering we were alone, and nature protected our tender moment from anyone.

Hopeful all of this open conversation will enlighten both of us more—no other way to do it—I jump right in. "I guess I'll start." I clear the lump in my throat that always seems to be stuck when I'm talking to him. "Kieran slipped a note under the door asking me to meet him."

Just with one sentence, he's stiff as a board, his hair standing on end.

"You want to know. Please, can you try to hold in some of your testosterone?"

The joke, thankfully, brings a slight smile to his face, and he nods at my recommendation. He motions for us to sit on the bed, and of course, I oblige.

"I left early because I wanted to write a letter to my dad. There are so many questions that seem unanswered for me that I was hoping, once I put pen to paper, it would clear some things up or help me process. I don't know. I didn't get to finish writing. I hate to admit that I am scared, not because of this new world, but because I don't want to let anyone down. Kieran has been a big help for me understanding things when no one else was there. He told me his mother was the Pureck who bestowed me with these gifts." I know I am leaving some things out, but that can be my bargaining chip for when and if he doesn't tell me something. It's sad that is what our relationship is. "All of this talk of destiny has me confused. Either people have no faith in me or all too much. Yet, everyone walks on eggshells around me, afraid I am delicate. But what makes me so is when people withhold the truth from me. I don't remember my previous lives much, so I need all the information I can get. And the only person who seems to be honest with me is the one person you don't want me near."

Taking a deep breath and closing my eyes for what comes next doesn't make it any easier to speak. "Aidan, I bumped into Marcus earlier, and he told me I would love you both. When Kieran and I saw each other, we kissed, and I let him." Could this cause me to lose my dream man?

"Ava, you kiss him because you have a linked soul with him, I believe … and because of my curse." Aidan looks ashamed. Words don't pour out of his mouth as expected. There is silence, deafening silence.

He gets out of bed and walks toward the glass wall in my room. "Ava, you were sat right there writing." He points into the forest. "You were singing the most beautiful tune as you were writing. You have always done that. You used to always sing, everywhere you went—to make your own songs—and it was so captivating. Seeing you like that gave me a glimpse of the woman I loved all those years ago. You are the same person. I stood from my glass wall and watched as Kieran approached you, and I knew it wasn't by accident. So, as much as I hide things from you, you also hide them from me."

My eyes roll into the back of my head; he has some audacity.

"He spoke of his mother, and I knew he was the one my curse spoke of."

As much tension as there is between us, he is vulnerable right now, and my urge to console him overtakes me. Within a blink of an eye, I am by his side, hugging him tightly and pushing my head into his chest. His heart is beating, not the steady, strong, and secure beat I'm used to but jumpy and scared. "Aidan, there is more. What is it?" I pry.

"Ava, I don't want to lose you again. Every decision I have made since the first time I laid eyes on you was to protect you and keep you mine. You can't leave me." The intensity of this, of us, is so exposing.

The fear in his eyes is apparent as he speaks once more. "Before you said you wouldn't leave. And I know I have left you, but I just don't know …"

"Do you have such little faith in me?" Walking away, I find some solace leaning back against the portal wall, feeling the electricity it produces running up and down my back. Out of the corner of my eye, the colors so vibrant almost blind me. Red, purple and yellow can only be seem at this exact angle. Something new and amazing always seems to shock me in this new world. I bask in this minor moment of wonder, until his voice pulls me back.

"The curse is more detailed than what you know." His words are short, sweet, and clipped. He remains firm in his spot across the room.

I shoot him a look that says, You know the deal; now hold up your end of the bargain—also known as the death stare to end all death stares. He paces back and forth, stroking his hands through his hair. We made a deal, and I am not going to cave now; he has to hold up his end.

My eyes dart to him, big and bugged. Out with it, Cross! I need to work on my patience with him, but he is so frustrating. I awkwardly wiggle around until I am able to talk myself into relaxing my arms, in an attempt to be more sensitive and to ease my body tension.

Finally, his mouth opens after what seems like an eternity. "You know the backstory that resulted in the curse. That is all true. That Pureck was the one who gifted you—Cassiopeia. However, the part of the curse that was left out was this: 'The one whose eyes change for his love will feel the sting of my heir stealing her away.' Werewolf eyes only change for their soul mate. I am the only one destined in my line to have a soul mate. He is the only suitor I feared. He doesn't even know about that most likely. I searched for him, but he did not exist after your first life. Cassiopeia was heartbroken, but when we heard she had found love again, I knew it was only a matter of time. She took her son into hiding and left his father. After that, no one could find him. No one here even knows who his mother is; he has kept it well hidden. I, not so shamefully, admit there was a point in my life before you came back into it, when I was with my ex, that I tried to find him with the sole intention of ending his life. Now he is here. Marcus called me when he pieced together who he was."

I choose to ignore the fact he went on an intended killing spree in order to ask the question running around the back of my brain. "I thought nothing could tear soul mates apart and that the curse wouldn't harm us?"

"I believed that for a long time, Ava. But still in the back of my mind, I worried and hunted him; it drove me mad. One day, my father pointed out the truth. When she gave you the gifts, she gave you a part of her heart with them. She was clever and worked some magic, literally, which has saved a place for her son in it. He is imbedded in your heart without you knowing. It's just a piece of your heart, not the whole thing. But you cannot remove him. The worst part is his feelings for you are genuine. It isn't like a magic love spell; there is a true connection. Our paths have all intertwined, and there is no way to change what has already begun. There is no greater revenge than taking away my love and giving it back to her family."

"I don't want these powers. I don't want to hurt anyone. I don't want to hurt myself either. Take them all back." I throw my hands in the air, begging the Pureck, who surely won't answer me.

"I can't do that, and neither can she." He looks saddened. "Your purpose here is far too great. If Kieran takes you away from me, I will experience the heartbreak required for me to die. At least, I would leave this world instead of having to bear the thought of seeing you with him every day of my life."

"I didn't choose this." He needs to be reminded. He cannot die. It all makes sense now—even why my breath changed color after Kieran's kiss. It has something to do with our connection. "I can't live this life without you. I would choose you, the man who walked out of my dreams." Am I just saying this to make him feel better? To convince myself I would do whatever it takes so he doesn't die?

"One day, Ava Buchanan, I will finally be able to call you my wife."

Sentimental Aidan is a rare sight—but so amazing. Everything is out on the table now. He walks toward me and leans down, about to place a kiss on my forehead, and his phone rings. He looks at me regretfully, and I know he has to answer, and I know he will be leaving.

I nod in approval as he answers and makes his way out the door.

Without even noticing my body slowly follows behind him, like an instinct, eavesdropping on his conversation. And as the door closes my ability to hear strengthens through the door. He is talking to his father. He has spoken to Isolde, a witch—not just a witch but a great sorceress. The call came at a toll to Elijah emotionally. I can hear it in his voice. She said the ring would have to have been made with the blood of the witch who injected it with magic. If they bring her the ring (she is somewhere in Montana), Isolde can trace the witch's location.

There are low grumbles as he starts to fade away into the distance beyond my hearing. But one thing he said was clear. He would steal it from me without my knowledge.

I flop onto the bed after a nice shower and start to create a mental to-do list in my mind. I have a night alone, for the first time in a long time. So I sleep without worry. Words can't even describe the solace that brings me—just to breathe without someone watching me or needing something or being worried about my safety, just a moment. Just when the night has provided me so much needed clarification, my subconscious gives me more to question and more to do. I am able to piece together my dreams the more I concentrate and practice. I can control my visions—turn them back and watch them. Now I know they are all subject to change. The nightmare from my childhood, where I was being tortured in the cellar, it is extended, and I can see the face behind the torturer. It was my imposter mother, looking for my real mother. What was the serum she injected into me? Maybe something similar to what she placed in the tea?

I need to find the imposter mother and question her. So I need to find Isolde. The question is, Why is Aidan going to hide it from me? He clearly said steal, so that means he won't tell me. For she who did the spell can undo it. Like Kerri said, something is holding my memories back. It could be my fake mother. It could be the amulet she used to harness her spells. Either way, it seems there is only one common link to retrieve my memories—and that means I must confront my imposter mother. Maybe when I retrieve my memories, I will also start to feel more of my full powers.

I think of my job and Harrison. I don't even know how to salvage that situation, and my stomach is wrenched with guilt for having left him in a bad situation at work. Add to the pile that he has probably seen the devastation at my house. I can only imagine the thoughts that must be running through his mind.

Then there is the big ticket item of my key necklace and finding out what that all means. I mean, my father was pretty vague about it in his letter in the first place. Find the old weeping willow and this key. Will I know when to use it? He mentioned someone being able to infiltrate time and time again. I wonder if that is Higgins, because then he never left.

On top of all of everything else, the Bermuda Triangle known as my love life seems so silly. Yet, I can't help but to crave intimacy and sex. I haven't been touched in that way in so long, a year, in fact maybe more. Aidan has been a total gentleman about that, but also there has never been good timing. There's always something going on, and I know he isn't repulsed by me; it's just bad timing. I almost let out all my sexual tension on Kieran if he would have come in the shower with me. At this point, I'm frustrated and like a pot ready to boil over. This is insanity.

I wonder how long the trial for Higgins will take and what other information they are going to try and get out of him. Then there's Cassiopeia—what to do about her? I wonder, if I met with her, could she reverse the curse? I highly doubt she would even want to do that for me or for Aidan. Either way, I feel like the only way I am going to get answers is if I go off on my own to get them.

Victor!

Chapter 14

For the first time in a long time, the natural faded sunlight wakes me through the glass wall. The morning stretch is long overdue and something simple that has always been taken for granted until now. My body covers every inch of the bed. I move from side to side, separating my toes and stretching ever muscle I possibly can like an intense but lazy Pilates session.

The glass wall is its own reflective portal that has been disabled. In a way, I'm in my own little jail cell, like I will go rogue at any minute. From here, it is apparent there is a search party meeting, and among the list is Aidan. He probably picked the positioning on purpose, knowing I would be able to see him. The group is dressed in black uniforms, similar to the ones we wore in our simulated battle. The uniforms seem a bit redundant, and I thought the point was to blend in, not stand out. Each member of the group holds up what appears to be a beacon tracking device, and all are nodding at Aidan intensely. He must now be running the show.

Laila is spry and almost knocks me over, bouncing around ready to start the day.

Somehow, the minikitchen in here is stocked with dog food—not the normal five-course filet mignon Laila is used to, but it will do. I take some pearly white bowls from the cupboard and fill them with food and water and leave her in peace to enjoy her meal while I shower and get ready for whatever this day throws at me.

Honestly, for the past, god only knows how long, I have pretty much looked like utter shit, a heaping pile of poop. And with no plans that I know of, why not spend all the time in the shower. Kerri pretty much got my body back in tip-top shape, so a clean slate it is!

"Son of a biscuit!" My feet feel like they are five feet off the ground as Aidan scares the shit out of me when I come out of the bathroom in only a towel.

Normally, I would be all about this fun-loving playful moment, but this is what I get for letting my guard down for only one second. I frantically search the room for my pooch; normally she would let me know if someone came in. But she gave me nothing, and she is not here.

The panic across my face forces Aidan to speak. "Relax, beautiful. She is fine. Marcus took her on a walk."

My body relaxes and it initiates in Aidan a playful mood I have never seen him in. Without a clue what's gotten into him, and without overthinking it for once, my body goes with the flow, craving some form of intimacy.

Lunging my body on his, I tackle him to the bed, wrapping my arms around his neck. Yet, he manages to flip me over in one swift motion. But there's no chance he will win this battle, so I flip him back. It's a miracle that my towel has managed to stay up and my wet hair keeps flopping in his face. He looks like he took a shower himself, at least from the chest up.

He lets out a loud laugh as I have his arms pinned over his head, knowing full well he can reverse this if he wants. His voice is low and seductive. "What are you planning on doing to me?"

Oh, that makes my mind wander.

Without thought, I kiss him, but not one of those sweet chaste kisses we have come to know—a full-blown make out, with our mouths and tongues searching to find that perfect harmony. It hits the spot, and my hips graze his as I press forward. He pushes my hair out of his face and cups my face in his hands, making me grin from ear to ear. "I am going to hold you captive in bed with me all day."

He can't even hide his grin at my request.

"Wipe that mischievous grin off your face."

Playful, fun-loving Aidan, it is. How can he flip the switch so quickly? "Make me." That accent melts me whenever he speaks.

I shoot a playful wink at him, and it's all over. He flips me around with one hand, so he's on top of me, pressing himself into me. He knows what he's doing, trying to drive me wild. He is hard, and it's pressing between my legs. With one hand on my face, he brings me in to kiss him while the other hand creeps under my lower back to lift me harder into him.

His sensual smell is invading my every thought, and his touch against my skin has sent goose bumps up and down my whole body, down to my toes. He changes the energy. "Ava, I forgot to ask you. Isabel." I cringe at her name and want to vomit. "She told me she stole the ring from Elijah's office, but she believes you took it from her. Do you know where it is?" There is a subtle desperation in his voice.

A barking at the door startles us both out of the intense moment, and it makes me jump inside, accidentally tensing my whole body. A pulse releases from me—and not the kind I was hoping to obtain—shocking Aidan and making him fall to the floor.

"What the fuck!" He doesn't yell but leans up on his elbow, glaring at me, as though all the love has evaporated from his body. And I know fun-loving, playful Aidan is gone.

"I am so sorry, Aidan! What can I get you?" I scurry off the bed to be by his side, making sure my towel is firmly wrapped with one hand.

He shakes his head and lifts his hand out to me. With the strength I have, I pull him to his feet. He feels as though he weighs about a ton. I'm not sure how that is possible, but he's like a bag of bricks. "I didn't mean to—"

He cuts me off. "Ava, I thought you were getting better at controlling yourself?" He searches my face for something. What? I don't know. Obviously, I feel terrible. "Never mind. I will be fine. Go put some clothes on, and I will get the door."

He recuperated quickly, faster than anyone else. Must be a wolf thing. I smile at my own dumb quiet joke and make my way to the bathroom to change quickly.

The door is locked behind me, and already I am displeased with the voice I hear. Chills run up my spine and not the good kind. But Laila is pawing at the door to let me know she is waiting for me outside, giving me some comfort.

"Sir, the tracking devices are put into place and monitors through this," Ray Smith says.

And I should give him more credit considering he did help save my life. But all of this is fishy. I still don't even understand Aidan's part in the Resistance fully. Based on conversations I've overheard or taken part in, I gather that people admire his strength. But does his pack hold sway over him? Or, based on what Isabel said, his father, who by all accounts seemed wonderful otherwise? At this point, I'm taking everything with a big grain of salt. But I'm always left with more questions than answers.

Abruptly, I make my entrance to the conversation—now that I am fully dressed in normal nonmilitary clothes, thank god, and a good old pair of Converse. Aidan has some watch on that projects a hologram, and he can scroll through each person and tap on the corresponding face icon to see the person's vitals and location.

"Very good." Short and sweet, he pats Ray on the shoulder, maneuvering him to the door. But Ray wastes no time shooting me an evil glance over his shoulder. "Anything else?" Aidan senses Ray's hesitation to leave.

"The other group heads are set to leave in thirty minutes. You want to get ready. She can go with the other group, if she wishes to participate." The way he said *she*, he was intentionally trying to be an asshole, saying I'm useless. He isn't even trying to make it hard to read between the lines.

"She," Aidan mimics his tone, "comes with me." Aidan is turned so there is no angle on his face, but it must be intense.

"Sir, the groups have been designated, and she is not in ours." It's like Ray wants to scheme and have Aidan all to himself. Anything he can do to get me out of the picture to whisper something in his ear to sway him. This is mildly uncomfortable.

Aidan is trying to get him to leave, but he just keeps pushing the subject. Back and forth, they keep discussing the arrangements previously made, and it is clear Ray switched it around so I am not with them. Perhaps his plans will start to unfold. The shift in the room is obvious in Aidan; he's gone from trusting Ray to questioning him. Aidan is getting more and more frustrated with Ray's words and suggestions. He has that boiling look to his face. Aidan opens the door with one hand and grabs Ray by the neck with the other, raising him inches off the ground and placing him outside of the door. It was so casually done that Ray is in utter shock. A few small drops of blood run down the porcelain skin of his neck. Aidan's claws must have nicked him. Ray meets my gaze with his mouth open as the door slams in his face.

Aidan's head lowers to the ground. "He has a purpose here, and we need him. Try not to look so happy I put him in his place."

"What exactly is his purpose? Give me all the details." Pleading is not my thing, but I have to work on it with him. It seems he only wants to give me answers if I am crying or in damsel-in-distress mode; it's rather annoying.

Was that what I was like in my past lives? Yuck. Finally,

probably after a good night's rest to myself, my emotions are in check, and I somewhat have my path sorted out. But I'm not sure how I will make it happen yet.

"Let's talk about that another time. For now, while you do look cute, you can't wear that. Let's get you suited up and ready to go."

Oh, lord, not another suit. My thick thighs literally cannot take it. Imagine going to the infirmary here for sweat rash on my inner thighs.

"Aidan, do I really have to wear this? You aren't wearing one. Again, what happened to the whole blend in thing? Looks like we are going to do one of those pop-up dances to 'The Star-Spangled Banner.'"

"That's because I am the boss." There is a hint of laughter in his voice, and I'm glad to see he's found his sense of humor again.

Walking out of the bathroom, I feel just as ridiculous and exposed as I did when I exited the locker rooms from the training facility. At least this one-piece is conducive to my body and doesn't make me overheat, although now I can't drink anything because how in the world would I go to the bathroom?

Aidan can't take his eyes off of me. He keeps looking me up and down. That's probably because this is ridiculously tight; it's the tightest one I have ever worn. And that's saying something, because in my college days, I wore some pretty scandalous jumpsuits, until I realized that wasn't bringing me the kind of attention I wanted. These military-style boots, though, have kind of won over a small section of my heart; they are just so comfortable and complete badass shit kickers.

"Stop looking at me like that!" It's a demand I have never given him before. In fact, I love it when he looks at me. But this all takes some getting used to. The uniform seems counterproductive and the total and complete opposite of blending in. "The other outfit I had on was fine."

"Can you work with me for once, please? If you don't see the need for it, don't wear it. But then you and I are never leaving this room." That low rumble in his voice kind of turns me on, and yet my mind wanders to Kieran.

My head shakes and clears my thoughts of Kieran. I turn around and peek over my shoulder and pull my hair to the side. Looking down, I gesture for him to zip me all the way up, just a few more inches. He saunters slowly over to me and obliges my silent request. He traces his fingers down my exposed spine before he quickly zips me up.

He exhales deeply as he rests his head on top of mine and breathes me in. "I can't wait to have you all to myself, once we are husband and wife." Oh, isn't he old-fashioned.

"You mean." My throat clears. "Have we ..." Gosh, I am mumbling a lot. "Done it before?"

He raises his eyebrows at my question.

"What? Can't a girl be curious? It's not every day you lose your memory, forget who you are, have to learn all over again, and get to be reborn century after century." I let out one laugh and then stop when I notice he doesn't find me funny at all. Honestly, the one trait I always thought I had going for me, and he doesn't even smirk.

"It hurts me that you don't remember. At least now you remember you agreed to be my wife. To answer your question, yes we have."

"Aidan, I'm sorry. I know this hurts you. At this point, we know what was done to suppress my memories. That is a step in the right direction. The other step is knowing I don't want to hurt you. I just want information, and maybe it will spark memories or feelings I had before. I know you're hurt when I can't remember. But imagine how I feel. You are having all these feelings, and I have just been lost, trying to figure out who I am. I know you shut down, but I am asking you not to. I am asking you to be honest with me. You are acting like I chose this, and I didn't. You think I don't want to remember every little detail, to see in me what you used to see in me all those years ago." Even through my mini rambling session there, the idea rumbles around in my mind. I really do wish I could remember everything. Yet, Kieran still flashes to my mind. What a scholar for covering me up in the bathroom.

He knows what I was thinking about, and he grabs me hard and places an aggressively perfect kiss on my lips. He begins to kiss down my neck, sending shivers up my spine, picking up where we left off earlier, before he brought up the ring and Ray Smith killed the mood. Now, I have mentally killed the mood. Laila is curled and hidden under the bed, and I pull back, feeling like I have been neglecting her after all she's been through. I sit on the ground, and she comes over and curls up into my lap.

There is a knock on the door, and Aidan looks down at me. He is burned, "When will he learn?" Aidan scolds as he opens the door, and Ray Smith is stood there once again.

Seriously, this guy is like a bad rash. Once you have him, you can't get rid of him. He smiles at Aidan and scoffs at me, and I make a weird face in return with my tongue sticking out like I am a two-year-old, but it felt good. I accept the fact that he won't be pleasant with me, like why even save me in the first place? I crawl under Aidan's arm that has the door propped up, and Laila follows me. I take a quick glance over my shoulder to check back on him. Ray once again, doesn't look pleased with his words.

My head should have turned forward before hitting the corner, but it doesn't. I watch them fade to the distance, and I manage to run into a stack of barrels and topple them over. Honestly, who places barrels right on the corner? Don't they know there are people like me lurking about the halls. My hands and feet are covered in a bright green substance. Hopefully, it isn't something valuable. I can't get my balance together to even get up on my knees. I am just starfishing it. So is Laila. And it has me dying laughing. Two peas in a pod and sometimes completely useless.

Marcus appears out of the blue and gives me a helping hand but not before snickering himself and trying to keep it together. How he manages to stand on the slippery substance without falling beats me, but he does it and with elegance; someone should give that man a metal. He takes hold of my arm, and all elegance on his part has evaporated, and now he looks like a bad excuse for an ice skater. Good news is this stuff doesn't smell bad; it's just sticky and goopy. He manages to get Laila up, and she immediately goes to a clean spot on the floor. As he pulls me up, my weight shifts him forward, and he is sliding on the ground. It reminds me of sliding across the wood floors in my house, and that is exactly what I am going to do.

These moments don't last long. Even Marcus begins to laugh as I start sliding on the floor and across the one hallway. I peek down it to see Aidan is no longer there, and a hard chest stops me from going any further. Kieran, in a T-shirt with his tattoos popping out of the sleeves and the top toward his neck, barely peeking through, or else he'd look like he had none.

I look back and see Marcus swirling around, having a good time himself. It's like we are kids in a candy store, and my laughter can't be held back. Aidan comes down the other corridor where Marcus is, standing with his arms folded, and that puts me over the edge. Now, I'm crying laughing to the point where it's contagious. Great, Aidan and Kieran. But now, even Kieran is laughing at me laugh, not caring at all about Aidan coming toward us with his hands on my hips preventing me from toppling over once more. Perhaps it's because I haven't had a good laugh in a while, and my body just needs this, but I am in all-out hysterics. I'm at the point where my laugh isn't making any sound, and tears fall down my face.

Aidan tosses Marcus a towel, which he uses to place his feet on and slide out of the gunk. Kieran slowly walks away before Aidan gets the chance to reach us. "We will talk later." He laughs, and I smile back at him.

Much to my surprise, Aidan isn't completely losing his shit. He tosses me a towel. "Come on, giggles. Your turn."

I do the same as Marcus and slide to the edge and pick Laila up on the way.

"Ah, good laugh, Marcus." I nudge his shoulder and try to wipe the tears from my face, forgetting I am covered in the green gunk.

Kerri opens her door, obviously to check the commotion and sees the mess and disappears for a second before coming back with a white potion in her hands. She doesn't speak and just throws the potion on the ground, and the mess is gone. She's miraculous really.

"Come, Ava. I have something that will work for you as well." She holds her hand out to me through her door.

"You have to come with me. I am leaving."

Oh, don't get your knickers in a twist, Cross. "I can leave with Marcus. Plus, Ray will enjoy the fact I am not there." Fact.

"Fine." He huffs. "The combination to my door is your birthday followed by mine. Take a shower in my room." He shoots Marcus a look he clearly understands, as he nods back. It's like they don't want me to go into Kerri's, but that's exactly what I'm going to do.

I don't know how I know it, but off the top of my head, I realize his birthday is December 1. A vision overcomes me. It's his birthday in a different time. His father and my father are there, laughing, enjoying drinks. There is no background, just faces. From the voices, it sounds like we're in Ireland, in a pub, Aidan's old stomping grounds.

"He is traveling with the group, but I will keep an eye on her."

What am I, a child? It's obvious who he is talking about, especially now the full details of his curse are out in the open.

"Can't you see she's had a vision?" Kerri stops the two men talking back and forth and grabs me around the waist, pulling me from my daze and into her room, not passing go or stopping to talk to the men. She shuts the door behind her without hesitation and sits me on the couch.

Kerri works her potion magic, and both Laila and I are squeaky clean, amazing, seriously. She tells me more about how her healing powers work and explains that, since she can harness power from certain ancestors, they grant her a tiny bit of magic to use, but in the form of potions; she is not a full-blown witch. It would be nice to have a good witch on our side. I respect her choice not to fight physically, and I envy it. I wish that could be me, instead of being pulled in different directions by different people. It's all par for the course of my life at this point.

Kerri is just so easy to talk to. And with her good nature and the fact she is a healer, I know she would not divulge our conversations to anyone; doing so would be against her morals and what she stands for. So we pick up where we left off last time, except I fill her in on absolutely everything I think she can help me with—for the most part everything, minus me being sexually frustrated. That isn't really something she needs to know.

She confides in me a secret of Elijah and Aidan. It's actually somewhat common knowledge, which is why she'll tell me, but they have hidden it from me. "Elijah was furious after the loss of his wife, but he was able to cope, knowing his son had love and that he would perhaps have a growing family. When you died last time, he met with the Grimmers to form a pact of some sort. No one specifically knows the details about what happened, just that he was looking for revenge and thought the Grimmers could help him and were safer to go to than the Militia. He made a vow in front of the Elders to do whatever he needed to do to save his pack. There is a reason he is never present at these meetings."

Wow, another thing just clicked into my mind. I always wondered why Elijah and other members of the pack were not at these meeting and held up in their safe house. Some of the things Isabel said now make total sense.

"But why is Aidan here then?" The dots are connecting but not this one.

"It was Aidan who removed his father from the council meeting when he stood up and confronted the others. He is here for you. I think a part of him always knew you would come back. However, him asking about the whereabouts of your ring with his father is suspicious to me."

She goes on to tell me Ray's purpose. She again states all of this is common knowledge and doesn't understand why Aidan hasn't shared the details with me. Ray is the definition of a rat. However, at this point they believe he has been discovered by the Militia and the Grimmers. Based on the timeline, Grimmers and Militia would have just figured it out, which gives us an advantage that we need to take right now—hence the search and report groups to see if Ray's information is accurate or if they are already changing locations. He was able to gain trust easily because of Elijah's public outburst. Ray's mother and Elijah had a known entanglement, so it made it believable he wouldn't want to be on our side, despite his mother always having the Resistance's backs. The timeline of events can be mottled, but I am following along. At the end of the day, Ray is a wild card that must be monitored closely. This is why Aidan is always with him at this point, so he can't get a message out if he was to switch sides.

As silly as it sounds to her, my feelings of guilt over leaving my coworkers high and dry without any notice really doesn't sit well with me. It's the same feeling I get if I leave a store and realize the cashier forgot to ring something up. I have to go back and pay for it. Or else I feel like I'm stealing, even if it wasn't intentional. Out of the kindness of her heart, she agrees to call my boss for me and tell him that, due to the wreckage at my house,I am in the hospital. She won't disclose a location even if he presses, and she'll let him know she doesn't know how long I will be in there for, just that I am making a steady recovery. I'm not a fan of lying or omitting the truth. But at this point I would never willingly bring someone into this crazy world. Look at what happened to Sofia. Imagine that happening to someone else—gut-wrenching.

She has left me to go to Higgins's trial. Apparently, the votes of the leaders of the search party have already been taken into account and will be read at his trial this afternoon. That means they got all the information they needed from him, and now he is standing trial. This is a much quicker turnaround time than I expected.

Kerri has left a parting gift on her way out the door. I didn't notice at first because I was in the bathroom, and it took me about thirty minutes to get this thing off and on just to go pee. There is a potion left on her table top with a note that reads:

> This potion will create a portal for you.
>
> Think of the destination you wish to go when you consume it.
>
> I have a feeling you will need to get out of a bad place at some point.

Well, that sure could come in handy. How in the world am I supposed to carry this thing around? It's not like I get to use a purse. Tucking it into my boot sock seems like the safest option. The bottle is small enough it won't shatter, and my sock will provide somewhat of a protective layer. I've become increasingly appreciative of Kerri recently, but I've never seen anyone with this potion. I wonder what lengths she went to to ensure I got this. It amazes me that Marcus hasn't shown back up to collect me yet.

Chapter 15

There's a light knock on the door. It's about time, only three hours later. This super speed of mine is something I don't know if I will ever get used to having. But, man, do I like it now that I can control it more.

"Ready, Marcus?" My voice trails off as I swing the door open. But it isn't Marcus who greats me.

"Marcus sent Kai to come get you—what a stupid move. And, well, here I am." Kieran gestures up and down his body while flashing a smile to me.

Lucky ducky, he is in normal clothes—jeans and a white V-neck T-shirt with a black leather jacket that has a gray hoodie attached to it, showing off that he, in fact, does have a chest tattoo; it's peeking through. I tear my gaze away, so it doesn't appear I'm gawking at him. I'm sure he doesn't mind.

His intense green eyes look into mine, and my smile reaches my eyes. "Marcus assured Aidan you and I wouldn't be spending time together on the ride there."

I look around and don't see my pooch, so I shout loud for her, "*Laila*!" and she comes barreling through the door and jumps into Kieran's arms. I close the door behind me as he gives her a quick scratch behind the ears before he puts her down.

"There are always ways around things. We will meet up with Kai and Efron before we walk to the bus."

My smile still won't let up.

"Hello … Treating you like a child much? He acts like he's afraid I'm going to take you away from him or something. That's all your call, no one else's. In the meantime … friends"—he's hesitant—"or whatever." He shoots me a wink as we walk side by side down the hallway.

The playfulness, ah, I cannot take it. He is too cute, and it melts my heart. It's just so easy to be with him.

We chat about things that are so unrelated to anything we have going on right now in our lives, almost as though we're normal people living normal lives. His favorite color is orange, and like me, he wouldn't know what his horoscope sign was, but he does due to the fact Efron is into that stuff, just like Sofia. As much as I want to inquire about every tattoo on his body, that's for another day. And I bring the conversation back to our real lives, just for a second. He needs to know about the ring and Aidan's call with his dad. This is something that would make anyone put up a boundary, but I know he won't judge me for my decisions.

"The strangest part about all of that is that he is keeping it from you, instead of bringing you into it. Why sneak around to steal something from you? Look, Ava, this will be the last sentimental thing I say"—he flashes me a huge megawatt smile—"for today."

I giggle. Even being serious he manages to lighten the mood.

"In the chance you pick him, I just want to say thank you. You taught my heart how to speak and open up, which I never thought would happen to me. You changed me for the better, not just in a romantic sense, but as a friend, even with Kai. I just needed to say thank you now, because I won't have the strength to later if you choose him. I will respect your decision, but I wouldn't be able to muster the strength to say it then."

Lord have mercy. What the heck am I supposed to say to that? Dagger to the heart. Someone come get me a wheelchair because I cannot move. Seriously, right through my chest bone and straight to the heart. Marcus was right. For whatever reason, I love both of these men, unconditionally, without time; it feels like no time at all.

"Ava! Toots!" Kai yells to me from down the hallway, and this moment is perfect for me to make an unexpected departure from Kieran's side.

Kai and I run toward each other, but he manipulates himself to multiply in front of me. Weird, how normal this all is starting to seem. "I will hug every single one of you, Kai. So you better show yourself, or else it's going to get hugtastic up in here."

All the Kai's have surrounded me in a circle. Honestly, how can anyone actually tell them apart?

With a snap of his fingers, the one and only walks in front of me, flashing me a huge grin. Boys really are such children; it's great to be surrounded by good spirits. He picks me up in an embrace and gives me a quick twirl around. He really is one of the most dependable people and has become such a good friend, even if it is through Kieran. I wish I had friends like that, but I don't anymore; it's just me. Dino and Sofia have gone AWOL. And the Marx brothers, well, like Harrison, I will not get them involved. Dino even has ulterior motives apparently.

Another boyish remark coming from Efron. "Finally the four musketeers unite!"

I don't ever remember him being this corny as he throws his fist up in the air. But I'm glad he has become a part of our new group, even if it was by force kind of. He's spent a lot of time with Kai and Kieran, and he looks like he has come into his own more.

Kieran walks over and puts Efron in a headlock, not even upset with Kai giving me a hug. Boys will be boys, but he is different.

I am part of the group here, not just some trinket to carry along like how I feel with Aidan.

Kieran and Efron start walking, leading the way to the bus, and Kai grabs me by the arm pulling me back. "Let them walk ahead so Marcus doesn't get his panties in a bunch. I don't know why he even asked me to get you. Maybe it was some kind of loyalty test to him." He shrugs.

"I'm jealous everyone gets to be in normal clothes, and I'm here like I have a Navy SEALs interview." I scoff. And Kia lets out a loud laugh, to the point Kieran and Efron turn their heads, and I blush scarlet. "Glad someone still finds me funny." I raise a brow. "Where are we going? I thought the portal was in the other direction?" I question as we continue walking down the sparse halls I didn't even know existed.

"Yup, you still have that humor going for you. What, Cross doesn't find you charming and funny?" Kai doesn't even wait for me to answer to continue speaking, even with Kieran and Efron out of sight. That was Kai's plan all along. "This is a good enough distance between us he wouldn't suspect anything. Those portals are for the forest. We're using a teleporting machine to send us to Marcus's old house. From there, we will go on foot to the portal entrance to the safe zone that services the northeast all the way down to the south. Then we'll each be given our missions for search and report. We'll meet other groups there with more locations to go to. At this point, we're relying heavily on Ray's intel."

Good old Ray Smith, coming in clutch; yet I find everything he does suspicious.

"Interesting. I didn't know Marcus had a house out here." There's so much about him I don't know, and I haven't even asked him anything personal. We have kept it pretty professional, minus talking about my dad and such.

Kai has some information to share. "The story goes that Marcus was once married with children. His wife was human, and his kids were born without powers because of his crossbreeding with her. The Grimmers were disgusted with him for this, so they killed his family. See, there has always been a war between the Grimmers and us, just because we don't care about crossbreeding or living among humans and hiding our secrets. But they do, and they want total domination. Yet, the Militia want all of us gone. So, this house we will go to is, in fact, the house his wife grew up in. He bought it in cash a few years back under a fake a name and now uses it to safely transport us. It's off the grid in a small town, so no one questions it; they think it's abandoned."

Kai and I, both stirred by the truth, wrap one arm around each other and keep walking.

"Poor Marcus. How long ago did that happen? My heart goes out to him." I sigh. There is so much cruelty in this world, more in this world than the one I was blissfully ignorant in.

We've finally caught up to Kieran and Efron, but Marcus was waiting at the door for them, or really me and Kai. Kieran and Efron open big, heavy, black metal doors with ancient door handles. They are large, about a quarter the size of the door and are gold, a harsh contrast against the black matte doors, with amazing detail that wrap from the handle into the door. The curves of the handles look like it would make the door harder to open, but Kieran does so with ease. Efron struggles but manages to get it open with a little help from Marcus.

They all walk into the room, and Kai and I run in after them, not wanting to have to open the doors all over again. The room is pitch-black, and we are at a standstill. I can't see anything around me, even my hand that I've lifted in front of my face. Laila remains still, her weight pushed against my leg, not barking, just leaning. The second the door shuts and makes a loud banging, the lights come on all at once, and the room transforms from a black wasteland to a multicolored, shiny, reflective palace.

My eyes can't focus to even see any walls, just different colors floating around us, like we're in 4D, and I could touch them if I reached my hand out. It looks like natural waves are floating around, and there are bursts of twirling colors for as far as the eye can see. This is deceiving. At some point, the room has to come to an end. With my hands out, I twirl around and try to catch some of the colorful specks, but nothing will land in my hands. I glide forward past Kieran and Efron, leaving Kai what seems like miles behind me. There is a spell on this captivating area. The further forward I move, the closer I get to Kai from the back. I can reach my hand out forward and seem to touch him but look over my shoulder and see him in my rearview.

How are we supposed to get out now that we have gotten in?

Next, we are overcome with darkness once again, which means someone is in the room who wasn't before. The lights turn back on, and Kai and I are face-to-face, so close to one another I can feel his breath against my cheek. Shocked by our proximity when the light of beautiful colors comes on, we jump back.

Marcus walks right past us and turns, standing and gazing out at everyone. My mouth nearly falls to the floor when Cornelia, the Ice Queen, walks to the front to get a good view of him. At this point, nothing is out of the question. Maybe her bitchiness was caused by someone putting a spell on her. What do I know?

I look around the room, and Efron and I lock eyes. Poor guy, he tenses up just at her presence.

Hopefully, I can bring some peace. I walk up to her and blatantly ask, "What are you doing here?" My tone isn't coming off the way I want it to, so I correct. "I don't mean to be rude, just a question." Maybe she will be more likely to enlighten me.

Marcus flashes me a look that tells me to play nice. She has tried to harm almost every single person in this room. So, at this point I am showing her a kindness by asking, instead of jumping to conclusions.

"Look … I am sorry about before." Her voice is meek and monotone; she is embarrassed of herself.

"Sure you are." Efron's voice travels to where we stand. "I literally had to thaw out." He is putting it on thick. And by the look on her face, she gets it.

"Give me your hand." It is a demand, not a question, and even Efron is sighing in disbelief. Unlike them, I have new eyes on this world; I've seen people do things for all the wrong reasons and resent themselves later, like David with Sofia I'm sure. Plus, if she tries to ice me, she will be in for a real shock.

She reluctantly gives me her hand in trust that I won't cause her harm. My eyes close to search her soul. She is vulnerable but puts up no resistance and lets me in. It's clear where she is and who else is with her. The vision focuses, and she's talking with Higgins. He's standing behind her with both hands on her shoulder. He's whispering into her ear—his voice grueling, evil, and callous voice. "Do as I say, or your family will be the cost of your inconsideration." She was told to come after me and anyone who stood in her way. He needs me alive but harmed, so he can take me with him. He's such scum. That's why she's here. The vision shows she testified against him this morning in private before anyone else got there, for her own safety. It's not my place to pry any further into her memories or feelings on this. So I drop her hand and give her a look that says I'm sorry and shrug.

On my way back to my spot, I purposefully walk past Kieran. "She's fine. Higgins."

My short words mean a lot to Kieran and he leans over to give an explanation to Efron. It would be unjust to expect Efron to forgive her. But as my father so clearly wrote to me, nothing is the way it seems.

Cornelia follows me. "How did you know?" She grabs my hand and looks flabbergasted.

"I could see him talking to you. That's all you need to know.

Don't worry, I didn't invade your privacy any more than I needed to in order to make sure everyone here would be safe."

Marcus is clearing his throat to get everyone's attention, so we turn to face him. "OK, is everyone ready? Ava—"

Before he can finish his thought, Laila jumps into my arms.

He nods. This is what he was going to bring up. For a medium-sized dog, Laila sure is dense and awfully heavy. Kieran was feeding her like a queen when I was gone. My grip is barely able to sustain as she moves around trying to get comfortable. Sure, girl, this is your world, and everyone is just living in it. She appears scared, and I snuggle her in close. I'm noticing this isn't like any portal I've taken; normally it is in individual units.

Marcus raises his arms in the air, like this is how the portal opens, and a whistle comes from the other side of the room. Laila jumps out of my arms, and I rush, following her. She must be thinking I'm no strong enough to hold her—how comforting. She jumps into Kieran's arms. He turns over his shoulder to shoot me a smile while petting my dog, so my run stops as the ground drops unexpectedly.

My stomach is in my throat, and the swirls of specks of color start moving faster and faster as my body becomes weightless. There is no gravity, and we are all floating in the air until the speed hits me, and it feels as though I'm flying through a wind tunnel. The force brings my hair in front of my face and runs through my hair, but almost instantly stops. My stomach falls back down as gravity abruptly comes back into play.

Somehow, my feet are firmly placed on the ground and my hands reach for my hair, and it's a bird's nest all over the place. Kai and Efron are completely toppled over, trying to pick themselves up quickly before anyone notices, playing it cool. Kieran is standing tall with Lala in his arms. Only he and Marcus are calm and collected. Even the Ice Queen is flat on her ass. Even though no one is saying it, Efron is smiling on the inside. Karma will always come around in some little way or another.

Kieran and I find each other through the small crowd, and I shoot him a smile "You must have done that before, not a hair out of place."

"You can't say the same," he jokes.

Laila jumps out of his arms, and he tucks my hair behind my ear, and I frantically try to tame my mess.

"My mother has taken me in portals like that since I was young. I had to try not to laugh when I saw everyone on the ground. This is an old way of transportation, so it's rarely used anymore, but still funny." He has a side smirk that's trying to hold back his laughter but makes me smile even bigger in return. And my eyelashes do the girly bat about fifteen times too many. He ignores my nonsense, thankfully and shoots me a wink. "Good to see you kept your balance."

Why can I not stop smiling? "Thanks to you for holding my baby. I wouldn't have been standing upright if I had her." She is by my leg, leaning in, almost like she is giving me a sarcastic thank you.

Everyone has already left where we landed, and I didn't even notice. We are in an empty brick garage, and he gets out one more quip. "I will hold your baby anytime." He was trying to be smooth, but it didn't quite work out, and he knows it and shrugs it off.

I laugh at him, and he follows me out of the garage. He clearly was talking about Laila, but my mind quickly runs to babies. Are they not in my future anymore?

There is no time to think about that right now, and I'm thankful. The garage is tiny, maybe the size for one car from the outside but so much larger inside. It's in the backyard of a small, quaint yellow house with black shutters. The colors remind me of a bumblebee. This yard is unkept, with weeds growing up to my knees; it's very apparent no one ever visits here. Marcus must not come here often because of the memories. There are other houses around this one on either side, but they're boarded up and look to have been vacant for years, with graffiti on the walls. I can't imagine how sad Marcus must be to see something that was once so precious to him run down.

Laila runs up the back porch steps and into the open door. Walking up the creaky old steps, I notice nails puncturing through and see the boards are protruding out; it's very unsafe, and there are a lot of them. My feet are lifted off the old stairs and floating in the air before I even have a chance to stop him from carrying me. Honestly, is he trying to get us both in trouble. I chuckle at him. And he knows exactly what is running through my mind, but I can't resist but to put my arms around his neck.

"I like anything that gives me an excuse to have you in my arms."

So cheesy, and it makes my eyes light up. "You know, you are hitting this friendship mark right on the head." My smirk is somewhat evil as I quickly place a kiss on his lips so chaste and tender and then just as quickly hop out of his arms. My face is going beet red. I can feel it from the inside out, and I cover my face with my hands. Marcus's disapproving eyes land on me and Kieran. Meanwhile Kai is shooting us an expression that say, *Oh, shit, you got caught*. Kieran was right. It's like I'm a child who needs babysitting all the time. But it isn't for my protection; it's for the protection of Aidan's heart.

Marcus throws a coat on me and tells me to put it on, so I'll blend in. Not like this was my choice of outfit in the first place. I did it to go along to get along. In these moments, there is nothing more that I want than to flee—to find my own way, my own answers, and Victor and to do what I can without risking anyone's heart or lives. It is so abundantly clear to everyone around us that Marcus is mad that Kieran has found moments with me. My eyes roll at the judgment he exudes to me right now. There must be a way to make everyone happy.

He changes his tone and finds his excuse to move Kieran. "Kieran, you walk up here with me, in case anything unexpected happens. The house is well covered in a trace so it shouldn't, but just in case." That's his way of saying nothing will happen here, but you cannot be near her.

We are walking around the outside of the deck to the front porch behind Marcus. I peer into the windows to look inside the house, and the shelves are visibly dusty through the dirty window. I'm barely able to see faces in the pictures on the wall. He hasn't touched anything inside the house.

"He wants us to look normal, but what adults walk single file down a porch and continue that way on the street?" I'm mostly talking to myself, but Kai catches wind of my sarcasm and shakes his head and laughs to himself.

He bends down. Since we are last in formation, it doesn't hold up the line, and he places a leash on Laila, while I ride the struggle bus to get this stupid coat on. We look like the only two normal disheveled people in the group, and I am in a Halloween costume to boot. Laila definitely isn't a fan of being on the leash, considering this is her first time ever wearing one.

After my workout putting on the coat, we don't worry about playing catch-up to everyone else and just move at our own pace, a breath of fresh air but a little tense.

"What is it? What aren't you saying?" I pry.

"As a friend, I told Kieran I wouldn't say anything, because I know he wants you to make up your own mind, and you deserve that. Also, he is my best friend, so I just have to say it. You know Kieran is in love with you, right? You guys have been through more together, and he is the only one who cared for Laila when you were gone. Today, he pretty much begged me to switch places so he could see you. That is unlike him in every way. He's always kept to himself and never been excited to see someone again." He stretched out his words to make them extra dramatic and added crazy hand gestures. I definitely got the picture.

"I wish it were that simple—to do what my heart wants. But it's not." I sigh. I know he doesn't know the whole story.

The people walking in front of us are so serious even in their movements. They are the ones who stick out like a sore thumb; they don't even look like they're friends. The closer to town we get, the nicer the area gets. There are no more run-down houses but, rather, a lively living area and kids playing in the front yards and on the sidewalks.

He is looking out for his best friend and just can't resist. "He mumbled some mumbo jumbo about how there are many average things in life, but love should not be one of them. If you tell him I told you this, I will deny it." He shoots me a playful smile but returns to serious. "Many things are run-of-the-mill, but you defy anything he has ever known. You are it for him, Ava. I can tell. He won't admit it to himself fully or say it outright to me. I have seen him with other women."

Why did that sentence leave a bad taste in my mouth in a way Isabel didn't?

"But he would never walk away from you or turn back. He would go Tom Cruise crazy for you and jump on Oprah's couch if you gave him a real chance—I mean a real chance to have an actual relationship. Right now, you are in a limbo in your life. Imagine what a real relationship would be like. Actually having one person giving you their all. That's just my two cents, for what it's worth."

"You're speaking with good intentions for your friend, and I admire that. I would have done the same thing for my friends. There's no question I feel something for him too. But this position I'm in isn't easy. I don't know what to do. Things aren't simple or black and white anymore; it isn't just about listening to my heart or gut. And my mind is overworked. There is more to it than Kieran even realizes."

Well, this was an unexpected conversation with Kai—no blame though, just unexpected.

"Ava, just talk to Kieran. Really talk. Tell him what you know. You would be surprised to see how much he understands. And he wouldn't jump to conclusions with you. The key word there is *you*."

The fact is this is something I already know. "I will take your wonderful words of advice into consideration if I ever get more than two seconds alone with him again." My joking tone causes me to raise my eyebrows too high, and I wish it were just a joke, but it is very real.

That mysterious grin turns up. "That can be arranged."

"Please don't go all Asian assassin hit man on people," I joke, and he laughs

It's great he can take a joke and kids back. Essentially, he's up for a nonthreatening roasting session. Kieran looks back over his shoulder, but I catch his glance, and he quickly looks forward. The main strip here reminds me of the main strip in my hometown. Kerri said she would call Harrison, but the guilt is still eating me alive.

"This is the most I've ever not shown up for work in my entire life. Bad timing, but I need to call my boss and apologize personally. He's spoken to other people more than he's spoken to me. It's so rude." This isn't something I want people to remember me by—simple.

Kai shakes his head at me in disbelief. "You're in a different world now. There are things far more important in life than work."

As right as he may be, how do people with no income survive? Work is still an obligation I agreed to, and Harrison needs to hear it from my mouth. Aidan has a bunch of money, so he has a steady inflow of cash. But others? How? How will I survive with no money.

"Do you have a cell phone?" I plead with him, not even realizing where we are walking to at this point.

He scoffs. "I wish. Many are afraid of being tracked, and I am one of them. My family and I haven't had the best of luck." He leaves it at that, not opening it up for discussion.

There's a diner on the corner of the street, with a flickering neon sign in the window. The diner is clean and small; if you can fit six cars in the parking lot, I'd be surprised. Across from the diner is a small Verizon store. Kai looks at me reluctantly as I convey to him to go on without me and that I will be fine. He knows I will be making this phone call no matter what. And at this point he doesn't need to get into any sort of kerfuffle with anyone. Me, on the other hand, it doesn't matter. He needs to know that he's appreciated. But at the same time, why would I risk him getting in trouble? After little debate, he leaves and follows the crowd into the diner, and I run across the main street to beg someone to use their cell phone.

There's a young African American woman in the store who looks to be about my age, and she's definitely eyeing me up. My frantic look isn't all that comforting to people. She hands her cell over to me without question to let me make my phone call. After a few moments, she realizes I'm of no harm to her, and her face turns to concern for me. She's probably running through scenarios in her head as to what's going on and why I'm in such a hurry.

"Greene House Contracting, this is Harrison speaking." His laid-back voice causes me to instinctively relax a bit.

The woman is not letting me out of her eyesight—and rightfully so.

"Harrison!" There is no reason for me to be this loud, but there is an excitement to hearing his voice. And the fact that he is actually in the office and not on the job is amazing.

"Ava, where have you been? Are you OK? The police here have been looking for you since your house burned down. Then a woman named Kerri called and said you were in the hospital ..." His voice trails off waiting for my response. The silence is deafening. I didn't think this phone call through.

"I'm OK, kind of. I'm so sorry I didn't show up for work. Or call—"

He cuts me off midsentence. "Ava don't worry about it. How are you? How is your mother? Where are you staying?" The list of questions is endless.

A loud bang comes from the back room, and the butcher from my hometown and his son appear through a misty fog. Vernon. Evil eyes, butcher smock with a cleaver in hand. They are running toward me. And before I even get the chance to react or speak to them, Kieran has appeared out of nowhere and taken the cleaver from him in one swift motion and has slit Vernon's throat. His son runs in the opposite direction but doesn't even make the door before the same weapon has lodged in his back.

"What the hell do you think you're doing? Get off the phone." Kieran appears by my side, trying to remain calm and quiet. But there is no hiding the worry and anger in his voice. His face is boiling.

"Ava, who is that? What is happening?" Now Harrison is overly concerned and worries even more.

"Harrison, I will call you—"

Before I can finish my sentence, Kieran has picked me up over his shoulder like I'm a toddler. He hands the phone back to the nice woman. She doesn't hide. She doesn't run. She just stands in shock the whole time. Clearly, she doesn't know Kieran and I are friends, and if she wasn't scared before, she is now.

We are in the middle of the street before he puts me down and grabs my face gently to look into my eyes. "What the hell were you doing back there?"

My eyes shift anywhere but to his face, even though his voice is tender.

"Ava, look at me!" He is firm but still doesn't raise his voice like Aidan does.

"Calling my boss was the right thing to do." I speak with conviction.

"Oh, Ava, please. You cannot believe that. Why do you think those people showed up here? The Militia knows you would make phone calls. You don't think they have someone waiting around outside his building or someone who's infiltrated his work to monitor his calls?" Now, he is pacing back and forth—thinking, pacing, thinking, pacing. He runs his hands through his hair. "Don't you realize what lengths they will go to get to you? The Grimmers and the Militia? The best way to protect people is to disappear."

Laila finally decides to step in front of him and growl at him to snap him out of his insane pacing.

"Let's go and we can talk about this later. Everyone went through the portal. Thankfully, Marcus had already gone through before we realized you were here." Kieran grabs my hand, but even with his voice so tender toward me and trying to make me realize, he grabs it in fury and haste.

We run into the diner and into the back room so quickly I cannot even get my bearings straight or pay attention to a single thing. We walk farther back into the room until there is no more space, and we are face-to-face with a brick wall. He draws the same symbol on the wall with his finger that was outside of the portal. The symbol becomes bright light, and he leans down to pick up Laila. The muscles on his arm are pulsing from anger, and he looks down at me and smiles. This is so different than arguing with Aidan. There is definite tension between us but not hatred behind our words. It's like when I argue with Aidan, he is disgusted with me. This feels different, like a normal argument with someone who still respects you even though they don't agree with you. For the moment, he has forgiven me.

"On the count of three ... jump." He looks at me with those green eyes filled with hope, and his words are eaten up in a smitten kitten kind of way.

"Jump where?" This is some platform nine and three-quarters shit from Harry Potter, and I get now why Harry and Ron wanted to shit their pants.

"Into the light." He grabs my hand and holds Laila with his other and lifts out joint hands and points to the symbol on the wall.

He counts us down. And with complete trust in him, we jump hand in hand.

Chapter 16

Kieran and I once again find we are overlooking everything from an aerial view but on a moving cloud this time. Thankfully, my face has some elasticity to it because that portal will do nothing but create wrinkles. My face still feels like it's being pulled back, and my eyes reluctantly keep opening until the picture becomes even clearer. This is absolutely magnificent and something that I only thought existed in books or mythology. My imagination couldn't even drum this up. The sun is shining brightly into the sky and lighting everything in this eutopia. We're underneath a physical rainbow, almost close enough for me to run my hands through the colored rays.

"Welcome to our very own fantasy land. Everyone had a say in what they wanted it to be like, and, well ..." He lets go of my hand to gesture to everything in sight.

"Where are we?" My eyes grow wide with wonder.

"We have walked into our own plane. Nowhere on any map. The sun is illuminated by magic. Wait until you see the stars when it goes dark." He looks reminiscent.

"If this exists, something so wonderful, why fight?" I didn't mean to ask; it just slipped out. Kieran and I have talked about this before. Why hide in fear? Yes, this is beautiful, but so is the world.

And imagine being locked up, behind a cage, even a beautiful one, and not being able to experience life and the different people along the way. "I just mean this is so beautiful."

He stops and smiles at me. "Sure is. Imagine your children one day not being able to do anything but live here in fear. Some might choose that path, but we won't. We do it not just for ourselves but for the future generations." In such dark times, he is still thinking of the future.

Tall trees form a circle around a large conglomerate of houses. The trees form a barrier between the houses and the rain forest, with clouds pouring over the one area, leaving the rest sunny. On another side, there is bright green hilly land that reminds me of scenes from *The Sound of Music*, with a spot filled with flowers. Separating the rain forest and the hilly area is a giant mountainous area—similar to the one we saw in the battlefield. All elements of life are living in harmony. The cloud we linger on hovers over the rain forest, producing rain; the cloud releases its tension and becomes even softer. Laila is clearly not fond of the height, as she digs her claws deeper into Kieran, but he doesn't seem to mind at all. I'm so thankful he saved my baby.

As the cloud descends, it takes us to an area not seen before from up high. It's another separator between the hills, a small training ground. No surprise, there are at least fifty people, if not more, packed into this area, and I barely recognize anyone. The cloud brings us down to the action. As we jump off, the puff vanishes instantly. You don't realize the vastness of this area until you're on the even plane.

"We have trouble." Kieran nudges my side and points out a very angry Marcus running toward us. I have never seen him do anything but a fast walk, but the fumes are practically behind him kicking up dust. Behind him comes an all-black werewolf with piercing blue eyes. As if Kieran didn't have enough stress, just from the happenings in town, now this.

Marcus is abusing his power and using his force field to move people out of the way (or maybe he's preventing them from getting clawed in the face by an overprotective soul mate beast). My body is tensing with each leg closer they get. Aidan's reactions haven't been the calmest, and Kieran's face is calm and reserved. He is not starting something. Aidan takes one last jump in the air to reach us and transforms midjump. A shirtless Aidan lands before me, and I barely am able to keep my jaw from dropping to the ground at his very low-hanging shorts that are his only covering—the way they cling to his hips and show off his perfect V that leads up his hard stomach. My focus shifts to Kieran's face, so unbothered by Aidan's aggressive scare tactic.

"Before you guys get all crazy, know that, if it weren't for Kieran, I wouldn't be here right now." My foot taps on the ground, and my arms are crossed firmly across my chest.

Aidan is uncomfortable with his words. "Thank you, Kieran, for getting her here safely and in one piece." Anyone nearby could hear the distain and disgust in his words. Just because he said it doesn't mean he didn't mean it in a different way. Still, you had to give the man some credit, as it couldn't have been easy for him to say it. Genuinely, I'm shocked.

Aidan reaches out his hand to Kieran for a shake, but Kieran does not take it. He just turns and walks away with Laila following him. Kieran acknowledges me over his shoulder with a head tilt and then leans down while walking to give Laila a scratch behind the ear. She is in good hands but doesn't want to be near Aidan. After all, he did leave her behind. She must know that. She's a dog, but they have feelings too. It's odd behavior for her to leave my side though.

As much as I want to run after Kieran, he knows I can't, which is one of the reasons I think he left the conversation. I follow Marcus and Aidan around the training facility, and there are skilled people here, not to mention the mass of weapons held up by wooden shelving. Anything you want. you can find it here—all out in the open. There are werewolves in one corner, none of them the same dark black as Aidan's fur. When we walk past the wolves, they all tilt their head down in recognition of him.

Then everything changes. Marcus is slowly moving backward, and I am standing in place, as is one other woman to my right. She is dressed in the same uniform as me. She has studied the opponents' moves and used that to her advantage. She rewinds time in small increments. She sees what her opponents are going to do and then stops it. Then it stops, and time is moving forward again.

"Who is she?" My finger raises to the small, purple-haired, dark red lip-stained beauty, fighting some hopeless guy.

Marcus, Aidan, and I are back together, and they answer in unison, "Sarah."

Marcus adds, "She has the power of time manipulation, but only knows how to travel back in sixty second increments, the most she has pushed herself to is five minutes."

"That's why Marcus was back there, and we are here." Aidan tucks hair behind my ears.

"Huh, interesting. It doesn't affect you?" Aidan lets out a chuckle and a nod, no doubt furious with my lack of memory.

"Her time warping skills do not apply to you for obvious reasons, and I have grown immune to that power centuries ago. It was one of the most common for a long time. Since then, it has faded slightly. My mind stopped falling for those kind of tricks." Even more interesting that he too doesn't seem to fully understand why, when Marcus has been around longer and is still affected.

Clearly, in this environment, they are doing this to train everyone on a fair playing field. Marcus stated bluntly, "She has never been defeated—each person more surprised than the next."

"That's because she's cheating. She isn't Cher. She can't just turn back time here. I'm surprised you allow it. But also how can you control it? Some people get lost in the time loop without realizing it." I leave the two men behind and walk over to her. She knows how to fight, and, well, I need the practice.

Her opponent scurries off, leaving her in the dust after she releases the knife from the side of his neck. I am totally unprepared, no weapon or anything; but I didn't think that far ahead. It's a plus, plus for me. She turns to look at me with a grimace; her eyes match her hair.

"What do you want?" She is so snide as she twirls the knife around her fingers. She is cocky, overtly so.

"My turn." I tilt my head to the side to give the same energy back to her.

And she stretches out her hand, motioning me to come forward. Her mischievous grin splatters across her face.

Aidan, once again, looks worried. But honestly however am I supposed to learn and adapt without any practice?

Taking two steps forward and without skipping a beat, Sarah shoots her leg into the air and tries to kick me in the face, but I deflect it with my forearm easily. This is perfect. I can already see her wheels turning in her head trying to memorize my moves before she turns back time. With my aura following behind me, with speed, I run toward her and slide on the ground past her leg, gently grazing it with my fingers, giving her a little warning with a small shock. I went easy on her, playing it lightly. She concentrates, and everyone around us moves, but she and I remain still.

This is my chance to do a goofy break dance; it makes absolutely no sense but feels so right. I'm letting her know her charms don't work on me. The smile wipes off her face and is replaced with determination as she lunges toward me, but I step gracefully to the side. Sarah is grunting, and it has caught the attention of others around us. A circle is being formed to watch us fight. I feel like I'm in middle school on the playground.

Since her powers don't work on me, let's make it fair. Mine

won't be used either; it would be too easy for me to take form of a bull and just run her over. She kicks herself up from the ground and lands on her feet. She pulls the knife out of her side holster and begins twirling it around her fingers. She gets lower to the ground, assessing what to do next, like a fox. Without giving her time to think, I move quickly as she moves her hand forward with the knife. I grab her wrist and deliver a precise strike to her forearm, just enough to release the knife from her grip. As it falls to the ground, I kick the butt of the knife and release her arm and turn to grab the knife midair and throw it out of sight.

She pushes me back with two hands, shocked to have met a worthy adversary and shakes her head. She backflips away to give herself more fighting room to see me coming. Got to give the girl credit where it's due. I would land on my ass or my neck if I ever did that. She's scared of close hand-to-hand combat without being able to rely on her manipulation. We run toward each other and are locked in a fight, reading each other's moves perfectly, almost as though it's a synchronized dance, until she loses strength. I keep up the pace and kick her right leg out from underneath her and pin her to the ground with my arm against her throat. She taps out. The wind whispers behind me, and I turn quickly to hold her foot that was aiming for the back of my skull.

"Don't make cheap moves after you tap out!" I release her foot from my grasp, and she is absolutely fuming, angry that I dethroned her.

Aidan pushes through the crowd to whisper in my ear and silently congratulate me. He looks like he wants to pick me up, but I wave my hand down saying no. She probably already feels bad enough. I am not trying to be extra.

Her eyes immediately are taken off me and put onto shirtless Aidan, looking over every inch. I don't blame her because he is quite the fine specimen. "Mr. Cross, it is a pleasure to meet you." She puts her tongue back in her mouth to get the words out. "I'm

Sarah." She is blabbering on to him about where she's from, what an honor it is to meet him, and how she's a huge fan of his. How the tables have turned when she was just death glaring me not that long ago. She goes in to give him a hug, and he awkwardly hugs back.

"Please, call me Aidan. You have good fighting tactic, Sarah. Just be mindful here we like to play fair without cheap shots, because we want to teach. Sure, in the real life there will be cheap shots, but this is for training with friends." Aidan gently scolds her, and her face turns bright red. Good to know he has that effect on someone other than me. He pulls me in by the waist, tightening his grip, and her eyes flash to his hands on me.

"Next time I will be more prepared." It's an open promise she left to me, but she gives Aidan a cheesy grin.

She turns on her heel and walks away to meet up with a man with light brown hair and olive skin, like he spends his time being kissed by the sun. He is just as tall as Aidan but is definitely walking his dad bod in confidence, as he should. They aren't too far from us, and I can hear him talking to her in an Australian accent. He calls her babe, and they share a quick kiss and walk off.

"Aidan, why did her hair just change color as she was walking away?" Seriously, always something new.

"She's part nymph. That's why her hair and ears appear purple. But then when she relaxes, they change color. She must be at ease with him."

I suppose so. Her hair went from long and purple to a light blue bob the second they walked off hand in hand. She has vitiligo; white patches cover her eyebrows and around her lips on her otherwise perfectly complexed, dark caramel skin. Looking at her walk away hand in hand, I see it also spread down part of her arms onto her fingers. They're a pair that some would never assume would be together just by their looks, but man do they rock it together well, like a yin and yang.

She would actually be a great person for me to befriend at this point—someone I could train with who won't go easy on me. Aidan continues to walk me around the training grounds, pointing out into the distance where things are. Apparently, there are thousands of people here. He advises me that he and I are to stay together, in the equivalent of a royal palace, but modernized. Was this my taste in the past life? Because it sure isn't now. I'd like a far house with some property and animals, not something fit for royalty. He looks so excited to show me around. Everyone lives comfortably here, in houses that accommodate the size of their families, but the larger homes, like the one he has are for the heads of the table, whatever that means. Amazing to think Rome wasn't built in a day, but this was built in little over a week.

He pulls a stick out of his pocket and throws it violently on the ground. It expands into a large circle. "This will take us into town center. It works anywhere within this safe zone, so we don't have to walk."

Kind of a shame actually, as I'd love to walk and see everything I possibly can. He goes to hold onto my waist, but I want to do this myself—to get a feel for how it works if I fly solo. We walk into the wormhole, and immediately, we pop out on the other end. No fuss, no muss, easy-peasy for once. It's like you close your eyes to nod off, and you're there; you don't feel anything, so different from everything else.

In the middle of town center, Aidan bends down to pick up his stick and place it back into the pocket of those shorts. How in the world did I survive humanity without these cool gadgets? How can he go on living a moderately normal life? That's what I strive to do.

It slips. "You know you should wear those shorts every single day."

All the ladies are gawking at him, and he chuckles and gives me a light hip bump that sends me flying across the sidewalk.

There are no cars but, rather, streets for people who wish to bike. It looks exactly like a miniature Washington, DC, and it's booming, with people walking to all sorts of shops. The air is clean and crisp, so refreshing for a city. It looks like something out of a magazine, with beautiful fountains and seating locations around a huge, white clock tower. I wonder where Kieran and Laila are. Probably meeting up with everyone else.

He points out into the distance. "Right on the outskirts of the main strip is the entrance to the living facilities for everyone else. There are houses for families and nice luxury condos for singles." I am in awe of him and that he helped arrange this and helped put it all together. It makes sense why he left Mexico now, since he was working on plans to start the build here.

"Here we are." He grabs me by the hand and stops me as I continue walking. We are standing in front of a massive building that looks exactly like a palace, with elegant spiral pillars and silver accent pieces and a fountain with a dolphin in the front. While this isn't my taste, I can surely appreciate it. The rest of the house is modern and perfectly sleek. With squared edges and a wraparound balcony with symmetrical lines, it looks like a house that would be oceanfront in California with all the rich Hollywood stars. There are six houses like this along the strip, this one more modern than others, which look Roman, and this one is Aidan's.

Aidan walks to the gate blocking the front of the house and stands near a panel. A scanner comes out that runs over his whole body, and the metal gate swings open. Honestly, it seems a bit unnecessary, given this is a safe zone, and there are no cars. But I guess he has things that need to be protected inside. Where is the rest of his pack? I pass by the fountain and run my hand in the water and watch as it doesn't make one ripple and the fish come up to nibble on my fingers, thinking I am food.

He calls my name, and I rush to join him at the front door, mostly because he is so excited to show me around. He has this boyish gleam to him. He pushes open the two large white doors, and we enter into the mansion. An elegant staircase, all black and very modern, is the centerpiece of the entrance room, and the sky-high ceilings lead to a circular skylight. It's not every day someone gets to see this kind of wealth dripping off the walls.

Based off of Aidan's room taste from New York City, this fits right in. The inside gives off a completely different vibe than the outside of the house, which has to look somewhat uniform on the main street. The wood floors are dark with different tones of gray. As modern as the house is, with huge windows, there is a hint of the antique style he likes. The art hanging on the wall gives a nice contrast to the room. He grabs my hand and leads me up the black stairwell to the second floor.

"Come with me. I'll show you our room." My walk is barely able to keep up with his long stride on these slippery stairs.

"Our room?" I really think I should be staying in the singles condo. Or do they have condo space for the anxiety-riddled, confused, new-to-this-world girl in her twenties? That's where I need to be.

"Yes." His answer is simple. We stand in front of another set of double doors with silver handles, "Our room—unless you get mad and kick me out." He raises a brow to me, and I giggle as he pushes open the doors pridefully.

I know girls date around and date multiple people at once, but that has never been my vibe. I can barely manage myself let alone multiple other people. And playing with people's hearts feels so wrong. It makes my decision easier and easier by the day.

The dark word floor is a nice furnishing against the otherwise minimalistic room. The rest of the house is over the top, but not this room—just a bed, no television. The room's main accent piece is a black and gray stone fireplace, and the large bed is covered with neutral down comforter blankets, so there is no sight of the bedframe. Laila's fur would show on every inch of the almost white comforter.

Without giving him notice, I run and jump on the bed and get swallowed into the comforter and feel the soft feathers against my skin. There is a skylight above the bed. I imagine it would be beautiful to see the stars I've heard about.

"Well, do you like it?" He is standing by the door with his arms crossed. He seems nervous and anxious, not like the confident man he is 24-7. I give him an aggressive nod, and he relaxes and lets his arms down before he jumps into bed. No need for a run—he can just jump from the door to the bed with ease.

"I love it all, but that ... There is no use for it." On the opposite side of the room there is a very large dog bed that made me laugh, like Laila would ever sleep in one of those. She always sleeps on the end of the bed facing away from me, her eyes glued to the door or window. She will get off the bed in the middle of the night and make her rounds and check the house before returning to the same position on my bed.

"We should really have the bed to ourselves." By the tone in his voice, I know he's going to stand firm on that point. "Let's have a nap and then get ready for the meeting."

Honestly, I need to find Laila, but I know she is safe. I've never been to more meetings in my life. At this point, I am pretending to sleep as he whispers, asking me about the ring. I know that tonight is the night I make a decision he will not approve of, one that will surely land me in his terrible graces. So for now, I will cuddle into him and enjoy the moment and ignore his inquiries.

Chapter 17

I'm dressed and ready to go to another meeting, but I cannot tear myself away from this bathroom mirror. Maybe my voice will be heard at this one. Finally, my body feels somewhat back to normal, dressed for comfort in bootcut jeans; a loose-fitting, white T-shirt; and, of course, my new military-style black boots with my ankle bracelet tucked away safe under comfortable tall white socks; and a black leather jacket. My hair is in its natural waves, and my face is without makeup. Part of me is also avoiding Aidan and his pestering questions about the ring. Maybe I should bring my uniform in a backpack just in case. Yeah, that sounds like a good idea—done and done. I'll throw something extra in there too, just in case it's needed, Aidan's portal stick.

Twirling the key my father gave me around my fingers relaxes me. It's almost like my mantra at this point to calm myself down and keep from overthinking. Boy, my counselor would have a field day with me if she talked to me now. Without closing my eyes, my thoughts drift to him and transform me into what he looks like. Although he looks funny dressed in my clothes, his face is a perfect picture, and there is a strong resemblance of him in me, especially in the shape of his eyes and his nose. He is rocking a scruff, and his hair is more salt and pepper, and his bright blue eyes pierce back at me. Then everything starts changing around me, and I am brought back to a memory. I'm on a playground, watching a father and daughter play. She is giggling and running around like a crazy drunk person, and he seems just happy to chase after her. He lets her think she has won the race until he picks her up and throws her into the air. She lets out a huge belly laugh when he catches her. I remember that pink dress now; it was my dress, and this is my sweet memory. The dress is an older frock, and the way he's dressed looks like he is from a different time, so this must be from my past life.

And just with a blink of an eye, the memory is gone, and I'm once more staring at my own reflection. I drop the key my father gave me and pick up the locket Aidan gifted me to look at the photograph of my mother. I have her smile. This is the only real thing I have of my mother's, and it's not the original, but I am grateful for it. All Aidan wants is for me to remember him and my family.

The same playground appears in the bathroom but in a cloud floating in the air. There's a beautiful woman walking toward my father and me. This must have been my first life in the 1800s. My mother is carrying a sun umbrella, and her peach dress has a bustle in the back. My father carries me over to her as I play with his pocket watch and notice a tree engraving on the back.

That's the first real memory of my mother I have ever had—not some false truth. Fact is, until this relic on my ankle is destroyed, my memory will not be fully back; my guess is it's the most important parts. She's here with me, my mother; I can feel her. She's alive; I can sense it in my bones. I see Aidan out of a corner in the reflection from the mirror. He's just leaning against the bathroom door watching me.

"I know it's hard." He speaks to my calmy.

But as I look back into the mirror, I see I look like her, my mother. I consciously change back to myself.

"You have lost so many people in your life and have been

through a whirlwind. I couldn't imagine having my mind tampered with. We can figure this out." He is sympathetic, instead of just telling me he wishes I could remember. Maybe he finally understands how real this is for me too.

"I know." My voice is meek.

I drop the locket from my hand, and he slowly walks over to me. He reaches for my face and holds me at arm's length, just taking it all in, looking deeply into my eyes; he is feeling what I feel. He lowers his hands to graze over my exposed arms since I have yet to put my jacket on and stops at the scar that is now permanently on my body from him. He hates the constant reminder, but I wonder why this scar won't fade but the others have.

"I hate myself for this." He can't stop running his fingers over the area on my arm and toward my back, looking at me with those sad eyes.

"Stop, please. It's OK. I'll just start wearing long sleeves." My attempt to help his cause doesn't seem to work. So, pressing up on my toes, I give him a kiss on the side of the mouth, knowing just by the look in his eye he will never think this is fine. Perhaps, when I get back to the real world, I can have scar removal? If it would work. Or maybe one of the witches in the infirmary can help me out? Add it to the list of things on the pile.

He doesn't say anything, so best I take it upon myself to lighten the current mood. "So, boss man, you ready to give your speech?"

He follows me out of the negative energy of the bathroom, through the vast closet, and into the bedroom. He throws me down on the bed and not in a graceful way; it's primal as he climbs on top of me. The blood is rushing through my body, and a different kind of electricity starts running through me. My hand grazes his, and his primal self wants me, right now. He wants to rip my clothing off and ravish every inch of my body, and I squirm happily under him at the thought. My breathing picks up as he places little kisses all along my neck and collarbone.

He knows what he is doing to me, and he's relishing every moment. My eyes close just enjoying this feeling. He plants a long, deep kiss on my lips, and they soak it up. He, much to my surprise, hops off of me and stands before me as I lean up on my elbows.

"We have much to talk about, like the whereabouts of that ring you seem to be avoiding for some reason. But for now, don't make a face; we can't be late." He raises a brow to me and makes me realize I was pouting. Just when it starts getting good, he gives me the female equivalent of male blue balls, and I am not happy about it.

"Fine, fine. Let's go." My words stretch out as long as possible for extra drama, and he laughs at me.

We walk out of the bedroom and down the hallway to the stairs. It's weird to not have to concentrate to walk down the stairs like I have been my whole life, but I am almost as graceful as a gazelle anymore. It's like he is withholding sex that I haven't had in ages, as a ploy or bargaining chip for information on this stupid ring. Son of a biscuit! He tells me how beautiful I look. But still, I can't help but think something is off and just not right. It feels off, and I can sense it.

I put that to the back of my mind but won't forget it; things need to be normal for now. So on our walk, I ask him if it's possible he might find the address of Louis, the man who helped me and Ray. His kindness deserves some form of acknowledgement beyond a mere thank you—even though he did it for nothing in return. Walking across the street makes me take in how beautiful this area really is—down to the streetlights that are silver and complete with elegant design and embellishment. If the world wasn't such a cluster, this would be such a happy space, a place for people to be of their own wishes and accord, not by force of hand. To the left, suburbia is lit up like a Christmas tree and streams of people are either walking or biking to the town center. Every soul here will be in attendance, minus the children, who will be in a daycare facility. Everyone will be watching either in person or on the holograms projected through town.

"Hey, babe. I'll meet you inside. I need to check on Laila. She shouldn't be left with Kieran for too long. Where can I meet you?" While I am completely fine with Kieran having Laila, I figured if it was phrased that way, Aidan would be more inclined to let me out of his sight, especially with the razzle-dazzle of the word *babe* added into the mix. Please eat up the lie; please eat up the lie.

And he does. "Marcus has Laila. He rang and said Kieran dropped her off to him because he didn't want to come to *our* house." There is no way Kieran said the part that he emphasized. Or maybe he did. Or maybe Aidan is ad-libbing that bit, but now I need to think on the fly.

"Did he say he was bringing her here? Or where can I get her?"

I am not much of an actress, but Aidan shrugs his shoulders.

"Look, she just helps me to feel more at home, and I can't wait to show her the new bed"—reluctantly the words come out—"the one on the floor." He looks pleased. This is good. Keep it going. "So, I'll just wait here for Marcus then. He'll either have her or tell me where to get her. And then I'll head in with Marcus. Sound good?" Normally, I wouldn't even ask, but Aidan likes that full control over my actions kind of thing.

"Sure. You can go with Marcus behind the curtain after I speak. Then we can sit together for the rest of the meeting."

"See you soon." I take a seat on the stairs as he walks off, and even the stairs have warmers in them, so my butt isn't frozen to the ground. Now I just have to wait.

People watching is a great way to pass the time; some look like humans and others do not. Cornelia walks past with the pale green ogre-like man from the battle and a few others follow who look like him with only slight differences. There are even a few Centaurs coming this direction from the woods. One woman shocks me the most. She has a snake full of hair like Medusa, but these could come off of her head and do her bidding. A year ago, if someone had told me all these things existed, I would have thought they need to be committed to a hospital. But now this is no big deal.

Marcus is one of the last to arrive. Thankfully, he doesn't spot me through the crowd of people. I have been sitting here for ages and didn't think of how to play this out in my mind. If I go up to him and talk, he won't let me away from his side. I don't see Laila with him, so she must be in his house safe and sound. Perfect, that's exactly what I need to know. Marcus was the last bit of the puzzle I am waiting for. Now he is here. When he goes inside, I can make my escape. I just needed to make sure Laila is safe. I hide behind the walls next to the stairs, and Marcus walks right up the stairs without noticing me. The other person who would rat me out is now inside the building and under the assumption I will be backstage with Aidan. So I bolt, bolt for the tree line nearest the battlefield, and with the wind pushing my aura forward, I will make it there in seconds before Aidan even takes the stage.

Insert Image 02.jpg

I look around the area for the first thing I need, weapons. The wooden shelves hold so many options. While I gaze at the tools in front of me, I start to take my clothes off. What I'm about to do actually calls for the uniform I resent so much, so I strip down to my bra and panties and begin to put my uniform on. This already feels better. My boots are back on, and I'm ready to go. My uniform is more of a deep blue than the black it was before; it must be adapting to something. There are small flakes on it. The sound of a twig crackling turns my attention around, but not in fear, rather, in curiosity.

"It's camouflaging with the night." Kieran's voice hits me in the heart, and my mouth drops at his appearance in from of me, in the same uniform from the training simulation, and his has changed color too.

"What are you doing? You are missing the meeting." My eyes bug out at him in surprise.

"So are you, sunshine." Oh, his sarcasm speaks right to my soul. Kindred spirits we are, "Don't be mad I caught you. Here, turn around, and I will zip you up."

There are no words that I can say right now. he totally called me out. His breathing gets heavier as he moves closer to me and his hand lingers on the zipper for a few seconds before he zips me up. At the top of my neck, he stops and runs his fingers along the back of my neck to push my hair to the side. I should have brought a ponytail. The touch of his hands against my skin has me taking deep breaths, releasing that pink aura from my mouth.

"How did you know I was going to be here?"

He is already smirking as I turn to him.

"I followed you." There is no shame in his game. He doesn't even sound reluctant to share that information with me. "You aren't as smooth and inconspicuous as you think; it's sad really. You were hiding from Marcus, and I was laughing my ass off." He lets out a chuckle, and I hit his arm playfully. "Honestly though, when that beast of a man attacked me and knocked you out, you kept mumbling about saving someone. So"—he moves his head in a weird, funny pattern—"I knew you were up to something. That's why I gave Laila to Marcus, or else I would have kept her. You know she loves me, right?" He shoots me a huge grin, and it makes me laugh.

I turn on my heel and head back to the weapons to pick up a few knives and place them into my leg holsters. "Well, thank you for that keen observation. You can go now." The wind flicks my hair over my shoulder, and I shoot him a get-out-of-here smile.

"You are insane if you think I'm letting you go alone. I know it has something to do with your brother." He is so nonchalant as he starts packing up weapons for himself.

"How do you …" Shaking my head in disbelief is an understatement; I'm almost giving myself whiplash.

"Ava, I just know. You don't have to explain anything to me. I can't tell you how I found out, or else I'd be breaking a confidence. You have to trust me."

A confidence with who? No one else knew besides me and he cannot read my mind. "One day you will tell me?" That's all I need from him because I do trust him.

"I promise one day I will tell you. It might come out sooner than that."

Now I am confused, but now isn't the time. Bottom line, I trust him; he wouldn't do anything to put me in peril.

We both reach for the same katana, but he pulls his hand back to give it to me. I take the sword and its crossover holster and place it around me. I'm ready to go. Kieran grabs a compound bow and the pack that goes with it to haul the bow and other critical gear. It's different than the traditional quiver; this gives an endless supply. Kieran looks like a badass. It reminds me of the first time I laid eyes on him. And as much as I hate to admit it to myself, he had me shaking in my boots.

"Come with me. We have about twenty minutes. I want to show you something." He grabs my hand without waiting for my answer and leads me to an edge between the battlefield and the rain forest.

"Twenty minutes until what?"

"Until they make their big announcement. Aidan is still speaking. My hologram will go off when the announcement happens—whatever it is." He is excited. "Ava, I see you in a house in the woods, surrounded by a lot of animals, taking in nature, not living on the main strip." Before I can even think of interjecting, his passion takes over, and he is speaking with understanding. "I understand now. I know. So, I just need to be here for you the best I can. I want you to remember this moment. Look down below you."

Without hesitation, I follow his lead like it's second nature and see people, walking below me, unaware we're above them. I look to Kieran's face for some explanation. "This place is the only spot where we can see down into the parallel human plane. They don't notice us here. If you look up, this is where the majority of constellations reside."

Boy is he right; there are more stars in this one area than above the whole safe zone. "It's beautiful, Kieran, the best of all worlds. And I get to experience everything at once; it's remarkable." The beauty of the night, the wind and mist coming from the rain forest, the people walking below us without a clue, and Kieran is just as amazed at it as I am.

"Dance with me."

It's another moment where he doesn't wait for my response. He places his hand on the small of my back and holds my right hand in position. I place my left hand on his shoulder and smile as he begins to lead me in a small circle around the miracle area.

"Someday, when I'm awfully low, when the world is cold, I will feel a glow just thinking of you and the way you look tonight." The tune of Frank Sinatra rings through my ears; only he is not the one singing it. Kieran is, and he's damn good at it too.

A strong blush comes across my face, and I can feel it take over my whole body.

He drops my hand and brings his hand to my face, and I lean into it. "You're so lovely with your smile so warm and your cheeks so soft. There is nothing for me but to love you and the way you look tonight."

"This is like something out of a dream." My head shakes, and my eyes widen as I focus on his smile. And in this moment, everything feels like it's supposed to.

"I want you to remember this moment—simple, perfect, and

easy, with just the two of us." In such dark times he makes moments lighthearted and good. He has a pleading sound in his voice, but I respect him for not pushing it more.

"I could never forget this."

He leans down to me like he is going to kiss me but stops unexpectedly. My eyes shoot to the left and then the right in confusion.

"Our time's up," he whispers in my ear and stands straight up.

Kieran walks fast toward the tree line surrounding the city, and I follow him. What the heck just happened? Why did he stop? It is good he stopped I guess because I am with Aidan? The fact that it's still a question in my mind shows my uncertainty.

I chase after him, but he stops abruptly right in front of the trees. I run into his back and bounce back as he says into the air, "Come on, guys! Let's go!"

Out pop Kai, Efron, Sarah, and her man friend from behind the trees. What the heck are all of them doing here? My look toward Kieran says it all—pissed, angry. How can all of these people agree to come for something they don't even know about? Not that I don't appreciate the thought, but who evens knows what I am getting into? And I don't want to lead everyone else into this—into what could be a huge disaster.

"Obviously, you know why Kai and Efron are here."

Both men nod heads in my direction.

"Sarah is Efron's half sister, and she wouldn't let him go without tagging along. Plus, she was impressed with you. Shamus wouldn't let Sarah go without him. So here we all are." It really is a domino effect. He widens his arms and shoots me a smile I cannot resist—like, This is us; the gang's all here. I respect Sarah more for this; I would do the same thing if I were in her shoes.

"Fine, but we need to work out some sort of plan. Thanks, everyone, in case I forget to say it along the way. I appreciate you all. I was going to run there. But, no offense, I doubt you guys could keep up. The location is near Massena, New York, close to the

Canadian border. Shamus, what do you bring to the table? Sorry. I don't mean to sound ignorant, but I want to make sure we're all prepared and on the same page."

"Come here, babe." He reaches his hand out to Sarah. With him, she's a giddy, upbeat schoolgirl, and she isn't that way with anyone else. He pulls her close and then vanishes and reappears behind Kieran and me.

"Obviously, I have the power of invisibility. What I can do that others can't is apply it to whatever or whoever I touch—like weapons or, in this case, my mighty fine girlfriend."

Sarah curtseys. And now it's official; she's a completely different person with him. Sarah chuckles as he holds her hand out and kisses it. I wish I had someone to show that much PDA with.

Kieran holds out his hand, and his little hologram device is beeping until a hologram of inside the meeting has appeared before us.

There is a stage with Aidan's speech coming to a close. He announces that, before they continue on and let the counsel speak and become open to questions, they have one more announcement to make, which is the reason children were not allowed to attend. It is the ruling in the Higgins trial. They have found him guilty on all charges and have extracted all the information they could from him. They bring Higgins out, and a few other coconspirators who I do not recognize. Aidan announces that, on this night before the meeting is continued, they will hold a public execution.

Kieran asks me if I knew this was happening, and I say no. Clearly, Aidan doesn't fill me in on anything. I am just as surprised to hear this as everyone else I'm with right now. We all thought the trial would be longer.

Kerri is at the side of the stage next to Judd and some woman holding a tonic. The woman is wearing robes that remind me of ancient Greece, with long brown hair. She walks elegantly and brings out the purple tonic to Aidan. He then throws the tonic on the ground in front of the guilty without giving them a chance for last words. But Higgins manages to open his mouth. Through the mist the tonic has created, Higgins's words are floating to the sideline, heading right for Kerri. Before she even notices, Judd steps in front of her and takes all the words in. The venom turns his face green, and he falls to his knees and cripples over. His fragile old body cannot handle the poison intended for Kerri, and he grabs his heart as it stops beating and lies lifeless on the ground. Kerri comes to his aid in distress, tears running down her face, but nothing will save Judd now.

Out of anger, someone from behind the curtain throws Aidan an axe. With one swift motion, he has beheaded all the guilty before the tonic can fully evaporate the air from their lungs. Higgins's head rolls on the stage floor, and the venom from his tongue and veins starts to disintegrate his head and his body.

"Guys, we have to leave, like now."

There's no time to process what is happening and feel badly for Kerri and grieve Judd. I know Aidan will be off stage soon. And even though the meeting isn't at a close, and he still has to speak, he will send his minions for me. Kieran telepathically sends his device far into town center; it cannot be tracked to us here.

"Here, Ava." Sarah hands me a little silver device. "Attach it to your uniform, on the wrist. I am wearing one too. If you need me to turn back time, click the button, and I will feel a vibration. You know I can only work in small time frames. But it will help. I can control up to a five-mile radius if I concentrate." She smiles and gives me a hug. Her smile reminds me of an American girl doll. She has a perfectly symmetrical face and white teeth.

I open my arms back to her for a quick embrace. "Wow, this is awesome. Great idea. When we get back, I can help you expand your gift maybe. It's something I've had to work on every day myself. I love your hair by the way. But right now we really have to go."

She whispers me a quick sorry about earlier, and we're off.

"Follow me. There's a secret portal to get us out of here. Don't ask me how I know. In my free time, I spy. Don't judge me." Shamus makes it sarcastic to lighten the mood as he takes the lead of the group temporarily. "There's a main entrance and exit portal, but the Elders and Manayunks always build in something extra for themselves in case shit hits the fan. Then they release its location in case of emergency. I heard about it, so Sarah and I scouted it for days, and no one ever used it or noticed it was there. We have to get to the mountainside." Shamus is leading the way, but just as it always has, a bright, shiny starlike lune directs me into the same path he is heading.

"I have something we can use." I pull out Aidan's portal stick from one of my many pockets. I'm assuming, since it's his, it can't be tracked. None of his stuff is ever able to be tracked or have a trace put on it.

I pull out the stick and gather everyone together.

Chapter 18

We reach the mountainside, and I had Kieran send Aidan's portal stick back to town center. Shamus says the portal is on the east side of the mountain, so we're walking there in a blizzard. Snow keeps hitting me in the face, but luckily is doesn't bother me. However, the rest of the group is shivering cold, and no doubt, the freezing cold brings back bad memories for Efron. So I run over to him and hug him first and watch him soak in my heat. Then I hit up Kai and Sarah. I give them just enough heat juice to get them through this blizzard. Both Kieran and Shamus are about two hundred yards in front of us looking down onto the ground. They must have found the portal.

The rest of us run over to then and stop behind both men, who are rubbing the ground in a circle, clearing off the snow—revealing, little by little, the see-through panel in the ground that appears to be leading to nowhere. Kieran whispers something to Shamus, and I don't have the chance to catch what he's just said.

"OK, so since none of us have used this portal before, it doesn't look like the one we're used to. This looks more like a transporter to me, which means we have to think of the location for it to take us there."

"Oh, yay." My sarcasm is showing.

Kai has a similar reaction. "This is the best time to try it out." Je shoots me a nervous chuckle.

"Sarah, I don't know if these will work through different planes. But how about I go first? If I land at the destination safely, I will click the button, so you'll know."

Sarah looks at my request skeptically.

So, Kieran steps up. "Give me the piece and I'll go first." He shoots me a look. "I don't need anything to happening to you in case I'm wrong." Oh, sweet, sentimental Kieran.

"Yeah, or Cross will have your head on a platter," Shamus interjects, not knowing the dynamic.

Kieran has an evil smile and rolls his eyes; he's up for the unspoken challenge.

We decide it's best to give up my clip, and he announces that he'll be landing ten degrees due west of Massena, and all of the faith I have in my body is energizing his way. He stands near the portal and, without hesitation, jumps into the air to land perfectly on the center and is gone. He wasn't sucked down; it was like he disappeared into thin air. A huge flash of light blinds us after he is gone, and I hope no one from town can see it. A force moves with the light, taking us all by surprise as we clench our faces to remain firm.

"It worked. He landed." Sarah holds up her wrist, showing the vibration coming from the device, "Who's next?" She jumps up and down, now excited for the adventure.

The order has been set—Efron, Kai, Shamus, Sarah, and then me. As all the men are getting pumped up and, not knowing what to expect, jumping in, Sarah approaches me with a side conversation. Another blast of light and pulse hit us, so Efron is gone.

"So, Aidan and Kieran, huh?" She shoots me a provocative wink.

"It's complicated." The line I previously dreaded hearing from anyone I was dating just came out of my mouth.

Another blast hits us, and Kai is gone.

"It's just us girls. You can tell me."

For whatever reason, I know I could tell her, and she wouldn't hold judgment against me.

"What was up with Shamus's remark?" Trying to change the subject but keeping it in the same ballpark normally works like a charm—something similar so I don't seem too overt.

"He and Aidan have been friends for a long time. You have actually met him before, I think? He's sensitive to the whole memory loss thing, so he didn't want to bring it up to you and make you feel like shit. Anyone can see how Kieran is protective over you but not in the dominating Aidan way, in a more natural, conscious-of-your-feelings way. That's quite the love triangle. I mean how romantic was that dance?" She has a lot of words, and she could talk forever. But my gaping is stopping her.

"You saw the dance? Ugh, now I'm embarrassed. When we get back from this, I will explain why it's so complicated, or at least try. Lord knows I need a girlfriend I can talk to." Especially since I no longer have Sofia, which is heartbreaking to even think about.

Sarah is thrilled by the idea, and honestly, her personality is infections—at least the personality she is starting to shine through with me but is full force with Shamus. "Perfect! When we return, we can have a girls' night, since Aidan will be mad at you anyway. We can be normal." She laughs, but it couldn't be truer. Not Kieran's head on a platter but mine, or maybe both of ours side by side.

"OK, you girls get ready," Shamus yells at us as he is midair doing a backflip onto the portal. And just like that, he disappears and another gust of light hits us in the face. But we're used to it now; we don't even bat an eyelash.

Like the lady she is when not on the battlefield, Sarah gently hops into the air. Her face becomes fierce in the sky, and her hair changes to that beautiful lavender. "Catch ya down there, A," she yells to me as she tosses me her end of her receiver. I grab it from the air and hook it onto my uniform.

A harsh wind is coming my direction and hits the burst of light; the wind is warning me. There is a man dressed in all black running toward me. My eyes squint in an attempt to see better, but my vision is impaired from all of the snow blowing around. His footsteps vibrate on the ground and up my spine. This is nature letting me know he is coming, getting closer and closer. He pulls something out from his side, and I am glued in position, ready for what is coming my way. The black figure tosses something at me, fast and hard, and it hits me right in the arm.

The wind angrily pushes me back, tossing my hair back and making me lose my footing. I stumble backward into the portal as the black shadowy figure approaches me. All I can see is the mask, the same mask I have seen before. Aidan caught on to me. He sent Ray Smith, his butt-kissing minion.

Soon, his face disappears, and the same burst of light that occurred when the others jumped onto the portal surrounds me, making it hard for me to see my direction. My eyes close, so I'm not blinded, and my back is consumed by what feels like pudding. I open my eyes and see my body caving into the ground and it bouncing back up, so I land softly. The earth is on my side. Everyone seems to be in shock from the ground acting like my personal trampoline. My closeness to nature is expanding. The more memories that come back, the more my connection is being restored.

Kieran is by my side and attending to my arm. "What the hell is this?"

I hadn't had the chance to take notice that, during the fall, a large throwing star was lodged into my arm. I sit up and bring my knees to my chest for support as I pull the star out of my arm before Kieran even has the chance to stop me to do it himself. It's in there deep, and pulling it out tears apart a piece of my suit.

The star has eight sides and a special black inscription all over the silver star. I toss it to the side, and Shamus picks it up and places it in his pack. Eyes linger on me and my exposed arm, showing the massive scar left behind from an unexpected attack. I close my eyes to cover my arm, and when they are back open, everyone has managed to tear their gaze away from me, all but Kieran.

He does me a kindness by not acknowledging my arm but still mildly scolds me out of love. "I cannot leave you alone for two seconds. What happened?"

There is dirt all over me, so I brush it off, and he gives me a not-needed helping hand to stand.

"It was Ray Smith." I shake my head just knowing he cannot be trusted. The fact Ray even created an opportunity to hurt me and no one questions him—maybe he is in love with Aidan and trying to delete his competition.

"He doesn't know where we are?" Kieran poses a good question.

"Unless he's a mind reader, like Efron here, I don't see how he could know where we're going? At this point I am thankful he is ordinary in comparison."

"Where are we going?" Kai asks me.

"Give me a minute." I search the surrounding are, and we're standing in the middle of a dirt patch in some field. This is great. That's about all I can see in the dark. We're about five miles out of the center of town, yet I don't see anything even close to me. There are snakes slithering through the tall grass, and the sound vultures make when they've found something to eat echoes. Taking deep breathes, centering my gravity, I breathe through and expand my whole stomach, down my feet to the ground to connect with nature. These snakes aren't supposed to be here.

My eyes open to the course we need to take; it's drawn out for me. Coordinates once again appear before me, and I am walking on a map, with a dot to the north that shows exactly where the

Militia is located. I don't want to disturb this moment. No words will come out of my mouth—not a word. I just begin the journey to the Militia base. I avoid all the roads through the main town, so we'll have minimal chance of being seen. The others know how to conduct themselves, so I know they're monitoring their surroundings and on guard. I'm trying to maintain a pace that everyone can match, so we can walk together and in formation, but it's hard when my legs want to run as fast as they can go to see Victor and see where he's being kept.

We are approaching the coordinates, and the line is starting to fade away. The sound of running water consumes the darkness that surrounds us, and I come to a stop in the middle of the woods.

"What is it?" Sarah is sure to ask quietly.

"We're close. Very close. Do you hear the water?"

"We're in upstate New York; it could also be a small dam," Shamus suggests and starts to lead the way.

He brings us to a stop at the edge of the woods. We hide behind the trees and peer out. He was right. There is a large dam to the right and a huge warehouse to sat at the back along the water, with many freight boats coming in to a dock next to the warehouse. Everyone is looking at things through their own tactic scopes.

We huddle in a circle to prepare a game plan, but I take the lead right off the bat. "I'll go in. Sarah, I'll beep if you need to rewind time. Kai, do you want to be my backup?"

"Definitely." He pulls his swords out in one swoosh. No offense to Kieran but Kai is a bit lighter on his feet. Plus, I would get too distracted with Kieran next to me. I'd be more worried about his safety than my own. With Kai, I know he has it covered—not that Kieran doesn't, but a girl has feelings involved.

"I'll stay behind here with Sarah, in case anything goes wrong or you need protection out here." Kieran surprises me, but that's for the best.

"I have experience in covert ops, so I am going in with you. Plus, Cross will go easier on you knowing I was in there."

I roll my eyes at him, but this is Shamus's area of expertise. It would be wrong if he didn't come in, just plain stupid actually. I don't want that comment floating out in the air and messing up my juju. "Good point, you have so much experience in tactical operations, so absolutely. As for the Aidan comment, he is going to hate me anyway, so let's ignore that." I try not to have an attitude, but the fact that the general population knows he will scold me like a child is very uncomfortable. At least Sarah thought it was funny, or she was trying to lighten the mood for Kieran's sake.

Kieran takes off his pack and kneels down. "Here, take these. We can use this to communicate." He hands us all earpieces; I'm not sure where he conjured these from. "Efron will stay back here with us and give you guys a heads-up if anyone is following you from here. Once you're inside, you've lost your eyes out here and maybe with each other." He tosses us the wireless ear communication devices.

We put them in our ears and turn them on. Kieran whispers from behind me, and we all nod in agreement that we can hear everything perfectly. There's no other way to do this but to just jump right in headfirst; it's not like we have blueprints of the building or any other information.

"You ready to rock and roll?" Shamus does a *Breakfast Club* fist into the air, and Sarah rolls her eyes.

"Really you find that attractive." A sarcastic nudge to her, and we both smile. It's nice being able to talk to someone in complete sarcasm. It's like its own language anymore; since people are easily offended, I don't get to do that often. I walk around in a customer service voice. So does Sarah.

Sarah waves me goodbye, as she is on the move.

Kieran, Sarah, and Efron look for a different vantage point closer to the dam, but still in the woods; they're off.

Kai, Shamus, and I stand covered in the same spot and scope out our entry points.

"Ava, the right side is less guarded. You enter through there."

I nod at Shamus and happily follow his lead.

"Remember, above all else, we are trying to gather information. So if we all can get inside to get information, that needs to be the main priority, not cause a scene. Ideally, we get in and out undetected. Kai, you can do a frontal assault once Ava gets inside if need be, if cover is already blown; it will buy her more time. If needed, use your skills, but keep them hidden unless in dire need."

Kai grins with his head moving up and down. He loves this. It is right up his alley and, oddly, probably the setting where he's most comfortable.

"I'm going to find a way in from the back and see what they have going on at the docks. If, for any reason, we need to get out, use the earpieces. If anyone needs help, just describe where you're located the best they can. Let's do this thang." He is a goof and can't hide it. He and Sarah are good for each other. "And find out what these bastards are hiding."

At this point, it's clear to me Shamus came to gather information and not just help me find my brother. He definitely is a two-birds, one-stone kind of guy, and it shows. Shamus is kind of growing on me. He is who he is and isn't afraid to be himself no matter the situation.

The electricity boils in my body intensely. As much as I wish I could shape-shift to a snake to get to the side door, I can't, or else I will lose all of my weapons. And there is no question I will need those, as much as I wish I didn't.

Chapter 19

It's difficult to ease the storm inside me. My heart is beating fast, as though it's likely to explode. It gets more difficult to blend in without changing form. At this level, crouching down is uncomfortable, as my head peaks through the tall grass, weeds stick to me, and I can barely make out the side entrance. The snakes' hissing gets closer and closer to me. A loud bang scares them off momentarily, and I drop completely flat to the ground. The sound came from the loading dock. Something slithering and slimy runs across my hand, and I keep still as to not startle the snakes into a frenzy. They were enchanted to project the woods. Their eyes are all glazed over, one red and one purple.

The marsh surrounding the warehouse is a snake pit, an intentional placement I am sure of it. As the snakes slither across my hands, my shoulders, and my back, the ground and I become one. I melt into it, giving them no sense of trespassing. My breathing slows down, and my heart mimics the vibrations of the ground, as I sink deeper and deeper, completely covering my face but not hindering my breathing. My lungs filter through the dirt and process the air. The snakes pass by, onto something more suspicious. So I rise, covered in dirt and soil, but come eye to eye with a timber rattlesnake. Thank you, high school, for teaching me this random shit. The snake pulls himself up and coils his bottom but doesn't strike as he looks down at me.

My body instinctively knows what to do; it's almost as though I'm talking to the snake but not saying a word. I hover my hand over the ground and move it all around him, enchanting him, almost hypnotizing him. The snake looks at my actions as the dirt slowly swivels between us, and with each movement, my hand makes the ground follows. The snake makes eye contact, telling me it's all right as he slithers under my hand. Like a dog, he runs his head under my hand, and I stoke him.

Hundreds of other venomous snakes come out as this one let his tongue out in a not harmful hiss. I can't count the number of snakes or breeds, but massasaugas, rattlers, copperheads, and timber rattlesnakes are some of the few I recognize in this marshy area. Oddly enough, there is no sense of danger; my heart is still. They come closer to circle me perfectly, standing up on end, giving me about a one-foot buffer zone from them to my body. Circling me, they hiss and fight with each other until they stop in unison and start creating a pathway for me to follow. They have pushed down a path through the thick marsh, around the back of the building, and about twenty feet away from the side door.

The warehouse looks old and as if it's withering away, but it's upgraded with all sorts of modern technology. From a distance, it would look like they barely keep this place up and running. There are rotating security cameras that match the gray exterior, and a high-voltage searchlight circles on the top of the building to help spot intruders. There are bound to be more tricks up the Militia's sleeves. The beam and the security camera rotate in opposite directions in a pattern that's harder to predict. Sometimes, it's fast, and other times, slow; there isn't any rhyme or rhythm to it.

Here we go—an open slot perfectly timed for me to run to the door. So I move my legs into position, but quickly duck behind a box that's conveniently located right next to where I'm standing.

Footsteps move closer and closer, getting louder and louder as the steps approach me. Part of a boot is edging over the box. Quickly, in one swift motion, I punch the end of the foot with all of my might, leaving a divot in the ground beneath the foot, and use my upper body strength to hold me as I lift my leg to kick him under the chin. And down, he goes. His eyes begin to close as he falls to the ground, releasing the gun he holds from his grasp. By the feet, I drag him behind the large cargo box with me to study his face and incapacitated body. He's out cold.

Small bubbles roll around inside every inch of my body, and the lumps move all over my frame. They are adjusting my body composition and color. I keep growing used to this feeling, but the sight will always be shocking. I am now dark olive and leave my neck exposed as my long hair disappears, transforming to short black hair. My physique grows larger to compensate for his masculine form. The change is complete and not painful at all for me now. The strap previously holding my sword has broken under the duress of the transformation. I stow the sword in the cargo box, along with his body after stripping him of his clothes and donning them myself. Thankfully, my uniform expands with the shapes I take—brilliant magic into these things. My knives remain, but in his cargo pockets, as they are less conspicuous, And I grab his gun and move.

The fact that I have never held a gun before seems a little ridiculous. You would think, with all the training, they would have taught us how to use guns. But now, I fumble around with it a bit before I drape the strap over my shoulder and leave it. My eye is read by a retinal scan on the side of the building, and the door clicks open. The halls are tall, wide, of neutral color, and very well lit, while the floors are black tile. There are boxes upon boxes against some walls, ceiling high. By all accounts, this does look like a warehouse on the inside, minus the tile flooring and LED lights. I speak into my earpiece, letting everyone know I'm in the building, keeping it short and sweet.

Walking around in a man's body feels weird. I exchange nods with other men and woman walking around the hallway in the same uniform I'm in—all red jumpsuits. It's honestly a little weird, but maybe because I'm so used to wearing black anymore. Seems anyone walking around with a gun is in a red jumpsuit; anyone without a gun is either in a lab coat or business attire. It's a very strange atmosphere. There is definitely more going on than a warehouse. There aren't even any regular workers here in proper safety warehouse gear.

There has to be something here, anything. But so far, I see nothing but people with poor judgment on their side, until I come across a narrow hallway. Honestly, I couldn't get back to this exact spot if I tried; it's like I've been looping around for ages. Someone has opened a large door, heavy by the looks of how hard it was for them to open—a real struggle. But it requires a fingerprint scan. Once the man who opened the door is safely in, I do a quick glance to check my surroundings. With only one camera in this hallway and the coast clear, now is my chance. I run as fast as I possibly can without letting my aura shine through and completely give me away. The camera has missed me, but the edge of the door knicks me and brings me back to normal speed as I squeeze through the open space between the heavy door and its industrial vault-like latching.

This side of the door is much different than the other. There are large dirty exposed wood beams and duct work, instead of a covered ceiling. The rafters stretch farther than I can see. I try to visually follow them, but there is a stop. The hallway splits at the end but not in a traditional squared off hallway. Rather, there are horizontal hallways that appear to get smaller and smaller, but it could just be an illusion. My blood starts boiling, and my head begins to ache; it's happening again. But at least this time, I'm stronger and can focus on multiple things. As I'm slowing walking down the dimly lit diagonal passage on the left, there is a sighting of Victor and me as children. I walk through the scene.

It's the day we were at a pool when we were young. He pushes me in, knowing full well I cannot swim. But part of my memory has come back, a new piece that must have been blocked. Victor's presence is growing stronger in side of me in this hallway, but the vision remains. He is standing by the side of the pool as I am begging him for help but with those dark eyes, the same that were in Mexico, stricken with hatred for me. He won't help. He just laughs. He smiles as I sink farther and farther under the water. He wanted me to die. He has been this way with me all along. The evil lurks in his soul year after year, life after life. Was there ever a time he cared for me? Why am I coming to help him now? This is a new revelation. At least I can gather information.

The profile of a face I know too well walks down the other hallway at the end of this diagonal one. He's at the intersection and stops upon hearing my footsteps and walks toward me. It can't be. He cannot be here. Dino, what is the part you play? Dapper as ever, still the same sense of style.

With a new intensity about him, he walks over toward me. "You do not have the authority to be in this section of the building." There was no question posed asking why I'm here, but he's stern and seems in charge. He's looking at me for a response, but I don't have one. *Dang it,* Ava*! Pull yourself together. Do not stand here like a goon.*

"Sir, someone let me back here. I have information on the Resistance you might want to know. The head of security gave me authorization to come back here and speak with only you directly." At this point the amount of sweat pouring out of my armpits is vile. He is looking me directly in the eyes and has no clue who I am.

"How did you come about this information?" His brow raises, questioning my intentions.

I appear to act skittish. "I met a girl when I was out recently, Saturday. Her name is Ava, sir. She was looking for someone named Sofia. She thinks I'm one of them. I've heard that name floating around here a bit. She trusts me and gave me some information." I seriously hope he believes this. After all, it was on a Saturday when I last saw Dino before he disappeared. My mouth uses every ounce of energy not to gape open at him. He is here—with the Militia.

"Follow me."

I do as he says as he turns to continue to walk into some obscure area. Either he believes me, or this night is going to go very badly. We hit the end of the dead-end hallway, and he places his hands on a tile on the wall and pushes, hard. It's a secret passageway that leads to an elevator. The door creaks open, and once we walk through, it shuts quietly. The room between is small; no more than three people could fit in here. And it's dusty and filled with cobwebs. But the elevator is sleek and clean and new. My reflection is not staring back at me, but I cannot help but just stare at Dino in the reflection, and he catches me.

"What?" he is rude and crass.

"Sorry, sir." I take a gulp, really playing it up. "I just know if she knew I were giving you this information, she would kill me—or have someone else do it."

He's buying it.

Dino smirks and clicks the elevator button, which also has a fingerprint scan on it. So he's been here a lot—enough to be trusted with whatever secret is hidden beyond this point. "Good thing you're here. But if you're lying to me, you will die."

"Good thing I don't want to die, sir," I quip back, and I'm deep into playing this character of someone I don't even know.

Hopefully, the real him is still knocked out unconscious. This will be bad if he isn't. I need to have Kerri make me something so I don't have to kill people to keep them from waking up.

We walk into the lift. He presses the button. And we're being lowered deeper into the ground. From the outside, it didn't appear there was more than one level, and with how far down we're going, I know there are several. And this is the only way down there.

The door opens to ceilings as high as the ones on the top floor, with the same rafters going through the top. But there isn't LED lighting, just dim, small hanging lights, very eerie like something out of a haunted house, only everything is clean and immaculate with the same black tile. Dino leads me down the mazelike halls with ease. But how? He was with me in Mexico, and he has a job and a lot going on in life. Or maybe none of that is real at all. He must have been here long before. That explains his move out east and his desire or obligation as my Shaddower to be close to me. It's getting hard to keep this form the longer I'm near him. The strength it takes is taking a toll on my body. He opens a door for me and advises me to wait here until he comes back. I am so thankful in this moment. I'll use the time apart from to rejuvenate myself.

There's no one in the room. It's bright with all white walls, flooring, and chairs. He slams the door behind him and locks it. This area is as large as a hospital waiting room but has a cold feeling. There are no cameras in here, yet I get the strange feeling they are watching me somehow; I can sense it in my bones. Or maybe Victor can just sense I am here. I cannot sit. I need to get out of here. I feel Victor and Dino's impact on my body; it's like I'm close to them and can feel it. I can feel Victor's pulse in my veins; I'm able to sense him and his movements. He's closer than I expected.

After about twenty minutes go by of doing many laps around the room, I feel the floor for movement. There's nothing. Those on the other side of the walls have left. Looking up at the exposed beams and grinning to myself, I silently thank Marcus for his training. It only takes me a slight jog to run and bounce off the chair with one leg and place the other foot on the wall, using that to shoot me into the air to grab onto the exposed beam that's about fifteen feet higher than my starting location. Parkour. Swinging from the beam, I use all of my momentum to shoot myself onto the next beam higher up into the cobwebs. They graze my face and find their way into my mouth. Gross. I take a minute and just lay here. But my current body is too large, and edges of me are hanging off the beam. While I'm out of sight, I change back to myself to be hidden by the beams—by a hair if that (dang these curves)—and give everyone a very quiet update as I remove the red jumpsuit. Dino must not be close by because I'm back at full force. I wonder what the proximity is for him to affect me.

Even with it being so dark up here, it gives me a clear idea of how large the space is down here. It's unknown how long I have until Dino comes back, so I have to make this quick. Those helpful starry lines appear once more, giving me aid in a time of need, a direction. The blood in my body boils, and I can feel Victor's heartbeat. The line is leading me to him. I crawl through the darkness and cobwebs on the beams over many rooms, until Dino's voice causes me to stop in my tracks, and the line has stopped guiding me. I hover over the edge and peek with one eye into the room below. I see Dino talking to Victor and a few other men. They're standing in an all red brick area. It's nothing like the vision I saw of Victor. His face is raw like he took a beating, but he's otherwise unharmed. In fact, he appears to be an equal among them. These man are standing around a black table and look angry as a few pace back and forth in their business suits, while Victor is in normal clothes, dressed down. The men who are pacing look familiar to me. They are two men from the boat! One operated the boat, and the other was the torture crusader, Lex.

Finally, Dino speaks up again, looking angry as he pulls a

knife out of his pocket. "You, sit down." He points the knife at Lex. This definitely isn't the Dino I know.

Lex looks frightened and does as he's told. Dino throws the knife to Victor, and he catches it. These two have the same energy as Kai and Kieran, like they know each other's movements so well they can predict what the other is going to do.

"You're aware you've ruined the main objective of our operation? So we had to plant a seed." Victor's voice is as cold as it was when he called me near my birthday. I guess some things never change. Crazy ass family. He walks around the table, and the knife makes harsh noises as he scrapes it along the white surface, making his way to Lex.

Lex is facing me, but he can't see me in the dark rafters. His eyes go back to the knife and then Victor and then back to Dino in a never-ending fear tactic. He takes a big gulp and, with fearful eyes, addresses Victor's comment. "Yes, Victor. I'm sorry." There is no way sorry will be enough for this man.

"What should your punishment be? You got ahead of yourself—wanting to torture her for killing one of your men. Yet she escaped because you couldn't follow the plan." He takes Lex's hand and places it on the table. With one quick motion he brings the knife down hard and cuts off his thumb. The sight makes me wince, but I cannot interfere.

Lex lets out a cry, and with each sound from him, Victor and Dino take turns taking fingers off of his right hand.

I scoot back into the darkness, unable to watch the torture, even of the one who tortured me. I do not relish in the fact that he is losing his fingers. It is in this moment I realize it was all fake. Victor took a beating to try and lure me in, and it worked. He wants to harm me still, just as he did when we were children, and I feel for it because he is family. Some people cannot escape the encroaching shadows that consumes their souls. Some dark shadows cannot be outrun.

Lex is silent. The screaming has stopped, and I peek back over the beam to see Lex lying on the floor with his mouth taped shut, gushing blood from his right hand that no longer has any fingers. He's rolling around in agony, and Victor is wiping the blood from the knife onto his shirt as he turns and starts addressing the other man.

"Now we had to lure her here since you couldn't do the job. We understand you were under Lex's command and the decisions were his. However, now we don't know where the Grimmer base is—or hers."

Dino walks around the table and stands in the pool of blood. "I gave her to the Grimmers on purpose so your team could follow them and find the base and kill as many as possible and then bring the girl back to me. The mission was not completed. You will form another task force and leave immediately. Do whatever it takes. Do not come back if you do not have results, or this will be your fate." Dino's tone is forceful as he looks the man in his eyes and leans down next to Lex and snaps his neck, leaving him completely lifeless on the ground.

"Yes, sir." The man doesn't bat a lash, just turns on his heels and exits the room.

Now Dino and Victor are alone with a body that is just bleeding out on to the floor. I cannot tell who is in charge of who at this point.

"How can we be certain she'll come?" Dino kneels to the ground as he slowly cuts Lex's throat, after he is already dead; he is doing it for pleasure. This is sickening, and the vomit wants to rise in my throat, but I swallow it down. He is a monster.

Kieran is muttering into my earpiece, just checking in to say everything is fine on his end and that the guy I put into the box is still in the box. Shamus says he's on the docks and looking into the cargo containers, while Kai has made his way around the building and discovered trip wires along with stockpiles of grenades and weaponry. But they haven't been activated yet. He said they look like they're missing a piece. And it isn't traditional guns but looks like something different, something of their own making. He's taken one to bring back to show everyone.

"You know her better than anyone after all this time and years of fake friendship, she will do anything to save a poor helpless soul. It gives her crippling anxiety if she feels like she hasn't done enough. Plus, I can sense her. She is near. I don't know where, but I sense she's on her way to the facility now."

If only Victor knew how near I really was. We can sense each other, great; but clearly, he can't sense as clearly as I do.

He continues, breaking into thoughts, "Our linked souls have always been able to give me her location. But this time it's different. She grows stronger as the Pureck grows closer to death. Unless she lets her guard down, I can't track her. However, I can still feel her if she is close, like a sickness of light." He rolls his neck, cringing at the thought of goodness in this world. Is Kieran's mother dying? Does he know?

Oh, boy, I'd better get a move on. Dino is talking to Victor about the man waiting in the exam room, which, coincidentally, is me but not me. I hide back in the darkness of the rafters and think of how the only exit down here is the elevator, unless I can somehow climb in here up to the top, but that doesn't seem likely. Maybe I can follow the elevator shaft up. My beautiful mind gives me directions again, illuminating the way with a path I graciously follow. It has more twists and turns than before. But now is not the time to doubt something that has helped me and never hindered me. Crawling and maneuvering on the beams is difficult. The friction on my elbows, even through my outfit, is like bad rug burn.

The sound of gears cracking and people talking catch my attention. This is where the light was leading me. I carefully go down to the lower level of rafters and turn slightly, hanging off them to see what the commotion is about since the main floor was dead silent. Steam fills the air, but I can still see the containers. There are at least fifteen full-size shipping containers down here, harboring humans. Wait, not humans, those with powers. The chattering below is telling me they are ones who haven't chosen a side between the Resistance or the Grimmers. Those caught inside are trying to use their powers to escape, but the containers are laced with something preventing that from happening. There are row after row of these clear shipping containers, with no way of telling how many people occupy them.

My sights search the room, and I land on a large, circular, out-of-the-future kind of machine. It has many people working on its intricacies, and it makes a loud bang. Some woman in a white lab coat waves her hand in the air, and six armed guards roll forward one of the large containers. She walks around the container inspecting it and makes another gesture. At that moment, the red-uniformed men remove a square piece of the container and attach a long aluminum-looking pipe to it that's attached to the machine.

It seems the people inside the container know exactly what this machine is capable of, as they bang on the walls, screaming bloody murder and begging for at least the children to be let out. A woman who looks to be about my age has tears rolling down her face. She has a G burned onto her forehead; my guess is that means she's Grimmer. She is terrified and sinks to the ground giving up all hope as the white-coated woman walks past the branding station that has a line of people and to the operation panel of the machine. The panel looks complex, something NASA would probably want to get its hands on.

The lab-coated woman flicks a switch, and the girl with the G branded on her face is brought up into the air with tears streaming down her face. She screams. As her mouth widens, she lets out silent screams while the life is literally sucked from her body. After her, every other member of the container she's in goes through the same fate. Once all in the container are dead, the coated woman leaves her position to talk to someone on the opposite end of the room near me, practically right under the rafter I lay on.

She seems pleased. A smile crosses her face. "We've done it. Now we can build this model on a larger scale." She looks back across the room at the now lifeless bodies lying in their prison cell and gestures for someone to turn the machine off. "We finally have the right combination to harness their powers into our machine. On a bigger scale, we can wipe out twenty at a time and use that power against them—either with the machine itself, or we can harness that power into our weapons. If only we had the girl, we would be unstoppable. You must hurry and tell the leaders about this!"

The man turns quickly on his heel and runs out of the room, while the woman skips back to her control panel in glee. Holy fuck. Seriously, I reserve that term for something insane, and this is it. They have made a machine that instantly sucks the power and life out of us and intend to use it against everyone. They're not looking to just exterminate us; with this, they could exterminate everyone on the planet—every person, woman, child, man, powers or none, everyone.

"There has been movement, Ava. The guy you knocked out is running into the building." Kieran's alarmed voice comes through my earpiece. "Shit, everyone get out!"

I know my time is limited, but there's something I must do, and this could end terribly for me. I move quickly, running on top of the rafters, until I'm right above the woman in the lab coat. Without giving it more thought, I float down aggressively to her level but make sure to land with either foot on her shoulders and my hands around her neck. Before she even starts to realize what's happening to her, I twist her neck, and her body falls to the floor. As an extra precaution, I reach into my holster and take a knife and stab her in the face. Crowds of containees go wild for freedom as I find the one red release button and hit it with all my force—Grimmers, undeclareds, and Resistance all contained together.

Someone from the container shoots fireballs from his hand into the walls to bring them down and let everyone run free. The sprinkler system goes off, but this whole building has to come down. I need to make sure Victor and Dino do not get these people back. And now I am 100 percent certain they will be looking for me. I need to bring this whole place down.

"Kai," I say into the earpiece, "do what you need to do. Move the trip wires and activate the grenades. We need to bring this place down."

With that, I silence everything on my end and haul ass to the elevator in hopes that, along the way, I can find some other things to help aid in the destruction of this place—this evil place.

My appearance has been spotted. Those in the machine room have spotted me even through the fire and destruction. I'm being fired at in all directions. But wouldn't you know? I am typical gun, bulletproof, thanks, doc. I disappear, running as fast as I can to avoid the fire and not caring if my aura is showing on the way. I'm in front of the elevator within seconds and hit the button.

Come on, come on. Hurry up. My feet won't stop moving, and there are knives in both my hands now, ready for anything that comes my way when it opens. The lift opens, and no one's inside. The door slowly starts to close with me inside but not before men turn the corner and run in my direction. Of course there's no door close button on this one to speed up the process. I throw two knives through the tiny opening slot and hit both of them in the legs, making them fall to the ground. The door is an inch from shutting when Victor and Dino see me, with mouths dropped to the ground. I have about one minute until the elevator reaches the main floor, and I'm sure there will be numerous weapons pointing at me when this door opens. Now is the time for me to speak one last time.

I turn my headpiece back on. "Everyone, get out. I mean it. I will lead them away from you and the portal so you'll have a chance. Kai, there are many people who are freed." I go on to quickly sum up as much as I can for him and ask him to bring those who need asylum back. I need to bring this weapon down.

They all can sense the seriousness in my voice. All of them unwillingly agree with me—all but one of course.

"I will not leave you." My sweet, sweet Kieran.

"Kieran, please." I am begging him. "We don't have the numbers, and there aren't enough of us to take this on."

There's no response from him. But Shamus goes on a private line to speak to me and tell me that they're together, and he will forcibly make him leave.

The elevator door opens, and an arrow flies right by my face, putting a small nick on my cheek, and a gunshot ricochets off my arm. The men look perplexed to see the bullet didn't have an entry or exit point. Unexpectedly, all the harsh electrical boiling in my body is at an uncontainable level, leaving my body shaking and my mouth gasping for breath. I fall to my knees and my hands raise in the air, and my mouth opens, letting out a loud stream of leaves from my mouth. This has never happened this way before. It's painful as all of the energy pulses out of my entire body. My hair flows around my face as the pulse hits every person in the hallway. When my mouth closes and my body relaxes, all others are beneath me, lying on the ground, their heartbeats weak; they have just been stunned. They're literally shaking from the shock.

There is not one second to waste, especially with Dino here. Who knows how badly he could suppress my powers? There is no hesitation as I begin to run and maneuver around all of the dropped bodies, down the hallways and through the door I entered, thanking that starry light for showing me the way. There are more men and women barreling down the hallway, sending vibrations from the ground up my leg and up my arm to my hand that rests on the exit door.

"That's her!" a random man yells into his watch at the top of his lungs and starts firing shots at me.

But I quickly open and slam the door behind me. I find the crate where I've hidden my sword and make my way back to the pit of snakes and out on the other side of them.

"Kieran, take care of Laila for me, please." These are my last words as I take the earpiece out and throw it to the wayside. Time to buy them as much time as possible.

One man comes hauling through the pit of snakes, getting bitten at each turn. He's the one with the laser eyes who opened the pathway for others to escape. Why is he after me? He is shooting bullets at me and lasering away all of the snakes. It's not their fault. His eyes glaze over, and I can see he's possessed. I can read his soul from here. I do not wish to be judge and executioner, but he is going to kill everyone, including those he let free, to prove to the Grimmers he is worthy of them. I draw my sword and run toward him, avoiding his eyes and his bullets. He is preoccupied with the snakes as I jump over his head and slash him in the back before he can even focus on me. It seems like a cheap shot on my part. Or maybe it's just well-played. My conscious will have to deal with that later. The snakes hiss around my feet as they start to feast on his body.

This makes my skin crawl, and I need to not see what's about to happen. I crawl out of the snakes and think about my next move until I realize they need more time. Still time. Focusing hard, this new power easily adapts to my body. My eyes shoot boxes next to the warehouse, and they go up in flames. Not only do I have full function of the lasers from his eyes, I also have the senses that came along with it. This is a different kind of focus, zooming in and out for what seems like miles or up close; it's like a video game scope. It's making me dizzy and nauseous. This will take some practice to get used to, but again, there is no time.

I wait. Making loud noise, I announce who I am, waiting to make sure all of the Militia see me. Soon, nothing but red jumpsuits are about a hundred yards away from me. Now it's time to take them through my maze, through the snake fields. Many drop as the creatures infect them with their poison. I loop back around to the dam and onto the cargo ships. They only have a few with powers chasing after me. How can they work for them knowing what they're harnessing in the depths underground? Or do they not know? Maybe they were promised asylum. Always so many unanswered questions.

From the top of one cargo ship, I count the grenades I've taken along the way off of their own soldiers. First, I toss off the smoke grenades and one MK 2 grenade while beginning to run, finding a new tactical spot. The impact and the heat from the grenade presses against my back; the explosion rockets my jump forward, and I land on the next ship. That must have been the cue Kai was waiting for; the explosives and trip wires he set up are going off around the complex.

I throw the remaining grenades on the cargo ships and toward the warehouse, which starts to crack and tumble to the ground. I run in the direction of the woods, dropping the last three remaining grenades on my way, leaving nothing but fire and destruction in my wake.

Chapter 20

The wind overtakes me, bringing me back to consciousness out of my run. It was like my body was so consumed by my run the outside world stopped for a second, including my consciousness. Already my body has grown accustomed to my new powers. Previously, my head would be splitting or something; the slight changes would be so drastic, like how I felt like I couldn't breathe when I was getting used to breathing under water, but not now. It becomes a part of me so quickly, there is no time to process. And my body soaks it up like its meant to do it; it doesn't hinder me or stop me or even take me down for a split second. There is no vulnerability to me in those moments at all. It's so strange.

My new vision searches for a sign—anything, even metaphorical to figure out where I am. But we land on something tangible, Seaway International Bridge. We're right between the border of the United States and Canada. Just great. I don't need to draw attention to another country. Lights from both countries slightly illuminate the bridge in the pitch-black darkness, showing a little island that also supports the weight of the bridge. Guess it's pure luck that there are no passengers coming to or from this entry. Snowflakes graze my nose and melt instantly on my face. It's a time of year I would normally love—the first snowfall, a real non-simulated snow. I would run out of wherever I was and find total happiness in sticking my tongue out to catch the first snowflake.

How is it there are no people? No cars? Nothing. I slowly walk down the bridge until I reach a center spot surrounded by water on both sides. The wind and water float around me in small partials, but I can see it clearly. I speak to the wind, but it doesn't listen. It must be listening to someone else. The feeling inside me is telling me that nature cannot listen to me and the Purecks at the same time. It's their only flaw—that they cannot wield the power of nature when another is doing it simultaneously. On my own then, I get a running start to jump into the air and gracefully land on the top of the bridge archway. This will give me a much better viewpoint. The cable connections do not budge as I hang my body from them on either side to look out into the distance. No one is coming, but the wind is back, warning me of a more imminent manifestation. The lights in the city closest to the bridge on the United States side have all gone off. Victor, Dino and their reinforcements are approaching as an encroaching shadow of darkness takes over all the lights for miles and miles; it gets darker the closer they get.

Now, there is dimness coming from both directions, and these new eyes of mine do not see in the total darkness that now consumes all around me. There is a stillness that surrounds me, a complete and utter silence. The only movement is the bridge, which sways softly beneath my feet, and the sound of heavy footsteps getting closer.

Until everything stops. There is not even movement from the wind or the water or the forthcoming people I sense in my body.

With the silence, I take my last breath as a violent bang coincides with a spotlight being turned on and pointing directly at me. My hand hovers over my eyes, softening the harshness of the illuminating light, only to reveal the rows of soldiers that line the bridge. No vehicles or tanks or anything that the movies would have prepared me for—just men, rows and rows of silent-footed men. There is no machine present that would suck the life out of me. So that's a plus at least—a grim one but a plus, nonetheless.

Some man is yelling from a bullhorn, trying to advise me to come down, or they will move back into town and kill the people off one by one. Well, look at that guy, playing on my emotions for being a decent human being. Is this what it's come to? Honestly, these people, for a lack of a better term, are fucking disgusting. As I release myself from the now swaying cables, it's obvious all of the Militia soldiers are on edge, holding their guns to their chests for dear life, clearly not knowing that now I'm bulletproof. Suck on that, assholes. I land delicately on my feet in the center of the bridge, and that boiling is growing inside of me again, painfully so, except I am able to control it from releasing. My hands and fingers are clenched so tightly my nails are digging into my skin, drawing blood, trying not to release the pulse yet. This is going to be painful when it's released. They must be able to sense the electricity coming off my body, as they all now have their guns drawn on me and begin to open fire.

The pulse releases through my body,and I scream. But this pulse doesn't electrify everyone; it turns into some form of radio frequency wave that disintegrates the bullets but doesn't bring anyone down. What? My body is doing different types of pulses now? This is going to be fun to figure out.

"*Stop!*" Victor's voice echoes on the bridge, and the soldiers in those tacky, ugly, horrific monotone red jumpsuits lower their weapons and part, leaving way for Dino and Victor to walk side by side to confront me from the back of the pack.

Maybe that's why my pulse didn't work. Dino is here. Victor has his hands raised in the air as he walks toward me. And with a flick of his wrist, he raises a Canadian ship out of the water miles away and flicks it onto land right behind his Militia. Then he violently flicks his other wrist that is still in the air above his head, and a lighthouse comes crashing down on the Canada side, destroying a few homes in its path.

"Stop this madness, Victor!"

He is face-to-face with me, and I loudly plea to him. My memory searches for any good moment of him. But there's only one—when we were swinging on the tree rope swings in harmony as children. But maybe that too is a fake memory. Still, with hope I hold on to that memory as he looks deep into my eyes with his cold glower.

"How is mom by the way?" He curls his lips up into a wicked half smile that makes me sick to my stomach.

"What happened to you? And you?" My eyes shoot between Victor and Dino with such disgust.

"Honestly, what is sickening is how stupid you are. How do you not know? Do you know how badly I want to kill you right now? Perhaps I should make it a tradition and kill you in front of Aidan again, break his heart all over." Victor actually likes this banter and is enjoying himself, while Dino remains silent, not looking at me.

I spit in Victor's face, and in a quick motion, he has a knife drawn. I cannot sense Dino as he moves behind me and grabs my arms behind my back. He is weakening me with each second he holds onto me. Dino deeply breathes in my scent from my hair. With one hand, he holds me still, and with the other, he grabs my hair and jerks my head to the side. Victor runs his knife softly over my throat, drawing a small amount of blood. I do my best not to swallow as the knife is pressed against me; but I can't resist, and the knife lodges deeper into me.

"Our parents chose you when they should have chosen me. Imagine the power I could hold right now. You are weak. The pretend mother dearest informed me of how you were growing stronger for good than you were before. You make me sick. Imagine what you could have. Imagine what I could have had. You make me sick." The spite just rolls off of his tongue. He's hurting others and doing all of this because of a choice neither of us had control over.

"All of this … out of envy?" I ask.

And immediately I don't even know why I bothered with him. There's no response, just more silence as Dino kicks the back of my legs, buckling me over to drop me on my knees. The blade razors off my skin as it goes from my throat under my chin. I lean my head back, trying to make eye contact with Dino, but it causes more blood to spew. Still, I cannot help myself. "Dino, why? After all this time … Was everything fake? Even our friendship—a lie?" Part of me knows the answer—that this was a game to him the whole time, but I want to hear him say it.

"Ava, I tried to get you to love me, but you wouldn't budge."

Gag, I hold back the vomit; this isn't love. A hint of sincerity glows in his eyes though. Maybe he still has a chance to be saved.

He loosens the knife, and it gives me the freedom to talk more clearly. "I do love you—or I did—but not this person who you are standing behind me right now. I don't recognize you." I have known him for so long. He has always been my rock. We know so much about each other. But it's simple. This man is not the friend I love or respect; he is someone else entirely.

"But not the way I wanted," he says.

I shake my head at him. How could I? I find it hard to believe that, if I simply loved him the way he wished or required, he wouldn't have traveled down this path.

The last inkling of the Dino I knew is floating away as his mouth opens once more. "We could have shared in all of this glory. The money. The power. The eternal life. The complete domination of those around us. We would have been treated like the king and queen we deserve to be."

"Who choses who is deserving of what?" These are my last words to him.

Screams and crying of animals sound from the end of the bridge; the loud ruckus creates reverberations that are coming off the metal framework of the bridge and smacking me in the side of the face. My vision zooms in, and there's a black beast, fighting with Huffnalgers. Aidan is biting them in the throat and tossing them to the side one by one. He is not killing them, just wounding them as they scurry back off into the woods. The firepower of the men does not seem to be able to stop him at all. He is on a warpath and coming in my direction.

"Perfect timing, as always." Victor beams and takes a step toward me. He mumbles something to Dino about how he got a message to Aidan letting them know where we would be after what I did to their warehouse.

Dino is turned looking at Aidan make his way here, so I'm able to use all my strength to back kick my leg and kick Dino right in the stomach. He cripples over and drops his knife. Without a running start, I press down, and the wind helps me jump back to the top archway of the bridge. Victor is trying to use his telekinesis to bring me down, but easily grows frustrated that, with the space between me and Dino, I am no longer vulnerable. The wind blows between us, acting as an additional shield to Victor's reach. His frustration has him lashing out at people around him, kicking and tearing them to pieces with his axe. Aidan has yet to break through the barrier on the other end of the bridge.

The wind picks up, and I release myself into it, using sheer balance to keep me in place as Victor tries to move the bridge in its entirety. But he doesn't have the power. I can feel the roots of the trees move within me, the breeze swaying me in place, and the hostility of the water below. They all power me and boil another pulse inside me. With a deep breath, my connection with nature grows deeper and more comfortable. I listen to the wind and jump off the side of the bridge, following that starry line, and open my eyes to see Aidan's werewolf eyes in a state of panic as I sink down closer to the water.

Gravity does not pull me into the water but hovers me above it. My arms spread wide as shots are being fired in my direction, but the water creates a barrier between me and the bullets, sinking them into the depths of its vastness. A wave pushes me higher, bringing me level to the bridge, looking through a one-way glass mirror of water. Without having to scream to release it, the pulse exits my body, ferociously knocking the men over. With a flick of my wrist, the water does my bidding and consumes the Huffnalgers surrounding Aidan, dragging them into the water.

The wave moves easily under my command and brings me above Victor and Dino. As I drop my arms to my side, the water disappears beneath me, harshly dropping me back onto the bridge and in front of Dino and Victor. That wasn't as graceful as I intended, and I need to quickly pick myself back up and onto my feet. Guess I don't have everything under control quite yet. With my last blast of energy with Dino so near, I drag the last of their standing men into the ocean, far into the distance.

"Dino." All the elements float around me out of control. I practically have to scream. "I am sorry I couldn't save you." A tear glides down my face. Every element I have ever tried to control is taking the control from me, lifting me high above them as water takes on the bridge, clearing everyone from my sight and devouring Dino and Victor into a tornado that takes them out into the middle of nowhere.

The elements dissipate around me and slowly tumble underneath my feet, bringing me down onto the now calm again bridge. Even though Victor and Dino aren't dead and the Huffnalgers are swimming for their lives, I consider this a win, without having to kill so many people. However, the problem has just been brushed under the rug and not dealt with.

"Thank you," I whisper to the water, and it drops by my feet, creating a huge flood on the bridge for me to walk through. But I don't mind, not with all the help it's given me, even if it did have some of its own control.

The black beast is on the trot to my location. A huge grin spreads across my face; I know he would have done anything to help/ "How did you get here so fast?" I wrap my arms around his furry neck and cuddle in, but soon arms are gripping me, and my face is greeted with the feeling of skin and not fur. His blue eyes match the puddle we're knelt in.

"Victor sent me another death treat, typical in his dramatic fashion. But I noticed Shamus was missing, and, well, at this point nothing is a coincidence. From the portal, I just instinctively followed the noise." He is sweet and comforting, the exact opposite of how I thought he was going to react.

My eyes can't help but gaze over his shirtless body in those shorts I love so much. He runs his hands over that witchy bracelet and is now fully clothed in jeans and a black T-shirt, but I frown when he rips a piece of his fresh shirt to place it around my neck to stop the bleeding.

"It's nothing." I mumble quietly, with butterflies in my stomach. It's like a constant anxiety attack around him.

"What the hell, Ava! Seriously. You could have gotten yourself killed. What were you thinking?" Now that he knows I am fine, all care is gone, replaced by anger, as I'd expected his original reaction to be. He is really laying into me, to the point where I have completely shut him out. Having selective hearing can be a beautiful thing.

"I can walk." I don't need him carrying me. Plus, that tone he uses when he is mad at me just puts me off. It's like utter disappointment in me rather than anger. He holds tight as I try to squirm out of the grip of his arm wrapped around my side.

"I need you to understand where I am coming from. Do you

not trust me? Why do you hide the location of the ring? Why do you purposely put your life at risk? What is going on in that mind of yours?" Now his voice is softer, and he has calmed down as we reach the end of the bridge.

I look into his hurt-filled eyes and try to come up with the best answer. But he doesn't stop and just keeps leading us into the wooded area. I shuffle out of his grasp and grab his hand and look him in the eyes. The trees lower and surround us, and his eyes flash across the safe cove they have built us in amazement. It's something I am getting used to, but it surprises him.

"Aidan." He brings his focus back to me at the sound of my voice. "You lie to me. It's not a lack of trust. I know how much you care about me, and maybe you withhold the truth from me to protect me in your own way. But there is so much you just don't tell me. I know how much you're trying to protect me. But how can I fulfill my purpose here, however vague it still may be, if you don't let me follow my gut? If we are really soul mates, you need to respect me as a partner and not look at me as some hindrance that you always need to protect, like I am an infant." He begins shaking his head, so I carry on. "I am not purposely putting myself at risk, but all great outcomes require some risk. Do you not understand that I also want to keep you safe and out of harm's way, just as much as you want to keep me out of danger?"

He doesn't seem to relax at all. "But why here? Why now? Are you questioning whether I am your soul mate? It is written in the stars. There is no changing it." The tone he is using basically makes me feel like he really didn't listen to anything I said and doesn't understand where I'm coming from. He just cares more and more about soul mates. But the vibe I'm getting isn't necessarily a comforting one.

I speak into his chest, exhausted, and drained. How do you make someone who isn't fully listening understand?

"Look, I saw Victor being tortured in a vision that came to

me. I had to save him. Believe me, I know he was playing me, and he will probably try to do it again. But now I understand; now I see. I got to see firsthand for myself how he is. And honestly, if I didn't see it myself, even if everyone told me he was evil, I wouldn't have believed it. I would have searched for hope, because that's what a family is supposed to do. Now I realize that's not the case, anymore."

He stops me from talking more by pulling me in quickly at the waist, like his life depends on it, for a passionate kiss. The trees surround us, but there is no other movement from them. I kiss him back, searching, feeling, and hoping this moment turns magical. I'm surprised; the moment didn't really call for it. It's like he's trying to solidify that we are soul mates and not listening to what I said or how I felt about Victor. He is searching for the passion between us, and it will always be there. I step back and look into those eyes. I would do it all over again, make the same decisions, piss him off that much. Chills run up and down my spine as the wind flows through my hair, whispering words into my ear that I cannot make out; it's like a different language.

I let my mind go as he pulls me in once more to a passionate kiss. I leave behind nature trying to talk to me. I leave behind Victor. I use this kiss as my release to forget it all for one second—to feel wanted. Yet I do not feel free. He pulls me in closer, kissing me deeper, sensing something is holding me back, and he wants me to let go. He wants me to embrace this moment. He is fighting for me in this kiss, and I cave in. We pull back at the same time, and there is that feeling, the irresistible electricity connecting us like it did in Mexico, like it did before Kieran. My eyes close, engraving this moment into my memory forever.

"As much as I want this moment to last, we have to go. They will be sending reinforcements. Plus, that will stop me from taking you right here and now on the ground." He lets out a low growl and shakes his head and releases me from his hold to run his hands through his hair. "The feeling is still there. I can feel that you feel it. You have to let him go." It is good to know he is as sexually frustrated as I am, but I know who he is referring to—the spiritual block between us.

He mutates himself and becomes hairy and snarling once more and tilts his head, as though he is telling me to follow him and bolts. I could have used a ride, but no. Maybe he's frustrated. It makes me wonder what lengths he would really go to in order to get Kieran out of the picture.

Even as Aidan is saying these things, I wonder what Kieran knows about his mother. When was the last time she saw him?

Chapter 21

The breeze from the cool mountainside feels amazing against my skin. But still, the lingering memory of my last moment here comes back to me in detail as a vision. Ray. He was here. He was trying to stop me or kill me. I'm still uncertain of his intentions. Maybe Aidan can provide some clarification. I place my hand on the exposed spot of skin on my arm, and Aidan stops me before I can even ask him and demands to know what happened.

"It was Ray. He was here." I explain to him in as much detail as I can the rundown of what happened. My fingers trace the spot on my arm; the vision keeps replaying. This scar remains, just like the one Aidan gave me, but all others have healed. I tear my uniform further down and run my hands across the scar on the top of my back and down my side, and I am brought back to a vision of Aidan and that moment. When I touch the scars, the memory appears. Again I run my hand over the scar from Ray, and I can almost see him and Aidan talking. My scars that still remain tell a story.

"Are you positive it was Ray?"

I don't know why but his question sets me off. "Now let's talk about lack of trust. Yes. I am sure." With that, I stomp off, still playing with the scar Ray has given me, and the vision becomes clearer.

Aidan is talking to him behind the curtains at the last meeting, telling him to stop me from whatever my plans are at all costs and to make sure I am kept away from Kieran. Aidan is so willing to trust him, and what he put on before for me must have been a show—another lie. Should I bring this up or not? What do I do about the visions? That this scar remains while the others fade makes sense—it was Aidan's doing.

He catches up after me. "I'm sorry, Ava. You can trust me, and I can trust you. Always."

Ha! Very funny, Cross. Just because we are connected and when we are alone I feel like drawn to you doesn't mean I will not try my best to do what is right for me. He is smart changing the topic, since he sees my wheels turn. Surely, he will put it together himself soon enough. Until then, he asks, "How did you move the water in such a way?"

"Honestly," I shrug, "it's weird to explain. I'm unsure of what to say. It's like everything in nature becomes more a part of me as the days go on and shares a spot in my soul. It has grown stronger. I am linked to it all. Sometimes it works for me, and sometimes it doesn't."

"You are a breathtaking angel." He speaks from his heart, his wording quaking as they fall out of his mouth. "My angel. I will have a word with Ray."

I'm sure you will. I nod and leave it at that. "When we get back, I have more to tell you about something I have witnessed. I would like to put a meeting together. I know it's late, but it's all of grave importance. Marcus and anyone else you deem appropriate should be there—including Kieran. Do you think you can arrange that for me?"

"Yes. Can it wait until tomorrow? I would like to have you to myself right now, before the daylight comes up."

As sweet as that is, "It cannot wait." I am stern on this and set on the matter, and he knows it now. The seriousness lingers in my voice and mannerisms. I look to the east, and now I know what he is talking about. The time has flown by. What seemed like a matter of minutes to me was actually hours of work scoping out and entering the Militia base.

"Fine, I will arrange it for tonight. But without Kieran. He left you anyway. So much for love," Aidan scoffs in a victorious manner.

"He comes. For your information, he trusts me enough to follow my lead every once in a while and respects me enough to listen to my opinion and try to see my side of things, especially when it comes to the greater good. So maybe we have different views on love."

As we hit the town center, all at once, like it's on a timer, the stars fade with Aidan's smile, and the sun rises.

"Ava, are you going to tell us why you called this meeting?" Kerri asks, nice and rude at the same time, still reeling over the loss of her beloved friend, Judd. She, among others, are growing impatient. But I need him here, as comfort, even if he is not standing by my side and Aidan is.

"I'm waiting for a few more people to arrive," I say innocently enough and calmly; it's the truth.

Aidan senses my anxiety and stands to hold my hand.

We are in Aidan's study, in his safe zone house. It's almost an exact replica of his shared study with his father back in New York City, including the liquor cart. Even though it's about only 6:00 a.m., I release Aidan's hand from mine and, like the typical lush I can be, grab a glass and pour whatever brown liquor is at the ready. The fancy tumbler is something one of my old friends,

Dino, would try to take from a bar or something; he and the Marx brothers loved taking them home. I swig it down and quickly pour myself another since Mr. Grumpy Gills himself is staring at me in an unapproving manner. At least I was classy and put it in a glass instead of taking the bottle right to the face like I really want to.

I would love to have a room like this one day, only with every wall covered in books. But after all this is over, I'm starting back at square one—no house—and figuring out whatever money I have in my savings and checking account add up to, probably not a lot. I'll starts back from the ground up and decide if I can even somehow rebuild my house or if I should let those ashes burn, along with the memories that go with them.

"Now we can start." Kieran walks in and shoots me a smile.

All my anxiety releases from my body. Aidan scowls seeing the effect he has on me and walks over to me and grabs my hand.

Kieran is followed by Efron, Sarah, Kai, and Shamus; of course the gang is all here. Marcus strolls in right behind them with Laila by his side, but she abandons ship and comes to sit directly on my feet. Kieran walks right over to me, with that boyish grin of his, disregarding Aidan's grasp on my hand and gives me a hug. My lips smack together and eyes dart to the side; well, this is such an awkward standoff.

"I was worried about you, but I had to trust your judgment. I know you would do the same for me."

Aidan tries to hide his scowl, but everyone in the room can feel it.

I let go of Aidan's hand despite his attempts to keep it. But not wanting to cause a scene in front of the Elders and Manayunks that have come, I give Kieran a quick hug and smile over his shoulder at our friends. Kieran and Aidan shake hands, but it's clearly just for show and they're trying to manage their dislike for one another.

Shamus, knowing full well we need to start this thing,

surprises me and comes to give me a hug with some more of his oh so wonderful comforting words. "Thank god you are in one piece. I didn't need Cross taking my head off.

Sarah shakes her head at his tact. Clearly, he is the only one who cannot read the room and the awkwardness of it.

I whisper in his ear. "He's a big teddy bear. He wouldn't dare."

Aidan overhears and lets out a loud laugh and mumbles something along the lines of he would be happy to take off someone's head. Sarah and I stare at each other. How is it women pick up on this stuff so easily, but the men are just plain clueless? She mouths to me that we will catch up later, and I nod.

I take a deep breath and look at Kieran. He moves his hands up and down near his stomach, telling me to take breaths and be calm; just talk. The way he eases my storm is something I have never felt before. There are some here I recognize—Ferma and Freya, with no Ray to be found. About twelve others I have never seen before, and Kerri introduces me to Judd's son, Flynn. Flynn looks like Judd in so many ways. They share the same eyes and facial features. Like his father, Flynn is of average height and build and has a kind, quirky half smile, with crooked teeth. His presence is no doubt painful to everyone in this room because he is a reminder of his father. He holds the hand of his wife. Even though she is not a Manayunk or an Elder, she has been invited here. She is a beautiful, stylish, black, plus-sized woman with light honey eyes and dreadlocks wrapped into a top bun. She holds her husband's hand with such concern and seems to be just waiting on his every movement; she is an attentive wife and holds him up. She is his support. It's beautiful to see.

I would later learn he stood firm and upheld his marriage by stating, if she were not invited, even with lack of Manayunk and Elder status, he would not attend, despite what happened to his father. She is now his whole world. It's clear just by their dynamic he would be nothing without her. He finds his strength through her and their marriage. It's beautiful really.

I turn to find Aidan staring at me, blushing. Apparently, my staring at them in admiration has made him feel uncomfortable—oh well. Laila leans against my leg, giving me extra security, always happy to see me no matter the circumstances.

"So, I have something I want to speak to you all about."

Before I can say more, Flynn speaks up. "Obviously. That's why you called us here at the asscrack."

His wife scolds him, "Thanks for pointing that out, Einstein," but tries to hide back her laugh. Kieran can't help himself and lets out a laugh.

Flynn proceeds to joke that he is older than Einstein and that he met him before and he wouldn't be as brilliant as he was if they'd never been friends and all the stuff I would normally joke and laugh about.

But not now, I continue on. "Not all of you are aware, but a few of us were able to infiltrate a Militia base up north last night, and I would like to share our findings. However, I just ask that you let me speak without interruption to just get it all out. You all need to know what lay deep in the ground within those walls but has since been destroyed."

I take a breath and exhale. "They have built a machine. I know many of you believe they are recruiting those with skills to help them with their battle, but that is not the case. In fact, only a few with powers have been trusted by Militia, from what I gathered, to do the work for them."

Ignoring my previous request, Freya asks, "Then what are they using us for?" Moving elegantly, she walks closer to me. She's wearing a similar dress to the one she had on before, but this one is light pink and more radiant against her skin tone.

"I saw lines of our kind in containers. They were being held captive and used in a device that sucks not only the power out of them but also their lives. Men, women, children, they didn't care. It was heartbreaking to witness. I saw the machine work and the lifeless bodies afterward. The woman operating the machine, well"—I take a big gulp—"I killed her. But before I did, I heard her say they were making more but on a larger scale, so the machine can have bigger working radius." I turn to my friends who were with me. "That's why I wanted you all to get out. I didn't know if they were just stashed around or what. But I knew—well hoped—it wouldn't work on me." Just a hopeful educated guess based on everything I know and what else has happened. "I didn't want to give it the chance, though. So, we took down the base."

Aidan shoots me a look and speaks cautiously. "If your Shaddower were nearby, my guess is they could get the machine to work on you too. He could suppress your powers enough to make it work."

"What exactly is the machine's purpose? To destroy us? What else do you know, Ava?" Kerri chimes in, worry spreading across her face. She grabs my hand, a gesture paired with a look in her eyes that shows me she is sorry for what I've seen.

"All I know is they're sucking the life out of us and using it to harness the machine and, potentially, weapons. They're using our own powers against us. I haven't seen the machine as a weapon, and I'm not sure what else it's capable of. All I know is what I heard." I shake my head and try to give them as much detail as possible. I speak to them of everything I saw—a play-by-play of it all, including Victor. And now, after what Aidan said, it makes sense why they need Dino. The fact is I don't have all of the facts. Can the machine reach a far radius? How many can it work on at a time?

"How is it Ray has been working undercover with the Militia and has not mentioned this to us? Where is he?" Kieran's voice is filled with anger as he looks at Freya.

She searches the room for her son, but he is not here, something I sensed earlier.

"He has answers we need." Aidan's voice is cold as he approaches Freya. "You are his mother. You find him and bring him to me immediately." I honestly didn't think Aidan could tell her what to do, but apparently, he can.

She has a tear running down her perfect face but shows no expression. The tear is from the realization her son might not be who she thinks he is. "I'm sorry I do not have more information to give."

Aidan is on a tyrant roll at the moment and I lower my head wishing I could help even more.

Instinctively, Kieran saunters over to me and plants a kiss on my forehead. "You did wonderfully, Ava. Without you, we wouldn't know any of this, no matter the situation that brought you there." His voice lowers as he whispers in my ear, "Can I speak with you privately for a moment?" He realizes Aidan is preoccupied at the moment, now with his cell phone glued to his ear, making multiple phone calls, no doubt to his father and his pack.

I whisper back, "Later." Marcus has his eye glued on us and the moment everyone else is pleased that Aidan missed.

Marcus spoke up louder. "What else did you come across when you were there?"

It's Shamus's turn to respond. And as he does I smile, knowing just how excited Sarah gets when Shamus speaks. "I went to the cargo hold and they have a lot of firepower."

"Not anymore." I scrunch my lips together. "I might have blown up a ship or two—or all of them."

I didn't think about us maybe needing evidence or wanting to do more recon on the area. After all, Aidan only said search and report to everyone and that we were not to get involved. At least that was with his planned stuff, not this. Kai lets out a laugh and says he knows he timed up his trip wires to go off when the first ship did; still, a laugh like that from him is rare for his serious superassassin Asian like self. "Way to go. But honestly, it all makes sense with everything we saw—what the machine can do and how it could power the weapons."

Aidan is off the phone and back to focus and immediately notices Kieran is next to me but speaks without acknowledging it. "They will need to acquire more firepower; that is just a matter of time. Unless all of their facilities have something like this. Based on everything you shared, this was the only one and the plans died with the woman you killed. But now they know it's possible, they will be relentless in making it happen. You have bought us some time but not enough. Tomorrow, the searchers will be back with more information. I am curious to see what they have that will line up with our new information."

"Do you think the Grimmers would unite forces with us if they knew what we were up against? The best chance for survival is if we work together somehow. We're outnumbered by their forces, and if they put these machines into mass production, how much of a chance do we stand?" It's a question that has been lingering in my mind since I was on the bridge, but now I have the balls to ask it.

"No," Flynn and Aidan say simultaneously.

"I agree with Flynn and Aidan. It's too dangerous." Shamus's accent softens the blow of his words.

"Ava, there is no way. It would be a death sentence for you, or anyone, to ask. You wouldn't even be able to get the words out before they attacked you." Kieran grabs me by both arms and searches my eyes for an explanation. "Of all people, you know this—after what they did to you." He is trying to be quiet. Aidan is upset Kieran knows more than he does. "They are monsters in every sense of the word. But if this is something you want to do, I will go with you. Just know they cannot be trusted."

Aidan immediately shuts down Kieran and causes a scene,

causing pretty much everyone to leave the room momentarily into the entryway, minus Sarah, Kai, and Shamus.

"I believe some of them would help us if given the chance." I lower my eyes to the ground.

"No fucking way are you going to speak to him." Aidan knew exactly who I was talking about.

"He would see me." I look up to Aidan from beneath my lashes. Now he is fully focused on me and not Kieran. David was even frustrated with how much Dillion was willing to discuss with me. I raise my voice a little bit louder. "He would listen to me. I would just have to get him alone."

Now Aidan is irate. "I said no fucking way, and I mean it."

Kieran jumps in despite my eyes telling him not to. "Ava, you don't have to listen to this bullshit. He can't tell you what to do. You're the one who's supposed to guide us all, and he won't even listen to you. Plus, given past events, I would be with you."

Shamus holds Aidan back to talk to him and bring him down off the ledge as I leave the room and Kieran follows me out.

"Ava, look." He pulls me to the side where no one can hear or see us. "You need to be careful. You know I have your back 150 percent. But have you ever thought they wanted you because your brother might know you can acquire powers? Think about it. If they force you to kill, you would be the strongest. And then they could kill you, with the help of Dino. Or not kill you but, I don't know"—he starts to stutter a little because he's frustrated and trying to process everything—"use you for your unlimited power. If you want to see Dillion, I won't stop you. But bring backup. And before you do, do some research. Please don't jump into this lightly. Let's speak to my mother or find the witch. Anything. But keep the word of your powers secret. No one needs to know what you possess."

I nod in agreement and walk off and to the front door.

"If you want to come, we are going to the rain forest," I say as calmly as possible to Sarah.

She nods her head as Laila jumps in my arms, and all three of us step at once into the portal from the stick I once again stole from Aidan's study.

"I don't have many friends. Efron and Shamus are my life." Sarah wastes no time just jumping right into it, with us being the only two here, waiting for anyone else who guesses where we might be.

I move my fingers around, controlling the trees and the wind with Laila snuggled into my lap. "I don't have many friends either. Everyone I've known isn't who they've claimed to be. My friend Dino is my Shaddower, and Sofia gave me up for a man; and my old coworkers and friends know nothing about this life, and I want to keep it that way." I scoff at the thought of Sofia choosing a man over me, but I guess he is her husband. "But at least she set me free in a way." It's unbelievable to think about what a short amount of time can do to a person and how it can change lives.

"How are you able to do that?" she questions, looking at the trees.

"Just kind of happens." I could really go into more detail since she is so open, but I'm just not up to it. Plus, the thought of Aidan and Kieran alone hashing anything out gives me anxiety. She must have picked up on my vibes.

"So." She moves closer to me, and we are sitting right next to each other Indian-style, legs touching, looking out into the silence and peace of the rain forest as the leftover water trickles off the thick leaves. "Tell me about Kieran and Aidan."

"There's a lot to tell, and I'm not sure where to even start ..." I trail off thinking about it.

"Start from where you like. Seems like we have nothing but time."

I know what she means and decide to live in the moment with her as a friend. Why not? "Ever since I can remember, I have been having dreams of Aidan. So I was surprised to see him walk out of my dreams and into life. I didn't know we were soul mates and have been together in previous lives throughout the centuries. I felt this powerful connection with him. But to cut a long story short, I have a connection with Kieran, too, thanks to the woman who gifted me with my abilities. Ever since I met Kieran, there is now no face at the end of my constant dream. Aidan is no longer appearing there; it's just a body without a face. I know I will have to make a decision, but I can't help but feel like there is a piece of the puzzle I'm missing. I love them both in so many different ways. Aidan, though, always causes me anxiety, while I feel like Kieran is a safe nonjudgment zone for me. They are two completely different people, and I don't want either of them to suffer. But Aidan is cursed by Kieran's mother, and Kieran would apparently …" I don't want to dive any further and stop myself.

Thankfully she just dives right in. "Wow, that shit is heavy," she says loudly, making her voice purposely deeper. We both laugh. But she sees the sadness in my eyes and leans her head on my shoulders. "Bottom line is, with matters of the heart, you have to follow your heart, not your mind. If you were to shut your mind off, who would you want to spend every moment with for the rest of your life? Not out of obligation but out of love. You are going to have to make a choice sooner or later, and it will be hard. And with the way things work in this world, it will be a choice that has to be made in an instant, without giving you any time to think about it. Just know you have a friend in me." She sighs.

"So tell me about you and Shamus." I stroke her hair, and man is it nice to just have a girlfriend again, someone to just talk to about boys.

"I am in love with him!" She lets out a giggle.

"Well, that much is obvious."

"Believe it or not, we met in a grocery store, about twenty years ago—"

"So you are one of the lovelies who do not age? I am jealous!" I lay my head on the ground, and the dirt moves as my cushion.

"Yup!" I can sense her smile. "You can thank my mother for being a nymph. I age slowly. I constantly joke with Shamus about dating an older woman, and he hates it. We actually met because some man was making fun of my hair, and Shamus interjected. Now, could I have kicked that guy's ass? Sure. But I liked how it was all damsel-in-distress in the grocery store, so I let it play out. We looked at each other, and we just knew we had to be together. And without saying a word, we both knew we had powers and walked out hand in hand. It's that connection. And we have been together ever since."

"Believe me, I know about connections. Can I read you something I wrote? It's a letter, and I'm not sure when to give it to him."

Sarah sits up. I guess by the tone of my voice she has become even more curious.

"Since you are older and wiser, you can help me," I lightly scold.

"Definitely." She smiles.

I think back into my memory of me writing in secret, and I visualize the paper in my head. I raise my hand and the ground slowly moves beneath us; the loose dirt flies into the sky creating an imagine of the words that are in my mind, and we both read simultaneously:

> So, a question remains, one many people choose
> not to answer. Have you ever
> Been scared to love somebody?
> Afraid to take the risk?

I was one who constantly would invade the question,
Because I knew the answer, and it is yes.
I am afraid of getting hurt,
Afraid of hurting someone,
Afraid of risking it all to get it all.
I am petrified knowing, at the end of the day, it is the scariest decision I will make.
But it will also be the best decision I will ever make.

Sarah's eyes grow big with wonder as the dirt moves around more, readying the next words for us to read:

You came out of nowhere and into my life beautifully
And all at once.
I need you to know how much I appreciate you
And all you have done for me, but above all else I need you to know I love you.
Many people say less is more and to keep it short, sweet, and to the point.
So,
Here it goes.
Thank you.
Thank you a thousand times over.
Thank you for showing me love in a way I needed.
Thank you for loving me for me.
Thank you for opening my heart.
Thank you for changing my life.
Thank you for, well, being you.
This feeling, whatever it is, is unconditional.

Sarah has tears welling in her eyes. "Well that could be a beautiful love letter. It could also be a heartfelt letter that you give someone before you leave them. Are you addressing it to Kieran or Aidan?" She looks at me, waiting for an answer.

She's right. it could be either, and I haven't decided if I'm going to love him forever or leave him forever. I just needed him to know how I feel and how much he means to me. Rain begins to break through our shelter and pour down on us. The sound of the rain has raises me to my feet; throwing my arms up, I twirl in the fresh scent that surrounds me. Sarah starts to giggle and does the same thing. The ease of this moment is amazing—light, not heavy, even though my letter still remains in the air. As it rains harder, the dirt becomes mud and sinks into the ground, but the letter transfers onto a leaf and floats into my hand.

"Come on! Let's go train in the rain!" Sarah exclaims while jumping up and down.

Chapter 22

"You are going to go anyway aren't you? Talk to that Grimmer man?"

I shrug at Sarah's question, but we both know the answer. Kieran did bring up some valid points. I mean there are a lot of things on my to-do list, but I feel like this would be the most beneficial above getting my memories back.

"To give Aidan peace of mind, I will give him the courtesy of letting him know I am going this time. I don't want to keep secrets from him."

We're about half a mile from the training grounds, but we decide to walk and talk, nice and slow, now that we are out of the rain and back in the run. A smile grazes my eyes. I'm happy at least my pooch is loving life and having a good time.

"Shamus would kill me for telling you this. But just be careful. Aidan's ex is floating around here somewhere. Word on the street is the reason he didn't come to look for you right away was because she showed up and stole him away to talk. Yet, as Shamus so eloquently says, you don't want him ripping someone's head off. By the way, you should really change."

I choose not to acknowledge anything about Aidan's supermodel ex-fiancée at the moment. No need to make myself feel worse, as my uniform is completely wrecked, and I hope they have someone here who can mend it. "A shower might be a plus for me at this point, I could scare the skunks off."

She laughs and holds her nose. At least she finds me funny. I still have a redeeming quality left. This anxiety is killing me really. It's like everything is all bottled up inside me. Part of it makes sense. When I was younger, my dad would let me speak openly about my feelings, but now that I realize who the imposter was, it makes sense. She always told me crying was a sign of weakness, that talking about my emotions was silly or idiocy. This essentially left me to process my emotions all on my own, which led to me bottling everything up and having crippling anxiety. I always slapped a smile on my face and was happy and kind to everyone, but I was a disaster on the inside. Makes me really think the person Aidan loved back then wasn't like the way I am now. Thank you to my old, wonderful, magnificent counselor for getting me into writing to have some form of an outlet. But here I am back at square one, unsure of what to do or how to process it.

Once again, my mind is spiraling, until Sarah speaks up, "By the way, thank you."

She leaves me stunned, "For what?"

"Doing the right thing whether you realized it or not. We appreciate that you made everyone leave, for our safety. Higgins didn't put anyone first beside himself, so it was refreshing to follow someone who put us first. I am just sorry I couldn't blow shit up with you." A light glimmer hits her eyes, and they look like rainbows. Being completely honest, without question, she would have loved to blow shit up.

As we walk closer to the training ground, her hair changes to that intense lavender. Normally, lavender is a soft, airy, comforting color, but she changes its perspective, making it fierce and controlling. She wears it so well.

Those training look surprised to see us together, especially given that, less than twenty-four hours ago, we were in an altercation with one another. This is by no means a normal friendship to the human account, but for me and her it works. Since I have been placed in this new world, everything is powerful and about connection; it is all at once and nothing less than extraordinary.

Speaking of friends, Kai and Kieran are getting their practice on too. Casually sauntering over to the weapon tower, I grab two draggers. I quietly notice that, for some reason, I've grown fond of knives, which is just wild. Sarah, meanwhile, picks up a flail. Her one-handed flail has a relatively long handle compared to the others, with a chain nearly as long as the handle and a large, spiked ball attached to the end. Seriously, is she familiar with every weapon ever made? This shows her dark serious side and why no one wants to mess with her, even if she doesn't use her powers.

"Who wants to fight us?" She doesn't waste any time announcing us to everyone in her overly confident, cocky way.

Laila moves herself off the battlefield as though she understood perfectly how forthcoming Sarah was. She moves off to the side and lies down, covering her face with her paws.

"Come on, Buchanan, move your ass." Sarah glares at me looking at my pup. She is ready to go.

I waste no time meeting her, and we stand back to back.

She waves her weapon in the air. "No one?" She laughs evilly. She has so much fun with this.

I know it's all in good fun, but I see why no one wants to be her friend. She's intimidating. Better to be confident than make yourself vulnerable to attack. At this rate, her sheer confidence will turn people away. At least now I really know how her time warping works.

"We accept your challenge, fine mademoiselle," Kai jokes as he and Kieran step forth and bow down like they're back in the renaissance time, and it makes me chuckle.

Cornelia takes my gaze off Kieran as she walks up to him and starts whispering in his ear, purposely making eye contact with me. Is she just trying to get under my skin? Or am I being too sensitive? Perhaps the news of Isabel being around really just took a chunk out of my armor. Ugh! I hate that I just got jealous of her lips being so close to his ear. That boiling starts to rise in me, and I guess, even though it isn't apparent to everyone else, it is to him.

Kieran reaches for my hand, and I oblige him. He places a tender kiss on it before releasing me back to our simulation. Sarah, on the other hand, will not let up. When her hair changes, so does her personality; there is no joking or messing about. Yet still, that pulse is rising in my body, building up, until I convince myself to ease the growing storm within me, like lightning that wants to run rampant through me. I have literally never in my life been a green-eyed jealousy monster this bad, not even with Aidan and Isabel. This is a side of me I do not like or recognize.

"Ava, I love you. You know that she was just wishing me luck."

Oh, boy, why can he read me so well? Kai is looking at him, confused. But Kieran is serious and now let his gaze linger on me for too long. Everyone is starting to notice and pick up on the vibe.

I playfully smile at him, hoping he buys the smile. The words couldn't be truer. "I love you too. Now don't cry too badly when I kick your ass."

He chuckles.

Our moment took up too much time, and Sarah is ready to pounce. All the spirits of the earth take over me, the wind runs through my veins, and I lunge forward and kiss Kieran on the lips. Somewhere, somehow, someone in the crowd got a blowhorn and let that thing rip. The loud noise takes us all back, besides Sarah, who pounces at Kieran instantly. Whoever had the horn must have started to hit the button before I kissed Kieran; that's how quickly it all happened. I don't know if he is more shocked that I kissed him or at her abrupt one-up on him. She pays no mind to what happens, and they are in their own little battle world.

Kai draws his sword and hits me with a mischievous grin, one that says I saw what just happened, and so did everyone else; and that smile is duplicating right in front of me—over and over. He replicates again and again, until I am surrounded by at least twenty of him running around me in a circle. Guess we're using our powers on this go-around. All the Kais come to a complete stop and stand uniformly in place and take one step closer to me. All the faces have the same thick hair, smile, and stance; it's literally almost impossible to tell them apart. I turn to look at all of them. They're all dark eyed, but there is a giveaway in the real Kai's eyes. One, only one, has a true soul, an apparent twinkle in his eyes, something that cannot be replaced or removed. It is my soul reading but from a distance, not with a touch. I look into those eyes quickly to not give myself away. But a memory of him comes to me. I see him spending every hour god sent him to train, to work; no friends, no life, just pain—until Kieran and he became friends.

I keep turning in a circle through my vision. This is what I was able to do before—to know people's hearts, what makes them and drives them, to see into them, what makes them good or evil, or to see their hope. My visions change all the time. I am beginning to suspect I can also sense what could turn someone or change a person's heart.

In one instantaneous motion, I stop turning and pull my knife and thrust it toward Kai, holding it at his throat, careful to not push it at him too quickly or deeply. He lets out a large gulp, and all the other Kais suck back into his body.

"How did you know it was me? No one has ever been able to tell us apart, not even my parents." He looks as though they would be disappointed in him, like he has done something wrong by my discovery. They are the ones who pushed him to train so vigorously.

Kieran and he really have such a strong bond. I look over my shoulder to check on him, and he and Sarah are still in the throes of it. She hasn't used her powers to turn back time; she must really be vested in this.

"Intuition I guess." I look back to meet Kai's gaze, and I can tell he is disappointed in himself and in my answer. "Honestly, I would like to say I could tell by your eyes, which is, in part, true. But I saw something when I looked into the eyes of the real you. I saw a vision of you training, starting off so young, maybe three years old or something, and growing up within the vision, until you met Kieran. It's like my powers are getting stronger and pointed it out to me. There is only one true original version of each one of us, and the eyes are the giveaway, the gateway to the soul."

"Interesting, you are the only one—"

His sentence gets cut short by Sarah vigorously yelling to change opponents and do it now. She yells and immediately starts her assault on Kai. My legs quickly glide myself back, watching her go at it and Kai beginning to multiply. I bump into Kieran's hard but comforting body, and he presses himself against me before quickly turning me around to face him. The wind kicks up my hair, like even the wind and elements are trying to pull me toward him in our own little bubble.

"You smell like the rain."

Well, isn't that quite the odd statement? But it's one that resonates with me and is endearing to me, since I love the smell of the rain. No one else has ever noticed it, just him.

"I'm sorry about before. I don't know what got into me. It's like I became jealous and, in a way, wanted to mark my territory. But you aren't even mine to claim. I haven't made a decision, and I feel awful. But I'm happy at the same time, because kissing you … well, it just makes me forget everything and reminds me to feel—"

He knows now isn't the time, and certainly we have people looking at us right now anyway; no need for more whispers to wander back to town center. "Don't worry. I liked it. Let's fight—see if you can kick my ass." He places a chaste, tender kiss on my forehead and pushes me away in the same breath.

I feel paralyzed just from his lips touching me, in the best way possible. He crouches into his fight position, hands at the ready, and all I can think is there is no way this fight position is real. If it's meant to throw me for a loop, so be it. He looks like he is about to play the human version of frogger.

"Oh, I can, and I will. Just a matter of how to do it, Mr. Kilic." I shoot him a playful wink. And let's be honest, I couldn't hurt a bone in his body even if I wanted to. So I'm glad this is just a game, even if Sarah takes it as though it's life or death.

I cannot take him seriously when he is trying to be serious with me. Instigating my attack on him, I lunge into the air. But he moves swiftly and holds me midair and moves me down on the ground. Clearly, this type of simulation isn't going to work for either of us as we start laughing. We care more about each other than getting a win under our belt. This is actually a bit pathetic.

I try to kick free of him, but it doesn't work, as he brings me down to the ground. I think we both know this is just us being playful. His sheer force holds me down as he moves my arms up and beings to tickle me with his chin on my neck.

"Stop! This isn't fair," I yell through a fit of belly laughter, like I'm a child all over again. We take turns rolling around pinning each other and trying to go for the tickles, not even caring at this point who is witnessing it. I haven't felt this free in so long, just to laugh for no reason and be playful with someone; there are no words for how amazing this is. Yet it's probably uncomfortable for everyone else.

I look over my shoulder, and no one is even paying attention to us. All eyes are on Sarah and Kai. And then he once again has me pinned. I feel like I am about to pee myself and yell stop through another mass of laughter.

Then all eyes dart to us, making Sarah and Kai stop. "She said stop." I would recognize that voice anywhere. Aidan. He is lifting Kieran off of me.

Oh lord, not this, not again. You have to be kidding me, like I can't have one moment where I feel myself—one moment of just happiness and laughter without it all coming tumbling down. It makes me realize more and more I need to sort things out.

"Aidan!" I quickly try to shuffle to my feet, but I'm not fast enough.

"Do not touch me, Cross." Kieran's voice is cool, calm, and collected as his left hook meets Aidan's face, hitting him square in the jaw. It actually catches Aidan off guard, and he stumbles back. Everyone is surprised to see him move, like it's impossible for someone to take him off his game. Those hairs start growing, long, thick, and black, from Aidan's forearm.

I place myself between them and hold my hands out. Talk about déjà vu. The last time this happened, it didn't end well for me. "Please, not this again." It is a demand. They exasperate me.

"Ava, do not let this asshole tell you what to do—especially when all he does it lie to you." Kieran isn't even looking at me when he talks to me. He won't back down from Aidan. He is standing firm, looking him dead in the eyes.

"Enable her. Go right ahead. But you'll have to live with her injury on your hands or, even worse, her death. You do not know whether or not they will just hand her over to Victor!" Aidan is doing the opposite, talking to Kieran but looking at me intently, giving me the chills.

"Aidan, can I talk to you please, in private?" I take a deep breath and look at Kieran and search for Sarah with my eyes, not realizing she was behind me this whole time.

She gives me a nod of approval, knowing what thoughts are running through my mind. Aidan hasn't responded. He stands tall and firm with his hands on his hips, clearly trying to restrain himself and the beast that lies within him. It isn't helping that

Laila is growling at him and tugging at his pant leg. I think she's pissed at him for the fire. Or maybe it's something else. Either way, she is no fan of his.

"Please, Aidan."

It's like he just wants to see me grovel and beg for him.

I grab his hands. I know if I tell him something along the lines of let's go home, he'll leave with me. But I can't. The words won't come out. Home. The word *home* resonates somewhere deep within me and makes me once again realize I don't have one. Yet I don't feel homeless in my soul. I have nothing tangible to offer anyone at this point. Home is not a place but a feeling, and I feel like my mother is alive, and so is my father, no matter where he might be. Having words that trigger me or my feelings is getting complicated. I plead with Aidan, hoping he can see in my eyes I mean it; we need to talk.

He shoots Kieran a look that just isn't fair and takes me by the hand and leads me off the training facilities. He must have found his portal stick, as he is pulling it out of his pocket. And I slowly mumble to myself under my breathe about how that field is bad juju, and he and Kieran anywhere together is bad juju, and now I just try to lighten the mood.

"Why so serious?" I make my best Joker impersonation, and boy, is it just bad timing on my part to even attempt to make a joke. He doesn't even turn to acknowledge it or me. "You are really mad. Fine. We will talk when we get to your house."

"Our house," he corrects me.

"It was Isabel's house the other night." That might have been a low blow, but it is out in the open now, and I can't take it back. "It's not my house. It's yours. I haven't contributed to anything. For all I know, I'm jobless right now, with no house, no clothes, and no belongings. My car that barely got me to work blew up, and there's not a whole lot of money in my checking or savings account." I stop my rant for a second to catch my breath. But you know what? I have always been confident in the way I speak. Why did I rant when the real issue is the first thing I said. "You lie to me—about Isabel, the ring, whatever you deem necessary, and you don't feel bad about it because you tell yourself it's to protect me, when it isn't." There. *Boom*! Said it.

And in typical Aidan fashion, he ignores it and goes right into flattery. "Ava, you are perfect as you are. As for everything tangible you're speaking of, that's an easy fix. This is our home. You and me. Always." He pushes the hair behind my ears and gives me a soft kiss on the cheek that I don't avoid, despite his gaslighting me. "Plus, you have more money than you realize. You just don't know where it is."

I forgot about that part in the letter from my father; it's under the weeping willow from his childhood. "Oh and you know where it is?" I question him.

Laila rubs hard against my leg, distracting me and reminding me once again she is here. I stop and pick her up into my arms quickly before we transfer through the portal stick and back to our home and whisper into her ears as I pet behind them.

"What did you just say to her?" Aidan's curiosity is peaked.

"I asked her if she knew where the money was, and she licked me."

"Strangest dog." He makes a funny face and says, "Let's go home. Our home."

Our home. I don't know if I love the sound of it. Or am I terrified of it?

Chapter 23

"Ava, you have to stop doing this to me. Stop doing this to yourself. I know you get frustrated when I control you, but it really is for your own good. Why can't you just listen to me and do what you're told?" He sits on the side of the bed, bent over with his face cupped in his hands.

There is just silence since I am just not sure what to say to him at this point. He treats me like a child who always does nothing but disappoint him. I wish I could be what he wants, but I'm not someone from ages ago. I'm me, who I am now.

"You run off on me, time and time again. I know I left you in Mexico, but that was for your own safety and to make others aware of the situation. Please forgive me." Now he's the one pleading with me. "Ava, you're the only person capable of breaking me and tearing me apart, and you do it every time you run off."

I kneel before him and remove his hands from his hurt face. "I don't mean to hurt you. I did what I needed to with Victor because you don't listen to me. You're so set in your ways, and only your way is the right way. I forgave you for Mexico so long ago, and none of what I do is in retaliation to that. You lie to me. You withhold the truth and pass by it like a leaf in the wind never to be seen again." How else can I possibly explain this to him? How many times can I have the same conversation but in different ways. The pain on his face kills me. "Knowing I cause you this kind of pain kills me. Maybe it would be better if—"

"Don't even say what you have rolling around in your mind. The day you leave me for good is the day I will rip my own heart from my chest and take anyone else's who stole you from me. You get angry or upset with how I feel, and you run—not telling me where you're going." He looks deep into my eyes. "The most beautiful green Ava." He touches the side of my face and sighs at our contact. "You could have at least left a note or something." The touch of his hand tells me there is something more, another piece to the puzzle I'm missing. His sincerity is real, but he's holding something back, keeping another truth from me.

Should I bring it up? Or drop it? Drop it. It is best, at least for now, to keep the peace. "I'm sorry. I promise not to run anymore if you promise to hear me out and at least listen to what I have to say, and process it, before you go all beastly on me." I give him a kiss on the forehead, something I have never done to a man before, and he pulls me onto his lap.

"OK." His voice is so meek and small I can barely hear him say the word. He pulls me in, cuddling into me, and I know this is the best time to bring it up.

"So, given this conversation, now would be a good time to let you know I'm going to see Dillion. I know you disagree, but try to see the logical side of this, beyond me just being in danger."

His arms tighten around me and his fists clench. He is trying to control himself and is really having a difficult time with it. "Ava …" He trails off, attempting to hold in what he really wants to say.

"Aidan, I know you think it's a death wish, and you aren't ever going to agree with my decision here. But it is the right thing to do or at least try to do. I cannot sit by and watch all of these people get hurt if I have the means to stop it. It would be like watching mass genocide. Imagine living with that on your conscience." It's the truth. I'm passionate about it.

"They have made their bed." He is firm, and his unwillingness to see past that and give people a chance at redemption is scary.

"I won't accept that. You know me better than anyone else; that's a fact. And I would love your support. Tell me, what do you think the old Ava would have done?"

"She would have stayed with me. She would have honored my wishes."

"Well, then, I guess I'm not the old Ava you knew. There is a difference between doing something for someone you love and being controlled by someone who says they love you. Would you stay back if I asked you?"

His silence is once again deafening. He knows he wouldn't. Did the old me really just sit around doing whatever he said? I mean, sure, if it really called for it and it was that important to him, yes, I would, but not with so many lives at stake.

"I am coming with you." He looks me in the eyes and I know this is a nonnegotiable. In fact, it might actually be nice to have him tag along. I mean he is, after all, Aidan Cross.

"OK." No argument on my part with him for once. "Do you have a phone I can use?" I ask him but then immediately question if I can even use a phone in this parallel universe. I mean, I've seen him use one, but was it like magic or just actual cell phone service?

He pulls his cell phone out of his jeans pocket and hands it to me. "It will work, but they won't be able to track it. The signal will bounce all over the place."

Honestly, I have a lot of questions about that from a technical perspective, but that's for another day. It works, and that's all I need to know.

I punch a number into the phone and saunter away from Aidan as it rings.

"Hello?" Her voice is so fragile, like it is not her at all, she has been replaced with an insecure, scared little girl, not the strong women I have always known.

"Sof, it's Ava."

She gasps on the other end. Clearly, she never thought I would be calling her or speaking to her ever again.

"Ava! You're OK! Dios mio!" She rambles off, speaking Spanish so quickly I cannot understand a word she's saying.

Just as she said my name, angry footsteps stomped toward her end of the phone. She was yelling, trying to say something as the phone was being taken away from her.

A voice I don't recognize breathes into the phone and starts speaking harshly. "What do you want? We have just buried her husband."

Sofia is yelling in the background, letting me know they are on speakerphone with others in the room.

"Give me Dillion." I am being as forceful as possible. Instantly realizing that isn't going to get me what I want, I know I have to play a part.

"Why?" the same voice asks.

Part of me wants to go off on this person. Why are you asking so many questions? Just do it. I channel my inner submissiveness. Sounding like the meek, submissive girl Aidan really wants, I talk to the crowd on the other side of the phone, knowing Dillion, knowing he wants the same thing. "Because I have changed my mind. I'm leaving Aidan and want to speak to Dillion. So put him on the phone, please." Fake tears will do the trick.

I look over my shoulder to see Aidan, looking green in the face, like he's holding in his vomit. He knows I had to say something to get Dillion on the phone. He just doesn't like that I had to use leaving him as the reason—especially to the man who was really trying to cause me pain.

Sofia is mumbling to herself in the background, or maybe she's trying to talk to someone. This goes on for like five minutes—a debate on whether or not to pick up the phone and talk to me, when the voice who is now disappeared told her not to. I really do not like what this has done to Sofia and what her life has changed into. In fact, it's repulsive. The footsteps approach, and the chatter in the room stops. Dillion is yelling at someone for not getting him the second I called.

"Ava, my darling."

Ew, god, just the sound of his voice makes my skin crawl. I hold in my vomit and gulp it down, remembering to channel my inner submissive.

"I hear you left that pathetic excuse for a man and want to see me."

Aidan is listening down the phone, but he cannot take it anymore and starts to pace around the bedroom.

"Yes, please forgive me for not seeing the truth you were speaking. Where can I meet you?" I need to sound more vulnerable for him to believe this. "You aren't going to hurt me again, are you? I am already scared." I let out a little fake sob.

"No, sweetheart, I only hurt you before to make you see. Now that you have your brains about you, there's no reason to hurt you. Let's meet back in your old town."

I cringe as he speaks so casually to me, like an abusive lover would do to a victim. I flash back to the inescapable changing dream, my town, blown to pieces. It can't be true. My house is already burnt to the ground, so how could that ever come to fruition?

"I will need some time to get there. I've been on the run, since, well ..." I trail off. He doesn't need to know anything, "I can make it there by tomorrow night. I will call Sofia's phone from this number when I get close." I am kicking myself. I need to keep in character and not act like I'm making some business transaction. He might catch on.

"I will meet you at the butcher shop."

I wonder if he knows the owners are dead.

"No one will hurt you as long as you are by my side."

Gag. "Thank you."

I hang up the phone and search for air to reach my lungs, but I'm overtaken by the vomit sitting in my throat and can't even make it to the bathroom before spewing it all over the floor. Laila curls into my lap to comfort me. Aidan looks completely and utterly uncomfortable with how things just went on the phone and doesn't even come over to check on me sitting in a pile of my own vomit. At least he did as he promised and remained calm, but I'm not calm at all. What the hell am I doing? Was Aidan right this whole time?

"We will just have to sort out a game plan. If they see me walking up with you, they will be up in arms. I cannot risk you getting hurt." He shakes his head, but my eyes are watering from the throwing up. I pick myself up off the floor and take my shirt off and use it to cover up the mess I have made before walking into the bathroom to clean up. Laila follows me in, and I shut the door behind me and quickly lock it before he has the chance to reach it.

We briefly talk through the door about involving Shamus and what game plan we should make. He wants me to open the door of course, but that phone call is probably the most uncomfortable situation I have ever been in. And to pretend like Dillion is a good person, even with seeing a glimpse of good in him just makes me sick.

Aidan's phone rings, and I can hear him answer it through the door.

"This is Cross."

I can hear Freya's voice on the other end. My hearing must be getting stronger too. Kind of crazy. Well, everything at this point is kind of crazy. I wanted to laugh at his greeting. Of course she knows it's you; she's the one calling you.

"What do you mean you cannot find Ray?" The serious version of him is in full force.

I start the shower and put it on full blast on hot, finally removing my tarnished jumpsuit. I'm going to steam up this whole room. I look around the perfectly modern bathroom to find adjustments on the wall, one for lighting, one for radio, and another for the skylight above the shower. I dim the lights, open the skylight, draw, the blinds and hit the play button. I'm not sure what song this is, but I can dig it; it's soft and relaxing, just what the doctor ordered.

With my toe in the shower, I jump right in, not giving my body a chance to acclimate. And nothing is too hot for me anymore. The sound of the music takes over my body as I tenderly sway back and forth, washing my body and rubbing the shampoo through my hair. I'm just rolling through the motions, of something I will never take for granted again, until the music shuts off, and it becomes eerily quiet.

Somehow, Aidan got in here, not like it would be difficult for him. I see him through the glass shower door. I turn the water off and, without one ounce of shame, walk right out completely naked. I give my best sexy confident walk over to the robe hanging up, grab it, and don it—all while knowing he cannot take his eyes off of me. I pull my dripping wet hair to the side and turn back to look at Aidan. He's standing there in his pajama bottoms, shirtless, and holding a small remote. He clicks the remote and holds one hand out to me while carelessly dropping the remote on the floor.

I recognize this song; it's the song we danced to in Mexico that first night, and it brings a smile to my face as he wraps his arms around me and plants a kiss on my lips. Is he trying to remind my heart of our moments?

"It reminds me of how you told me I came right out of a dream." He flashes me the biggest smile. and it melts my heart. If only he could be this loving and sincere all the time. I love him. There is no doubt. But my heart is torn in two. And Isabel. Where has he stashed her? He pulls me in, and we dance right here, on the bathroom floor, not caring about the puddle my wet hair is making or the fact that we constantly disagree. This moment is about us.

He lifts my chin. "I have loved you my whole life, and I will love you for the rest of the lives I live." In that moment, we share a passionate, vulnerable kiss, a kiss that shows what we really mean to one another. I know what I must do.

We spend the rest of the night dancing, laughing, and getting to know each other all over again—something we've never made time for. He gives me a tour of the grounds, including the movie room, game room, spa area, and garden. We find pure relaxation in every corner of this vast estate, and Laila loves the large backyard—although she disappeared in the tree area for like forty minutes.

Aidan is cooking me dinner to end the night off. Just everything about the way he cooks, the way he moves so confidentially in the kitchen, the way he gives me little tastes of food, and mostly how he throws pasta against the wall waiting to see if it sticks captivates me. This is a side of him that's rare, like it's bottled deep down, and he only lets it out once in a blue moon. Speaking of Blue Moons, I could go for a beer. He spends this time getting to know someone he already knows inside and out, but I get the joy of learning everything about him all over again, even if he still avoids certain topics. I know he loves me, and it is a constant, never-ending love. But in a way, I have been blessed. Not only is he my soul mate, but I get to fall in love with him time and time again—no matter how much he pisses me off. Only this time it's different because of the Pureck's wishes, something I'm having a hard time processing. Laila is even starting to come around to him, although I don't think I could ever completely block what happened from my memory.

Of course, Aidan brings up the whole marriage thing, like really pushing it, like really hard this time around. As in, he wants to set a date. But this all feels wrong to me, so soon. I mean, only tonight has he really taken the time to get to know me as the new Ava. When I brush it off, he keeps making sure to say he's going to make me his wife; and that's it, no further discussion on how I feel about the matter or what my views are. Honestly, he is taking such a sweet subject and turning it into something not romantic. Right now, it doesn't matter, and I let it go because there's no way it could ever happen in the near future with everything we have going on.

Yet, the thought lingers in my mind. If I were to marry Aidan, I would be losing Kieran in the process—even though he respects me, and I know we would remain friends. I'm not sure I'm ready to take back the piece of my heart he has. So, in a way, I'm happy the marriage talk can't progress right now. This is all so selfish of me. But for once, I'm thinking of my own happiness and what that actually means and how to accomplish it. What if I forget what would make Aidan or Kieran happy, like Kieran has pretty much told me to do, and just concentrate on what would make me happy?

I cannot lose Kieran, not yet.

"For as long as we live, I will carry you across the bedroom threshold every night." He lifts me and kicks open the door to the bedroom, and places me delicately on the bed.

"Until you get old and can't lift your own arms." I giggle away any of my earlier thoughts.

"Lucky for you, I am a beast who ages very slowly, so my body wont decay," he quips back in a serious tone.

Let me bring it back to the funny side. "Good, you won't have old saggy balls." I laugh loudly, and he gives me a scolding look.

"No sagging here." He places his hand over his junk and gives it a cocky lift while shooting a wink my way. I was expecting him to make some reference to how, in previous lives, I wouldn't say such things. Instead he says, "You always had a morbid sense of humor."

Boy, if he thinks that's morbid, he hasn't seen anything yet. If only he could have heard how Kieran and I talked to each other after the battle. He pulls me in closer and snuggles into me, against the robe I never took off, and I purposely rub my butt against him.

"I know what you are thinking and no. Not now. When we are married."

"You know times have changed. And we have done it before. So,why not now?" Something more lingers in the air.

"Well, you don't remember last time, so this time it will be right. Plus, I won't do it while Kieran is still in the picture. I want it to be about my love for you and not staking my claim."

Well, as much as I hate to admit it because my sex drive is running through the roof with my sexual frustration, he is right.

"So, you never did tell me where your ring went."

With that statement, I roll over and place my head on the pillow and drift off into sleep, ignoring his last question. I guess I should be thankful Aidan doesn't want to take advantage of me while Kieran is in the picture. I wish I could explain or comprehend this feeling my gut is giving me that's telling me there's more. Maybe I will ask Kieran. But how? I mean I know Aidan thinks I leave him, but I have constantly left Kieran time and time again. It doesn't feel right. A tear wells in my eyes, but I dare not sob and make Aidan think I'm awake.

Right now, I have a man lying next to me who wishes to uphold every ounce of my moral fiber when it comes to sex and not ruin me, until we are married. Why can't I accept that? Because of his lies. My dreams slowly take over and shift me into a familiar scene, with bombs in my small town and a man grabbing my waist. But no face appears.

Chapter 24

"Sir, we were not able to penetrate the base, but we did see them moving some objects up this way, including a large metal machine. We were not able to get a good look at it before they loaded it into a trailer."

Aidan has a firm hold on my hand as one of the high-pitched searchers tells him about what they've found.

We're standing outside the convention center. Beats me why we didn't actually go inside. But the poor guy nearly burst all of his words out at the first sight of Aidan. The other groups stand behind him nodding in agreement.

"So, all of you have seen the same type of machine?" Aidan asks them and then looks down at me.

"Yes, all of us. Now, Jacoby, you know, Flynn's brother, Judd's other son, was able to hear one Militia talking on the phone, saying they have found a way to harness it, but the plans were blown up with their other facility, along with the woman who created it. She had just figured it out and was unable to log in her instructions."

I am waiting for Jacoby to answer, but he doesn't, he just waits for the attention to pass by him, but I cannot help but notice how much Jacoby looks just like Flynn. No surprise there; they look like the younger version of their dad, except Jacoby has huge curly hair that's barely able to be tamed.

"Hey, Marcus!" I yell at him passing by and into the convention center, disturbing Aidan's conversation.

I tug my hand away from his, and he lets go when he realizes it is actually Marcus there. So much for any form of trust, but OK. I run over to him with Laila closely following, stepping on my heels.

"Hey, Marcus, can I talk to you for a second?" I grab his arm and stop him on the middle of the sidewalk, like he was purposely trying to ignore me.

His gaze doesn't break from the destination where he wishes to be but for a second to glance at Laila.

"Look. I know you want to get in there, but this will only take a few minutes. I promise!"

I'm not used to him being so withholding of information. He sighs and sits down on the small brick wall that lines the sidewalk, and I join him, sitting with my hands folded in my lap. "I just want to kind of confirm something with you."

"I'm not surprised. I forget that you have forgotten sometimes." He chuckles and instantly the mood lightens and puts me at ease.

"So, for as long as I can remember, I have been having the same dream, over and over again, which now I believe to be some sort of premonition. I know premonitions change based on decisions people make. At the end of the dream, it would always be Aidan, but now the face has been muffled out, like he's being removed. I just don't understand why."

Laila jumps on the brick wall too and lies across my lap. The intuition that animal has is unlike any other I have ever come across, not like I have had loads of pets.

Marcus sighs. "Kieran." Then he starts shaking his head and presses two fingers against his temples on either side of his face.

"Kieran?" I repeat after him. I know what he said, but I'm just grasping his words.

"Yes. Kieran. You and Kieran weren't supposed to meet. That's nothing new to you now." He is getting frustrated but is quick to change the tone back to normal. "Aidan and I knew of this curse and what the Pureck has said, so we were just going to keep you two apart. Plus, Kieran's resentment towards you at the beginning was a great help. But you are drawn to one another; the closer you get, the more Aidan will disappear.

"Then, as always fate took its course, and we couldn't keep you two apart any longer. You said for as long as you remember Aidan was the one in your dreams, but he is fading now because you have met Kieran, and even destiny is not sure who you are ending up with. The choice is yours. You just haven't made it yet, even if you think you have. Aidan was the one you loved through the centuries, the one you relied on. Please don't tell him about this fading dream; it would crush him. If only I could have kept you and Kieran apart longer, he would have gone to the other side. But my moral compass came into play, and I couldn't kick him out of the safest place for him. My loyalty to Aidan is strong, but so is my loyalty to doing what's right—can't sacrifice one for another. Plus, Aidan tells me you two are getting married. Once that happens, everything will solidify and will go back to the way it should be—"

"What do you mean once we are married it will solidify everything?" I sternly question him as though this is an interrogation. I knew something wasn't right with the way Aidan talks about marriage, like it is a chore and not just about love.

"Ava, you don't know?" He genuinely seems perplexed.

"There is a lot Aidan doesn't share with me, obviously—"

"Aidan or Kieran, neither of them told you?"

Come on. Out with it Marcus! Now Kieran is withholding from me? That doesn't seem right. I want to shout at them from any rooftop I can find, but now just doesn't seem like the right time.

"Well, there is no easy way to say this. I mean, are you and Aidan getting married? He made it out to me last night like we should start planning the wedding."

Laila huffs at my side.

"I cannot marry someone who hasn't even proposed to me. And I'm not even sure that's what is best for me at this point."

Marcus shifts gears a little bit. "I cannot stand to see that man lose you again, and this isn't my business to share. I thought you already knew. We are like brothers."

Poor Marcus, I know he feels responsible for the fact Aidan and I aren't the way we should be, but it's not his fault. "Marcus, you are a wonderful person, inside and out; none of this is your fault. I won't hurt him. Please tell me."

Even though I speak with conviction, I can see he does not feel any relief. "Ava, with all due respect, you don't know that yet. Even if you don't want to, it might happen. And if it does, may whatever god exists save us all."

He stands and walks away. And I feel torn, right through the middle of my heart, like a dagger is ripping it open. I am a lump, and there is no point of moving. Guess I never really did make my decision, or my vision would be clear.

"Ava, are you OK?" Aidan's voice is filled with apprehension.

I look at him from beneath my lashes and reach my hands to his face. I hadn't realized I had been crying. Thankfully, it's early in the morning, and there aren't as many people walking by as normal. I can't imagine what a goon I like right now—sitting alone on a brick wall, crying to myself, like I'm some old crazy cat lady.

"I'm fine." The second my feet touch the ground and I stand, we are not even an inch apart; there isn't even personal space to breath.

"You are not fine. Was it something Marcus said?"

For whatever reason, the tears won't stop flowing. I'd rather die than hurt Kieran or Aidan. "Tell me why you want to get married."

"Because I love you."

It's a truth but also not a whole truth.

He goes on to tell me I would never hurt him. I know there is a falsification in his words, just to make me happier and lift my spirits, but I can see through it. Aidan sees Shamus approaching, and I nudge him in that direction to give me space, and he actually listens to me. Aidan walks into the center and tells me he will meet me later. I am actually surprised he's leaving me on my own. He must know I'm actually really upset and think it will keep me from doing anything. Aidan and Shamus walk into the center together, and I am astonished to see that Sarah is not with her man. But I guess everyone needs alone time.

I walk alone.

Where to go?

That spot.

The spot Kieran showed me.

My feet start walking, following that starry line once more, leading me to my destination.

His comforting arm reaches around mine, and instinctively I lean into him, smelling him, breathing him in; and all butterflies are gone and replaced with calmness. Kieran plays with my hair and leans into me, and I lean back into him, so comfortable, so at ease. I'm not surprised he's found me here—at our spot. I'm just looking for clarification, for answers to a never-ending cycle of questions rolling around in my mind. We sit silently for a few moment, or maybe an hour. I'm not sure how long. I just know his presence makes me feel at peace.

"Whatever you need to talk about, I'm here." His words are mellow and willing.

"What is so important about marriage for me? Why does Aidan push it on me? Marcus said you knew something." Plain and simple, no hostility at all.

"I didn't even know Marcus knew to be honest. I knew Aidan knew, which is why I have always had such an issue with him." He takes a deep breath, and his shoulders relax, and I just rest my head on his shoulder, letting him speak in his time. It's like there's a judgement-free zone between us. "How do I even say this to you?" I give his hand a reassuring squeeze, and a few moments go by before he talks again, really searching for the words. "I never wanted to put pressure on you the way Aidan did, which is why I never said anything. I believe that your choices, especially with your heart, should always be your own and free from anyone else's influence."

"And I can't thank you enough for that, for always letting me be me."

He leans his head on my head resting on his shoulder, and a weight is lifted from his voice with a secret he has been keeping. "I always wanted the choice to be yours, no matter what that meant to me, or no matter how long it took you—months, years, or longer. I would have waited. Aidan is being impatient and, quite frankly, an asshole and wanting you to marry him because he knows what that means. It's the last part of the curse, or more like a foretelling, something my mom never even told me. I had to figure it out on my own, because in her own way, she wanted the decision to be yours as well. When there is a split connection like ours—it has never happened; it is unheard of; you are his soul mate, but we literally share part of a soul—it is told that, whoever you marry and then consummate the marriage with will win your heart, while the other will be destroyed. This is what his curse meant; only if his heart is broken can he be killed.

"It's probably why he wants to seem so generous withholding sex before marriage, because of how things will play out. You need to sleep together after marriage to solidify the bond and connection for it to overpower the other. Marriage will unite your spirit—a vow given in front of Mother Nature herself. So, he would need to marry you and sleep with you to overpower our connection, and that is the only true way I could get him out of our life. But you see, I never even wanted to bring that on you. I never told you because it didn't matter. If you chose him and that's what made you happy, so be it, but not out of guilt. I would never force you to marry me or even be with me for my own benefit or to save my soul. I would rather die than use you like that or play with your heart like that. I would only want you to marry me out of love, no other reason. So I withheld it from you because you didn't need that on your conscience too. I truly believed it didn't matter, and I'm sorry that now you have this weight on you." Just by his body language alone, I know he really didn't want to have to put that on me.

"How do you know this if your mom didn't tell you?" There is no animosity between us, just respect.

"Do you trust me?" He asks me so sincerely and with hope in his eyes as he turns to look at me, breaking our cuddling comfort position.

"With everything I have." Just truth.

"Remember how before you asked me how I knew certain things, and I told you there was something I would tell you when the time was right? Well, this is part of that. Believe me, I wish I could tell you, and I never would withhold something from you unless it was absolutely necessary. And this, this is for your protection and safety."

There is something different about the way he conveys that to me than how Aidan does. It's something serious, and because he doesn't play the safety card often or at all, I know it to be true. I can look into his eyes and see his soul—not that I even need to do that to trust him with everything I have. Every fiber of my being would trust him with my life.

"What if I wanted to make love to you right now. What would that mean?"

He closes his eyes at my question, taking it in, knowing the thought has crossed his mind, but he has never acted on it. When he opens his, our eyes connect, and the passion between us is stronger than ever before.

"Ava, as much as I wish we could—and I would if you really wanted me to; the desire is there, trust me—to answer your question, I really don't know. I think, if we did, you would still be connected to Aidan, and then forever this battle between us would go on, if we broke the sanctum of what the curse entails. To me, it is not a curse. It led me to you. If you chose him, I would respect that. I would become the villain that everybody expected me to be. I would take that role on without hesitation if it meant you got to choose your own path." He runs his hands through his hair. This is the first time he has gotten frustrated, but his voice is still kind. "You get to make your own decisions, and I just want you to be happy. And that has nothing do with the curse or the prophecy; that is just how I feel about you."

That's a kind of love I don't think I ever expected to come across in my life, one where someone would give literally anything, including their soul to make me happy. He would watch the world burn if it meant I was happy in it. I can see now that I could cause his darkness to rise; the same is apparent with Aidan.

"I love you, Kieran." I can feel a tear start to swell in my eyes. So, I switch the subject, based on something I previously heard, before he even has the chance to talk me through it more; it would just add more tears to the stream. "You said let's go see your mother. When was the last time you saw her?" There is no easy way to just ask this part. But with how we always have been together, there is no holding back now. "Kieran, is your mother OK?"

He leans me back in to the comfortable position we were in before, me leaning on his shoulder and his head rested in line with our hands intertwined, my fingers grazing the tattoo that peaks out of the bottom of his sleeve. "Every second the prophecy comes closer to the moment of truth, the weaker she gets, especially given the fact Purecks cannot wield nature if another one is doing it, and they heal through nature, too. As your powers get stronger, hers get weaker, and she is not able to heal herself, especially if one of the other Purecks is using magic, which I get the sense is happening. It has been a while since I've seen her, but we are always able to find each other with a guiding starry light."

"A starry light." I look up to him, and he sees it too—a starry light surrounding us in a circle on the ground where we sit. The wind, earth, trees, everything moves around us, in beautiful colors, but we remain steady in the center of the circle. It is like the wind is singing a sweet melody as chimes come from the rainforest.

Our eyes lock, and in this moment, there is nothing but love, to be solidified when our lips lock. Laila jumps off my lap and exits the circle as Kieran and I find passion within each other. Our heartbeats sync up; this is a kiss to end all kisses, one I never want to end. I shift onto his lap, straddling him, and his hands softly graze my back, down further and further, until he passes over my butt and pulls me in closer to him from the back of my thighs. We lose ourselves in this moment until the wind stops, and everything comes crashing down harshly.

"Ehhhemmm." Sarah clears her throat aggressively, and I let out a laugh, not moving off of him as he keeps gazing deeply into my eyes. "While I hate to break up this moment, which, guys—totally happy for you." She is joyous, giving off some of those overly happy vibes she does with Shamus. "Aidan, well he is looking for everyone. And so is Marcus ..." She trails off.

And almost in unison, we all say, "Marcus always finds what he is looking for."

Kieran and I both shake our heads.

"But seriously though." She shoots us a wink and two thumbs up, almost imitating the Fonz.

Kieran and I take our time getting up, stealing a few kisses along the way. We walk hand in hand with Sarah leading the way back to town center. This moment has me giddy like a schoolgirl. Kieran and I actually agree to keep our happiness and our hands to ourselves right now, for so many reasons.

Sarah walks next to me, and Kieran gets the hint to scoot along. "Girl, good choice, for what it's worth. Aidan does nothing but hide the truth from you." As your friend, I need to tell you something," she adds, starting to ramble. "And I'm not trying to add fuel to the fire, and I also don't want to ruin this happy moment, and I know you have a lot going on—"

"Sar." I chuckle. "Out with it."

"Well rumor has it, Isabel showed up here because—"

My eyes get bigger and bigger looking at her. Come on, my neck moves forward, nudging the information out of her.

"She's pregnant. Now I don't know the logistics if they can even or if that's even possible, but that's what Shamus told me."

"Excuse me? What?"

"Yeah, Isabel is pregnant. Aidan found out the other day when she came to speak to him. I assumed he didn't tell you—especially now the whole town is planning some like elegant wedding."

I don't know how I am able to even focus on anything anyone is saying at this moment with that news being dropped on me. Is it even possible? Can they? I guess I have never thought about the logistics of any of this. But I mean, they do have to repopulate somehow. Do they do it in werewolf form or human form? OK, enough of this train wreck going through my mind and back to the conversation surrounding me.

They have finally determined what is going on. My town is tiny, which is probably why Dillion picked it in the first place, so they will most likely have other Grimmers walking around to make sure I'm alone. The best bet is for me to go in alone, and everyone else be on the outskirts in case they're needed. I'll wear the bracelets Sarah and I used to communicate before. Kieran didn't attend the meeting. I guess there's no way he could not look smug. And I didn't even get to tell him about Aidan yet. Honestly, he is my best friend, and I share almost everything with him; it feels weird not to.

Shamus says that Kieran told him to tell the group that Laila needs to come in with me. It would put up a weird front if she wasn't; everyone knows we're inseparable. Aidan rolls his eyes, but since Shamus is the one who actually said it, he agrees. They hand me a fancy-dancy contact lens that will project everything I'm seeing to them in a hologram. It also has the capability for them to hear my conversations, which I'm no entirely pleased with. But I can't be too picky at this point, especially since everyone is going along with me. I plop it in my eye without even using a mirror—skill. My face is sour and scrunched when I realize how much thicker it is than my normal contact lenses.

"For fuck's sake, Ava. It's a contact lens, not a bowling ball. You don't have to tilt your head so much to compensate for it." Aidan is flabbergasted at my ways.

"Frustrated because you are now a baby daddy, huh?" Oh no, it slipped out before I even realize it, and I am standing here mortified. So is he.

But his confidence exudes through. "We can talk about that later."

Of course we can, just like everything else.

His demeanor shifts closer to me, in a dominant way. "You love me just as I am. And we will marry in front of our friends and loved ones. This will not be a hinderance."

Well, nice to know he thinks so, but what the actual fuck?

Finally, I'll be going into an uncomfortable scene not in my uniform but in normal clothes—dark wash bootcut jeans; Vans; a white, long-sleeve V-neck; and an actual knee-length jacket with a cool multicolored pattern. Perfectly comfortable and normal. But I need to give myself that friendly reminder that, if I morph in normal clothes, I will be completely nakey. So let's not do that under duress. I wear long, high socks so I can stash a knife in the side, and it's completely unnoticeable under my jeans—win! I tinker around with the idea of stashing one in my waistband, but it looks too bulky under my tight shirt. I reach for the grenades, just to look at them.

"Ava, what the hell are you planning to blow up? Put the grenades down." Aidan shoots me a quizzical look, and Shamus laughs.

I think blowing stuff up is my new thing—not very healthy, but it was kind of fun. I would so get out of hand if I brought these along, but I can't really bring anything—nada, zipolla.

This is the first time I have seen Shamus in a T-shirt, and he is proudly flaunting his buff arms in Sarah's direction. His arms are covered in brands that are raised on his skin and look to be of an intricate design.

I hate that I am still attracted to Aidan, no matter how much I want to hate him. It is literally impossible. Even dressed down, he is still looking ever so hunky and dominant.

This just sucks. I guess that's what it means to be connected to someone in my case, until marriage, until unity of the sexual acts. I make myself chuckle, sounding so professional in my mind, just thinking about doing the dirty. Damn that sexual frustration, and this isn't making it easier.

Shamus fills his bags with gadgets and weapons, pretty much grabbing one of everything that will fit in it as he goes down the line of weapons hidden behind a hideaway wall in Aidan's study. He has a full walk-in armory. Aidan doesn't pick anything out of his weaponry room, but I guess Shamus stocked up enough for the both of them. We're lucky he isn't leaving here with a bazooka.

Everything is all set, the plan and my nerves. At least I know they will be able to see me if anything goes astray. He and Shamus have gone over scenario after scenario with me—escape plans, and procedures, anything I need to know—yet my brain won't process it all. Aidan leans into me like he's about to place a kiss on my lips before he begins to speak again. My eyes widen as I lean back away from him.

"It won't change anything." Is he talking about his baby? Isabel? The plan? I'm not sure, but it was a promise on his tongue that he quietly whispered and then continues on more loudly, "We are going to use the portal you entered through. I want to stop off at Marcus's house to leave behind a few things in case anything happens." Aidan is serious and making sure everything is covered. He has a backup plan for his second backup plan, which is a lot better than me flying by the seat of my pants.

Within moments, we are going through the motions, and time starts passing by rapidly. Everyone has already left except Aidan, Shamus, and me. Out of the house and to the portal we go the same way I came, on the cloud. We ride the cloud up to the entrance and look down on the place I've grown so fond of. Or maybe it isn't the place but, rather, the memories it holds for me, whether good or bad. Yet a feeling sinks in my stomach, having me believe this is the last time I will be looking at this place from this view or even the last time I will get to see the majesty of the rain forest and that secret spot where I can see all parallels and the spot it holds in my heart. With a deep breath, the trees slowly wave back to me as the wind blows through my hair, taking it out of a ponytail and loosing it so it falls down below my breasts—affecting no one but me. Shamus looks at me with raised brows, but Aidan doesn't question a thing.

The cloud stops, and Aidan places his hand against an invisible wall and advises me to jump through. I pick up Laila in my arms and hold her tightly and, without breathing, jump right through the cushiony, soft, cloudlike wall. The same suction feeling I recall from the first time around overcomes my body, and I'm back in that dark room with miscellaneous objects all around. I do not let Laila go. She is making me feel safe and comforted, and I know I provide the same thing for her—or at least I hope so. Who knows anymore?

Minutes pass by and no one has joined me, so I make my way through the darkness and into the diner. The diner is packed full. It's everything you would expect from an old-school diner—red bar stools, milkshake signs, a juke box, very retro everything. It seems not one detail has been changed since the day it opened. The paint is chipping off the walls, and there's a teenager behind the counter. She and I make eye contact. She's dressed like she's from the '70s. I wonder if she is and just hasn't aged. She looks to be no more than seventeen. She nods her head to the front door like she's speaking to me, so I take my cue, quietly walking. Not one person has turned his or her head in my direction, and it's oddly quiet, not a lot of chatter at all.

As I start exiting the building, I press too hard on the door, and the bell goes off, all too loudly—turning the heads of the diners, as well as the six policemen strolling the otherwise quiet street. One police officer sees me and starts running across the street, rushing over to me, looking as though he has seen a ghost. He is saying something into his cell phone. I take a few steps back cautiously but remember who I am. I look into his eyes and his movements don't stop. He barges through the door of the diner and brings me back inside with him and looks at the scared teenager behind the counter.

"We just swept this area. How did she get in here?" Then he looks down at me and places his hands on my shoulders. "Are you OK, Ava? My name is Agent McGuire. We've been looking for you."

I wouldn't have thought that at all based on how frantic he was with the people in the diner. I am confused and really don't know what to say, so I keep quiet, but Laila is practically howling in my arms, so he continues walking through the diner door and down the street. "Come with me." His voice posed it as a question, but it wasn't. He has his hand around my lower back, guiding me where he wants me to go. "Your boss, Mr. Harrison Greene, filed a missing person's report."

That makes me smile. My boss is such a good person. But it also makes me sad at the same time. The agent gives me a funny look, searching my face to decipher the mixed emotions. "It's nice to know someone was worried about me."

Agent McGuire relaxes his face, and even the wrinkles on his bald head go away. He looks like a typical police officer to me—nothing appearance wise stands out. But then again, that would be hard in that uniform I imagine. His demeanor changes as if he's gone from thinking I'm some sort of psychopath to seeing me as a lost woman. Boy, some men really do love the damsel-in-distress bit. They want to be the hero. And hero is written all over his face. He is tall, unlike his partner, some lady cop, with a serious attitude problem and a rocky jawline. She's sporting a unibrow and a short, red bob hairdo.

He leads me over to the edge of the ambulance and asks me a bunch of typical questions—none of which I answer, simply because I don't know what to say. And honestly, I'm still terrified of lying to the police; that's the human side of me. McGuire reaches out to take Laila with his large hands, but I hold her tight, and she growls at him.

"I guess she will be staying with you." He turns his lips up to a half smile and seems entertained. His eyes are as green as mine. He looks far too young to be an agent of the caliber he's claiming to be. There is a whole police force out there, so I'd rather have one point of contact and try not to doubt him. Plus, the more he looks at me, the more I can get snippets of his life. He has taken his younger brother in since their parents died. And recently, he bought him a puppy to keep him company while he's working. He is a good man.

"How did you manage to find me, Agent McGuire? How is Mr. Greene?"

He studies my face, curious those are the questions I've chosen to ask him.

I feel an overwhelmingly compelling need to apologize. "I'm sorry." I fold my fingers together and look down at my hands.

He sits next to me and places his hands on mine and gives them a reassuring squeeze, something I've seen in a lot of TV cops do. "Please, call me Liam. Your boss said you called him, and we tracked it here."

Of course they did. Silly question on my part.

"He said there was a struggle on the other end before the line went dead. We did further investigation and saw that your house had been set ablaze; it has been categorized as arson. Your boss is on the way to the precinct to see you."

Liam gestures for me, and I go inside the ambulance, and he shuts the door. He advises me to sit up on the stretcher, and I just do as I'm told. He smacks the inside of the vehicle hard two times, and we take off. He takes a seat next to me on the stretcher, and I bring my legs as close to my chest as I can with Laila sitting on my lap. Aidan and Shamus and everyone else are going to flip when they realize I'm not there and see the police combing the streets.

"What police station are we going to?" We have been in the vehicle for quite some time, and I have forgotten to keep track of the path. Most police stations are local and wouldn't take this long.

"We are taking you back to the local police station near where you live. They have questions for you. We would also like to take you to the scene of the arson and ask you a few questions there—maybe walk you through it. It will help jog your memory.

I haven't forgotten one thing, other than my previous lives. But this works in my favor. They are taking me exactly where I need to be anyway, so this kind of works out for me for once.

Chapter 25

My house is in pieces. Vomit rises in my throat. All the lies make me sick to my stomach. The only remaining parts are the porch and the entranceway. The rest of the house is in ashes on the ground. Laila jumps out of my arms and runs around the debris-filled yard, barking and stomping on everything. How can I still be having my dream when I'm standing on the ashes of my house and everything it held?

"So … you never leash that dog?" Liam seems surprised that she's just running around. He kicks up the soot with his foot, and it creates a cloud around us, so dry it causes me to cough. There hasn't been any rain here. This area is perfectly preserved, and not one ash has been washed away or carried away by the wind.

"I have never leashed her. She won't go anywhere. Between me and you, I think she has a little separation anxiety." I speak to him over my shoulder as I walk around my old stomping grounds. Step one, have anxiety. Step two, get a dog with anxiety. Step three, have emotional separation anxiety from each other. Done and done and done.

"I can see that. Your boss, Mr. Greene, has already set up for his company and other contractors to come here tomorrow to start the rebuild for you, and it looks like you own the land with no previous mortgage, so you will be in a good spot."

My mouth drops to the ground as Liam hits me with this bomb. "You can't be serious. I don't have money to rebuild a house." There's no way I could ever afford this even if I found the buried treasure.

"Don't worry about the cost." Harrison wraps his arms around me to give me a huge hug from behind.

I turn to look him in the eyes, and his sincerity exudes out of him. The soot begins to settle back down to the ground, and I give him another hug.

When I pull away, he has to know how I feel. "I can't let you do that—not after everything I have put you through. Why would you do this for me?" I shake my head, and only god knows what face I'm making. But I'm sure flabbergasted doesn't even begin to cover it.

"But I want to. We want to. We are in the slow season anyway, so many of the men will be working on it, too. minus Shane. He never showed up for work after the charity event. My father heard about what has happened, and he and I both came to the agreement this was the right decision." He tries to lighten the mood and make a joke. "Plus, it's a charitable donation—a total tax write-off."

Oddly enough, that does make me feel better. At least it's helping him too. His smile makes me smile. I give him another hug and whisper a sweet thank you into his ear.

When he releases me from his care, Liam walks over and extends a hand that, without hesitation, Harrison takes. Oh, to be normal again—when a handshake is just a handshake. They shake hands and banter like they have known one another for years, and I just zone out and walk away but catch the ending of their conversation.

"Thanks for finding her, Liam."

"Of course. I still have to take her to the precinct to get a statement and actually talk about what has happened." He sounds more agent-like now than he did earlier. I guess at some point we have to get down to business.

I shift through the rubble and move toward the remaining front porch. I place my hand on the barely there railing gently, and it collapses immediately upon my touch. I put a foot on a stair and the same thing happens; it crumbles beneath me.

"Don't go in there."

What the fuck? I jump back, startled to hear Aidan's voice next to me. I turn in a circle like a crazy person and have to stop myself from acting like a strange bird. It takes me a minute to realize he is speaking to me somehow through the lens I'm wearing, and it sends vibrations through my body with each word he says. I definitely don't think it's meant for two-way communication, and it scares the shit out of me.

I stand still, turning my back to Liam and Harrison so they can't see me talking to myself.

"First off, no way is he paying for this. I will have the cost taken care of." Yet again, Mr. Serious has made his presence known.

"You were listening?" I shouldn't be surprised, but I am considering the fact I even forgot I was wearing this stupid thing.

"I will collect you from the police station." His words are short and clipped.

"That's probably not a good idea. I'll meet you at the location we discussed."

How could he even want to do it when we decided as a group collectively that everyone needs to keep a low profile? Plus, right now, all of this is working in my favor. The Grimmers are watching and seeing my every move.

While I turn on my heel to walk back to Harrison, Aidan keeps speaking to me, but I do not let it faze me. "All of this will come to a close soon." Again, there are so many things Mr. Secretive could be talking about, but now is not the time to dive into it.

Harrison and I are face-to-face once more. "We'll add a security system here for you and your mother," he says.

But my eyes fall to the ground. "My mother …" I try to get the words out. "She won't be returning here anymore. She's the one who started the fire."

Liam gestures for me to move to the side so he and I can talk in private, but I remain firm in my spot.

"Ava, I'm so sorry." Mr. Greene goes to wrap his arms around me, but Liam stops him.

"Let's discuss this further at the station."

"Yes … I think this place is haunted." No one questions me, especially not Harrison with those sympathetic eyes, looking at me like I am a lost puppy dog or a charity case.

I call for Laila, and she comes running from the field. Liam smiles and whistles that he's impressed with her recall. Liam opens up the door of a large black SUV his partner is driving, and Laila jumps in with ease, while I stumble all over the place.

Harrison closes the door behind me and tells me he'll meet me at the station. The ride to the station is a little uncomfortable. Liam is questioning me about my relationship with Mr. Greene, asking why would he spare no expense to rebuild my home, with improvements, not just the way it stood before? Liam said Harrison went over all of the plans with him, and it's quite impressive. His partner is blissfully ignorant, and the tone Liam is using is turning harsh. Like I planned this myself for my boss to rebuild it? Like that even makes any sense at all? He is on a fishing expedition, but he is barking up the wrong tree. Point-blank, I ask him if he's trying to insinuate something—no need to beat around the bush here, just being extra ballsy.

He apologizes me to and insists that people these days just

aren't that kind. But Harrison is; he's a giver. As a police officer, he shouldn't be so quick to judge—talk about a character fail for the line of work he chose.

He jumps right in asking questions about the fire, and as odd as it sounds, I would rather answer them here in the SUV than in the precinct. It might cut down on my time spent in there. In hopes that, if I keep talking now and keeping the dialogue open, he'll be more forgiving and let me leave, I dive right in headfirst. I give him information without giving him too much information, just keeping him on a need-to-know basis. I talk to him about my mother and her problems and claim that she's always been emotionally unstable. Her whereabouts are unknown to me, but she did set the house on fire when she got upset with me. Only, first she attacked me, knocking me unconscious. He is taking everything in but seems a bit lost and asks what the argument was about. Point-blank, I tell him it was over a man. He leaves it at that and doesn't ask who.

He then goes on to tell me there is evidence that a bear was in the house. He believes my story about my mother but accuses me of withholding some information. The bear could have happened after the fact, rummaging around for food or something. I play dumb there. Then he starts getting to the good questions. If I was knocked unconscious how did I get from point A to point B? And how and why did I make a call to Harrison? His questions are asked in a nice way, not an abrasive way anymore? He's changed up his tactic, realizing quickly the latter isn't the way to get what he wants from me.

It's right about now I am wishing I didn't make that phone call to Harrison at all. It might have caused more problems than good; this is what Kieran warned me about. If only Sarah could turn the past back farther. I wouldn't even have to worry about this. I made my bed. It's time to lie in it and accept that my decisions led me here. The police are so blind to everything around them—us, the

Militia, the Grimmer. It's amazing another world exists within their own without them having any knowledge of it. I am living proof of that. All of this seems so trivial in comparison.

Maybe this will put his mind to rest. "Even if I told you the truth, there is no way you would believe me, not for a second. Just believe I didn't want any of this to happen."

"I can tell by the look in your eyes that you mean what you say. Believe it or not, I have been doing this for a while, even though I look young, and normally I can sense a lie. I believe you. But could it be something so outrageous and out of this world that I wouldn't believe it?" He's confused, but I suppose, as an investigating agent, there isn't much he hasn't heard.

"Yes." Simple and to the point.

Knowing Aidan is listening in to my every word makes me uncomfortable. He's probably going to ream me a new one for even saying some of the things I've already said and can't take back.

The car comes to a stop, and Liam leans in closer to me. "I would believe you." He is short and sweet and to the point. He is being true.

He gets out of the car and shuts the door behind him. I try to exit, but the handle is on child lock, Liam has opened my side of the door, and I hop out, with Laila following. Liam gestures for me to carry her in the building, so I open my arms to her, and she jumps right in without me even saying the command.

The interrogation room is chilly and bland—just the typical two-way glass you see in all of the TV shows and the table with two chairs. Someone tried to take Laila from me when I entered, but that didn't go so well for them. Simply reminding them that, if I am not under arrest, I can leave at any point shut him up really quick. However, the one thing I did have to comply with was the body frisking, during which they found all of my knives. I knew I shouldn't have shoved that extra one in my shirt last minute.

The door flies open, and in comes a livid Liam. "Ava, why the hell were you carrying so many knives on you?"

I expected this reaction to come. "I need to defend myself, plain and simple."

"Defend yourself from what or who? What is going on? Is someone after you? Did they cause the fire to cover their tracks? Where have you been? I need answers in order to protect you." Oh, the famous words.

"No one can protect me other than myself. I am the only one with the power to make the decisions that could protect me." At this point I have already said too much, and I keep putting my foot in my mouth. But what am I supposed to do? Blow up the police station with my laser vision? I mean, come on.

There is a bunch of chatter on the other side of the two-way glass, getting control over my powers does have its benefits, my sense of hearing has never been so good, there are so many voices, some I do not recognize and I know it's time to shut up. Liam keeps digging and digging but isn't getting anywhere with me at this point, and I feel kind of bad; poor guy is just trying to do his job.

He raises his voice to me and turns around. "Ava, how can I help you if you won't talk to me."

Oh, good, he is playing along with this good cop routine now. I keep quiet, and he storms out of the room with the same hostility he came in here with.

I wish I could say I'm shocked at who is just casually walking through the door, but I'm not in the slightest. The door doesn't even have a chance to close before Aidan is entering the room and walking over to me.

"I told you not to come here. It is too dangerous. You could blow this whole thing!"

He shoots me a look telling me to keep my voice down and leans on the edge of the table. He speaks so softly that the conversation is private, "There are no Grimmers in here, and Shamus is on guard. Relax, baby. They have a terrible stench to them. I can smell them a mile away; it's a wolf thing. We cannot leave you in here. Come, let's get out of here." He reaches his hand out for me, but I don't take it.

For once, I would like him to listen to me. I'm sure he covered all of his tracks, but this area could have someone else watching it in a matter of seconds. They know I'm here. They have to. He grabs my arm and pulls me up. Fortunately for him, I do not decide to act like a toddler and become dead weight but, rather, shake him off and stand up myself, while whispering to him and letting him know that, for the record, I am mad. I pull open the door, and Liam is looking at me questioningly. I roll my eyes as Laila follows behind me.

"Mr. Cross, it is a pleasure to meet you." Liam extends his hand out to Aidan.

Sometimes I forget that, even in this world, he is a big deal. I continue walking, and Liam runs behind me, trying to catch my ear in a free moment. All the men are asking Aidan about his football team and business stuff and what investments they should look into—typical guy bullshit. The kiss-assery is above and beyond.

I navigate my way through the small police department and Liam is just chiming questions in my ear about how I know Aidan and why he barged in here demanding to take me home. Then Liam bursts into laugher, and it stops me in my tracks. We lean against the same wall and are only inches apart, and I can feel the goodness radiating from him.

"So, how long have you two known each other? How did he know you were here? You might not want to run off without speaking to your boss first. That man was worried sick about you.

He is in the waiting room." He taps his fingers against the wall in what appears to be a nervous tick of his.

I ask him to lead me to the waiting room, and his face lights up as he pushes himself off the wall, waits for me, and starts leading the way. Liam clears his throat, prying for me to answer his other questions.

"Guess you could say I have known him my whole life."

Strong arms grab me from behind and wrap around my waist. "Don't be modest; it has been centuries." Aidan chuckles. "At one point, you even agreed to marry me."

Well that makes Liam look at me twice. Sure, Liam might not think I'm unattractive, but I'm average in comparison to Aidan; everyone knows it.

I shake my head and laugh it off. "That was a long time ago." A random sighting of playful Aidan almost draws me back in, and I know it's to mark his territory despite everything we have going on.

"But you two aren't married now?" Liam looks at my hand and sees there's no wedding band.

Aidan releases his arms from around my waist and walks to the other side of Liam just as we enter the waiting room.

"Nope," I quip, and that is that.

I scurry off to Harrison, who is anxiously flipping through a magazine. "Harrison." My voice is so meek and heartfelt. What do I even say to him?

"Ava, what's going on?" He's shaking his head at me, and I try to formulate the best answer I can.

"I wish I knew." That's all I come up with, but I speak to him mildly as he holds me at arm's length. "My life turned into a whirlwind, and I'm sorry you're involved even in the slightest." Even deep breaths aren't helping me in the slightest at this point, and I feel like I am going to have an anxiety attack. My palms become sweaty, and my heart is beating faster and faster, until I feel light-headed.

"Then where did you go? Were you kidnapped?"

I wish I could answer his questions. But like Kieran told me, the best way to protect people is to let them go and live on in their lives.

There is a woman in my vision. Her face and hair are covered in a dark cloak. This vision takes over me. I'm not able to navigate through it like the others. She has two different colored eyes that are pierced with pain. The eye that is bright green looks deep into my soul. The other, a deep blue, looks in the opposite direction, on purpose. She is trying to talk to me. She is feeling the room spinning, just as I am. Harrison keeps repeating himself to me, but his words fade, and my voice won't speak.

Aidan and Harrison are arguing with each other. Harrison quips back about how, whenever Aidan is around, bad things tend to happen, and everything spirals out of control. He insists on taking me to a hospital, but Aidan denies him. I manage to get out a few words to Harrison, using all of my strength.

"Mr. Greene, I am so sorry, but there is something I have to do."

My ears are losing the ability to hear sound through the spinning. The woman pulls her hands to her face and covers those storytelling eyes and falls to the ground. My body naturally responds the same way. There is no control. I know it's her. It's the Pureck. Cassiopeia. I can feel her. She is whispering to me.

"Ava!"

Aidan's sweet voice trails off into the distance. The two different colored eyes are back staring into me. She is not here, but when she drifts, she takes me with her. I try to open my eyes but have serious difficultly; it's like they're anchored down. I let out a squeal, and then I'm going into the darkness.

Chapter 26

Aidan and Shamus are speaking to one another casually. As my eyes peek open, I see am in the woods, woods that I recognize, ones that were close to my old house. My eyes perk open to see them hovering over me. They look confused about what happened, but aren't asking any questions. They know that time is of the essence. Shamus mumbles on, as I'm still coming out of my fog, about how somehow, he diffused the situation between Aidan and Harrison and convinced the detective to let me go into his care. The last thing I am even concerned about right now is asking questions. Talk about being pulled away from the mission at hand.

Aidan places his hands on my arms and keeps talking, but I only catch the tail end of it when my mind is clear and back to full focus. "Now, let's get you into that base." His voice gives away that he is not thrilled about the idea still but is going along with it still. "This is where their stench starts to grow strong. Shamus and I will be invisible from this point on. You will walk to the butcher shop, and we will be on the rooftop across the street."

"So, this means you two will be holding hands for the remainder of the day." I laugh pretty loud given the circumstances but immediately cover my mouth; the last thing we need is more attention, not like anyone can hear me out here.

Shamus shows a large grin. "And we will enjoy every minute of it, right, pookie?" He smiles at bats his eyelashes at Aidan, who returns the favor with a barfing sound.

Shamus takes his hand, and they disappear before my eyes.

Aidan speaks a few words, but I am too far ahead to understand him. Whatever he said was enough to shut Shamus up from his never-ending chatter. There must be Grimmers in this area. I'm on edge more now than I was the first time I ran into Huffnalgers in the woods. There could be more of them, along with unlimited Grimmer forces—how comforting.

I decide to take the shortcut to the butcher shop through the woods and around the back of the shop, instead of directly through town near the police station. A tightly closed tree canopy lies above me, preventing any light from being shed in this area. The trees have once again created a path and close behind Laila and me, not even letting Aidan and Shamus pass through. The roots of the trees are moving, kicking up dirt and leaves into the clean air. The path is leading directly to my house; it has looped me back around. There are forces trying to break through the barrier the trees have created. Laila jumps into my arms, and we run to the house, peeking through the path. So close, yet so far away.

Growling and pounding against the barrier, something large is trying to break through, but the trees leave me covered in encroaching shadows. One light remains toward the end of the path. The tree branches and roots are moving and swatting away the opposing forces with ease, and the wind breezes across my face, assuring me everything will be just fine and pushing me out into familiar territory.

My house now has a mass of supplies in front of it. I guess whatever Harrison's conversation with Aidan was, it kicked him into overdrive—as opposed to what Aidan probably wants. Do I really want this place rebuilt, with all the lies and memories? Even if I didn't, I couldn't tell that to Harrison. I wish the memories would have burned with the house.

My thoughts are interrupted by Laila's growing. She circles me and growls into the abyss and kicks dust up with her hind legs. She looks like a bull at the ready. All too quickly, she moves from behind me to directly in front of me. She points her head to the sky. A beam of multicolored light appears from the sky, landing in front of me. When it disappears, Dillion stands in front of me, accompanied by a man I've never seen before. There is no hint of color as the beam quickly evaporates.

"You look ridiculous." I laugh and joke to him, hoping he cracks a smile, and he does.

"I wanted to impress you." He turns his lips up in a wicked grin and runs his hands over his finely pressed suit.

Now, I have always been one to think a man in a suit is attractive. However, given the circumstances, he is just being an over-the-top egotistical bastard.

"How did you find me? I didn't call yet." My eyes shoot back and forth between Dillion and the nameless man. He is short in stature, round, and kind of looks like a really hairy dwarf. He too is dressed in a suit. I am getting some serious Dr. Evil and Mini-Me vibes.

"We've been watching your house. I wanted to make sure you were completely honest with me."

He moves and circles me like a lion does its prey, and it sends chills up my spine. That boiling is growing deeper and deeper inside of me. I have to control this. I have to act as though I trust him, unconditionally. I mean I'm the one who begged him to see me. "And? What conclusion did you come to?" My brow raises at him, and U turn my lips to the side, trying to ignore the fact that everything Dillion does makes my skin crawl.

"You are innocent. You came alone. For whatever reason, your boss is rebuilding this trash hole for you. And that cop Liam is far too nosey for his own good and now must be dealt with."

Great. Now he means to harm the cop, just to prove a point. Awesome. I want to defend everyone, but I need to get through this portal first or gain Dillion's trust.

"And who is this sour-faced gentleman?" I point to the man next to him.

He runs his hands through his greasy long hair and wipes the sweat off of his face. "Hector." He barely gets his name out as he hacks up mucus. He extends his hand to me for a shake, and I take it.

The handshake's lasting far too long, and Dillion breaks it up.

"Hector here still hasn't learned his manners." Dillion speaks down to Hector, and it makes my stomach churn, but his Mini-Me keeps quiet as he continues to berate him around. "But he has some skills that do come in handy. Show her what you have there." He slaps his short companion on the back of the head hard, and Hector walks over to the crumbling house and hits the remaining standing part hard with his two bare hands.

The few spots remaining fall at his touch. Not one inch of the house is now left standing.

"Your boss is rebuilding it anyway." Everything he says and does disgusts me.

The wind picks up, and I turn to look over my shoulder. The barricade from the trees has softened, and the trees are back in normal position. Aidan's aura is coming this way but not close enough.

"So, he is essentially your bodyguard? I figured with you being such a strapping werewolf, you wouldn't need one of those," I bitchily tease him, and it feels good, and he loves it.

"Now, Miss Buchanan, that's no way to treat someone when you are going to be a guest in their house." The low rumble in Dillion's voice shows me I struck a nerve and not a playful one.

Laila jumps into my arms and starts growling at him. She bites him as he reaches to touch my arm, drawing blood.

"Fuck! That damn dog is not coming with." He tries to rip her out of my grasp, but I don't let him.

The escalation of what he is willing to do is showing in his eyes, but there is more behind them. Pain? I need more time with him to figure it out; there is more beneath the surface. Anguish even, masked with rage and oblivion. My gut instinct tells me to run, faster than my aura can keep up.

That's exactly what I do, but it doesn't stop the blood from Laila's teeth from dipping onto my shirt. I turn back to look for him as I hit the mini city center, and no one is following me. I must have lost them.

I bring my head back to center, and he is right in front of me. "How did you do that?" Why am I even asking him? It's not like he's going to tell me. But there is no way he can outrun me. Is there? I should burn him to bits with my special eyes, but maybe I can still salvage this.

The town is completely destitute. There is not a soul in sight. If I were in an old western movie, there would be a lone tumbleweed floating around the center of the road. Shit. Of course I would stop right in front of the butcher shop on accident.

Hector appears through the air in front of me, holding a stick similar to the one Aidan carried around with him in the safe zone. Dillion looks at me smarmily. He was pushing me to see what I would do. He raises his hand to me and stops right as his hand is about to harshly graze my face. He was going to hit me, but something inside of him made him stop as he is locks eyes with mine and lowers his hand to the side. I release Laila from my arms and tell her to run. She is my weakness—my everything. I would do anything to keep her safe, and I cannot have them using her against me. I would crumble. Dillion knows that. He gestures for Hector to track the dog down, but she is long gone by now.

He shoots me a curious look. "Why did you let her go?" A hint of evil touches his smile in his eyes.

"Because even though I want to be here, I cannot risk her." Well I should pat myself on the back for that answer; it was brilliant, and his wicked smile fades from his face.

"Very well then. Come." He kicks the glass of the butcher shop door down and insists on walking through the shattered glass. He just wants to leave carnage in his wake.

"Will I get to see Sofia?" My voice becomes a bit higher pitched in excitement. I hope I get to see her, just to lay eyes on her and know she's fine.

"David would have never allowed it if he were still here with us. But now it's up to me." There is the glimpse of what I was seeing behind his eyes—him wanting to do something for me. However, those nice eyes soon glaze over once more as though he is in a trance, and he leads me to the back of the butcher shop. He opens a heavy white door that leads to the large, refrigerated storage room. Large slabs of meat and full pigs hang from the hooks in the ceilings, and my body keeps smashing into them as Dillion leads me on his path.

We continue walking through the never-ending maze of pigs, lambs, and other animals. I try to keep my wits about me and my stomach from churning as he walks me past the human section. He is keeping people on ice here. This row seems like it's taking an eternity for us to get though. All I can see is the blood and hanging dead carcasses.

This place is absolutely massive. But finally. we reach the back—the darkest place in the whole shop. But there against the black wall is a symbol—illuminated in red, it looks like fire is about to pop out from the background surrounding it. The fire moves against the symbol on the wall. The symbol itself looks like an upside-down Y with a G intertwined inside a square box.

Dillion places his left hand inside the box and the symbol on the wall, all while mumbling words that make no sense to me.

Just like that, the portal opens, and he reached his hand to me to take it.

"Are you ready to pay the price to enter?" He coolly looks at me, and I nod.

He pulls a living body off of one of the hooks, while the portal still runs open in the background. It is Officer Liam hanging with a hook through his chest and tears streaming down his face. There is no time to even comfort him as Dillion picks up a butcher knife and lodges it into his throat. I am the last face he sees before he dies, and I cannot even shed a tear for him like he deserves. I just reach out to grab Dillion's hand, bringing him back to the entrance of the portal with me.

"Good girl. There is potential for you yet."

My gut is sinking to the ground, and disappoint in myself runs raging and unchecked.

My eyes cannot believe what they are seeing as we leave the freezing darkness and walk into the blinding, flaming eternal heat that even makes me sweat.

Chapter 27

Their, I guess I can call it, safe zone, is like ours. However, a few less elements create it. The burning and flames are coming from the two large volcanos that spew lava and bubble over. No one is bothered by the overpouring, since there is a magical netting that stops it from destroying their town. Their town is vintage gothic looking, very medieval. They have a training field just like we do. Their eyes must be used to the shadows, as it's constant dimness here. Part of me expected them all to look evil and like devil creatures. But while that's the vibe the town gives off, the ones who reside here don't look like that. They have diverse, eclectic taste and different styles. They look every bit normal as they train and work, continuing with their day-to-day, preparing just like we are.

I am not brought down on a cloud but, rather, on a burst of lava, with Dillion still firmly grasping my hand. The lava doesn't even burn my Vans. In the back corner rests a tiny mountain, about three-fourths the size of the one located in our safe zone, and it looks to be used for cooling off the weapons they've made. No machine in sight here. Their town gives off dark and gloomy vibes, but it's so much vaster than ours, with amazing, tall architecture. There are no cute suburban-style homes but, rather, tall, dark metropolitan-style buildings that shine silver metal and give a beautiful contrast to this otherwise murky place.

"We are constantly surrounded by darkness. No light shines here," Dillion says as we jump off the lava and onto a huge metal slab that now brings us down to the ground.

I feel like I'm being drifted down through the gates of Mordor into the poisoned lands. Despite everyone looking normal, there intentions reek through their bodies. None of them believe that humans and our kind should intertwine. Humans are peasants to them and should be destroyed or used as their slaves, not treated as equals. They are willing to destroy anything in their way. How are Dino and Victor with the Militia and not the Grimmers? What is the Militia offering them at this point?

As we get closer to the drop zone of the training field, pieces of ash cling to my body like saran wrap. I want to be in and out of here as quickly as possible. Fireballs scatter right past us and land on the ground, leaving huge indentations that the students make use of. Dillion takes off his suit jacket and throws it to the side, not caring that it gets incinerated before even touching the ground; it turns into burning ash and blasts into our faces. A piece of burning ashes gets into my eyes and causes me to temporarily lose vision.

Dillion is actually concerned for me, but I can feel the contact melting in my eye. I cover my eyes and blink it out. He reaches out his hand to me to make sure I'm OK. I take it and jump off of the hunk of metal and onto the ground. No doubt Aidan and Shamus are freaking out at the lack of vision on their end now, as I flick the burned contact to the side without Dillion noticing. Thankfully, I still have on my bracelet to alert Sarah. Hopefully, the boys take that into account.

They have so many people training down here—their numbers are far greater than ours. Granted, I do not know the numbers in all of our other safe zones, but if they have just as many as we do, this is a hard call. I cannot believe so many people think the way they do. Light outshines the darkness. The Grimmers have all sorts of beings here—from Golfenites to Centaurs. There even are a few Medusa-looking men and women here.

"No Huffnalgers?" The surprise rings through my voice as Dillion leads me through their battlefield.

Everyone stops when they realize my presence here. The intensity of their glares is overwhelming—along with the fact they want to kill me. Yet no one makes a move toward us.

"The Militia control most of them. Whoever controls them must be very powerful and not a human; that's for sure. I've managed to obtain a few, and I use them to keep nosey people, such as your boyfriend, away from this base."

"Which boyfriend?" I joke to him, but boy he doesn't find it funny. Good thing the device is gone so Aidan couldn't hear me or Shamus.

Dillion stops to look me in the eye, and even though those training haven't made a move, they are intent on us as he tucks a stray hair behind my ear. "He has been searching for us, Aidan, but he'll unable to ever find us. Now that you are here, I can use you against him." I hate how his hand is lingering behind my neck, inching me closer to him.

"I doubt that will work. He is back with his ex anyway. Can we talk in private?" My exhale reaches his face, and his lips are moving closer to mine but stop an inch away, and they turn up into a half smile. I have stopped breathing, just waiting to see what he will do.

"Of course. Come this way." He takes my hand once more, and I am able to breathe as we leave the battlefield and head to no-man's land. We are walking farther away from the city and battlefield to an open area that appears to have nothing in it—just a blank space between the mountain and one of the many volcanos. There are two large ones, but up close you can see there are hundreds of small ones. My newly acquired vision gives me the ability to zoom in and search the area. There is a house, surprisingly large but tucked away so it's not easily visible; it just blends into the scenery, making it appear obsolete.

"Oh, Ava. I am just so excited to have you here. The possibilities." He runs his fingers up and down my arm, making my skin crawl. Now he is excited, creepily so, when earlier he was about to strike me in the face. He needs to be on medication, but what dosage could help a werewolf?

"I am glad to be here." What a lie. I force a smile, but part of me knows he isn't quite buying it.

We pass by another volcano, and he is practically pulling me in the direction of the hidden house. Once we get through the heat, a cold chill takes over—the chill coming off of the mountain is pressing against my face, relaxing me. The heat and the chill are in constant collision with each other in this exact spot.

"Wow," I say in astonishment when I look up, and Dillion turns back to look at me in awe of this magnificent sighting.

The heat and the cold are colliding with each other. You can see them. It's like they're dancing together, not fighting. They're working together to keep this exact spot neutral. Even in this dark, evil, malevolent fiefdom there is a mutation, with the elements, in a natural way, trying to keep the order.

"How do you notice this stuff?" He is actually making an honest inquiry. He walks closer and looks up taking it in. "I have been here for a while, and I have never even realized this exact spot exists in this way." He reaches his hand above his head and twirls his fingers in the middle of the two elements, fire and ice.

"Unbelievable, isn't it?" It brings a smile to my face. He looks like a kid right now. "My body just senses this stuff."

He pulls his hand down quickly, making eye contact with me along the way. I look into those childlike vulnerable eyes and see his truth. He has let his guard down. There was a huge wall put up, but in this instant, I can see everything. I can see what the Grimmers have done to him. They held his family captive—his mother, father, and sisters. They slaughtered them right in front of him and only left him and his bother alive. They needed to use him for his position. He was famous, so people would follow him and turn to their side. They made him a symbol, a face of the cause. But he is not the one pulling the strings. They are keeping his bother alive and use that to wield him in whatever direction they desire. He has gained their trust enough he believes they will let his brother go. He is doing all of this for his family, and they have him under a spell to do their bidding. But it is moments like these that break him free, allow me to see his vulnerable side. There is so much more to his story.

I try to dig deeper, but his eyes glaze over and turn wicked again. "David's brother is coming this way. We must go."

He grabs my wrist violently and leads me to the house. It is clear there are reflective mirrors on the outside, making it camouflage in that scene. David's brother has just walked out of the house when we arrive, and Sofia is cowering behind him, afraid to make a move. His brother is his identical twin; there is no telling them apart. I have to get her out of here, but would she actually leave?

I peer over Dillion's shoulder and try to make eye contact with her. But she won't even look me in the eye; in fact, she does everything she can to avoid my gaze. When he realizes what I'm trying to do, he maneuvers himself so I cannot even see one inch of her. I want to throat punch him, but I have to play nice right now.

"Dillion, I need to talk to you without him in the room. That is what I meant by private, please."

Knowing now that he is just a puppet, I figure he's probably forbidden from talking to me, I have a feeling he's just a pawn in a larger scheme, yet he makes the exception time and time again.

"I told you I would speak to you privately and I will." Even though he's trying to speak with sincerity, it's clear there is something up his sleeve.

This is not the time. No. Please. I beg to my body to not let this happen, but another vision is coming to me. It's one of her again and those eyes. I wish she would speak to me. Instead, I can just feel her pain growing inside of her as she screams, letting it release her body. The same spins are taking me over. Vision after vision of her suffering is torturing me. My body begins to convulse, and Dillion is standing there in shock, but he picks me up. The last thing I see is his childlike eyes once more, as he carries me through the door. I reach to touch his face, knowing he is vulnerable in this moment and try to show him my vision. I pass out without knowing whether or not it has worked and fade once more into stillness.

I have been transplanted into a beautiful log cabin with high ceilings and a magnificent stone fireplace, a beautiful contrast against the cherry wood that covers the walls in the house. There are banisters and walkways that lead to the levels above. I am lying on a bear rug that covers most of the space in front of the fireplace. I sit myself up on my elbows and glance around the room until he locks eyes on me again.

"Are you OK?" he actually sounds concerned, and his eyes aren't glazed over. Maybe this is vulnerable him.

I choose not to answer and go with a poorly timed joke. "This doesn't offend you? I mean, you're animal too." I look to the rug and then back to his eyes.

A hint of a smile reaches them. He has no words and just shrugs as he saunters over to me but sits on the plush, brown leather couch directly in front of me. There is no sign of Sofia or David's twin anywhere. Dillion is patting the seat next to him, and I bring myself up and swerve around the glass table and sit next to him, leaving a small bugger space in case he decides to go beast on me. It's not like I could burn the house down without people searching for me, and I don't even have a way out.

Perhaps I just need to say what I came here to say. "I have to be honest with you, there's more you need to know." I take a deep breath and prepare myself to speak, but he interjects.

"You tried to show me before you passed out. I'm not sure how you did it, but I could see some of what you've seen. It was enough to pull me from my trance that I walk around in, day in and day out, waiting on their will. But I'm listening now. Part of me knew it wasn't because you wanted to see me. There had to be another reason." There is no backlash.

It's all out on the line now. My storytelling abilities get right to the nitty-gritty, and I lay it all on him, well as much as I can about the Militia base and what I saw. I tell him about Victor and how he will hold nothing back and would kill even more of those Dillion cares about just to get to me. I explain the machine and how it works and how they plan on expanding its range. Just because the person who created it died doesn't mean it isn't possible now they know it works. Even with all the powers in the world, if this machine had long enough range, it could kill us in a fight before it even started or we got the chance to stop it. Really, I just conveyed that there isn't enough time to have two wars.

"So, where do I fit in? What do you want of me?" He looks almost perplexed that I had the audacity to even come to him.

"I need your help. I don't just want it. I need it. We need the best of both worlds to make this happen. We have to track down the rest of their bases. If we can get enough of us to rally, we can invade the bases and destroy the machines before they bring in a new doctor or scientist to put it all back together and figure it out. We could burn them to the ground before they had the chance to attack us."

"Then what? They will just rebuild." He can't resist turning up a smile though. "Now I see it—the intensity within you. Perhaps a little darkness too."

My face goes red at his observation. Perhaps I should choose my words more carefully around him.

I need to play at what rules him still, "Maybe you coming forward with this information to whoever runs the show will mean they let your brother go. If we unite, we can take down every one of the Militia. We at least owe it to our kind to try."

Even though I want to see it is a way to save innocent people from the turmoil of this war, I don't. There could also be the chance that, even if he agreed and got others on board, they would turn around in the end and attack us. I've made it this far into the Grimmer den, and I still remain alive and breathing; that's a promising sign.

"We could watch them burn together, even your brother and Dino. You know I never liked that kiss-ass Shaddower of yours anyway."

His words don't worry me as much as they would normally, perhaps because I saw into his soul, perhaps because he is actually contemplating this—joining forces. He is actually thinking of helping me instead of helping himself. Even he knows the larger the numbers and the more skilled fighters the better chance the Militia will come to a forced halt.

He scoots closer to me.

"So what are your thoughts then?" I pray for him to give me more information as his eyes widen.

"I support anything that would make the Militia fall even faster and harder. I will talk to a few people in the morning and see what I can put together. See who would be willing to work together … temporarily. Who knows if Archibald will go for it?" He can see the confused look on my face. "David's twin." He sighs and rests his hand on my knee. As long as he doesn't try anything further, I'm fine with this, just because of the progress he's making.

Sofia's beautiful face brings me some relief as I see her walking down the staircase. And as soon as Dillion sees her, he removes his hand from my leg. I'm getting the strong feeling that, with David gone, his brother has taken over every aspect of his life, including Sofia. She is just as soulless as she was when I saw her last, just following the rules that are laid out for her. That is no way to live. The sadness in her eyes is unbearable. But the willingness to stay now shouldn't be there for her, now David is dead. Aidan is controlling, but he's not this bad.

Hopping up from my spot on the couch, I run over to her and greet her with a big hug the second her feet come off the stairs. She doesn't even put her arms back around me. She just drops her head into my shoulder and slowly beings to weep and mumble, "Ava, forgive me. I am so sorry."

Even though she's probably apologizing for luring me to the hotel, she helped me escape. And I've already forgiven her, even though our dynamic will never be the same.

Archibald makes his presence known. "I refuse to let this girl change our plans, Dillion. What is it about her?" His voice echoes through the house from the top of the catwalk. He has a smug look across his face like he's planning something, and Sofia keeps weeping into my shoulder that she's sorry. Maybe she isn't apologizing for the hotel but for something that hasn't happened yet.

"She makes sense to me. She understands me. If you spoke to her, she would understand you as well and show you what you need to see. Maybe there's a different way to defeat the Militia, and that is by us joining forces temporarily. Think about it. We would end them all without causing so much harm to those who stand with us. Now, I still do not care for the humans like she does, but the rest makes sense. We could take over the world if we united. Imagine a land where no one had to hide or shelter themselves from the humans. We would be the masters of our own destinies."

Well, he certainly has put a not-to-true spin on the things I've said, and I am not sure if he's doing it for show or if that's what he really means. We cannot wipe out the entire human species, and he knows it. This is not how I wanted it to go, but I believe he is stretching my words to get Archibald on board. Archibald places his hands on the banister to use as leverage to throw himself off the side. He lands perfectly and sturdy on his feet but walks over to us with harsh, determined footsteps.

"No humans at all … How does little miss feel about this?" Archibald walks past Dillion, giving him a pat on the back, and stands face-to-face with me, all while Sofia doesn't have the courage to lift her head. He runs his right index finger along Sofia's hair and moves toward my face, but Dillion lets out a feral growl from deep within him, and it pulls Archibald's hand back. This could turn bad.

"I can see you don't like me touching her. Let me introduce you to someone who she knows very well—someone who might be able to kill her. The question is, Will she kill him before he kills her? Let's put it to the test. Can she actually harm someone?" He looks me over intently and walks back to two large French doors that do not fit the esthetic of the cabin.

He's unaware of the fact I have actually killed before. Even though I don't relish it or wish to do it, it wouldn't be my first time, so that's helpful. Sofia is here, and I will need to protect her too.

Archibald disappears and then reappears within seconds. But this time, he's dragging a cage behind him. A man sits on the floor with his back to me. All I can make out is that he's holding his arm in pain and rocking himself back and forth. It isn't until he begins to speak through his caged walls that my mouth falls to the ground. Now I know why Sofia was apologizing to me. That voice—one I could never forget—rings through my ears. She has told Archibald about Lucas, my life way before any of this way my life. He has brought him here.

I haven't seen him in years and years. In fact, I spent most of my life after him trying to forget his existence, forget the memories, forget the pain, forget the sadness, forget all of the hurt he caused me. But they will be disappointed to know, there is no love, no linked connection between us. I know what real love is now. There is no way he could ever kill me. Here he is locked in a cage in front of me. Still, even after the way he treated me all those years ago, there is no part of me that would be happy to take revenge out on him.

I circle the cage he's in and look him in the eyes. He's petrified, and even more scared to see it's me. Who knows how long he's been trapped in here? He doesn't appear to be the strong-willed, aggressive boy I once knew. He's scared and timid. They've shaved his once long, black hair down so only his head shows, and his gray eyes are dim. He looks as though he is slowly withering away. His clothes are baggy for his frame. He looks as though he hasn't eaten in a while, and his clothes are torn. He is covered in ash. There are no shoes on his feet, exposing his open wounds, and he shakily holds one arm. This doesn't resemble the person who once caused me harm; even if it did, I couldn't.

"Ava, I am sorry for everything. Why is this happening to me?" He is quaky and scared. Lucas drops his hands to the ground and tries to pull himself together, but I catch a glimpse of a bite mark on his arm.

"Who is this man to you?" Dillion asks in return to my gruesome expression I shot in his direction at the bite mark on his arm.

"Someone she cared about once. But he hurt her—time and time again." Archibald laughs smally but evilly. "Sofia said he is the only other one she thought Ava loved. We will put that to the test. After Mexico, it's clear she doesn't remember her other lives. I mean she looked at David right in the eyes and had no recollection of him. Even now, she doesn't remember me—the way my brother and I hunted her for the bounty on her head.

Archibald walks over to Sofia and pulls her off of me to aggressively press a kiss on her lips, bringing tears to her eyes. She doesn't want to accept it but is forced to.

"That is why you had me bite him?" Dillion speaks, and it is clear that the wool has been pulled over his eyes. "You wanted me to turn him to kill her? This is not what we agreed upon. This is for her to deal with on her own."

This is turning into a weird loyalty test. They want me to kill Lucas as proof of my willingness to work with them. My hands are placed along the bars of the cage, and I rest my forehead on the cold metal. Lucas lunges at me and bares his teeth. Great, he is going through the transformation. It doesn't seem painful to him, and his only objective is to harm me. They clearly told him it was me or him; someone is dying.

Archibald speaks harshly. "You see, the new werewolves who are changed and not born with the gene can be programmed to do whatever we want. They do not have control. They just want to kill. They do not have their humanity like those born with the gift. They want to fight. It's in their blood. And boy is he mad at you for putting him in this situation. Kill or be killed, Ava."

I hate everything about David's brother—right up there with David too. Look what havoc they have caused. Sofia is following him around like a puppy dog, even as he walks over in this direction; she is captivated by his every move. This is so wrong and gross. He laughs and creates lightning in his hand and throws it against the cage, releasing the beast inside that has his sights set on me.

Lucas crawls out of the cage and growls as he slowly walks toward me. With each bone of his body that breaks, he lets out a squeal. But then it is covered in red and brown hair. His hair is short in comparison to Aidan in werewolf form. I keep trying to talk to him, to calm him, but I was never really good at that in the first place. Hence, the dynamic of our relationship. I say anything I possibly can to keep him from coming at me, but it doesn't work. His neck is the last to break, and as his new form is growing it, it incapacitates him for a moment so I can search the room. I do not love or connect with him, but he still did nothing to be put in this situation. My back hits the couch, and I use one hand to throw myself onto the other side. I harness all my momentum to run and use the force of my legs hitting the fireplace and push as hard as I can to the elk antler chandelier.

There is nothing in his eyes now. The transformation is over. They're just bloodshot and red with thirst for my death. He is much smaller than Dillion and Aidan, but he's still fierce with the taste for my blood.

Trying to reason with him isn't working. He jumps high and swats my legs, causing the bolt in the ceiling to loosen with each passing swat. Blood runs down my legs from him scratching at me. I cannot hold myself up here for much longer, so I swing back and forth, gathering the inertia to fly myself onto the catwalk. Lucas almost grabs me midair, but I shoot him with a little pulse, causing him to whimper.

Nothing is stopping him, and he climbs up the railings, destroying the house to get to me. I close my eyes and brace for the impact. And *boom*, like a ton of bricks being hit by a freight train, I'm taken down. We tumble through the air, and all of his force lands on me, pushing me into the wood floor that has broken off around me and gouges into my skin. Drool covers my face, and as I open my eyes to search for some glimmer of him, there is nothing. His eyes are red and filled with resentment toward me. Sofia starts screaming at the top of her lungs.

Lucas's force is lifted off me by Dillion, and he throws him against the wall, overpowering him even in human form. "Stop this! This isn't your decision to make. It is our Elders."

Thank god. That pulse was building inside of me, and I didn't want to use it. If it went off this time, I don't know if I could control it. I could have killed everyone.

Lucas comes to a complete halt and does not move from the corner he is cowering in. I am not sure why all of a sudden he stopped, just when Archibald said they were uncontrollable. Maybe it has something to do with him doing Dillion's bidding, since he is the one who turned him.

"They obey the ones who have created them when they are not born but turned. I am in his blood." Dillion looks at me. I'm surprised given the current mood of the house that he even took a second to say that to me.

Dillion jumps over me, landing in front of Lucas, and Lucas submits to him on the ground, whimpering.

"This is bullshit. We are not the good guys." Archibald walks over, lightning in his hand, and throws it in my direction, but I dodge the beams. Assault after assault he throws my way, but I avoid them, until he strikes me one time. Dillion is too busy calming Lucas in his manic newborn stage to help.

Then suddenly, Archibald is falling to the ground, lifeless. Tears overcome Sofia. She stands behind him as his body hits the ground. All the electricity shocks through the house, but her hand never stops shaking, even with the fire poker covered in his blood; she cannot release it from her hands.

Lucas turns back into his human form, and before I can say anything to him, another body hits the ground. Sofia has taken the knife from Archibald's holster and slit her wrists. Blood is gushing; she must have cut deep. I lunge to her to be by her side and place her head in my lap as I try to take care of her wounds. I rip edges off my shirt to wrap her wrists, but it doesn't stop the blood from seeping through. I yell to Dillion and Lucas for help, but they just stand there with their heads looking to the ground.

They won't say what I feel in my gut. She is dying. The life is slowly leaving her body.

"Sofia, why?" I pull her in close to me, not caring that I'm being covered in her blood.

"How could I live with myself? With all I have done? Ava, I have done worse. You will come to know soon enough. I told them things—things I wouldn't have thought would matter, but they do. I can go be with my love now." Her eyes close, and her hand releases mine, falling to her stomach. With her last breath and blink, a final tear comes down her face. She is gone.

I panic and try to give her CPR, knowing it won't bring her back. I scream, yell, start throwing things around, but none of it will bring her back.

My senses are tingling as the wind howls at me. Even here it offers a warning, I look over my shoulder to see Hector peering in through the window on the porch, barely able to even see he is so short. Fear strikes his eyes, and he bolts from view.

"Ava, Hector is going to the Elders. He thinks I have been compromised. There is nowhere else he could go. I have to stop him. Now go. Take Lucas with you."

"Dillion." I don't know what to say to him or how to say thank you. "How will I know when you have made your decision?" I touch his arm as I am opening the door to leave, a simple thank you, and Lucas trails behind me.

"I will find you. Now go, before Hector has more people show up. Remember I wasn't always like this."

As I step off the porch into the snow filled atmosphere, he yells his final direction. "There is an exit behind the mountain. You will know it when you see it. Stand in the center, repeat the words I used to get into the other portal, and think of where you want to go. See you soon." It's a promise.

Chapter 28

We are nearly to the side portal on the back of the mountain when Lucas drops to the ground holding his hand over his face. It takes me a minute to loop back around, as it's been more difficult to control my run, especially when I so desperately want to get out of this place. He is unable to control himself and keeps changing between his human and wolf form. He keeps spasming, and in the bitter cold, it is not good for him to be buck naked. It's not like there was a part in my Psychology 101 class that taught me how to handle something like this. What did college actually prepare me for? Absolutely nothing.

He is shirtless, bleeding from his chest, and looking up to me with vulnerable eyes when I make it to him. The snow is violently smashing into his face, and he can't hold his balance any longer. He lies on his side, clutching his center. Trying to mimic my conjuring of the ground, I reach my hands above my head and try to do the same with the snow, keeping him safe in a confined bubble.

Searching his body with my eyes, I see there is no visible wound; there is blood but no known source. He is flashing between wolf and his battered, weak, and bruised human form. There is so much agony in his face, and I don't know what I can do to help him. He cannot speak, just keeps gripping his arms around his stomach tighter. I try to free his arms so I can look at his stomach. But we struggle with each other, and he growls at me, making the hair on my arms stand up. He holds his arms tightly across his stomach and winces more and more with each passing second.

Through agony, he starts speaking to me, struggling to get the words out. "When that wolf left, the other guy made me drink something and told me that, if I didn't kill you, I would die. It was a potion or something. I don't understand any of this." He is shaking his head, and his body starts to convulse slowly as he moves his hands away from his stomach for me to see.

My eyes can't even comprehend what I'm seeing. There are large red boils surfacing on his stomach, the source of the blood. They're surrounded by a black matter, something I can't identify. But with each new boil growth, the blackness takes over the surrounding area. It looks like molten lava covering his skin. Now the boils start to move around on his stomach, causing him to scream and cry out in pain. He sounds like a fox dying in the woods. The bloody, dark red boils stop moving and suck back into his body, and he is left with nothing but a black circle left on his belly.

He lies there naked and vulnerable, I look into his eyes that are now frozen. I strike him across the face and yell at him, but there is no response. He's gone. Just like Sofia. Gone. The bubble that surrounds him violently shatters, sending the icicles that surrounded it off into the distance as my eyes fill with fury. It feels wrong, not being able to give either of them a burial. So I start covering him in the snow. I wish that, even with all the harm he caused me, he ends up in a good place. It is unfortunate he spent the last moment of his life in this condition and in such fear. I do not shed a tear for him as I look over his snow-covered body. But I feel sorry for him, sorry for the person he was and the person he had become.

The snow is pushing even harder against me, and I have no control over the wind now. As I am running to the back of the mountain, a terrible pain begins ringing through my head. It feels like someone is stabbing me in the temple. Why? Why can't I just have one good moment, where something, anything goes to plan.

A faint whispering echoes through my mind and I know it's her again. Cassiopeia is trying to speak to me, but the pain is distracting. Pushing through the wind that is giving me so much resistance, I am able to see the large portal. It looks like a helicopter pad, without a snowflake in sight on the blue circular surface with a big red R in the center. The portal acts as shields from the elements.

Standing in the portal, my body falls to the ground and soaks up the heat. The neutral temperature warms my body, and it's soon back to being a furnace. My knees are in excoriating agony, evert bone in my body feels as though it is being broken, and my skin feels like it is being ripped from my body. Cassiopeia is there. She is not screaming or tensing from the violent stabbing she is feeling. She knew this moment was going to come, and she is embracing it. She has such strength. The pain is too much for me to bear. Every eyelash feels like it's being ripped out, and my fingers are being slammed in a door over and over again. I feel her pain, yet she shows none. There's too much going on. I cannot even decide what part of my body to hold and console. The more I fight, the worse it is. She keeps talking to me, but I cannot make out the words.

A shadowy figure appears through the snow, running full force, and breaks through the barrier and onto the portal with me. The brown werewolf is alone as he transitions back into himself.

"Ava, what's wrong?" He takes a knee and is looking over me, but there appears to be nothing wrong with me.

It's all on the inside. Everything is exploding. My screams would be enough to awake every Grimmer in this place.

He picks me up, and my breathing is labored. Full sentences

escape me, but my eyes widen, like they are fighting to see. I will not let go of this sense.

"Where are we going? Tell me where to take you! What do I do?" Dillion is screaming at me for answers. He knows he cannot save me from this, and he dare not take me further into the Grimmer den. He repeats himself trying to figure me out. "Damn it, Ava! If you don't answer me, I will take you somewhere far away from here."

"Home … my home."

And he speaks his not understandable phase and repeats the word I hold dearest to my heart. We are sucked into the air and into a pitch-black beam. Does the portal know what I meant? I am weightless in his arms, and the blackness somehow shelters my pain for a second. I am able to crawl out of his arms and stand in the beam, just as we are transplanted to the rooftop across the street from the butcher shop. It's dark outside, but still my eyes adjust to it being so much lighter than the portal. The stars shine brightly, and my mind feels like I'm going loopy, like I'm coming off anesthesia. The portal drops its invisible walls, and the pain overtakes me once more, so my body drops to the roof.

"What is happening to her?" The fear in Dillion's voice echoes. He leans down, trying to hold me steady, but I cannot stop shaking.

Another cry pierces my ears, one that instantly breaks my heart into pieces. Sarah is with Shamus, and Kai is kneeling over Kieran as he cries out in pain. Kieran turns his head to me, and for a second, our eyes lock. He can feel his mother too; he can feel her dying.

Everyone is shocked, even Aidan as he starts running toward me. Clearly, this wasn't in any of the prophecies he has heard of or part of his curse. He is genuinely surprised. At least he didn't keep this from me. I take all the strength I have to lean up and search for her. My eyes dart to Laila. She is coming. She is safe. She barks in my direction, and I let the feeling take over me as my face hits the cement, and I am consumed by Cassiopeia's pain. Everything fades from around me, and I am welcomed by her eyes, one blue and one green, so piercing. She is smiling at me through her pain. There is a slight sting in my body, but my body relaxes, and she reaches out her hand to me. She is elegant, but hers is a rare unique beauty. She is very tall, probably over six foot, but elegant and timeless. Her skin is pale with freckles. She has long, curly, untamable hair that's the same color as Kieran's. Even with the hood on her head, her hair has so much volume. Her fingernails are immaculate. I take her long slender hand in mine, and we walk—a stroll down memory lane.

She searches my memories and watches every single one. She dives into my soul and starts off from what I can remember. She transfers me back to the cold room first, the one where my fake mother held me, looking for the whereabouts of my real mother. There are no lights, and I am standing in my memories with her. We're holding hands. Silent, not speaking a word to each other.

We jump to more memories. These are of Aidan, but I do not know if she has me focusing on the painful memories and the things I sweep under the rug with him, instead of the good stuff. She replays them over and over, just taking everything in. Remaining silent.

The memories cause me to violently shake. A high-pitched scream that shatters glass is yelling in my mind. Maybe it's me—the sound and the scream I have always wanted to let out to feel some release. I am swirling in a loop of madness as all of my memories from the past surround me, but I am unable to reach any of them. The witch's hold on my memories still remains. Some things cannot be broken by others and only by the one who created it; it is a rule of nature. A balance. All my memories fall out of sight.

Her voice is like a voice from a classic old movie, sweet and graceful. She pulls me back as she whispers, "There will be time. You will get your memories back. Come to me."

She is in the sky above all the white that surrounds me. It is evident these are the Pureck's last moments here. And with that power she connects us. Kieran and I have the ability to see each other. She brings us both to this plane, high above all, just living in the clouds. But we're separated. She stands between us. He calls to me, and I try to wave to him, but my arms won't move. There is a shine, an angelic light shining around him.

A whisper once more surrounds me—her voice, telling me to blink. When I do and open my eyes, she has transplanted us to an open, hilly field, made of the purest green grass, with sunflowers growing wild and free. Her eyes linger on us from up in the sky as Kieran and I run to each other. He picks me up, spins me around, and places a kiss on my cheek as I snuggle into him. There is no pain anymore, just peace and calmness. This place blocks everything out.

We pull apart and look at each other quizzically. We both have a sense of what is going on, but our appearances have changed. I am in a beautiful, low-cut, white dress that hugs me down to my waist and then flows into a beautiful movement as it grazes the ground and loosely moves in the wind. My face doesn't have the feeling of blood, soot, or dirt on it. I am perfectly clean, down to the fingernails and toes that I can see are barefooted. Kieran is dressed in all white as well, without shoes. His button-down is rolled up to his elbows and is unbuttoned to reveal all of his chest tattoos. He looks perfect. I follow his eyes, looking to the sky. Her eyes are in the sky, but slowly she brings herself down. She wants to speak to us.

She is no longer in the cloak-and-dagger routine, and her eyes aren't the only of her features that are exposed and stunning. Cassiopeia is in a Bohemian-style, solid yellow, long-sleeved dress that matches the flow of her hair and the sunflowers that stay in her hair. She has silver streaks in her hair that I now notice glimmer in the sunlight. She walks toward us with elegance and poise and moves straight to Kieran. She stands inches away from him but does not embrace him in the motherly way I expected. Instead, she places a soft hand on his shoulder and gestures me to move closer.

I abide her silent instructions. She reaches out and places a hand on my shoulder, while one remains on his, pulling me in closer. "I want you two to see everything—why I have become the way I am, why I have made the decisions I have. This is my past, and it cannot be changed." He voice is that of an angel, soft and sweet and just angelic. Her full lips speak but this time only to Kieran. "Son, are you comfortable with Ava seeing these parts of your childhood?"

"Ava can see everything. There is nothing I want to hide from her. I would share my soul with her if she would take it, all in the right time." He looks at me with such longing, and I know he wants a decision made between him and Aidan. Yet he is still sharing this part of himself with me despite that.

"Very well then. Let's get to it." She claps her hands and seems awfully chipper for someone who is dying.

"How is any of this possible?" I look to Kieran as we follow her. "I could see you, feel you in such pain. And now we are here?" He clearly knows more about this than I do.

"Ava." Kieran is upset, and it's difficult for him to get the words out. His mother reaches back to him and hugs him closer and speaks words he is unable to say.

"This is my before death moment. As a Pureck, we are granted this gift. It may take as long as we need. I am able to share my soul and go through my memories with those I choose. It is a way for me to complete my cycle here, without leaving anything to chance, to put everything to rest. I was experiencing the pain of my death. So, I am already dead. After death, I get this moment, the moment in between, a moment of happiness to do this. Then the process will continue on. All of my business is finished here after this."

She turns to me, and Kieran's eyes have so much hurt, pain, and sadness in them. Even though he hasn't seen his mother in some time, the sting of this is real, and I am here on top of it. My every desire is to hug him and console him and be there for him, but Cassiopeia has us continuing on this path. So I reach for his hand, which he gladly takes, and we stroll hand in hand to the field of sunflowers. This is her very own version of a safe zone, created deep within her mind. And only those who connect with her can see these memories. We are barricaded in here, a beautiful place, until she allows us to be released. And even though the situation isn't ideal, and neither is looking at a heartbroken Kieran, we are safe here for once.

"Each one of these beautiful flowers holds a memory for me, some darker than others, but this is where I have hidden them. Some I am not proud of. Like the curse. Yet it leads you two to each other. So for that I am grateful, as a mother. Some light in my word … Some"—her eyes light as she looks to Kieran—"some are the reason I was able to live this long. Some gave me more peace and happiness than I could have ever imagined. You, son, are my greatest gift and creation, and I am so proud of you."

It is clear she never spoken to him in this way before. They did not have the best relationship from what Kieran has told me. But she really does love him, and he loves her unconditionally in return. These memories might help Kieran to understand, to see a different side other than his own. Her memories might just be able to set him free from any grudges or resentment he has toward her. This could be the closure he needs. Her memories could very well be the key to mend a relationship as her last act.

"Let me show you." She reaches her hand to the sky and pulls her sun down. It is gravitating down toward us but does not blind us.

My eyes widen in curiosity as the sun drops in front of us, and we naturally form a small circle around it. Even with the sun here, as a large ball in front of us, this place still shines. She moves her fingers, and the sun changes to a memory viewer. All are memories of Kieran. He is her sun. He made her world rotate.

Memory after memory shows Kieran running, playing, jumping in the snow, singing, swinging, playing sports, just being a happy kid, what every kid deserves. Within all of those memories is a mother's faint, distant smile as she watches him. He is the life that sustained hers once he was born. He makes her world go around. I peel my eyes off the memory and focus on Cassiopeia looking only at her son. He is shocked to see she was watching this whole time and cared, even though she didn't show it to him the way he needed to feel loved.

She moves away from the sun, and it quickly darts back into the sky, not even causing any winds or any movement in this area. No flower even shook. Without speaking, she picks up a sunflower and twirls it in a circle above her head, and a memory is dropped down, taking over our reality. We are standing in a living room of an old house, with creaky stairs and pictures on the wall. The rest is a blur. The space itself is nothing spectacular or memorable, but the people yelling at each other are the main focus. At the top of the stairs is a young Kieran looking sadly down on his parents arguing, yelling, and throwing hands in the air.

She pulls a vision up and shows it to her husband. Kieran's dad has brown eyes and gray hair but looks like a silver fox. His father seems of average height. Kieran is much taller than him and his mother, which is saying something since his mother is over 6 foot tall I would guess. He must have gotten his height from his mother's side, but he looks like a dad, dressed in jeans and sneakers with a sweatshirt on. Flames illuminate the vision, and her husband's eyes are filled with evil; he is working on a machine. I know that machine. It is the one I saw in the Militia base. My head shakes. This cannot be. She was having a premonition. She is yelling at him, saying that the money and security are no reason to help the Grimmers or the Militia. He doesn't understand what is going on and begins to yell at her. Young Kieran runs up to his father sobbing as his dad holds him in his arms, all while yelling at Cassiopeia.

We are back surrounded by the sunflower field. "Mom, I don't get it. Dad was working on the machine Ava saw?" Kieran is pacing back and forth frustrated, upset his mother has never told him any of this. He is trying to wrap his mind around this one truth bomb his mother dropped, and there is a field of them left to go.

"I saw a vision of your father—one where he had made an agreement with the Militia for more money and our safety. But in return, he would be creating a machine that could kill millions. He created the machine but was working with another woman to harness power. He had the ability to make it all work. I told him I was going to leave him because he was making the wrong decision. I couldn't have you be a part of that. You father didn't understand that I could see something from the future, when all he would do is live in the present. So we left." She makes sure to speak to him softly, giving him time to process everything. He sits down on the ground and sinks his head into his hands, a vulnerability from him I have never seen. So I waste no time going to him and pull him into a tight embrace, the only thing I can do.

He holds me back and directs a question toward his mother. "If you saw the future, couldn't you change it? How do you know his decision wasn't made by you leaving?" Valid questions.

Her response is not so simple. "You are not wrong. My leaving him could have caused that. Maybe if I stayed, it wouldn't have happened. To an extent, we create our own destiny. Things can change. Ava knows this, as her visions have changed. But this one of your father remains unchanged. You stopped speaking to me and were determined to live your own life, Kieran, doing everything possible to escape what I had told you. Even with that, your fate is holding your hand right now. All decisions lead to the final path, the prophecy. Look what has fallen in your lap." She is looking fondly over to me, holding Kieran, and the look in his eyes shows he is contemplating her words.

"Son, some things cannot be changed. They are written in the stars. Your fathers' actions are one of those things."

Kieran nods his silent understanding of the decision his mother had to make and why. There is relief in her face, as she has been waiting to show him that exact vision for years but struggled with it because she also wanted her son to create his own path and find his own way in life. She had hope that fate would have him back here with her. She picks up flower after flower, showing us her fond memories of his father before that day, memories of Kieran as a child, memories of what her mortal mother and father looked like, and her memories from childhood—all of which were happy. She had twelve brothers and sisters, and they lived on a farm. It's like we're getting to know each one of them through her eyes. She shows us what her life was like before she became a Pureck.

She pulls another flower, the smallest one of the bunch and shows us how, one night, she woke in the middle of the night with hot cold sweats in a hut. This was very long ago. She knew something was wrong. Her mother said they should call a doctor, but when the doctor showed up, he refused to treat her saying nothing is wrong with her, and it will pass by morning. Her mother and doctor left the room, and she was left to figure everything else out on her own.

Soon, she realized she could control nature and the elements. It wasn't long after she also came to the conclusion she could see the future. She witnessed her predictions happen but wouldn't say anything to anyone. And back then, people would have thought she was crazy; they still would now. She couldn't understand what was happening to her and why. Like me, her powers developed, minus the one I was born with. It was soon she realized death was no longer on her doorstep and that she was becoming more powerful. She never realized how powerful she was until she met the one who changed her life. She has lived longer than any Pureck, making her the strongest and most powerful as the centuries passed.

Another flower is pulled. This one show her gathering with other Purecks in the middle of a mountainous desert. All are dressed in brown robes, their faces hidden. All are coming to the realization that they were put here to maintain the balance between good and evil. They always believed that, when one died, another was born or gifted. But they still search, realizing some are in hiding.

That is a shame. It would have been nice to actually get a look at their faces.

"Now let me show you how you two are connected and why." She drifts off, searching the field for the biggest sunflower, one that stands taller above all the others, by easily two or three feet. It is wilted though; it looks like it's about to die with her. Now I will get some information on the one sharing the same bloodline as Aidan. This is a different side of the story, another truth to be told.

She picks the petals off and drops them to the ground. A gust of wind picks up and sends the petals flying into the sky. They circle us, and we are once again taken back to a different time entirely—standing in and living through someone else's past. We go back hundreds of years to where a woman in her perfect youth smiles kindly at a man who looks like a perfect mixture of Aidan and Elijah. The two stroll down the street with her hand draped over his arm. She was his perfect accessory, and they seemed to be so in love. I cannot tell when this actually look place, because the vision is so focused on their faces. They spend time talking and walking, just getting to know each other; their contagious laughter has smiles reaching to their eyes. She can feel the presence of other people, envious of what they have. The vision goes on, with snippets of their relationship over the years, many innocent kisses stolen, many happy tears shed from laughter, and her heart was stolen by him. It is a montage to him.

The happy scenes fade to one of great damage. It was a perfect night under the stars, and she could not contain her excitement to tell him something.

"Beauford, I'm pregnant." The glow beams across her face as she starts to hop up and down where she sits. Every ounce of excitement is pouring out of her. She reaches over to hug him, but he does not reach back for her.

He pulls her arms from around his neck and places them in front of her. "Cassiopeia, I am sorry." He can't even fake being sorry well.

He goes on to tell her how, even though he loves her, he has found someone else who he is more in love with and that she is also pregnant. He explains that he will have nothing to do with her from this point out because he wants to make a commitment to the other woman and get married. He cannot have Cassiopeia soiling his good name and bring this news forward. And even though abortion doctors didn't exist at the time, he tells her how he has learned of ways for people to terminate their babies. She doesn't know what to say or do but refuses to get rid of the baby; this causes him to be irate, so she runs off.

The memory gets darker. She went from having everything to having nothing. Everywhere she goes, people brand her as a whore, being pregnant out of wedlock. There are only voices remaining in her now black vision. A woman approaches her aggressively, demanding she leave town and leave her and Beauford in peace, so he doesn't have a constant reminder of his past mistakes. She refuses to give the child up or to move. The child will know who the father is, regardless of what that means for him.

The vision becomes lighter, more visible again, and we see what caused her to hate. There she lays at the bottom of the stairs, bleeding, holding her stomach, crying out for help, with Beauford on the top of the stairs looking down at her.

That is where Cassiopeia's spite came from—her moment of vulnerability, her moment that she thought was weakness, letting him get close to her again and causing the end of her child. She never thought she would be able to conceive again, so Kieran is her miracle. She wanted to protect him from his father, something she feels she couldn't do for her last baby. It was in that moment as she was lying there bleeding that she realized her power of evil and that the curse could cover generations.

She confronted Beauford when she was well and able and cursed him and his family. He knew nothing of her powers, so he thought it to be a silly girl joke. But he was wrong. She cursed that they all would feel her pain, and one day, she would birth a son despite all he put her through, if the spirits let her, who could cause the one whose eye changed color more pain and heartache than a lifetime of cursing could do. She could see how powerful Aidan would grow to be and that he would be the strongest and bravest of their bloodline. She cursed them, with the only evil she had in her body. It manifested, and not even the destiny of soul mates could stop it.

Everything stops. My mind is filled with emotions. She blessed me, yet there's this and her bringing her son into this. Was she thinking? Was she just blinded by the rage?

At least she accepts who she was and what she caused from that. The vision falls, and we are back with a lot fewer sunflowers to go through.

"I love you for bringing her into my life, but I still hate you for giving me this great love that could very well run away from me." Kieran breaks his silence. "You cursed someone else but still could break my heart. You don't know the outcome."

Well, I certainly cannot make eye contact with anyone right now.

She speaks softly once more. "That was the first and last time I have done something of that magnitude. I am not perfect and admit to having let my rage get the best of me." She is stumbling across her words. She knows our hearts break with what she went through, but we are living today and not in the past. "I was led by rage. What little I had in me, I just used to conjure up that curse. I live with my choices every day, and I am sorry to the both of you that you are having to live with my choices as well. Nothing can change this. A decision will have to be made."

It is the first time I have heard her voice quake. Even still, she sounds elegant, but the quaking in her voice doesn't fit her demeanor; she annunciates each word so carefully with thought.

It's time for me to speak my thoughts. "Why did you pick me? You could have picked someone else." Disappointment ripples through my voice as I try to remain confident to this powerful being.

She takes a step closer to me and farther away from Kieran. "My dear, don't you see? Aidan was destined to be with you regardless of whether you had these gifts or not. That's how a soul mate works. You are his equal pairing on this planet. You were also destined to be the one who could bring this war to an end. All signs point to you. Even if your destiny weren't to have these powers, with my curse, you would still have to make a decision between the two loves and would still hold this power over them. Your two destines have intertwined." She looks at me with eyes that say she is sorry, but what has been done is done. There is no changing it now, but she chooses to impart some other wisdom. "Remember you can change your destiny. Your Shaddower is supposed to be neutral like Switzerland. But after time, he took control of his own destiny as well. He broke the yin and yang, and you can too. You also might want to take into consideration the man who was the alpha before Aidan and what he had to do to get there. There is more to the puzzle, but time is of the essence."

Kieran and I glance at each other, not even knowing where to go from here. There is so much to say to each other. No matter how absurd this moment is, and all of this is, his mother is still dying or dead. But I am thankful that he gets this closure.

"Kieran, it is time for you to go. Take this. It has the rest of my memories on it." To my surprise, she hands him a little gadget. "Ava and I have much to discuss. Goodbye, my son." She walks toward him, but he takes a step back.

I can't help but shooting him a look, knowing full well he will regret it if this is his last chance to give his mother a hug and he doesn't.

He embraces her. "I love you, Mom." He gives her a kiss on the cheek.

She lets out the happiest of giggles. "I love you, too." She pulls back and places her long hands on either side of his face. "My son. I am so proud of you and who you have become." She holds him and does not let go for at least five minutes. And when she pulls away, her tears are filled with more tears.

She releases Kieran, and he walks over to me with a smile. "Thank you."

"You're welcome. I just don't want you to regret anything."

He pulls me in close, and I wrap my arms around his neck, snuggling my face into him. I love the way he smells, even after the stress of the day. I loved being here for him and sharing this moment. Now I have to go it alone. Before he can attempt to give me a kiss goodbye, he is being evaporated from my arms in a pixelated dust.

Chapter 29

"Come, let me show you something." Cassiopeia takes me by the hand, and we glide over the sunflower petals and green hills, hovering, floating just inches above the ground, back to where we first stood when I was taken here. The wind blows through my hair, making me feel elated and high on life.

"Look down below you." She speaks melodiously as we are still hovering in the air.

There is no grass, just a reality beneath me. It's similar to what Kieran and I witnessed before. She explains to me that no matter what reality you are in, there is always a view into another. Across the world, across the planets this holds true. You just have to find the spot. Aidan is holding me in his arms, trying to speak to me, but I don't even bat a lash. I am out cold. She explains that, if I were to listen closely, I could hear him. But I choose not to, not now. I don't want to miss a word she says. The others just look frightened and confused. This isn't something anyone is accustomed too.

Shamus holds Sarah tightly, and her hair and eyes have changed color to a deep red with yellow accents; this shows her sadness. They look to me and to Kieran, rattling ideas off, but Aidan shakes them all away. Kieran wakes and immediately pounces to his feet and runs into my circle of view, wearing his all-white attire. He runs his hands through is hair. He's trying to explain to them what's happening and where I am, but he's simply pointing to the sky.

Aidan looks down at me, hopeful once more and kisses my forehead, and Kieran doesn't even wince.

"Why are you showing me this?" There is always a reason with her.

"I want you to see that Kieran's heart is one as good as yours. Look at him. Not starting a fight for the betterment of everyone. If Aidan saw you that way, he wouldn't do the same. Kieran respects Aidan's feelings for you and wants you to make the choice yourself, while Aidan is forcing a wedding on you, not even having asked you to be his wife." She wants to say more, what she is really thinking. "Please. Please save my son. That is all I ask of you, and I know it is not a small ask." Her eyes widen with longing and hope for me to give her an answer.

I look down to the ground to see Aidan and Kieran once more and the heavens that have opened up. Her tears are the rain, and Kieran knows it. He looks to the sky, not blinking as the rain covers him. I have felt her pain and seen her face through all the excruciating pain she felt earlier, and not one tear was shed on her part. But for the love of her son, she will make the sky fall.

"Please, help me." My fingers are intertwined and my head shakes. "He is such a great person. How could he be anything other than that?" He has done everything to prove to his mother that he is good. I can see it in him. No shed of darkness lies within his soul.

"Even the best of people can turn into darkness." She is cold.

"Maybe Kieran is different." My train of thought has escaped me as I look down at the worried faces below.

"The part of the riddle that is left behind. You know now in order to solidify the pairing, there must be a marriage held before

Mother Nature herself and the love of consummation; then the other connection will disappear. You will no longer be drawn to both. When I let the curse free on them, there were repercussions for my actions. The curse remained intact, but a price is to be paid at the final act. This is when the evil will shine through either man."

Here she was blaming it on a broken heart, when that is only part of the story. The last missing piece now fits. She made a curse not fit for this world and was punished for it. There has to be a balance; this is something even I know.

"I know after what happens next, you will want to run to Aidan. But please, keep my son in mind before you make a rash decision." She is pleading with me, and finally the rain and her tears stop.

"What happens next?" I bite my lower lip and just wait on her words.

With a deep breath she speaks. "You will remember. But don't let a lifetime of previous memories make you forget who you are now or the life you live now."

"I will remember?" The thought makes me smile, finally. "Everything?"

"Almost every memory. There are a few that cannot come to pass. The witch, the ring, all of these things are not to block your memory in general but, rather, one very important memory it seems. She has made it appear as though it was just to hold back your memories as a whole. But as I am preparing to do the enchantments, I see that it was all just for one specific memory. It must be important for her to want to block that or for whoever's bidding she is doing. She is the only one who can break that block. Otherwise, yes. Everything will return—every memory. The serum has already grown weak. But once I leave this world and you stay, you will be too strong for it to hold any longer. Your power of foresight will still develop, and it might take a while for your body to accept everything. It will be like sifting through a puzzle trying to put the pieces together. Then all at once, it will hit you and make sense. You will need rest—lots and lots of rest."

She has more to say, but I cut her off. I don't mean to be rude, but I need to tell her before she disappears. "Thank you. For all of this."

Even though this has been and continues to be a whirlwind for me, she has been a huge factor in making me who I am. Thanks to her, I still stand here. Thanks to her, I get to live.

There is one thing I know she wants to hear. "I will not make a rash decision." My conviction doesn't seem to sell it to her.

"I know you believe that now. One last thing. That starry light that has guided you, that has been me, looking over you. Now you need to learn to find that within yourself and trust your gut and instincts. Goodbye, Ava. Take care of my son." And just like an old memory, she fades from my sight into the sky through a ray of sunshine.

As my eyes focus on the sky, waving to her in her departure, a smile reaches the top of my cheeks. My memories. There is a power arising within me. She is gone. All of my memories scatter in front of me, like a line-up for me to pick and choose what to see first. Where to start? As the Pureck dies and her soul fades from within me, the power grows. The serum cannot control its hold, and more memories spin in front of me. I keep trying to grab them, but my arms are not moving as I can feel the serum peeling off of every organ and vein in my body. It's like a flash of lightning, pulsing through my body, is killing off each bit of the memory blocker. My body starts convulsing once more, and my neck churns in a welcoming, satisfying pain.

It is gone. The serum has left my body, and the enchantments blocking the memories is gone—minus the first memory I search for. It's the blocked one. And it's out of reach. I walk through aisles and aisles of my memories, feeling like I am in *The Matrix*. But instead of a blank white room, it is the sunflower field. My eyes are being forced shut but opened to every memory my mind has been blocking. I am not choosing; the memories are choosing me.

Wow, the first memory I see is from this life. My fake mother must have really done her job well. The vision is of David and Archibald. We were friends or friendly by association of our parents. David and I are running around a large yard playing together. I must have been around seven years old, so this was after the time my father left, but my real mother stands in the yard with us. She is beautiful. I can see how the impersonator had a resemblance to her. But my mother's smile shows crooked bottom teeth and straight top teeth, and the smile is kind. She has long, straight, brown hair that flows down her back and ends right above the lower back dimples she has showing. She is wearing a crop top and jeans with wedge heels. She has olive skin that looks sun-kissed. What happened to her? Where is she now? Where did she go and how did the imposter get here? This must be part of the memory she's blocking from me, the only one I can't retrieve. To be so young and innocent again and feel those moments as if I were living them now is amazing.

Centuries spin in front of me, and my eyes are eager for as many memories as my mind can hold. I see my brother and I happy. I see moments with my mother and father and all the love a child could experience. Even memories with my grandparents who have since passed away still remain in my mind. All the corrupt and fake memories fade and are being replaced by the happy lives I have lived and the saved moments where I have passed away.

One in particular catches my grasp. It's one Aidan has spoken of to me, the one where he could not save me because I chose Dino over him. Dino has always been a Grimmer, through the centuries. He has chosen to be reborn each time as such, wanting to be the reason for my demise. He was created to help people prevent my destiny. Every memory I have of him from this life has been due to blindfolded ignorance, him claiming to be someone he was not, a friend. Dino has blinded me before in another life in a way that led to my death. My memories scatter, but it plays out right before my eyes.

Dino runs over to me as Aidan and I walk hand in hand through a park. This was the perfect moment for Dino to strike because Aidan had somewhere to be, and I would not let him miss it. I conveyed to Aidan that he could trust me, and I trusted Dino, even though he didn't. Aidan pleads with me not to go, but I do it anyway. Maybe this is why he is the way he is with me. It's history repeating itself. Dino is yelling that there is something wrong with Victor, and I must go to tend to him. He needs my help. There is a reluctance in Aidan's eyes, but he cannot miss his meeting. Dino leads me to a field, and I search for Victor. Victor strolls out casually from the woods and thanks Dino. As he does. Dino leaves, and Victor goes on to tell me how much he hates me and that he loathes me entirely. He tells me to fight, but I refuse. We struggle, but I will not cause his death. And then he strangles me, and my life drifts way. But I can see as I am dying this would not be my last life; another would come.

Aidan lies over my dead body, blaming himself, saying he shouldn't have let me go and that he would do anything to keep my safe. Wind speaks through my breath, letting him know I would be back—never letting him know exactly when.

Now I know why he is so protective and the way he is with me. Even when I have begged him to trust me before, he's had to live with the consequences of my actions. He wants to trust me but knows history will repeat itself and knows I can be blinded by my own passion sometimes. He has always had my best interest at heart. I love him for that. I see the weight he is bringing upon himself, even now, holding himself responsible for my death. But I made the Pureck a promise—to not let the memories blind me from the life we have now, the lies he has told me now, the things he still omits.

Then like a tidal wave, every moment he and I have ever shared is rushed back to me. Every kiss. Every hug. Every moment where I have fallen in love with him. It is clear we are destined to be together. There are centuries of love—so many moments of love that have never faded. She knew I would not be able to control the overflow of memories or emotions that came along with it. Rush after rush, his love for me shows more and more. The moments come back, including the time he proposed to me, this time more real than the last vision I saw; the feeling is there. I see our families sharing meals together, and he and my father have friendly banter back and forth, all while he looks at me with longing and passion from across the room. I have dreamt of a man looking at me, especially when he thinks I don't notice and seeing that longing, and here it is. Now I have seen it thousands of times, all from his eyes. Years of memories come back to me, but more than memories are the feelings that go along with it.

The Pureck speaks to me through a memory, one she implanted for me to see last. Her eyes linger in the background. She is dead but has given me one last parting word. Her eyes fade, and she stands before me, giving me a message, dressed in all black but looking radiant and surprisingly filled with life. Her voice is the same and she says, "When you pass, you too will have the power of transference. Make the right decision."

The wave of her memory is gone, the pressure released from me, and I am able to open my eyes and stand, not even realizing it has knocked me down. My eyes slowly peel open, and I am once again in real time. At first as my eyes adjust to the darkness of night, no one is nearness. But when my eyes have adjusted, he is there. Aidan smiles from his mesmerizing blue eyes as he lets out a sigh of relief. His smile is bright, and his eyes light up. He embraces me so tightly I am barely able to breathe.

"I remember everything," I whisper into his ear.

He pulls me back to stare into my eyes, and he can see it in me, the memories our love holds. It is so hard to keep my promise when all the memories of Aidan, all the years, all the time, all the dedication is staring back into me. My mind is flooded with him.

Now, the rooftop filled with my friends can sense I'm awake, and they rush over toward me. I'm wearing an all-white outfit, matching Kieran's. They know we were together. I look over at Sarah, and she shoots me a look, one saying we'll have to talk, but I'm glad you're all right. Crazy how girls can just communicate with their eyes. With men, they would never understand that level.

Aidan doesn't bring the memories up again but just lets me have a moment with everyone on the roof. Still, I can tell he's having a hard time containing the excitement in his voice. Finally, his one wish has come true.

"Where is Dillion?" I ask to anyone who is willing to answer.

Shamus speaks up. "He'll help us. He's going to speak to his people and his Elder group tonight. He'll be in touch."

"You did it, girl! You crazy son of a bitch!" Sarah's voice is filled with surprise and excitement.

At this point, these people are family, more family than any of my blood is. Kieran is hesitant to approach me. Perhaps he's unsure of what happened in my remaining time with his mother. I smile to him, and he relaxes and joins the crowd of us talking and hugging.

My dress blows in the cool night wind, and Kieran and I make eye contact and laugh. We look ridiculous in our white get-ups, looking like we're going to do a beach shoot in the winter, in Pennsylvania—like a pair of crazy people. And with that laugh, my memories with him, my best friend, my place of comfort rush to the front of my mind.

I cannot help but look back at the memories of me from before. It's a whole different world, a whole different life. And I still know I'm not that person anymore. Aidan loves someone else.